THIRSTY RIVER

aflame books

Aflame Books
2 The Green
Laverstock
Wiltshire
SP1 1QS
United Kingdom
email: info@aflamebooks.com

ISBN: 9781906300104

First published in 2009 by Aflame Books

First published in Dutch as Dorstige Rivier
by Meulenhof/Manteau in 2008

British Library Cataloguing in Publication Data
A catalogue record for this book is available from the British Library

Cover design by Zuluspice www.zuluspice.com

Printed in Poland
www.polskabook.com

This book was published with support from the
Foundation for the Production and Translation of Dutch Literature

THIRSTY RIVER

RODAAN AL GALIDI

TRANSLATED BY LUZETTE STRAUSS

For the victims who never
became the perpetrators

Thirsty River family tree

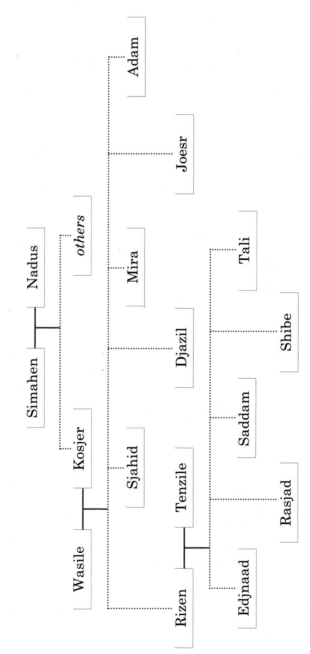

CONTENTS

Family tree   Facing page

CHAPTER 1

A brief history of a family
that had no history

In the south of Iraq flows the Thirsty River, so-called because in the winter it dries up and people can walk over the riverbed. In the summer, fresh water flows, first as a small snake and later as a dragon, which spews not fire, but waves. On the banks of the Thirsty River lives the Bird family, which for many generations had been strong and stood firm against the famines, plagues and wars that had fallen on them from the unsettled skies of Iraq. Their problems began when a stork came down to earth.

Nadim once built a high tower and on the tower he built a large nest. That is how he wanted to encourage storks to come to Boran. Nadim liked birds. He had built a number of cages and spent all his time on his birds. He enjoyed listening to their song. One day he saw a stork flying through the heavens. He had no idea of how big a stork was, because he had only ever seen them high in the sky. No one in Boran knew how big a stork was, because no one had ever seen one close up. If he had a stork, he would be the first in Boran to have one. So he began building a tower with clay bricks. The tower grew higher and higher, and when it rose above the house, his family began complaining behind his back that he never paid any attention to anything except birds and his tower. But they said nothing to Nadim. He was the strongest man in the family. Although he had seven older brothers, all of them were scared of him.

One day the sheik of the mosque knocked on the door of their house. He said that God would be angry if Nadim's tower became taller than the minaret of the mosque. But Nadim, who believed more in birds than in God, chased the sheik away. People say that he grabbed him by the beard, as one would a goat, and shouted in his face: "Make the tower of the mosque higher than heaven, and I won't complain. But don't say anything about my tower. I won't accept that. The tower will go up and never down." It was said that the sheik of the mosque trembled with fear in Nadim's hands.

Nadim slept soundly after long days toiling on the tower, while the men and women of the house were busy working all day to earn money. He kept on building until his tower was higher than the minaret. Nadim's tower could be seen from further away than the minaret. When it was complete, Nadim tied big branches together and built an enormous nest on top of his tower, big enough for a man. After that he sat beside his tower for the whole day awaiting the moment when a stork would land on it. Sometimes he clapped wooden slippers against each other, because he had heard that it made the same sound as storks made with their beaks, but no stork landed on Nadim's tower.

The sheik of the mosque said during Friday prayers that storks did not land on Nadim's tower because there were devils sitting on it, but Nadim did not believe that. He said there were no devils sitting on top of the tower, only a nest. Nadim climbed the tower and sat in the nest with two wooden slippers. The people believed what the sheik of the mosque had said. They thought that the devils were sitting in Nadim's head, which made him think he was a stork.

A while later, one of the women from the household fell ill. She lay on her deathbed and began to see devils coming in through the windows, doors and holes in the walls. The woman complained about Nadim's tower and she was taken to the home of her family, far from the tower and the devils. Everyone, except Nadim, became fearful of the devils. They begged him to make the tower lower than the minaret, but he refused. "I have already told you. The tower is not going down. If you are scared, then make the minaret higher than the tower."

After a while the faces of those who lived there became paler, as if they never slept, and one by one, they started dying. Still Nadim refused to make his tower lower. He built a wall between the house and the tower. The deaths stopped and this time the residents of Boran expected that Nadim would die, but he did not. The people saw him staring into the sky for hours on end with two wooden slippers in his hands. Sometimes they saw him sitting quietly in the nest, while daydreaming about a stork landing there.

When spring arrived, Nadim was awoken by a noise that resembled the sound he made with the wooden slippers. He jumped out of bed and ran outside. There he saw a large black-and-white bird with two long, thin legs standing on the nest. It was clapping with its red beak, which gently drew the residents of Boran to his tower. That day no one went to the mosque when the sheik called them to prayer. Everyone looked at the wonder of Nadim's tower.

"If there were devils up there, the stork would not dare land there," Nadim said softly, because he did not want to scare the stork away. He watched the bird for the whole day. If it flew away, he became anxious and wandered around like a sleepwalker, just as Adam would many years later. The family members avoided talking to Nadim if the stork was not on the tower, because then he would not say a word. They thought that the stork took Nadim's soul with it into the heavens and brought it back when it returned, because when the stork landed on the tower again, Nadim came alive.

With the end of the season, the time of the birds' migration arrived and the stork flew away. This time it circled for longer than normal around the tower and looked at Nadim, as if bidding him farewell.

11

"Shoot at the bird, perhaps it won't come back," said one of the women, but Nadim was not listening. The stork flapped its wings graciously and flew higher and higher. Nadim felt that day that the bird would not return. He went to lie down on his bed and shivered with fever. He began to hallucinate and only ate and drank when the wooden slippers were clapped behind a screen. He was wasting away and five weeks later he died.

The family broke the tower down until it was lower than the minaret. They burnt the stork's nest, because they thought devils were occupying it, but the following spring the family was awoken by the sound of clapping slippers. The stork looked even bigger this time, because the tower was lower. The family wanted to chase it away, but they were afraid that it would take away the soul of one of their family members.

The founding members of the family were the first inhabitants of Boran. They were named Star. It was said of Dajim that he fled from the desert fearful of revenge, because he had murdered a Bedouin who had used the name of his sister in a poem. He had sworn that he would not dismount from his horse until he had killed the Bedouin. So he had been supported on his horse by two men, one on either side, to prevent him from falling off while he slept, and he had used a bucket for his bodily functions. Once he had killed the Bedouin, he immediately jumped off his horse, fell down next to the Bedouin's corpse and screamed from backache.

One night he had slept with a group of travellers at the place where Boran would later be founded. Dajim wanted to live in that place. One of the travellers, a soothsayer, smelt the earth and told him that it would be better to move on, because the ground there smelt of dried blood. Dajim, fascinated by the breeze coming from the Thirsty River, decided to settle by himself in the place where they had spent the night and, when the sun rose, the first inhabitants of Boran began to build houses with cellars underneath in which to sleep during the heat of summer. The first house completed was that of Dajim Star.

Years later the men of the house fled into the cellar in fear of the Ottomans, who sought to take all the household's animals and men to fight in the wars of their vast empire. During this time, the inhabitants of Boran learnt two things: the size of your moustache indicated how much of a man you were, and the better you listened to the sultan in Istanbul, the better a Muslim you were. Apart from the women and children, the Ottoman soldiers saw only a horse in Dajim's house, which he had been unable to take underground. The Ottoman soldiers tortured the women with fire, after which one of them led them to the secret cellar. The soldiers dragged all the men, goats, sheep and chickens outside and took all the men and animals with them to Istanbul. From that day on, the cellar's trapdoor was buried, until the day of the murder of Baan, when Joesr opened the wooden trapdoor to become the final inhabitant of the cellar.

The Star family were not well liked. Nevertheless, they were one of the most respected families, esteemed above all others, because no one ever saw their women. There was not even any proof that the women existed. The men of the household had built a high wall and shuttered the windows with clay. At that time there were ten men in the family with thick, black moustaches. Their mother said proudly that if she were to weave their moustaches together she could make a rope that would be able to hold back a randy bull. The men were so preoccupied with the honour of the family that they banned any sex in the house, even if it was making love with their wives outside the house, behind the palm trees, in hidden corners. One day one of the rams of the household jumped on one of the ewes. Because the girls in the house could see what was happening, the men immediately shot the ram.

This was one of the sheep that brought misery to the family, as was later to be the case with Kosjer's ram. Rumours were spreading that Dime, the only sister among ten brothers, was the most beautiful woman in Boran. After she had seen what the ram had done with the ewe, she began dreaming about men. She could not talk about it, except with one of the other women, whom she trusted. The woman said to Dime that she would be slaughtered just like the ram if she repeated even just one word about it. Dime, who was never afraid, laughed in the face of the woman who warned her. "They killed the ram, not the ewe," she said.

One day a young man from Boran accompanied by his mother knocked on the family's door. The boy said that he wanted to marry Dime. The ten brothers told him that no woman with any such name lived in the house and said it would be the last thing he ever did if he knocked on that door again. So the young man, who had heard of Dime's beauty but who had never seen it for himself, disappeared.

Then Dime entrusted her fate to the sheik of the mosque. The sheik went to the ten brothers and told them that God forbade what they were doing. He spelt out to them how sex was good for the soul. He became so enthusiastic that he even told them how many positions there were and those that were and were not permitted by God. "Your wife is your field," he said. "Plant it any which way, except from behind." To clarify that the doggie position was allowed, but not anal sex, he continued: "Take your field from behind, but not *in* the behind. From behind and not in the behind is permitted, but from behind and *in* behind is not permitted by God." When he had finished explaining, one of the ten brothers grabbed him, just like Nadim had long ago, by his beard, and dragged him outside like a goat.

Dime was like a flower that happened to blossom in a desolate place. She grew up alone. The seasons stretched out without her being plucked, without her being smelt or being treasured. Her beauty was unsurpassed and it protected her from hands that might have hit her; no one in the family hit her out of respect for her beauty, no one screamed at her or spat in her face. She was not asked to work hard, as were the other women in the house, where they worked harder than the men. For that reason when the hormones started swirling, they had a lot of room in that graceful body. From that moment on, Dime no longer had any peace in her life.

In a house full of chickens, cows, flies and dogs, surrounded by walls of clay, Dime grew up in a few square metres. She was like a sea contained. With a needle in front of the mirror she searched for pimples on her face and then carefully pierced her skin, as if opening a tunnel of light in a dark mountain. If she found no pimples, she pricked her skin with the needle just to feel it. Then she pushed the needle deep into her skin and looked at the growing drop of blood until the moment when it ran down, and she touched the edge of her lip with the needle. That is how she translated her desire to kiss or to touch someone. Sometimes it looked as if her face had been stung by bees. Her mother admonished her, but she did not listen.

Dime became a tall young woman, and as she grew, her ten brothers made the walls higher, so that no one from outside could see her. After she had gone to the sheik of the mosque, the only time she had been out of the house since her breasts had begun to grow, her brothers held her like a prisoner in her room. Once a day she quietly tried to open the door. If it was locked, she tried again the next day. Every day she opened the curtains in front of the densely plastered window, listened to the clapping of the stork and dreamt that it would take her far away from Boran.

In the light of the sunshine that streamed into her room through one little hole, she began digging into her face with the needle. Every day she cut off a piece of her dress. She began with her sleeves, until she came to her shoulders. Then she started on the collar, until her nipples were visible. She cut away at the hem, until the dress no longer covered her knees. After that she stuck the needle in her face, until the blood dripped from her round cheeks and her face became a mask of blood with two captive dark eyes.

One day one of the women of the house forgot to turn the key in the lock when she removed the pan that Dime used as a toilet. This time, when Dime tried to open the door, it moved. Without anyone noticing, she slipped outside. She looked briefly at the stork and then began running naked through the streets of Boran. She screamed the words that are still being repeated, the words that changed the surname of the family from Star to Bird. "Hunter, hunter, my cunt has become a bird."

She ran to the Thirsty River and threw herself into the water. Her ten brothers mounted a search for her and took a blanket with them. This would serve to cover her if she was found, so that no one would see her naked body, but they did not find her. Only when the Thirsty River ran dry the following winter, did one of the brothers come home with her bones and her hair in a sack. He had found her in the little stream at the end of the Thirsty River.

After Dime's death the strong men of the family fled the Bird home with their wives to faraway cities out of shame at her nakedness on the streets of Boran and the family began to lose its prestige in the town. The men earned their daily bread by weaving carpets, and nothing of the previous glory of the family remained, except the high wall around the house. The generations who had forgotten Dime thought the family had the surname Bird because they were fond of doves and because of the stork's tower, but some of the older women in Boran still recalled the story of Dime. Some women said that the Thirsty River had devoured the flesh of Dime and thrown her bones into the stream. That is why it dried up every year, out of a sense of remorse over Dime's death.

Chapter 2

Simahen

Because the Bird family had lost its reputation and its glory, the women could find no marriage candidates for their sons, especially not for Nadus, who was renowned in Boran as a master weaver. No family wanted to offer him a wife because weavers, due to the nature of their work, are always at home and therefore not respected. When his mother had lost all hope, such that she had resorted to looking for the daughter of a weaver, she heard of a girl named Simahen. She was the daughter of a rich landowner and her brother wanted her married off quickly so he could take her land. Thus Simahen married Nadus.

Simahen grew up among date palms, rice paddies and canals filled with sparkling water from the Euphrates. When she went with the girls of the village to pick grapes and gather figs and pomegranates, the air above them was strewn with birds and light that seemed to have risen from the green earth. In her town there were no cars or tanks, and people knew nothing about Baghdad and who ruled over whom. The only thing she knew about Iraq were the names of the cities where the holy Shi'ite imams were buried. The older people from the village had been there on pilgrimages.

Simahen had asked her father, who never denied her anything, if she could go to Samarra to visit the holy graves of Imam Ali Al Hadi and Imam Al Hassan Al Askari. Actually, she did not really want to visit the graves of the imams, but Samarra was the most distant place she knew from the village. If she visited the imams' shrines, she would see a great deal on the way. On the day of her departure, she rode on a donkey to the road where she would wave down a bus, but when she got there Simahen became scared and longed for her village. So she went back with the man who returned with the donkeys. Simahen talked eagerly about her pilgrimage from the village to the road. She related everything she had seen on the way.

When pilgrims returned and told of what they had seen during their journey, Simahen used their stories as if she had participated herself. Each time in her stories she went a little further than the road from where she had returned with the donkeys, as if she had really been to Samarra, and not only in her imagination. When she eventually travelled to Samarra four years later and did not come back with the donkeys, her stories remained the same after her return, as if she had travelled in her imagination this time and had not actually gone to Samarra. The only thing that changed after her actual visit, was her great longing for her village and her anxiety that the way back would be much longer or would disappear. The pilgrims recalled how Simahen ran crying to the donkeys that were waiting to take her back to the village. After that she never left the village again, that is until her only brother Abbas had her married off so he could inherit her piece of land for himself.

Her father had said that he would leave each of his daughters a piece of land, but if they married their inheritance would go to Abbas, so that the land that had been in the family's possession for a hundred years would not fall into the hands of strangers. The father did not know that Abbas, after the forty days of mourning, would have his sisters married off in a few weeks so that he could take ownership of their land. Simahen resisted the marriage, but the wife of Abbas, who hated Simahen, spread a rumour in the village that her sister-in-law refused to marry because she was no longer a virgin.

"The bastard," said Simahen when she realised that the wife had even been incited by Abbas. "He exchanges his honour for a piece of land." Because everyone in the village now believed that she was no longer a virgin, she agreed to get married, but not before one year had passed after the death of her father.

Because of the rumour, no one from her village wanted to marry her and so she was married off to the carpet weaver, Nadus. Thus she came on a donkey to Boran, the town far from her beautiful, green village. For her entire life she complained that Abbas – may God refuse to bless him and send him to hell – had let her marry a carpet weaver because he wanted to steal her land. When Simahen entered her husband's bedroom for the first time, she pinched her nose tightly. "Abbas, may God break your neck in this life and the next. You have married me off to rubbish!"

Nadus entered the room with a white handkerchief in his hand to be able to prove her virginity. Outside the family heard a racket. It sounded like screaming and hitting. The men and women thought that their young man was getting busy, but after just half an hour Nadus came running out covered from head to toe in blood. He stepped over the threshold and fell over.

"Idiots," he said as the men helped him to his feet, "you have let me marry a tiger."

The door was opened once again. Everyone saw the hand of Simahen, which threw the handkerchief out, still as white as snow. It fluttered down on to Nadus's head. The door closed again. Simahen fell asleep, crying silently.

For days on end Nadus dared not enter the room. The women of the house treated her like a queen. One evening she summoned Nadus, who went into the room cowering like a little rabbit. Only after she had made the decision, did she let him touch her. Before she had sex with him, she told him to close his eyes tightly. He slept with her, exactly as she wanted, with all their clothes on, so that nothing of her body would be visible, except what was essential. When Nadus was finished, he took out the white handkerchief that he had kept in his trouser pocket until that moment. She immediately began beating him on the head with her shoe.

"Filthy weaver, do you want to prove that I'm a virgin? To whom? Ask your mother how many times she was screwed in her arse before your father let that handkerchief get bloodied."

With his sharp white teeth Nadus bit into his own wrist until it began bleeding. He dabbed at the wound with the handkerchief and went out. In those days families did not test the blood on the handkerchief. People say that in Boran many a cat had been killed in a room to use its blood to prove that a woman was a virgin. Many cats paid with their lives to assert the virginity of girls who had done something before marriage. It was said that before the custom began to disappear in Boran, a girl once went to a doctor and said that she would be killed if her prospective husband discovered she was not a virgin. The doctor sewed a piece of rabbit skin in place of the hymen. When her husband tried to have sex with her, the rabbit skin proved too thick and too strong for his penis. He howled and howled, and his mother, who was standing behind the closed door waiting, called out to him. "My dear son, have you opened her?" "No, but my balls are going to explode," he wailed.

When Simahen became pregnant with her first child she started to save money that she took from Nadus's wages. When he resisted giving it to her but gave it instead to his mother, she hit him hard. With some of the money she bought groceries and with the rest she bought gold. She hid it for the dark days, under the floor of her bedroom or between the bricks in the wall. She would have preferred to buy land. In her view that was better than gold. In the village where she was born and grew up, people with a lot of land had more power. Land could not be stolen, but it also could not be hidden away. However, the money that she saved was not enough to buy land, but enough for a few hundred grams of gold. When her children had grown up and gone out to work, she also took money from them and hid even more gold. No one knew she was doing it. The only one who knew her secret was the jeweller in the big market in Najaf, a descendent of the Prophet Mohamed, which was why Simahen trusted him.

Since the day Simahen had left her village to go to her husband's house, she had never been back to her brother's house for a visit. She longed for her village, but never went there because she did not want to cross paths with Abbas. He had tried to visit her, but she refused, even when he asked if he could see her children. On his deathbed Abbas asked her to forgive him. Because she could not write, she sent her words back with the messenger. "Let him ask forgiveness from God."

Her brother sent the messenger again, this time with a calf, and asked her again for forgiveness, but Simahen sent the calf back. Then Abbas sent a calf and a cow. "Do not send me back with a single animal," the messenger pleaded. "Your sister forgave him after a hen, a goat and a sheep. I've come such a long way, please take the cow and the calf." He knelt tearfully in front of her and explained that Abbas had promised him a pregnant ewe, if he came back without the cow and the calf. Simahen looked at the cow's udder, full of milk. For a moment it appeared she would grant forgiveness. Nadus and her sons were standing behind her and were hoping she would accept the cow and the calf, but they dared not ask her and waited breathless on Simahen's answer.

"Take it back," Simahen said eventually, with an anguished voice, because it was difficult to refuse a cow. But the pain inflicted on her by her brother was greater than the udder, the tears she had cried were more than the milk it carried, and the grief weighing on her shoulders was surely heavier than the calf.

"Noooooo," squealed Nadus. Simahen took her slipper off and hit him.

"He made me marry a weaver. I swear, I will never in his life let him forget that," she said to those who criticised her for sending the cow back.

Days later, Simahen discovered the cow and the calf still standing beneath the date palms behind the house. With a slipper in her hand she stalked around furiously, looking for her husband and her sons, who had fled in the face of her anger. She did not want her brother to die believing that she had forgiven him. It was a few hours later that she managed to get hold of Nadus and hit him with her slipper, until her sons rescued him. She wanted to send the cow and calf back. But, with his face black and blue, Nadus begged her not to.

"The man is dead. We can't send the calf and cow to heaven."

So the cow and the calf stayed, but Simahen swore that she would never drink a single drop of milk from that cow.

"Is the butter from that cow?" she asked every day for weeks on end.

"No," everyone said, and then she ate it.

"Is that cup of milk from the cow?"

"No." Then she drank it.

Sometimes she sent the milk from the cow to a friend who also had a cow, and swapped it. Sometimes she screamed that the bitch had shaken the milk to get the butter out.

Like most of the inhabitants of Boran, Simahen did not know the date of her birth. When she had gone with all her children to the city hall to get an identity card for the first time, the official asked for her date of birth.

"When the English came," she said. The official wrote '1920' in her file, because he did not know that the English came to Iraq in 1917, but he did know the year of the uprising against them. Years later Simahen went to the city hall to get a new identity card because her old one had been eaten by a goat. To avoid having to pay, she told the official she had never had an identity card. He asked for her date of birth. "When the English came," she replied. This time the official gave her an identity card with the date of 1917.

So Simahen acquired two dates of birth, one with the arrival of the English and one with the uprising against them. When Simahen went to the city hall years later for a passport to go to Mecca to become a *hajja*, the official opened the older file and discovered the two dates.

"You have two dates of birth, that is not permitted," he said.

"My son, may God bless you. I was only born once and not twice, but I have died a thousand times. Do not prevent me from seeing Mecca," said Simahen. The official let '1920' stand.

"So, we have made you three years younger," he said laughingly.

Simahen reacted graciously.

Simahen paid little attention to her children, except to Kosjer, her youngest son, who was difficult to understand and slow to comprehend. He was thin, and a stream of slime ran from the corner of his mouth. He had nothing to his name, not even slippers, because his brothers took everything he had.

One day one of their aunts came on her donkey to visit the Bird family. That day Kosjer watched the donkey for hours and the donkey watched him. Kosjer liked the donkey. He begged to be allowed to ride on it and the following day his wish was granted. He sat for hours on the donkey behind his aunt, who could not have any children, on the way back to her village. The aunt's husband saw how half-witted the boy was, how much he liked the donkey, and how long he stared at it. He realised that the donkey understood Kosjer or that Kosjer understood the donkey. Either way we have a big problem, thought the aunt's husband. For that reason he began teaching Kosjer the alphabet and began to work on the boy's brain.

Long before that, in 1908, the first motor car had arrived in Boran, from Aleppo in Syria. The father of Kosjer's grandfather had slid under the car to investigate the horse that had to be in its belly, because it was unfathomable how a cart could move without a horse. Once Kosjer had learnt to read and write, he was looking at a book with photos of cars. Kosjer repeated the question of his grandfather's father.

"How can the car move?"

"Because it burns gasoline," said his aunt's husband. The boy was perturbed for days on end, staring deep in thought at the donkey, and the donkey at him.

"If I burn gasoline then will I also be able to move like a car?" asked Kosjer.

The husband of the aunt felt that Kosjer was not becoming any cleverer despite having begun to read and write, but he had begun to grasp his own stupidity. He regretted having taught the boy to read, because the more Kosjer read, the more he looked at the donkey. That was when the husband of the aunt decided that the best solution would be to send the boy back to his family.

Back at home, Kosjer spent much time sitting and thinking, as if he was busy in his head with a big problem. The family thought he had gone crazy and took him to a traditional doctor in Boran. He examined the boy thoroughly and ordered him to choose an egg from a pot full of eggs. Kosjer picked one and gave it to the man, who put it in a pot full of water. The egg sank to the bottom.

"If there is a chick in the egg, it will float. If there is no chick in it, it sinks. Your egg is empty." The traditional doctor gave Kosjer a green stone that was as round as the egg and read a sura out of the Koran. Then he wrote a holy passage on a piece of yellowing paper and ordered Kosjer to put his head on the ground and to lift his feet up and put them on the wall. Kosjer stayed like that for two hours, while the doctor smeared him with stinking creams, read verses and burnt incense. After that he sent him home and told him not to drink anything for a day and not to eat anything for two days.

Thus Kosjer was cured of the alphabet. Nadus had thought that his son would weave carpets, but he decided to become a sheep trader because, when he was still able to read, he had read that every prophet had begun as a shepherd. Kosjer built a pen behind the house, where Adam would later lie, and became a respected trader of sheep, albeit one who was laughed at behind his back.

One day Simahen noticed that Kosjer's moustache was getting darker and that he had begun shaving the first soft stubble on his chin. The time had come for her son to be married. The only problem was that it would not be easy to find a wife for Kosjer, even more difficult than it had been for his father. The older women in the household asked other women to identify suitable marriage candidates, and discovered a girl who went by the name of Wasile. She lived in a village behind the date palms of Boran. She cropped her hair short, rode a horse like a boy and was not scared of snakes and scorpions.

Her father had wanted her to be born a boy, because then she would have become a strong man.

Wasile married Kosjer when he was sixteen. In the clay room, which he had built himself to see his wife in for the first time, he removed the veil that concealed her eyes. He thought briefly that she was only nine years old, although she had just turned thirteen. Kosjer had the little handkerchief in his hand, which he had received from Simahen with the instruction to come out of the room only when it was red, otherwise she would boil him – despite the fact that she herself had furiously fought when it was expected of her. He was nervous, a sliver of slime ran from the corner of his mouth.

By the light of the lantern he saw Wasile sitting on the edge of the bed, that had been made from date palm branches. She was wearing a white dress, full of dust from the journey from her village to Boran on a donkey. He saw her black hair and eyes that were not afraid. He wanted to lift the hem of her dress, but she brushed his hand away. She took off her plastic shoes and her colourful socks with little flowers. For a minute Kosjer sat and watched her. Then he lifted her dress with trembling hands. He looked for the first time at her thin legs, threw himself on her and began to pant and quiver.

When he was finished, he went with the lantern in his hand in search of the white handkerchief, which was shining like a white flag in the darkness. After he had dipped it in her blood, he went outside. He held the bloody handkerchief in one hand and the lantern in the other. The men of the household fired into the air and everyone was glad for Kosjer, who had reached a milestone as a man, and for Wasile, who had passed the test of her virginity.

Wasile trembled at the shots and sat on the bed like a little bird. She thought about running away, but she was scared, not of foxes and wolves, which hid away among the date palms, but of her brothers. The following day she found herself among the women of the household, who hit her on her bottom and screamed at her to do it like this and not like that. She could not sit or lie down for a moment, except when night fell, and Kosjer returned.

Months later Wasile had been transformed from a child into a woman. Before her second year in the Bird family household was over, she had given birth to Rizen. She had learnt to make bread, to cook and to fetch water – in the summer out of the Thirsty River and in the winter out of the well. The flesh of her childhood years had developed into womanly muscle. Because Wasile was always testing Simahen's medicines, it was said that as she grew older she began to look like a man. Wasile hated everything around her, especially the women who followed her with their eyes, as if she was a shadow of herself.

One day her patience ran out. She ran out of the house, not naked, as Dime had done, but with her clothes on, and not to the Thirsty River, but to her family. The following day one of her brothers, after giving her a hiding and telling her not to come back again, returned her to her husband. "The girl is still young. She will learn," her embarrassed brother said to Simahen. He left without having seen the inside of the house. When Kosjer returned from watching over his flock, Simahen called him to her bedroom. She gave him a switch that she had broken off a pomegranate tree.

"The slut ran away from you, because you did not fill her eyes with yours," she said. "You are not a man in her eyes. Take this switch and break it on her head. If you don't do it, I am no longer your mother." She began to wind him up like an old clock. She threatened, cried and clucked like a hen until Kosjer began to tremble with rage.

He grabbed the switch and went to the room of Wasile, who had managed only one full day with her family. He began to hit her without looking at her, while her child Rizen, whom she had left behind when she had gone to her family, sat crying in a corner of the room. He hit her until blood started dripping from the switch and Wasile could no longer move.

Kosjer came out of the room carrying the bloody switch and the women looked at him with admiration. Proud of himself he strode up to Simahen, who had heard Wasile's screaming. He laid the switch down in front of her.

"Now you really are my son," she said. "The milk that I let you drink from my breast was not given in vain."

The next day Simahen saw Wasile creeping to the toilet like a bird with broken wings. Her heart broke. "Who did this to you?" she screamed.

"Kosjer," answered the women of the house, in chorus. She threatened, cried and clucked like a hen and called Kosjer. He came to her room, she shut the door and began hitting him until the same switch was smeared with Kosjer's blood.

The women of the household looked on with amazement at Simahen.

"The idiot!" she cried with a tremor in her voice. "How dare he hit such a little girl and a stranger." She ordered that one of the young cockerels be slaughtered and cooked for Wasile, at which all the women of the house began to chase after one of the birds.

After that Wasile never thought of running away again. At night, when everyone was asleep, she went to the banks of the Thirsty River and cried. One day she heard from an old woman that if someone fasted for forty Wednesdays as Zachariah had done, and spoke with no one, they would meet the prophet Khidr in their dreams. For forty Wednesdays she did not eat and she did not speak, and in a dream she saw a man wearing green clothes smiling at her. She knew immediately that it was Khidr. She asked him to free her, from herself or from everyone in the house.

"Patience, Wasile, at the right time the ram will bring the solution," Khidr said to her.

When Wasile gave birth to her last child, Adam, she was freed from everyone in the house, except from Simahen, and her six children. Kosjer had bought a ram with large horns, from a distant village that was renowned for its lusty rams, to impregnate his ewes. The ram was the reason for the disappearance of the men of the Bird family. Some people in Boran said that the ram had emptied the household, others said that it had been Saddam Hussein.

The residents of Boran joked that Wasile had been transformed into a man after the men of the house had disappeared, and that her body was as hairy as that of a monkey. Some thought that it was for the best that Kosjer had disappeared and Wasile no longer became pregnant, because every time Wasile had borne a new child there was a change of power in Baghdad – except with the birth of her only daughter, Mira, who was five years older than her last child, Adam. With the birth of Mira nothing happened in Baghdad, except that eight ministers were hanged, a few hundred soldiers were murdered and two cities were bombed. The residents of Boran became concerned when Wasile was pregnant, and when her labour began, soldiers carrying guns were to be seen on the streets of Boran.

"I think Wasile must be going to give birth today," said one of the neighbours when he saw a soldier.

"She has given birth," said Kosjer, "otherwise no soldiers would appear on the streets."

When coups d'état no longer took place in Baghdad, no one knew if it was because Kosjer had disappeared and no new children were being born, or because Saddam Hussein had come to power. When Naji had completed the first huge mural of Saddam Hussein in white clothing and with a Cuban cigar, Wasile saw Saddam Hussein in a dream. Just as she had asked Khidr to free her from everyone, she asked Saddam Hussein to bring everyone back.

"Sir, God bless you. Simahen goes to the party's house every day and asks after the men of this house. Every time she says that the party took them."

Saddam Hussein appeared very clearly in Wasile's dream. "Yes, Wasile, it's true. He who gives life, takes life away. God gives, God takes away. The party gives, the party takes away. And you, Wasile, will no longer become pregnant. If you become pregnant, they will drag me through the streets on a rope or riddle me with bullets."

Wasile saw that Saddam Hussein had an enormous stomach. She asked him if he was pregnant.

"Yes, I am pregnant and will shortly give birth to Iraq."

After the dream, Wasile no longer dared look at the murals of Saddam Hussein, which appeared on every street and in every neighbourhood of Boran and on all the buildings. Saddam

Hussein dressed as a Bedouin, Saddam Hussein in American cowboy clothes, Saddam Hussein in Kurdish clothes, Saddam Hussein in pyjamas, Saddam Hussein in a bikini, Saddam Hussein on a horse, on a camel, on a tank, on the shoulders of the people, Saddam Hussein in an aeroplane, in a helicopter, on a ship, in a submarine. Saddam Hussein in a taxi, on a mountain, in a valley, on a hill, on the clouds. Saddam Hussein with a gun, with a knife, with a pistol, with a sword, with a pen, with a lighter and with a match.

One day a taxi driver from Boran was very drunk, and he shouted at a mural of Saddam Hussein. "We need a painting of Mr President with no clothes on. I really want to see his dick, out of which we all, Iraq and every Arab nation, come and with which he will screw Israel and America."

The taxi driver did not come home that day. Men said that he worked for the secret police and had received an order to sow fear in Boran. That he fled suddenly in his taxi. No one dared ask after him at the secret service, the party's house or the police, not after what had happened to Kosjer's father and his brothers, who had asked after Kosjer.

CHAPTER 3

The three coincidences

On the same day that Saddam Hussein came to power, Adam, the last child of Kosjer and Wasile, was born asleep. The midwife who brought him into the world thought that he was dead. "He was a boy," she said quietly, as she picked him up by his feet and laid him on the ground.

Then, suddenly he moved his tiny hands. The Bird family gathered around and looked at him. "He's dead!" they all said at the same time.

"He's sleeping," said Mira, his sister, who at the very moment Adam was born was exactly five years old – one of three coincidences surrounding the birth of Adam. No one paid any attention to her words, but Mira always believed that Adam was sleeping. At the same instant that the midwife picked Adam up by his feet, the other two coincidences occurred.

Kosjer was just returning from the distant village, where he had bought a stout ram with big horns that would impregnate his ewes. On the way home he passed the teahouse, where everyone had gathered to watch the one and only television in Boran, a black-and-white set. Kosjer was glad to be back in Boran after his long journey with the ram. On the way he had given it food and water, and was so happy with it that he had allowed it to look at the date palms or the sky and regularly, every half-hour, let it lie down. From the teahouse he heard applause, which sparked in him the allergy of clapping – an incurable disease in Boran – and he began to move his hands. Kosjer laughed happily, making his golden tooth glisten. He had not clapped in a long time. He forgot about the heavily pregnant Wasile and began clapping his hands, in which he was still holding the rope by which he had been leading the ram. The ram was taken aback; he could not understand how Kosjer could move his body so energetically after such a long journey. Kosjer tied the ram to a metal pole in front of him. He had not seen the pole before and he did not know that it was the aerial for the television in the teahouse. Applauding, he went into the teahouse with his face covered in dust.

The television had two wooden doors and four legs. It stood in the middle of the teahouse like in a puppet theatre. The tall aerial outside pointed towards Baghdad. If the wind moved it, the teahouse boy went outside and moved the pole from left to right until the picture returned. If it was raining or there was a storm, the picture from Baghdad disappeared and vague images from the neighbouring countries were visible or the image was made up of vibrating black and white dots.

On this day, the reception was clear. A newsreader with a large moustache filled the screen and bellowed like a car stuck in the mud. He said that Comrade Saddam Hussein had become the president of Iraq. Saddam Hussein had been second in charge to president Ahmed Hassan al-Bakr since 1968. When the people in the teahouse heard the name Saddam Hussein, they began to applaud.

"With our souls and with our blood we offer ourselves up for you, Saddam." The newsreader disappeared and the national anthem boomed out. Then everyone in the teahouse saw the Iraqi army marching rhythmically through the streets with tanks, rockets and cannons, which were adorned with Iraqi and Palestinian flags.

Suddenly Saddam Hussein filled the screen. Every visitor in the teahouse stood up, as if a scorpion had simultaneously stung everyone on the arse. The applause grew even louder. Saddam Hussein looked each and every one of them in the eye, as if he were not on the television, but standing in the flesh before them. No one dared turn their head or look Saddam Hussein in the eye. Everyone, except the children, looked at the ground and kept absolutely still, because Saddam Hussein was about to speak. Kosjer smiled and promised himself that he would name the new child Saddam if it was a son and if it was a daughter, Sabha, after Saddam Hussein's mother.

Saddam Hussein began his speech. After every word he left a silent pause to give time for applause. "Beloved." Applause… "People." Applause… "Great." Applause… "Arab." Applause… "Nation." Applause… "Marvellous." Applause… "Iraq." Applause… "On." Applause… "This." Applause… "Momentous." Applause… "Day." Applause…

While everyone in the teahouse clapped energetically, Saddam Hussein suddenly disappeared from the screen. He transformed into innumerable black and white dots. The audience was nailed to the spot with dread when they saw how Saddam Hussein with his moustache, his military uniform and the insignia on his shoulders and swords and stars on his chest was transformed into black and white dots and his voice into crackling noise. Everyone was afraid that a coup d'état had taken place in Baghdad again and that the broadcast had been interrupted. No one dared look at anyone else. They expected that Saddam Hussein would immediately fill the screen again, albeit covered with blood, as had happened with the first president of Iraq, General Abdul Karim Qasim, who, after the broadcast had been restored, appeared lying on the floor next to his chair as a soldier spat in his bloodied face. Kosjer even thought that Wasile must have borne twins and he had to do his best to suppress a smile.

"Long live fighter and Comrade Saddam Hussein," shouted one of the members of the Ba'ath party in the teahouse.

Everyone began to call out after him. "Long live, long live, long live." Applause filled the teahouse anew, which made everyone feel safe, because no one could be accused if they were applauding.

"But he's gone," said a child. A hard slap followed. Silence. Only the crackle of the television could be heard. Everyone anxiously watched the screen, stared at the countless black and white dots, which were moving on the screen like powerful bacteria under a microscope and just a short while ago had been Saddam Hussein. For a moment the dots began to come together, allowing Saddam Hussein to fill the screen and the crackle to become his voice, but just a moment later he became black and white dots again, and his voice a crackle.

"The." Crackle... "K..." Crackle... "Iraq." Crackle... "K..." Crackle... "K..." Crackle... The children laughed as they heard Saddam Hussein shouting at one moment and then clucking like a chicken the next. Here and there slaps could be heard, followed by silence and crackle filling the teahouse again.

The black and white dots came together again and a presenter emerged to be seen, this time, without a moustache. "The bloodthirsty criminal Saddam Hussein has deposed Ahmed Hassan al-Bakr. This man will drown Iraq in blood and burn it."

The people in the teahouse could not believe what they were hearing.

"I call on the Iraqi people to rise up against this criminal." Hadi the Rocket, the chairman of the Ba'ath party in Boran, drew his pistol from his belt, held it in the air and screamed, as if it was not the presenter on the television, but the public in the teahouse who had uttered the threat.

"Silence!" The presenter with no moustache disappeared and a woman, with a bunch of lettuce in her hand, behind a table with pots, vegetables and fruit, filled the screen. She disappeared again just as suddenly and a woman singing in Turkish on a boat in the sea became visible. After that they saw someone with a long beard shouting in Persian, while thousands of people listened to him. When he disappeared, the screen was filled with a man and a woman screwing on a table. Coincidentally, the man had the same moustache, the same hair and a comparable arse to Saddam Hussein. Everyone was afraid. Was that the penis of Saddam Hussein? Why was he screwing the woman on a table and not on a bed?

The boy from the teahouse went outside to check the aerial and came back shouting. "The ram! The ram!"

Everyone stormed out, as if they had been waiting for an excuse to evacuate that room. Outside they saw a large ram, larger than the ram Dime had seen jump on the ewe. The ram was butting the aerial pole with its enormous horns. First it looked angrily at the antenna and then lunged at it vigorously. Then it took a few steps back, as far as the rope would allow, and rammed the pole again. The antenna, through which Saddam Hussein fell upon Iraq from out of the heavens and made him appear on the screen through a thin cable to threaten and cackle, swayed. Hadi the Rocket brandished his pistol and walked up to the ram, which showed no fear of the pistol and kept its concentration fixed on the aerial. Hadi the Rocket pointed his pistol at the large head and fired at the moment the ram jumped into the air. The ram, riddled with six bullets, fell dead at the foot of the aerial.

"Who does this ram belong to?" screamed Hadi the Rocket, swaggering with his pistol. No one answered. "Who tied that sheep to the aerial?" Kosjer kept quiet. But a little later two comrades from the Ba'ath party grabbed Kosjer by his hands, which were still hot from clapping. Hadi the Rocket looked at Kosjer, from whose face the blood was draining. "Take him away!" The two comrades ushered Kosjer away and beat him about the head.

Everyone stood where they were. They dared not go inside nor did they leave. The boy from the teahouse turned the antenna until Saddam Hussein reappeared on the screen, where he remained for years.

"Do not let this aerial move," said Hadi the Rocket to a party member carrying a Kalashnikov. "If your mother's cunt turns into a bird and lands on the aerial, shoot it dead." Thus he referred to Dime's words, which were still remembered in Boran.

The party member remained standing near the ram's corpse and everyone else went to sit in front of the television. After seeing what had happened to Kosjer and his ram, they applauded even harder this time round.

"Pity about that sheep," whispered some. "If he had slaughtered it according to ritual, we would have been able to fill thirty pots, but now we must throw it to the dogs." No one had any pity for Kosjer, who was taken away with his hands bound in rope, in a car with a blue number-plate, while the party member hit him in the face with the butt of his Kalashnikov.

"How many enemies will our revolution have?" said Saddam Hussein on the television. "Twenty thousand? Thirty thousand? A hundred thousand? I will cut their heads off one by one without disturbing a single hair on my body. Comrades, it is no exaggeration that I have a soft heart that breaks when I tread on an ant."

When his speech was over, beautiful women in colourful clothing sang a song in Arabic and Kurdish. "Precious, precious, Saddam is precious."

On a table in the teahouse two party members placed photos of Saddam Hussein. Large ones for the wall, small ones to hang round the neck. As they left the teahouse, everyone took one large photo and one small photo.

The owner of the teahouse picked up one of the large pictures from the table. On the back was written: "Saddam Hussein, his excellency the president of Iraq." He wanted to hang it next to the photo of Ahmed Hassan al-Bakr, the previous president, but Hadi the Rocket told him that the photo of Ahmed Hassan al-Bakr was no longer necessary. So the owner of the teahouse took the photo of the previous president down and hung the photo of Saddam Hussein on the wall.

In the same frame, behind the same piece of glass and in the same place, the photo of King Faisal had hung from 1921, until he had died in September 1933. After that the photo of King Ghazi was hung next to it. In April 1939 King Ghazi died in a motor accident. He was succeeded by his young son Faisal II, under regency of Prince Abd al-Ilah. The photo of King Faisal I remained hanging after his death next to that of King Ghazi, the only person who remained in the frame until he lay in his grave, until Faisal II was inaugurated as king in May 1953. King Faisal II remained hanging undisturbed on the wall until a military coup d'etat in Baghdad in July 1958 brought General Abdul Karim Qasim to power.

That was the end of the monarchy; Iraq became a republic. General Abdul Karim Qasim remained hanging on the wall until he was murdered in 1963 by members of the Ba'ath party, and the photo of Abdul Salam Arif appeared in the frame in the teahouse. His place on the wall was taken by the photo of Abdul Rahman Arif, his brother, who came to power after Abdul Salam Arif died in a helicopter crash. When, in July 1968, comrades from the Ba'ath party ordered him to leave Iraq after a military coup, a thin layer of dust settled on the frame. The wall behind it was still as white as in 1921. The photo of the bald Ahmed Hassan al-Bakr appeared in the same frame until the day in July 1979 when Adam was born, Mira turned five and the photo of Saddam Hussein took pride of place in the frame on the wall.

On the evening of the day on which Adam was born, everyone in the Bird family household was waiting for the return of Kosjer with the ram, but he never came back. Half an hour after the ram had been shot dead by Hadi the Rocket, a boy had shouted from behind the wall around the house: "They killed the sheep!" The women of the Bird family started screaming before they knew which sheep was being referred to.

Only after an hour did his brother dare go to the police to ask after the sheep and Kosjer, but he never came back. Another brother went there to ask after Kosjer, but he also disappeared. A third went to look from a distance at what had happened to those who had gone to ask after Kosjer and the sheep, but he never returned. The following evening a group of Ba'ath party members and the secret police came into the house. They brought all its inhabitants together in one room and searched the house. When they found nothing, they took the rest of the men with them.

Adam became the black sheep of the family because the ram had been killed, the men of the house had disappeared, only women and children remained in the house and Saddam

Hussein had become the president of Iraq. The Bird family believed that Adam had been born to mark the end of the family, which had existed for many generations. Some women thought it was for the best that Adam had been born asleep, because if he had opened his eyes and looked at someone, the earth would have opened and that person would have fallen down into hell.

On the subsequent days one of the wives of the men who had been taken away would slip out each night, quietly into the darkness, back to her family. Wasile, who had just given birth, thought that after a little while she might be able to run away for good, but after a month there was no longer anyone in the Bird family household, except Simahen, herself and her six children. Although she disliked Simahen, she dared not leave her behind all by herself. Simahen always said that she would die in that house and would never leave.

Wasile had five sons and a daughter, Mira, who looked after Adam. She dribbled milk into his mouth, especially after Wasile forgot about him after she began making bread, which Rizen sold on the streets of Boran to earn what money they could, now that there were no longer any men. Wasile believed that Adam, not Saddam Hussein, was the reason for her life changing and her having to bake bread all day long to feed others.

Rizen would never forget that during his childhood, after his father had disappeared, he often walked with Simahen to the Ba'ath party's house where she would ask after her husband and her sons. In the party's house a young man sat in military uniform on a stool, a Kalashnikov in his lap, a thermos flask of water next to him on the ground.

"My son," said Simahen breathlessly to the young man, while wiping the sweat off her forehead after the walk, "they said that they took them away because the sheep pushed Mr President around with his horns. That can't be possible? Mr President is in Baghdad and the sheep is here. A sheep has got horns and not rockets. God bless you, my son, and Mr President. Where are they? Are they inside?"

"Who are they?" asked the young man.

"Everyone," said Simahen.

"I don't know," answered the young man.

"The party took them. Can you tell me where the party is, so that I can go to him to ask him myself?" asked Simahen, who, like many in Boran, did not know exactly what the word 'party' meant.

"You are at the party's house," said the young man.

"Is the party here too?"

"The party has no time for you."

Simahen, who could no longer hear very well, bent towards Rizen to hear what the young man with the Kalashnikov had said.

"Gran, he said we must go home, because they're coming back tomorrow," said Rizen.

The young man with the Kalashnikov appreciated Rizen's answer, understanding that he wanted to get his grandmother back to the house.

"When are they coming tomorrow? In the morning, afternoon, night?"

"At night," said Rizen, because he did not want to bring her to the party's house in the morning and because she never left the house at night.

Simahen sighed, as if she had been freed from a great weight on her shoulders, and settled on the ground.

"Not here. This is no cemetery for old people," shouted the young man with the Kalashnikov, angrily.

Rizen pulled Simahen by her hand. She got to her knees, struggled slowly to her feet, took a few steps and sat down again. She closed her eyes and fell asleep. After half an hour Rizen woke her up and led her home. On the way Simahen thought about the party. She knew every hen, every rock, every person in Boran, she even knew which milk came from which cow, but she did not know who the party was. She tried to recall if she had ever seen him anywhere.

"Does the party have a shop or a pharmacy?" she asked Rizen. The word 'party' appeared together with photos of Saddam Hussein on walls, windows and on people's chests in

Boran. In the past the people had talked about "the king", "the president", "the government", but after Saddam Hussein had come to power, people began talking about "the party".

"They say that the party took them, and not Saddam Hussein," Simahen said to Wasile after they got back home. Her face was red from exertion. "They said they were coming tomorrow evening."

Simahen looked at Rizen. "Who said that again?"

"The party," said Rizen and he ran away to hunt birds with his younger brother Djazil among the date palms.

When Simahen smelt her bedroom, she felt at peace. She crept over to her bed, holding the edge of the frame like a drowning man clutching a lifebuoy, gathered all her strength and pulled herself up on to the bed. Adam lay on a mat next to her surrounded by flies.

"Mira, take him away," called Simahen. "He is the reason for all this misery."

Mira picked Adam up carefully and carried him like a precious treasure to the stable. In a corner, where the animals could not stand on him, she lay him down. She did not know what she should do. He was blue from the heat. She looked at how his hands were moving like little worms. "He will wake up," she whispered. His lips were cracked from the heat.

Mira, summoned by her mother to chase the chickens out of Simahen's room, left him behind and ran away. Before the sun had set, Mira remembered him. She took a cup of milk from the kitchen and dribbled the liquid into Adam's mouth. Adam was like a frail plant that had almost died of thirst and swallowed the drops greedily.

"Mira! Where are you?" called Wasile

"He's sleeping!" called Mira. "Shall I bring him to you? The rats will eat him."

"Leave him there," said Wasile, who, after a long day of baking bread, fell exhausted on to her bed.

Chapter 4

The party is their father

The Bird children will never forget the day that their mother Wasile took them to the house of Hadi the Rocket, the chairman of the Ba'ath party in Boran. She begged him to release her husband Kosjer and his father and brothers if they were still alive, or to release their bodies if they were dead. She had even taken Adam along. Wasile walked in front with Adam leaning on her arm with Rizen, Sjahid, Djazil, Mira and Joesr following behind.

Hadi the Rocket was a middle-aged man. He had a thick black moustache, from which he always plucked the grey hairs with tweezers. In his chest pocket was a comb and a mirror, with which he kept his moustache in shape. Hadi the Rocket came from a poor family in Boran, whose members sold ice in the summer, and coal and oil in the winter. His father had owned a cart and an old horse. After primary school, Hadi began to work with his father. He had thought it was his lot to get old sitting in the cart, until he became a member of the Ba'ath party.

"God in heaven, the party on earth," he always said when the Ba'ath party was still underground.

"The party in heaven, Mr President on earth," he said when

the Ba'ath party seized power and was the only party remaining.

"Mr President is the heaven of the fatherland, the party his ground," was his slogan when Saddam Hussein seized power.

Sometimes Hadi the Rocket forgot his own house, which the party had given him, his wives, which he had also received from the party, and his children and he slept in his uniform in the party's house. Every time people became more afraid of him, he felt safer and became friendlier. Little photos of Saddam Hussein were pinned on his clothes and he wore watches bearing his image. He gave the photos to everyone, and the watches to people who were higher up in the party than himself, as if it were an offering to the gods. No one was as attached to anything as Hadi the Rocket was to the Ba'ath party; not medieval suitors to their lovers, nor knights to their swords, nor believers to their gods.

During the first days after the Ba'ath party had come to power and he was merely a comrade, he spent the whole day walking around Boran so he could be everywhere at once. This cost him a great deal of time. During this period he was thin, but when the party gave him a Toyota with a blue number plate to show that it belonged to the party, he went everywhere in the car. He became fatter and his neck became fleshy and he developed an enormous belly.

He was seen everywhere, at all hours simultaneously, as if he had been cloned and transformed into hundreds of Hadis. Only when he was sick did Boran's residents not see him, but never for more than two days in a row. On the third day he rose again, despite fever, sore throat or diarrhoea, and he made his rounds through Boran in his military uniform with his pistol in its holster. He had an eye on every corner of Boran, an ear to every wall and in every brain a thermometer to measure the ideas in them.

After Hadi the Rocket, it was his mother who believed most in the party. The women of Boran brought her chickens or lambs and asked her to prevent Hadi the Rocket from writing a report against their husbands or sons who wanted to get a passport or get into the army. Once the house was filled with roosters that were fighting each other, and sheep all butting their horns against each other, Hadi the Rocket became angry with his mother. He told her that she should not accept all those animals, because the party would be angry.

"My son," his mother replied, "does the party have ears with which to listen? Does it have a nose to smell with or a hand that can hit? God made heaven and hell, angels and devils, and still the people make him angry. Let the party be angry."

When the party gave Hadi the Rocket a piece of land, money to build a house and a new Toyota with a blue number plate and air-conditioning, his mother began to believe in the party even more. Especially when Hadi the Rocket decided not to install his first wife in the new house, but to consecrate it with a new wife. That is what Hadi the Rocket did with each new house. When the Americans invaded Iraq, he had six wives in the six houses that he owned.

His mother saw how the families of Boran offered their daughters to him. They were the most famous and richest families and the most beautiful women and girls. Because of this Hadi the Rocket's mother came to believe even more in the party, which could perform such wonders, because previously, when he was just normal Hadi and not Hadi the Rocket, he could not find a single woman who wanted to marry him, apart from his ten-year-old cousin. Her belief in the party became greater than her belief in roosters and sheep. That is why she no longer accepted them.

"Hadi has nothing in his hands, everything is in the hands of the party," she said to a woman who stood at the door with a gift.

When Hadi the Rocket received a farm, his mother not only believed in the party, but also became afraid of it. "My son, whoever makes God angry, has time to ask him for forgiveness. But whoever makes the party angry, has no time for that," she said to Hadi the Rocket when she saw the photos of Saddam Hussein on his clothes and on his watches and the pistol in his holster.

Hadi the Rocket was not surprised that his mother and the rest of his family also believed in the party, because he saw the party as God and later as even more than God.

"What did God give to Moses, who believed in him?" he once shouted out during a drunken moment. "A stick. But what does the party give to those who believe in it? A rocket!"

That is how Hadi came to acquire his nickname; The Rocket. People called him Hadi the Rocket, or usually The Rocket behind his back, but if he was nearby they called him Comrade Hadi.

Hadi the Rocket gave his first two sons the names Saddam and Hussein. His other children were given the names of Saddam Hussein's children, the sons Qusay and Uday, the daughters Raghad, Hala and Rana. The following daughters he named Sabha, after Saddam Hussein's mother, and Sajida, after Saddam Hussein's wife. One daughter was given the name Samira, after Saddam Hussein's second wife, but he did not dare say this out loud. Samira Al Shahbander married Saddam Hussein after he had ordered her husband, the head of the Iraqi national airline, to divorce her. He gave one of his sons the name Ali, after the son of Saddam Hussein and Samira Al Shahbander.

When the names of Saddam Hussein and his family were used up, he made up other names, such as Saddamhussein and Raghadrana. The only child who had a different name was his first daughter Fatin, because she had been born before Saddam Hussein had come to power.

Just as devoted as Hadi the Rocket was to the names of Saddam Hussein and his family, so was he equally devoted to the work of Saddam Hussein's photos. He hung them everywhere in all of his houses, except in the toilet. The photo which pictured him with Saddam Hussein, was his most precious. He had even had a plan to have the photo made into a mural in Boran, but he was afraid it would be seen as a fantasy and not a real photo, or that he was comparing himself to Saddam Hussein and he decided not to do it.

One day he wrote a report to the government in Baghdad. In it he requested permission to ask for gold from the people to make a gold statue of Saddam Hussein and, for future generations, to shoot it into space as a measure of his fame, but the government sent him a letter thanking him and made it clear to him that the people were busy with a war against Iran and that it was not an opportune moment to make such a marvellous statue. The brilliant idea should be shelved and kept for the right moment.

Hadi the Rocket was proud of his idea of a gold statue in space and he was proud of the letter thanking him, which he had framed and hung on the wall in the sitting room of one of his houses. He hung a copy of the letter in the party's house.

When he heard that the people of Boran whispered behind his back that it was the party who had screwed his mother and made her pregnant with Hadi, and not his father, Hadi was proud. "If the party had a dick, I would believe more in the party's dick than that of my father," he said drunkenly.

When Wasile saw Hadi the Rocket in front of his house, she began to cry. Although she had prayed that she would be freed of everyone, now that all the men had disappeared she found it very difficult to feed the children and look after the household. She knelt down to kiss his shoes, so that Adam's face bumped against them, making him cry. The other children also began to cry, except Djazil, who never cried.

"Not necessary, not necessary," stammered Hadi the Rocket. He wriggled his foot, so that Wasile let go of his shoe and stood up. "An Iraqi woman must not kiss shoes, stand up," he said. Uncomfortable and a little bored, Hadi the Rocket looked at the row of children behind the woman in the black shawl and the child on her arm.

"We have asked everywhere about the father of these children, his brothers and his father, by they haven't come back," said Wasile. She tried to grab his hand and kiss it, but he pulled his hand away.

"Where did they go," Hadi the Rocket asked innocently. He tried to make his voice sound virtuous.

"They say the party took them. Please. I spend the whole day baking bread. My back is breaking. These children need a father," begged Wasile.

"Don't you worry," said Hadi the Rocket. "The party will look after them, the party is their father." Absent-mindedly he pressed five dinars into Wasile's outstretched hand.

Wasile grabbed the money, kissed it and pressed it against her forehead. She tried again to kiss the hand of Hadi the Rocket, but he pulled it away.

Wasile walked home with the children behind her. She believed that the party lived somewhere and that Kosjer was there because the party wanted it. When she got home she remembered that she had forgotten to ask Hadi the Rocket for the address of the party, so that she could go there. She did not believe, as Simahen did, that the party lived in the party's house.

The word 'party' was an indistinct one in Boran, especially for children and residents of forsaken villages. The moment the word 'party' began to be heard in conversations, people saw buildings protected by armed men and on which 'house of the party' was written. The people understood what a hospital was, or a garage or a shop, but a party house was new.

The word 'party' was used as the name of a person. It was the only word that was linked to the president, like God and devil were linked to each other. The president did all that was good, the party did the rest. "The president gave the order for the bridge to be built," it was said if a bridge was being built. If war was being waged, it was said that the war was begun to protect the party. "The party took him," it was said if someone disappeared. If someone was released, it was said that the president had secured his release. Eventually the word 'party' became a mythical word, which gave Simahen a headache for which she sought an aspirin in her medicine bag.

Simahen always had a black plastic medicine bag to hand. She opened the bag and put her hand in, as if her hands had two eyes which could see. Then she grabbed drops, an ointment, a syrup or a pill. If she bought new medicines from Kamel, the pharmacist, she tested it on Wasile before she used it. "You are young and strong. You still have many years to live, but I'm old. Drip that in your eyes and tell me how it feels." Wasile then put two drops in her eye. She put it in one eye, one ear or one nostril and after a few hours answered Simahen's questions as to whether she itched or experienced pain or if she could still see well.

When Mira was old enough, she let her try out the medicines. "Your grandmother is old and weak," she said. "One bad drop will kill her, but you're still young." Mira always listened timidly and did as she was told. She did not mislead her grandmother by just testing one eye, one ear or one nostril, as Wasile did. "You are not like your mother," said Simahen when she was alone with Mira. "Your mother also says she has an itch or pain that is not there. I don't trust her."

Each time Simahen felt weaker, she bought more medicines from Kamel the pharmacist. In the beginning the pharmacy was purely homeopathic, but with the passing of time new medicines were added. Kamel believed a pharmacist was better than a doctor, because a pharmacist could prescribe medicines without seeing the patient. He knew the inhabitants of Boran, the diseases that appeared in the families and the appropriate medicines for them. He also sold his remedies on credit. "Illness cannot wait, but my wallet can." He took medicines back if the patient found they did not work well or swapped them for others.

When the party came to power and medicines without a prescription had been banned, Kamel complained at the door of his pharmacy. "The party, which should ban disease, bans medicine."

When the party made it illegal to work in a pharmacy without a diploma, Kamel employed a young man with a diploma. After a few months the young man disappeared, but the diploma remained hanging on the pharmacy wall. If someone from the party came in, Kamel pointed to the diploma. No one from the party did anything against him, because he had treated them or their children at some time. Kamel, who protected everyone against bacteria and viruses, was protected against the party.

Simahen came regularly to the pharmacy. Kamel listened to her and gave her medicines. As she grew older, she sent her grandsons with money so they would not to forget her symptoms. She sent dates, butter or milk for Kamel. "If someone is no longer able to go to Kamel's pharmacy, the only place they will ever go again is their grave," she repeated self-pityingly on her bed. When the medicines were finished, she gave the empty bottles to her grandsons for them to go and buy some more of the same. She compared the old medicines with the new, always praising the old and complaining about the new.

Although she kept using the same medicines until the end of her life, she nevertheless continued to test them on Mira, the only one she trusted. If she asked her grandsons, they would drink all the contents of the sweet bottles and say it had spilt on the ground, or they refilled them with water. The bitter tablets they threw away without tasting and claimed that they were good.

Years later Simahen unexpectedly appeared with a walking stick at the door of the pharmacy, which had been taken over after the death of Kamel, by his son. Simahen did not know this and could not believe her eyes. Before her stood a young Kamel. From that day on she not only believed that Kamel could cure illnesses, but old age as well.

Because Wasile had only been thirteen when she was married, her oldest children sometimes seemed more like her siblings than her children, but because she aged so quickly, Mira sometimes looked more like a granddaughter than her daughter. Adam had never been a son for her, except on the day when she had taken him on the visit to the house of Hadi the Rocket. Because Simahen spent her time in the shadow of the party's house after the men of the household had disappeared, and Wasile was baking bread, Sjahid, Djazil and Joesr grew up in the date palm orchard and the rice paddies. When Sjahid and Joesr started going to school, the streets and date palms of Boran continued to be Djazil's world. He only came home at meal times and to sleep.

Djazil stole everything from everyone. No one knew who had taught him that. He stole to buy ice lollies from the van that came once a day from Najaf to Boran. He could never eat enough of those. Wasile hid the bag in which she kept the money she earned from selling bread, so that nothing could be stolen from it. If she caught him, she twisted his ear and he promised pleadingly that he would never steal again. "Learn not to steal from your flesh and blood!" she screamed. Sometimes she bit him until the blood flowed.

Djazil had a great talent for disappearing. He would dig a hole in the ground or find a cave, into which he would disappear like a fox, or he would climb a tall date palm like a monkey, build a seat high up and hide himself there like a bird. He could hide himself for days on end and could fall asleep anywhere.

One day a man found him asleep on the roof of his house. Djazil woke up and saw the man aiming his gun at him. Behind him stood women and children looking at Djazil on the roof and the bouquet of chickens tied up next to him that he had killed, so that they would not make any noise and he could sleep. Djazil begged, cried and said that his father, brothers and sisters had been murdered and he was the only one left alive. He swore that he had slaughtered the chickens in the Islamic way and that they could keep them. The women began to cry and asked the man to let him go with the slaughtered chickens. So he escaped a bullet, but from that day on Djazil slept with one eye open.

One day Djazil sat on a scorpion. The scorpion stung him on his arse. Djazil screamed in agony, ran home with his hand on his backside and did not come out again. Wasile thanked God that he had created the scorpion. From that day on Djazil spent most of his time standing up, and if he had to sit he would closely examine the place where he intended to do so. One night Wasile heard something fall over. She ran to the kitchen. There was Djazil who, having dropped off to sleep standing up, had fallen to the ground with a thud.

Wasile decided to take her son to the traditional doctor, who had cured Kosjer of the alphabet. The traditional doctor examined the scorpion sting and sent him to a famous woman in Boran by the name of Farha Jabbar, who made tattoos. With a needle and charcoal she tattooed an eagle in the attack position around the sting. The place where the scorpion had stung became the eye. Djazil was held down by four women, while Farha Jabbar pushed the needle into his arse until the blood and charcoal merged in the wound. As Djazil's arse grew, so the eagle became fatter, until it eventually looked more like a chicken than an eagle.

People complained about Djazil when he began pestering girls. Sometimes he came home beaten black and blue, but he could not stop doing it until the day he came home bleeding from the head. A man had hacked off his right ear when he saw him following his daughter into the date palms. "If I see you again, I'll remove your head," he had screamed. Because of that Djazil stayed at home for weeks.

"If I had known that hacking off his ear was the solution, I would have hacked them both off," said Wasile, who was glad that Djazil appeared to have eventually found the right path. She asked Sheikh Abdullah al Najafi to show him with one ear the true path and she took him every day at dawn to the mosque, because Djazil, who was up before the wind, would now not dare set foot outside the house. In the afternoons she fetched him again. If she was busy and forgot about him and was late in coming to the mosque, Djazil would be sitting quietly waiting for her.

Sheikh Abdullah Al Najafi had a group of children. Their parents preferred having them educated in the mosque, rather than the school. They were mostly the religious families, because the school was the party's, but the mosque was God's. Djazil sat quietly in the circle for months, writing in chalk on a small blackboard on his lap what Sheikh Abdullah Al Najafi had said. He also copied sentences from the Koran and so learnt to read and write.

During one lesson Shiekh Abdullah Al Najafi said that God had created sexual desires for people as a test. Sexual urges served all creatures as a means of reproducing themselves and this only occurred once in every season, except for man, for which it was a test during all seasons. Djazil put his hand in the air. Sheikh Abdullah Al Najafi was surprised that this had happened after all these months and gave him permission to speak.

"What you say is not true," said Djazil.

"What is not true," asked the sheikh.

"What you said about people."

"So do you with your missing ear know what is true?" asked the sheikh.

"Yes," said Djazil.

All the children were quiet. All that could be heard was the sparrows, which inhabited the empty mosque between prayer times.

"My mother had a rooster that screwed the hens all through the year. Did God give the chickens a test just like the people?"

The sheikh scratched his head. "You have a point. With your missing ear you have stumped me."

One day Sheikh Abdullah Al Najafi asked the children why Flying Djafer was called by that name. Only Djazil and one other child put their hands in the air. Sheikh Abdullah Al Najafi gave the opportunity to the other child.

"Because he could fly," was his answer, at which Sheikh Abdullah Al Najafi gave Djazil his chance to answer.

"Because there was a rotor on his head and a helicopter engine in place of his heart," said Djazil.

The children burst out laughing and the sheikh screamed at them to keep quiet.

"Flying Djafer was known by that name because, during a war, he carried the flag of the Prophet Mohammed first in his right hand. When his right hand was chopped off, he held the flag in his left had, until it too was chopped off. That is why God gave him two wings in heaven, so that he could fly everywhere," bristled the sheikh.

Djazil put his hand in the air. "Which is actually faster, an F-16 or Flying Djafer?"

Everyone laughed, this time even louder.

"Your missing ear is the fastest," shouted the sheikh, grabbing Djazil by his other ear and twisting it slowly but steadily. Djazil shrieked from the pain, at which the sheikh twisted even more. In a flash, Djazil grabbed the sheikh's hand and bit it. Those sparrows that had not yet been chased away by the screaming of Djazil and the laughing of the children, flew out of the mosque at the scream of the sheikh. It reverberated just as loudly as when he made the call to prayer when there was no electricity. Djazil bit and bit and then ran away, until he arrived unnoticed at the farm where his ear had been hacked off. He climbed over the mud wall and saw that the man who had severed his ear was sleeping. He threw a large stone in the man's face and fled over the wall.

Later he proudly told his brothers what he had done to Sheikh Abdullah Al Najafi and to the man who had hacked off his ear, and began again with his life among the date palms and canals, just as he had done before his ear had been hacked off.

After Djazil had the eagle tattooed on his arse, he was to be found everywhere, just like Hadi the Rocket. He was everywhere and nowhere. While Rizen sold bread, Sjahid and Joesr went to school and Mira worked in the house, Djazil wandered through the streets and date palm orchards of Boran. He fought and came home wounded, stole chickens from nearby villages and sold them to a woman at the market. As a child he stole from his family. Wasile hit him, but he did not stop. When he was bigger than her, she dared not hit him and always kept her bedroom locked. If she thought that she had left her bedroom unlocked, she ran to the door, let the bread burn in the oven and scolded Djazil. When he became stronger, he began to steal not only chickens, but also lambs, and when he was bigger than she was, he stole sheep and then calves. When his moustache had become thick, he thought that as proof that he had become a man, he should steal the biggest creature in the south. He regularly failed to come home for days on end. On those days he stayed somewhere outside Boran and came home with dusty clothes.

Wasile saw him come back one day, not with a clean heart, as Simahen hoped, but with a camel. Wasile chased him away from the house, because she knew that he had stolen the camel. So Djazil trekked from one town to the next to try to sell the camel, but he did not succeed.

Two days later three Bedouins came looking for the camel. They had heard that they must look for Djazil to find the camel, but Djazil was nowhere to be found. People spoke with amazement about Djazil, because he had succeeded in hiding the camel from the three Bedouins and if the Bedouins could not see the camel, then Saddam Hussein also would not be able to find Djazil without the camel. It was said that Djazil had sold the camel to a butcher in another city on the other side of the desert.

The three Bedouins set up a tent in front of the door of the Bird family house. They knocked on the door as the sun came up and as the sun went down to ask after Djazil. Wasile swore that he was not at home. Simahen began taking food and drink to them and they began using the toilet in the house during the day, because, while in the city, they could not adhere to nature's call in the street.

Days later soldiers came to ask the Bedouins what they were doing there with their tent.

"We're waiting for the camel," they said.

The soldiers asked them when the camel would come.

"When Djazil comes."

So the soldiers burst into the Bird family house with their Kalashnikovs. Wasile and Mira screamed in terror and the soldiers searched in every room.

"Don't be afraid," they said to the women. "We're looking for the camel."

The Bedouins heard the screaming of the women, packed up their tent and had disappeared before the soldiers came out of the house.

During their childhood years Sjahid and Djazil fought with each other the whole day, like two cockerels. As they grew older, they began to draw away from each other and fought together against other children. After Sjahid had been going to school for a few years and had started drawing, the distance between them became even greater, such that Sjahid would avoid him when they were outdoors to prevent others from seeing that they were brothers. Sjahid began to paint on every piece of wood he could lay his hands on and so refined his drawing technique. Sjahid was proud. If he was enthusiastic about an idea, he discussed it with everyone in the house at length until everyone believed in his idea. Then he began with a new idea about which he had heard or read. He despised those who would not listen to him and subjected himself to those who were stronger than him.

If Sjahid needed money, he went crawling to Wasile. Once he had the money, Wasile no longer existed for him and he ignored her questions. During his puberty, the difference between him and the rest of the family became evident. Sjahid looked after his appearance. He combed his hair, used oil to make it shine and had his own shampoo, which he hid away so that no one else could use it. He had even bought an old flat iron for his clothes, after a day of crawling to obtain money from Wasile, money that she had been saving to buy a car for Rizen in order that she could one day stop having to bake bread.

Wasile was more proud of Sjahid than of her other children. "Look at him, he deserves a 'doctor' in front of his name," she said if she saw him walking around in his smart clothes. Sjahid used every cent he got from Wasile to buy clothes, perfume and shoes. Sometimes he bought books. He looked eagerly at every picture in books about Spanish and Italian artists. Sjahid was like a window for the family, through which events and ideas entered the house. Between the chickens and the smell of the bread that Wasile baked, events and ideas remained suspended in Joesr's head. If Sjahid introduced a fresh idea, Joesr got a headache and Mira would bring him lots of tea. Joesr was tormented by ideas, because he was a sensitive soul, and had a strong sense of responsibility.

Sjahid had two good friends, Mohamed Mansour and Yasin Al Terref. They came to visit him with books, which they hid under their clothes, and which they discussed with each other. Joesr enjoyed sitting with the three friends and relished the secrecy with which the forbidden books were brought into the open. He listened to their discussions and clung to the strange names that they used, such as Jean-Jacques Rosseau, Marx, Voltaire and Lenin. The ideas of the three friends flew through the room, landed on Joesr's head, settled in it, laid eggs, hatched and the chickens grew, until they flew to other corners of Joesr's head, where they made new nests and laid eggs. Joesr really wanted to join in the young men's discussions, but dared not. Not because he was younger, but because he had not yet read any books with strange names to use as examples.

"The three greatest literary characters are Faust, Hamlet and Don Quixote," said Mohamed Mansour one day, when the friends were sitting at the Thirsty River.

Joesr noted down the names on his hand and the next day sought out the books in which those names appeared. He read the books over and over and for a long while was preoccupied with those characters in his head. Thus he developed a theory, which he dared tell only to Mira.

"The lowest three characters in history are Saddam Hussein, Michel Aflaq and Hadi the Rocket," Joesr said secretively.

Mira knew who Saddam Hussein was, and Hadi the Rocket, but did not know who Michel Aflaq was.

"He was the founder of the Ba'ath party," said Joesr, glad that he had taught his sister something.

Sjahid joked about his brother's theories with Mohamed Mansour and Yasin Al Terref. It irritated Joesr that he did this. After a while Joesr discovered that Sjahid and his friends discussed, but did not believe in anything. He allowed himself to be influenced by Sjahid as if he were a tail wagging to the left and to the right. Just as Simahen tested her medicines on Wasile and later on Mira, so Sjahid tested his books on Joesr. Every book that he gave his brother, was devoured by Joesr. If Joesr was not at school, he did nothing but eat and read. "If that child would only read the Koran, he would become an ayatollah like Khomeini and take us all to heaven," Wasile sighed deeply.

Joesr was slim. He had eyes that shone with energy and sharp thoughts. From a young age Joesr had always been against something or someone. Against one of Wasile's roosters, against one of Simahen's sheep, against one of his brothers. The discussions of Sjahid, Mohamed Mansour and Yasin Al Terref and the books that Joesr read, ensured that he was bounced back and forth between all sorts of political and literary trends.

The party was one of the first philosophical problems Joesr encountered in his fluctuating thoughts on philosophy and politics. The family was accustomed to Joesr, after having sat in his room for days, coming out with crazy ideas. This is just what happened after he had spent a long time thinking about the party. It was a sunny winter's day. Mira, Djazil and Sjahid were sitting in the yard. Suddenly Joesr appeared, eyes red from lack of sleep.

"So you've emerged?" said Djazil laughingly.

Disoriented, Joesr dragged his fingers through his hair and stretched his back. "The party doesn't exist," he said. "The party is merely another name for Saddam Hussein."

Djazil laughed loudly, as he always did when he heard Joesr's thoughts. "For days on end you sit like a chicken trapped in an egg only to discover what everyone already knows? Even the yoghurt sellers in the market."

Joesr ignored what Djazil said and began a discussion with Sjahid about the significance of the party.

When Sjahid once told Joesr that capitalism ended with communism, but communism ended with hunger, Joesr no longer believed in the words of Sjahid. After long discussions about socialism, Joesr went to El Mutanabbi street in Baghdad with Hassan, the father of his best friend Samer, with his books about surrealism and exchanged them for a box of second-hand books about socialism. He devoured the books and felt that at last he knew why he had been born: for socialism. Wasile watched in amazement at how Joesr followed Mira around and explained to her that as a worker she had rights in the home and that she could refuse to do something if someone asked her. Wasile was also surprised at the red clothes that Joesr began to wear and how he took down the photo of Imam Ali from the wall and replaced it with one of Lenin. Wasile was used to the photo of Imam Ali, to whom she complained about the pain in her back and her knees.

"Who's that?" she asked him angrily, pointing at the photo of Lenin.

"My new friend," said Joesr.

"Who did you get the red clothes from?"

"From my new friend. These are the clothes of the revolution." Joesr told his mother that religion was the opium of the people and that God did not exist.

Wasile thought about the word 'opium', which she did not know, and did not listen to what he said after that, that God did not exist. Shaking her head she went to the clay oven, where she began to bake bread and spoke to the oven. "It would be better if he, just like his father Kosjer, had been a sheep trader."

One summer's day Joesr went with his friend Samer and his father to Basra in a Soviet-made car, called a Volga. The car drove slowly. After every few kilometres Samer's father stopped, opened the boot, took a watermelon out, cut it in two and put one half on the bonnet to cool the engine down. Joesr looked with large eyes at the American cars in which the Kuwaitis drove and how much faster they were. During the trip he decided that he was sitting in the wrong car. So, when he returned from Basra he burnt all his red clothes and turned his back on the Soviet Union, on socialism and their Che Guevara.

"Socialism is stupidity. It needs watermelons so it doesn't burn out and has to stop every few kilometres to recover," he said to Wasile to justify the burning of his red clothes. He removed the picture of Lenin from the wall and in its place put a photo of Brooke Shields, the star of an American film. In it she was swimming in a blue lake. He had seen the film many times in the Sinbad cinema. In the height of summer Joesr sat in the darkness of the cinema and watched the American girl lying naked on the sand, and dreamt about the West. Wasile tore up the photo of the unclothed girl and threw it into the clay oven, because she was scared that the house would cave in on itself because of God's anger if a naked American girl was hanging there, where Imam Ali had previously been. Joesr had his hair cut just like Elvis Presley's.

"The most beautiful and greatest mistakes of humankind have been the mistake of Adam and that of Columbus. Adam's mistake formed the world, Columbus's mistake America," said

Joesr. "I cannot imagine the world without America." Joesr read translated American books by Walt Whitman, Edgar Allan Poe and Ernest Hemingway.

Sjahid wanted to change his brother's mind. "The Americans could have dropped the two atomic bombs in the sea and said to the Japanese that, if they did not surrender, they would burn up just like the sea. But they didn't do that, because they like taking revenge," said Sjahid to Joesr while they were swimming in the Thirsty River on a hot August afternoon.

"Don't be so stupid," said Joesr, who was no longer a timid youngster, but had become a young man with a moustache. "You have a gun in your hand and your enemy has a gun in his hand. What do you do? Do you shoot the wall and tell your enemy that he should throw away his gun, or do you shoot him through his head?"

Sjahid pushed Joesr's head under the water so he would not burn from the heat, while Djazil lured Baan to a place on the bank, a few hundred metres further away, to make the most of her body.

"Be careful!" said Sjahid at the moment when Djazil threw himself on to Baan's trembling body.

"Be careful of what?" asked Joesr.

"Be careful," repeated Sjahid. "Anyone who has ever been for America has then turned against the country all by themselves, let their beard grow and join forces with Khomeini, or let their moustache grow and join forces with Saddam Hussein. Or shav them both off and turn against themselves."

Joesr pushed Sjahid under the water. After a few seconds he resurfaced and saw Joesr standing like a statue staring at something. Sjahid called out to him, but Joesr did not react. Sjahid shook him back and forth, at which Joesr shook his head and woke up.

"What's up with you? Isn't your head working any more."

"Did you know there was a war?" said Joesr. Sjahid began to laugh loudly at the joke, but Joesr stared with his eyes fixed on a rocket soaring past in the nearby blue, pure sky of the summer, in the direction of Baghdad.

Chapter 5

Love and peaches

No one looked after Adam, who lay in the stable as if he did not exist. Apart from Mira, who kept on believing that he was asleep and would eventually wake up. She had looked after him like a mother since she had been five years old, and refused to get married when she was older, even after the scoldings from Simahen and Wasile, because she knew that then Adam would be forgotten and would die of hunger and thirst. Every now and again she also forgot about him and did not drip any fruit juice, milk or lentil soup into his mouth. At these times she knew that she had forgotten something, but did not know what and if she became thirsty, he shot into her thoughts again and she would immediately run to him. Sometime he lay in the stable like a mummy and relaxed his mouth with every fresh drop.

If thirst was not enough to remind her of Adam, the chickens would begin to cluck and the sheep to bleat at the extreme anxiety in Adam's eyes. Then Wasile would scream threateningly at Mira, as if she was guilty for the fact that Adam was still alive. Wasile never spoke about Adam and never mentioned his name.

No one actually mentioned Adam by his name. The custom in Boran was that the father or the grandfather would name a child, but Kosjer, who had been applauding for Saddam Hussein on the day that he had bought the randy ram for his ewes, and so had decided that his son should be named Saddam, never came home again. Because the child was born asleep, no one had any need to call him and no name had ever been given to him.

When Adam was two, he began to say puzzling words in a strange little voice. Mira called Wasile and Simahen so they could hear it.

"He's talking in his sleep," said Simahen.

The boy said Mira's name many times, one after the other, the name which was called out of every corner, from every room and from behind every door throughout the day.

"Mira, wash your body and pray to God. You're undoubtedly going to die. Listen, death is calling you," said Simahen.

Mira turned pale with anxiety, when she heard what her grandmother said, but after hours of uproar in the house she no longer thought about it. The child repeated the name of Mira and said all sorts of unintelligible words, until, a little later, he began to say the name 'Adam'. Mira could not understand how the child could know the name. No one had said it in his presence and there was no one in Boran who went by that name. If it was not too hot and if a gentle breeze was keeping the mosquitoes and flies away from him, the child repeated the word 'Adam'. After a while Mira began to call him by that name, but when he no longer said the word, Mira forgot what it was and had to wait for him to say it again to remind herself what his name was, but he did not say it again.

"Who is the man who stole the apples from God's orchard?" Mira once asked Simahen when she took her yoghurt and dates. "And whom did God run after to give his ears such a twist that he would never do that again and was banished from heaven by God?"

"Adam," said Simahen and she complained. "If he had not stolen the apple, Saddam Hussein would not have stolen the men of this house. I don't understand God. Why was he so angry with Adam over the stealing of one little apple and he is not angry over Saddam Hussein who makes people disappear…" Simahen began a long monologue to the wall of her room and God.

Mira grabbed the broom, because Wasile had called her to chase the chickens out of her room.

Adam was a living doll for her in the beginning. She washed him and dressed him in clean clothes every few days. She pulled the ticks from his small body and dripped soup on his lips. Adam grew slowly and began to crawl around the stable with closed eyes. He pulled himself up on the sheep and learnt to walk. He wore Mira's old clothes or those of other family members. Mira cut them shorter in front, so that he would not trip over them.

In the silence of the night he stood up slowly and carefully like a plant just emerging from the earth. Then he held out his hands in front of him and began to walk. He felt his way through the darkness, walking with small steps through the stable and turned himself around if he walked into something. Only if the door was left open, would he walk over the courtyard. He wandered to places which were quieter than others, as if he could hear the silence. He walked carefully from the stable, as if he did not want to rustle the straw under his sleeping feet, over the courtyard to the front door of the house. If it was closed, he remained standing, as if he was waiting for the wind or an unseen hand to open it. If his thin legs trembled with tiredness, he turned himself around and wandered back to the stable. If the front door was open, he walked outside to places which were even quieter. In forgotten corners in the city or among the date palms he could remain standing without getting tired, as if supported by the silence. In the mornings, when the silence in which he was standing disappeared, Adam turned himself around as if he was balancing on a rope between two high roofs, and went back home. If the sun came up while he was still on his way, he stopped in his tracks. Then he could no longer find his way through the noise of the day and would be taken to the Bird family household by a resident of Boran.

It was as if he found it necessary to move to quiet places in his sleep to stand there, as if he was part of it. Adam wanted to find a quiet place in this noisy world to stand there like a tree and never to move from there. When he had turned fifteen, Mira saw him once trying to push his head through the keyhole of an old wooden chest in the stable, in which Dime had put her clothes and it had never been opened again since the day on which she had thrown herself into the Thirsty River. Mira did not know that Adam wanted to escape from the noise of the bombardment into a quiet place. She called Wasile to let her see what Adam was doing.

"He thinks he's a snake," said Wasile, her eyes wide in amazement.

Once Adam was taller than Wasile, Mira no longer let him wear women's clothing, but mended Djazil's and Sjahid's old clothes for him. Sometimes he said words which made Mira nervous. Words that were turning in her head. She did not know if she had said the words to him or if he could read her thoughts.

One day Adam continuously repeated the name of a young man. Mira made a racket when he did that, chased the chickens around so that they would start clucking, banged pots and pans, and sang like she had never sung before. She did not want anyone to hear the name of the young man. He sometimes came to the house and she had locked him away in her heart and dreamt about him, because he was the only young man she had ever got close enough to to smell.

Mira was never Mira in the Bird household. She was an oven, a fridge, an iron, a teapot or a remote control, but she was never Mira. The only one who felt her existence was Adam, in his mysterious sleeping world, and Joesr, when the photo of Lenin had hung on the wall. He sat in his room and called Mira. She came in with tea, because her name at ten in the morning meant tea. She put the tea down and turned round, but before she had gone out of the door, Joesr said her name again. For the first time in her life, she heard the sound of her name, as a name and not as a summons. It was a day in April and Rizen had just returned to the army. She vaguely heard her name, but when Joesr spoke for the second time she knew that it did not mean tea or lunch, but that it was her name.

"Stop with this running around the house," said Joesr.

"Everyone can look after themselves. Stand up for yourself! From today onwards, refuse to do what others want you to do."

Mira laughed and went to Simahen, who had called her to milk the cow. From that day, for a while, Joesr fetched his own meals and made his own tea. When he was the best in his class, he received a watch as a gift from the school. He gave it to Mira and taught her to tell the time and to recognise the days of the week and months. The watch was a Seiko brand. If you moved it, it wound itself up. Mira thought it marvellous that the watch would die if she did not move. The watch told the time, the days of the week and the date. She proudly wore that timepiece and never took it off. Even when Djazil tried to get it off her by saying that he would give her a women's watch with batteries.

Wasile started calling her when she wanted to know what the time was, and no longer waited for the call to prayer from Sheikh Abdullah Al Najafi.

"Time is going so fast," Mira once said to Wasile. "It was born yesterday and has a beard today."

"Don't look at the clock too often," said Wasile. "You'll get old before your time."

Gradually Mira turned into a watch herself. She no longer looked at the position of the sun, as she had done previously, but at her watch to know if the sun was high or low in the sky. Sometimes Mira seemed to be telling the time herself, just like the watch, because if someone asked her what the time was, she closed her eyes tight, first said what the time was and then looked at her watch to see if she had it right. Most of the time she was not far wrong. Everyone asked Mira for the time, except Rizen, who asked her for the date so as to know when he had to go back to the army. Every month he had five days off. With his first leave he travelled from the war to his home and on the final day he travelled back to the war, to which the commission for the determination of people's ages had decided to send him when he was sixteen.

At the time that the men of the Bird family had disappeared, Rizen began selling the bread that Wasile baked on the streets. "Hot bread!" he called, even when the bread was cold, while covering many kilometres through the streets. Sometimes he was beaten if the bread was cold, but he did not find that too bad and he kept on calling out that the bread was hot.

All the years he spent selling bread led to him looking a lot older than his brothers. He left the house as the sun came up, came home before lunch if he had sold everything, took fresh bread and before the sun went down went for a third time with fresh bread down the streets. He regularly nibbled at the bread that he should have been selling, which led Wasile to complain that he ate more bread than he sold. Hard work taught him not to take insults seriously.

Rizen was the only one who had inherited a love of doves. He had made two dove cages on the roof of the house, one for the doves to fly around in and one for the doves to breed in. When he was free, he would sit on the roof between the two cages and watch the flying doves. In summer he would fill bowls with water and watch with pleasure at how the doves bathed. Before Rizen had changed in the army and came to drown cats and dogs himself, he paid Djazil if a cat was pestering the doves, to catch the cat and throw it into the Thirsty River in a sack with stones. Djazil liked throwing cats and puppies into the Thirsty River, more than Rizen liked doves, but he never let Rizen see that, because he was also now getting paid to do it. Djazil negotiated with Rizen over the price for the cat and after a while held out the sack with the cat. Rizen paid him and went out through the door to go and sell bread again. Djazil then went to Mira, who was then still too young to put cats and dogs in sacks herself, and talked to her about the drama of the cat, which he had to throw into the river, at which Mira bought the cat's life from Djazil with the little money that she had. Djazil did not let the cat go without biting its tail off or burning it so that it would be so scared that it would never come back to the Bird house where Rizen would see it.

On the day on which Saddam Hussein turned all workers into officials, as proof that he wanted no differences between Iraqi subjects, Rizen saw a girl walking to the Thirsty River to fill her urn with water. Without knowing why, he followed her. He

felt his heart beating as it had never done before. He breath quickened. The girl had her hair covered with a black scarf, but he could see a few loose strands. They had a red henna colour.

Rizen hid behind some reeds and breathlessly watched the girl. At the bank of the Thirsty River, she hitched her dress up, so that it would not get wet. Her legs, which never saw the sun, were not as dark as her face. She filled the urn, let her dress fall into the water and bent over to splash water on her face. Then she looked around fleetingly and when she saw no one, she untied her headscarf and wet her hair. She let the headscarf float on the water and put it wet on her head again.

In his secret place, where Rizen had hidden himself to watch the girl, he did not feel the midday heat, but something in him that descended from his chest to his feet, only to shoot to his head. He did not know if he felt like laughing, or screaming or crying. A few minutes later he saw her walking away from the riverbank with the filled urn on her head.

Her name was Tenzile. She lived in one of Boran's clay houses. In the afternoons, when few people ventured out into the heat, her mother sent her to the river to fetch water. The following day Rizen hid himself, with his bread, in the same place at about midday and he saw her coming. She was wearing the same clothes. This time she filled the urn and went straight back to her house.

Days later she came again. She put the urn down on the riverbank and looked to see if anyone was watching. Then she went into the water with her clothes on, up to her neck. Rizen left his hiding place and walked to the riverbank. When the girl saw him, she quickly waded out of the river. She filled the urn while her clothes were dripping, and quickly walked away without talking to him. He saw her dress clinging to her body, painting it forever in his memory.

The following day he saw her again. She looked around and then filled her urn. He was glad, because he knew she was looking for him, waited until she had gone and then left. The day after that he dared to walk behind her to the riverbank. She was not surprised to see him and said that someone would see them if they stood there for a long time. He did not ask her to join him and hide away, and also did not think of it.

One day he followed her to an open place among the reeds, the willows and the date palms. She trembled like a reed, scared that someone would see them. Coming to the open space, she stopped trembling and he began trembling.

"Tomorrow don't come to the riverbank, but wait here for me," she said, while she looked calmly at him. Then she went away, leaving Rizen, breathless and stunned, behind. He stared after her and saw how she now and again playfully looked over her shoulder and smiled.

With a beating heart he remained out of sight in their hiding place until it seemed safe, came out through the reeds and hurried away. He ran through the dusty, desolate streets of Boran with the bread. He ran like Dime had run naked through those same streets and soared with happiness. The sun was hot on his face and he ran back to the Thirsty River, shouted happily on arriving there and threw himself, bread and all, into the water at the same place where Dime had fallen into the river out of despair. He saw the soggy bread and thought of Wasile. He wanted to feed the bread to the fish, but was afraid that she would think that he had sold it and did not want to give the money to her.

With the wet bread, he walked home. Rizen's love for Tenzile was, without her knowing it, good for Wasile because Rizen stopped eating the bread. He had the feeling that he could get through life by only drinking water, breathing and seeing Tenzile.

"I fell in the water," he said to Wasile when he let her see the bread.

"How on earth? Did you fall asleep?" she shouted in his face, while a rocket fell in the distance. "If you're not eating it, you're throwing it in the river! Ach, go and fetch your grandma at the party's house before she melts in the heat. Then perhaps you'll be making yourself useful."

At the party's house Rizen saw Simahen sitting in the shade against the wall. Rizen rolled her mat up and carried her thermos flask filled with water, which she always had near her when she sat at the party's house, with her black string of beads wound around it. With heavy steps she walked home with him.

Alongside her Rizen also had heavy footsteps. The whole day he had been thinking about Tenzile, about what would happen if they never saw each other again, all the feelings that he did not know. He did not know if he should kiss her, touch her, bite her or stay far away from her. He thought about what would happen to him if the Thirsty River dried up in the winter and she would no longer come to fill her urn.

When he arrived home with Simahen, Djazil stood waiting for him with a cat in a sack. Djazil negotiated with him over the price, but when Rizen had bought it, he did not want Djazil to throw it in the Thirsty River and he let the cat go, after he had bitten it gently on its tail, so that the creature would not come back to his doves.

Rizen stared straight ahead for hours on end. Sometimes he was cheerful and jumped around, sometimes he was depressed and quiet. He asked Djazil what guys and girls did when they were alone. Djazil told stories, but Rizen did not want to believe him. He could spend his whole life with Tenzile, even without touching her. During this period Djazil and Rizen became closer to each other, until Djazil said that he, if Rizen wanted to, could show him the party in his own house.

The last thing Hadi the Rocket received from the Ba'ath party was a large farm on the banks of the Thirsty River. The farm had belonged to Abdullah Al Sjamil. It was thought that Abdullah Al Sjamil had at some time spat in the face of Hadi the Rocket when he was still a minor member of the Ba'ath party and the party had not yet come to power, and that he had said that the party would not last forever. It was whispered that Hadi the Rocket, who continued to respect Abdullah Al Sjamil and even feared him, never forgot the spitting. Then the party came to power and Hadi the Rocket became even more important. It was alleged that Hadi the Rocket had written a report in which it was stated that Abdullah Al Sjamil listened to Iranian radio stations on the sly and that he was in favour of Khomeini. Three cars from the party took everyone from the farm away. Some family members had jumped over the wall, swum through the Thirsty River to the date palm orchard and never returned. It was said that after that the party had gone to live on the farm.

Children from the town dared not come near the farm of Abdullah Al Sjamil to steal peaches because he threw stones at them, but when Abdullah Al Sjamil disappeared, the children were scared of approaching the party farm because there was an electric fence that turned each and every child, who went to the farm to steal peaches, into ashes. All the children were scared, except Djazil. He managed to get a little closer each time, until he could steal the peaches. He crept through the peach orchard to discover those amazing creatures of the party. No one had ever seen them. The children told each other that the party had the animals because otherwise it would get bored, that he not only had the peacock, which everyone could hear as the sun went down, but animals that could talk and birds that could laugh and cry.

Djazil dragged Rizen along to go with him to see the party. Rizen dared not, because it was said that whoever saw the party would turn to stone, but he went along and they crept together towards the farm. Djazil slipped between the fruit trees and led Rizen carefully through the orchard. He showed Rizen the places where he should stop and let him see the ominous electric fence. Coming to the peach trees, Rizen snatched peaches up from the ground with both hands and stuffed them into his mouth.

"Don't throw the pips on the ground. Then they'll know that someone was here. Bury them," whispered Djazil, as he adroitly buried the pips in the ground with his feet. "Walk on your toes. Otherwise they'll see footsteps."

Rizen would not have believed that Djazil would dare do it if he had not been standing there himself.

"Look," whispered Djazil again. "The party lives behind the wall." Djazil pointed to the high stone wall which encircled the farmhouse. He had never dared approach the farm by himself and had to swallow to make sure that Rizen would not notice his nervousness.

"Why don't you climb over?" whispered Djazil.

"They say that whoever sees the party turns to stone." Rizen's teeth were chattering from fear. He was scared that the party would see them through the wall and would turn them into stone.

"That's not true," said Djazil to calm his brother. "Why don't the guards then turn to stone?" Alongside his brother, Djazil felt a little braver. He crept between the trees, quickly climbed the wall and looked over it. He signalled to his brother to follow him. Rizen dared not, but because Djazil began to whisper and Rizen was scared that someone would hear him, he slid to the wall and pulled himself up next to Djazil.

What the brothers saw behind the wall, they would never forget. In the fading twilight, coloured lights lit up the whole garden. They saw a fountain with a coloured light throwing water into the air. They saw grass and soaring drops of water. They saw flowers and trees that they had never seen before. They saw deer walking around, the saw peacocks and all sorts of birds, filling the branches.

A white parrot sat in a cage on a grapevine. "I love Saddam," it repeated. "I love Saddam. Down with Israel, long live the Arabs."

Suddenly they saw a boy wearing white clothes. When the coloured lights from the fountain lit up his face, he glittered. He was about fourteen years old and sat on a swing chair. Together the brothers dropped their heads down behind the wall, so that he would not see them and turn them into stone.

"Did you see him? He must be the party," whispered Rizen.

"He is the party," said Djazil.

"He's so young," said Rizen.

They raised their heads from behind the wall again and saw Hadi the Rocket coming between the branches. In his hand he held a red apple. He went to sit next to the boy and caressed him tenderly over his hair, while talking to him. They could not hear what he was saying. The boy looked at the ground, as if he wanted to say that he did not want to or that he wanted to go away or that he was tired. Hadi the Rocket stood up and led the boy by his hand into the big house. Darkness began to fall.

In the room opposite the wall a lamp was burning. They saw Hadi the Rocket touching the neck and lips of the boy and kissing him. They saw how Hadi the Rocket took the boy's shirt off and kissed him on his neck, on his chest and on his mouth.

"What's Hadi the Rocket doing?" whispered Rizen.

"He's kissing the party and he's going to screw him," said Djazil self-confidently.

Rizen, who would always recall this scene on hearing of the party, let himself down fearfully. Djazil stayed watching with wide eyes and hissed to his brother that he must watch something which could end at any moment. Each time he hissed louder. Rizen climbed up, because he did not want anyone to hear them, and he saw the pain in the boy's face. Hadi the Rocket stood behind him with his trousers around his ankles and had unbuttoned his shirt.

Suddenly a dog began barking at the foot of the wall. While he was busy with the boy, Hadi the Rocket looked into the darkness without seeing anything. The two brothers fell to the ground. Rizen grabbed Djazil's shoulder. He did not know what he should do in the pitch darkness which had covered the land in the meantime. They heard the dog barking from the other side of the wall and were scared that someone would open the gate for it.

"Don't rush," whispered Djazil calmly, as if he was not scared. "Get past the electric fence and only then run."

They heard that barking of the dog was getting ever closer and when Rizen heard his brother say "Now!", he began to run so fast that he could not feel the ground beneath his feet.

After half an hour they arrived at home. Rizen was still trembling with fear, but Djazil, panting, took the peaches out of his pockets, proudly counted them and began eating them.

"How many have you got?" he asked.

"Two more," said Rizen.

"Why don't you eat them?"

"One is for Tenzile and one is for Mira," he said. "I also had one for mother and grandmother, but they fell out. So give me two of yours."

"No," said Djazil. "Unless you pay for them."

After some hard bargaining Rizen bought two peaches for Wasile and Simahen.

"Did you see what Hadi the Rocket was doing there with the party?" Djazil asked Rizen.

Rizen nodded. "That is what guys do with girls when they are alone."

The next day in their hiding place Rizen told Tenzile that he had seen the party. His voice betrayed fear more than pride.

"The party? Where?" asked Tenzile.

"In its house," said Rizen.

"It's not true. You're lying. No one dares go there. You just want to try and prove to me how brave you are."

He gave her the peach. "From the party's orchard."

Tenzile, who had never eaten a peach before, took the fruit in her small hand, looked at the delicious proof of Rizen's honesty and began eating it, while Rizen gently laid his hand on her clothes and began to search for her breasts.

"They're still small," she said, while biting into the peach. "You must put your hand under the hem to feel how small they are."

As if putting his hand into a snake's hole, Rizen put his hand under her dress and searched for Tenzile's breast. He could not find it, until she pressed her finger on her nipple and he slid his hand under the dress to her finger. There he felt her small nipple, which would later feed his children. She stopped chewing. Peach juice ran from her lips.

Each time, Tenzile stayed a little longer with Rizen in their hiding place between the reeds. Each time she lifted the hem of her dress a little higher, so that he could see more of her body, but when the hem came just above her knees, a bolt of lightning fell from a black cloud on to their heads. Rizen left the bread behind, ran away and left Tenzile with her mother, who hit her mercilessly with her two slippers. When he saw that Tenzile had to take all the punishment herself, he went back and put himself under the slippers. Tenzile's mother hit him even harder and when the pain was greater than his love for Tenzile, he fled, this time with the bread.

"I sit at home worried that perhaps you've drowned in the river and you're sitting here!" Tenzile's mother screamed, while sparks leapt from her eyes.

Only days later did Rizen dare go back to the Thirsty River. He checked from a distance to see if he could see Tenzile, but she was not there. He wandered around Boran in the hope of seeing her, but she had disappeared, as if she no longer existed. He discussed it with Djazil, because he thought that someone who could let him see the party in his own house, could also arrange that he could see Tenzile.

"I'll take you there once for free, but after that you must do it yourself or pay for it," said Djazil.

In the evening they slipped through the streets. They jumped on to the clay wall and saw Tenzile in the courtyard in front of her house, sleeping under the moonlight.

"Get back down," whispered Rizen, because he did not want anyone other than himself to see her.

The next day Rizen went back by himself to see her, but the dogs barked and the chickens sleeping on the wall clucked softly. He went back not having accomplished anything and paid Djazil to take him there. In the full moon Rizen could see Tenzile clearly. Her hair dyed with henna lying in waves next to her white face.

When Rizen no longer had any money, Djazil took him for free, until the dogs and chickens became used to Rizen and he climbed the wall every night and looked at Tenzile. Once he was bold enough to throw a little stone at the sleeping Tenzile. She opened her eyes and looked straight at him, as if she had expected to see him on the wall. She straightened her dress. Rizen stared for a second, which seemed like an age, into her eyes. He felt as if he was standing on solid ground, as if the earth had risen to support his feet, as if the earth was saying that it was good that they were looking at each other. In a daze he looked down and saw that her mother had grabbed his feet, as if she was helping a beginner rider down from a horse. On the ground he got a beating. He struggled until he escaped.

Rizen came home with a black eye and Djazil started laughing.

"Before you get to screw that girl, her mother's going to screw you. Not with a dick, because she doesn't have one, but with her slipper."

After that there were no further opportunities for Rizen to see Tenzile. The wall around her house became higher, like Dime's wall long ago. Broken glass was cemented in to the top. Rizen became even thinner and when he walked down the street to sell the bread that Wasile baked, sometimes he called out her name instead of "Hot bread!". Thus the whole town knew about his love for Tenzile, except for Wasile. Rizen dared not tell her.

Wasile became concerned about her son, who was getting ever more emaciated. She wanted him examined at the clinic.

"Worms are not the reason for your forlorn son being underweight, it's a girl," Djazil said laughingly to her, but she did not get the hint.

During this time Rizen began listening to songs and buying books of traditional poetry. Every time Rizen longed to see Tenzile, he went with the poetry books and asked Joesr to read them to him, because he could not do it himself. In this way Joesr himself began to develop an interest in poetry. He immersed himself in poetry and brought a box full of poetry anthologies from the book market. He began reading poems to his brother by Bedr Shakir Al Sejaab, Naxik Al Malaike, Hafez Shirazi, but Rizen understood nothing of them and asked for the traditional poems. When Joesr had exams, Rizen asked Djazil to read for him, but Djazil read without any feeling and had to laugh at the emotions. If he could not find Djazil, he walked past the door of Tenzile's house. He also felt better if he saw the door, until her mother discovered him and pelted him with stones.

Djazil thought that Rizen would forget Tenzile if he slept with another girl. He took him to a whorehouse, where it smelt like a mixture of urine and incense. Rizen gave the fat madam of the house three dinars, which he had been saving up for months, and went with a stout, short girl into a room. The girl shoved the door closed with her foot, went to lie on the seedy bed and pulled her dress up to her breasts. Rizen immediately turned around with his hand over his mouth and looked for a place in which to throw up. Djazil negotiated with the madam to be able to sleep with the girl himself, but the woman refused. Djazil did not want to leave without the money or without having slept with her. She agreed that he could bite the girl on her breasts.

"You paid the whore three dinars and all that we get is a little nibble," said Djazil angrily.

Until the war made him forget about it, Rizen could not look his brother in the eye and they grew apart from each other, but Rizen thought that his brother thought that he was not able to have sex with women.

Years later the first rocket fell on the town. Everyone came to stand around the enormous hole the rocket had caused. Among the throng Rizen saw Tenzile. She had become a woman. She surreptitiously smiled at him. Suddenly the rocket, the hole and the people disappeared. The houses, the soldiers and the world transformed into Tenzile. She let him see her ringless fingers. He understood that she wanted to tell him that she was not yet betrothed. She went home. He did not follow her. He was too old for that. He also went home and decided to ask Wasile to have her betrothed to him. On the way back home he saw Djazil giving something to a child, at which the child ran to the house of Hadi the Rocket.

"What are you doing?" asked Rizen when they were back at home.

"I'm busy screwing with the party."

Rizen understood nothing of this.

"Fatin, the daughter of Hadi the Rocket," Djazil explained. "If I screw her, I screw the party."

While the two brothers were talking with each other, Wasile pulled her door shut and counted the money she had been saving to buy Rizen a car, so that she could give up baking bread.

CHAPTER 6

No men in this town

From 1534, when the Ottomans governed Baghdad, the Iraqis learnt that the government should not know how many animals and goods and what food supplies were in their house, otherwise the authorities would take them. The number of men in a household was also kept a secret as far as possible, so that they would not have to go into the army. In 1917, the English came from the south of Iraq and the Ottomans went via the north back to Istanbul.

After the English left and the Iraqis came to power, they sent commissions out to the localities to record the families, and how many men and women lived in each house. The families gave the names of their sons as girls' names, so that the commissions would not return to their houses when the boys turned eighteen to enlist them into the army. So Nasir became Nasira, Hassan Hasna and Saïd Sade. "In this town there are no men, while all the women are pregnant," said the surprised head of the commission on leaving Boran to go and count the men in other towns.

After that, armed commissions came and made the families stand in line. They wrote their names down and estimated the ages of the boys and men by the length of their moustaches.

That is how everyone came to have a birthday on the first of July.

Because Djazil stood before Sjahid in the line, when the commission came to the Bird household, he was noted down as being one year older then Sjahid. Sleeping Adam was the last in line.

"Wake him up," said a soldier, pointing with his gun at the small, thin Adam surrounded by lice and flies.

"He's dead," said Wasile.

"Why hasn't he been buried?"

"He ..." began Wasile, but was not sure how to explain what she wanted to say.

"He what?"

"He's still breathing."

"Write his name down," said the officer to the soldier who was noting down names in a thick book. Rizen was sixteen, but the commission decided that he was eighteen years old. Because he did not go to school, he was sent to the army. With a piece of paper with his name and a photo stuck on it, he had to go to the training camp in Mahawil. Sjahid tried to persuade him to run away, but Rizen would not listen. He was scared he would be caught.

Wasile woke Rizen the following morning before the first call to prayer. She packed bread with egg and a drink in a knapsack and gave him money for the journey to Mahawil.

The car full of sheep, chickens and people set off on its journey. For Rizen it felt as if he was travelling to another world. In the darkness he looked at the date palms and the old houses. It was the first time he had left Boran. Now and again the car stopped at control points and soldiers in uniform or civilian clothing stepped up. They looked at the faces of the people in the car and asked the men for their papers. When Rizen showed them his paper, they examined it, gave it back and let him remain seated. He felt how important that paper was, that allowed him to sail through the control points, where some travellers had to get out and walk and were not allowed back into the car. After a few control points, Rizen did not return the paper to his pocket, but kept it in his hand. He blew on it or dried it on his trousers if it became wet from his sweat.

When the sun began to shine, he looked out of the dusty window towards the south that was just waking up. In one village he saw a girl herding sheep next to the road. He thought of Tenzile, felt a longing for home and had to suppress a tear. In Najaf he asked if there was a car going to Mahawil. A car was pointed out, with the driver standing and shouting. "Five more passengers!" Even when someone climbed into the car, he continued shouting. When the man dozed off and later woke up, he still continued shouting out the same words without looking into the car. "Five more passengers." Meanwhile, the car was filled with sweaty faces. So the man took his place behind the steering wheel and began driving, hooting to clear a path in the bustle and to greet other drivers. The hooting and the heat of summer drained Rizen's head. He fell asleep with the paper in his hand. After a while the driver woke him and dropped him off at the gates of the training camp.

He handed over the paper to one of the guards and was taken to a hall full of young men from all over Iraq. At four in the morning, a whistle woke them up and, each in their different clothes, they followed a soldier. Their hair was shorn, each young man received a green uniform and an order to be ready in half an hour for the start of training. The wall around the courtyard of the camp was emblazoned with slogans. "Saddam Hussein is the roof and walls of Iraq" and "The sweat of training lessens the blood of battle".

The young men stood close to each other and behind each other in rows in the courtyard, while a corporal addressed them. "This is the most sacrosanct ground in our fatherland, where men become lions. Whoever spits on this ground must lick up his spit."

One of the men laughed and was called to the front by the corporal and punished. He had to crawl over broken glass with no clothes on and was beaten with a stick until he bled. When everyone saw what had happened to that man in the very first quarter of an hour in the army, they fell silent.

During those first weeks every young man underwent similar punishment.

When the corporal discovered that Rizen had not shaved at four in the morning, but the night before, he had to crawl through faeces while being beaten with a rope. Rizen did not scream. His work as a bread seller had taught him to endure a great deal. After the punishment, when he was covered in faeces and mud, he was glad, because he had proved to the corporal and the others that he was a good soldier.

After one month Rizen was given five days' leave. With his shaved head, his green uniform and his heavy army boots, he went home. He arrived at the moment Sjahid was taking his paintings to the clay oven to burn them.

To be accepted in the art academy, Sjahid had to fill in forms about himself and his family, whether he was a member of the Ba'ath party, whether anyone in his family had been detained by the government, whether anyone had been hanged, whether the extended family, uncles, nephews, had been involved. If the answer to just one question was yes, the student was not accepted, and that is what happened to Sjahid. The day he failed to get the party's approval and returned from Baghdad with the rejection from the art academy, he went straight to his room without greeting anyone and took all his paintings to the clay oven.

"Use wood as well," he said to Wasile, and he added more when it was paintings of Saddam Hussein and the party, to make sure that Wasile would burn them. When she heard that, Wasile immediately threw the pictures, which Sjahid had spent a long time painting, into the clay oven.

She held one in front of her and looked at it. "But these are trees," she said.

"The trees as well," said Sjahid.

Wasile did not know what he meant with "the trees as well". She merely thought that it was a pity she had to burn that wood now, when she could have made a profit from it. She thought that it would be better if he sold bread instead of painting. Then she would, most importantly, be able to buy the car sooner.

Sjahid was the first in the Bird household after Kosjer to learn the alphabet. But while the alphabet was like an illness for Kosjer from which he was cured, for Sjahid it was a medicine.

During the first year of school, when the teacher asked the children if they wanted to paint a fish, Sjahid discovered that he could draw well. Sjahid painted a wavy fish, different to all the others.

"The fishes of the others are all dead, except mine. It's alive," said Sjahid when the teacher asked him why.

The teacher admired his answer and hung his drawing up in the class.

From that day on he often told his friends Mohamed Mansour and Yasin Al Terref that he wanted to go to art academy. When he was rejected by the academy, he paced back and forth for days in front of the house.

"Thousands of people are dying in wars, prisons and the cells of the secret police and your son is depressed because he can't study how to throw paint on to wood," Joesr said to Wasile.

Mira often found Sjahid's food untouched. A few times she warmed it up and brought it back to him, but Sjahid did not eat and grew thin. What hurt him most was that no one knew the extent of his pain.

"Just have a look around you," cried Wasile. "No one knows whether or not a rocket is going to hit their house."

When even Mohamed Mansour and Yasin Al Terref no longer listened to him, Mira saw him one day sitting next to Adam's head and talking.

"Imagine that I had been born on the other side of the border. Somewhere else. Far away. Would that not have been better for my soul? I don't like weapons or war. I don't believe in the fatherland, family or God. The only thing I believe in is my head and not even in that sometimes."

"You're talking to yourself," said Mira. "Have you gone crazy?"

"I'm talking to him," Sjahid waved the flies away from Adam's face and looked at the fine moustache and beginnings of a beard, which Mira had not shaved in days. "Just look at him. He has no concerns about war or the heat of the damned summer or of Saddam Hussein. Ah, perhaps his way is the best way."

"I don't understand what you're saying," said Mira.

"I'm saying that he's got it right, sleeping his life away and never waking up. Do you understand now?"

Mira looked at him with vacant eyes. "Do you want me to warm up your food for you?"

Mira left the stable where Adam was lying on a mat made from palm fronds. She ran after a hen to catch it. Sjahid looked at her and at the hen. The hen ran back and forth with round, red eyes. Mira hit at it with a slipper.

"If only I could also chase a hen with a slipper in my hand. Ah."

"What are you saying?" called Wasile from behind the clay oven, when she heard the groan that Sjahid uttered. "Have you been stung by a scorpion?"

"Yes," said Sjahid.

"Suck on the sting until it bleeds," she said.

"That's difficult."

"Why?"

"It stung my brain."

"Joker. I thought you'd really been stung."

Simahen, who had been awoken by the noise from a falling rocket, asked from her room what was going on.

"I heard Sjahid groaning and thought a scorpion had stung him and I said that he should suck the poison out, but he said it was his brain that had been stung."

"Where?" asked Simahen.

"In his brain!"

"What in his brain?"

"A scorpion stung him!" said Wasile while taking bread out of the oven, which she had been selling herself since Rizen had gone to the army.

"Tell him that he must suck the sting out before the poison gets to his heart!" said Simahen.

Joesr came out of his room and laughed at the conversation between Simahen and Wasile.

"You must find a course that will accept you, otherwise you're going to the army," he said to Sjahid.

"I'm never going to the army."

"What are you going to do then?"
"I'll fade away. Evaporate like water."

When night fell, the sparrows on the vine rested and the mosquitoes around the light buzzed, Sjahid sat on his bed. His life was held tightly in the hands of Saddam Hussein. His fear of the war became greater than his disappointment over the fact that he had not been accepted at the art academy. He had never thought of the war as part of his life. He saw the black shrouds with the names of the dead soldiers, the places where they had fallen and suras from the Koran in front of him. The freedom he had when he had been at school and had discussions with Mohamed Mansour and Yasin Al Terref had disappeared.

To set his mind at ease he went outside. On the streets of Boran he saw homeless dogs scratching through rubbish, cats sitting on walls and rats running away. Yasin Al Terref's mother said that her son was not yet home and Mohamed Mansour's house was far away, so Sjahid decided to go to the teahouse. He heard the air raid siren and then saw all the windows being blackened out. In the darkness he saw Naji's spotlight shining, indifferent to the soldiers patrolling to make sure everything was in darkness. Sjahid jumped towards the bright light like a traveller in a great desert beginning to make out the silhouette of date palms around an oasis on the horizon.

Naji was busy concentrating on his work. On a ladder against a wall he was painting over a mural of Saddam Hussein, obscured by dust, smeared with bird shit, and faded by sunlight. Naji had a spotlight focused on Saddam Hussein's face, which had just been done, and was busy painting over the clothes. Sjahid greeted him. Naji returned the greeting without looking, until he sensed that the person he had greeted was standing still.

"Why don't you paint during the day?" asked Sjahid.

Naji focused the light on the speaker beneath him and looked down. "Are you from around here?" he asked when he saw that Sjahid was neatly dressed, had nice shoes and oil in his hair.

"I'm from the Bird family," said Sjahid.

"Where're your wings then?"

"They hacked them off."

Naji began laughing and climbed down. He looked for his cigarettes, lit one and offered one to Sjahid. Sjahid declined, but Naji persisted.

"Take one. Burn something."

Sjahid repeated his question. "Why don't you paint during the day?"

"During the day, it's too dusty, it's too hot and it stinks of shit," said Naji and looked Sjahid in the eye. "How can you paint shit, while you're smelling it?"

Sjahid looked carefully at Naji, who had called Saddam Hussein shit, and was not sure how he should react. Many people dared not even mention the name of Saddam Hussein and merely said "Mr President", because there was no other president.

"Can I work for you?" Sjahid asked shyly, because it was the first time he had ever asked for work. The idea had just come to him and he had blurted it out without thinking.

"Work for me? What can you do?"

"I can help you with painting." He wanted to tell Naji that he had wanted to go to the art academy, but did not do so.

"What I do can endanger your life," said Naji. "Even the tiniest mistake can cost you your life." He looked at Sjahid's pale face, from fear or from confusion – he was not sure. "Imagine, if you will. You make a mistake with the cigar in the mouth of Mr President and you paint it like a carrot. Or ..." Naji looked with a sardonic gaze straight into Sjahid's eyes. "Imagine that the cigar looks like a penis. Can you imagine what would happen then?" Sjahid was at a loss for words. "You don't have a reply, because you don't know what would happen then and how dangerous this work is that I do. There was an artist in Mosul who had made a mural of Mr President, with eyes that were so ringed with black that it looked as if they were made up with kohl. He was immediately hanged. In another painting in Basra the lips of Mr President were painted too red, as if he was wearing lipstick. They took the artist away, just like your father, grandfather and uncles, just because a randy sheep butted a television aerial. Who knows what they did with the painter. They say he had to bite off his own lips and eat them, but that's not true, because no one knows what happened to him. Not even Mr President."

Sjahid looked at Naji, who was talking and smoking, and could not work out for whom and against whom this man was.

"Take the paint and the brush. Get up in front of the jacket. It is completely white, as you can see, but be careful. It is the jacket of Mr President."

Sjahid took the paint and the brush, and climbed in his neat clothes up to the jacket of Saddam Hussein, which had been transformed from white into a yellowish hue, while Naji sat below on his chair, smoking. After quarter of an hour he looked at what Sjahid had done and went back to sit down again. "You're good at colouring in," he said when Sjahid was finished. "From today onwards you can colour in the clothes of Mr President from his neck to his shoes." He gave him one dinar and told him to come back the next day at the same time.

Sjahid did not go straight home, but carried Naji's things back to his house. Naji walked behind him with a barely noticeable limp.

When Sjahid got home he gave the dinar to Wasile. He had wanted to keep the coin, but because it was the first one he had earned through work, he gave it to his mother to show that he could earn money for himself.

"Where did you get that money?" she asked.

"From the President's jacket."

"From Mr President's jacket? Did you steal it?"

"I painted it."

"Take your trousers off," said Wasile and she washed the paint out of his clothes. "Next time, don't let the paint from Mr President's clothes drip on to yours. That is dangerous."

The following day Sjahid waited for Naji far away from the painting, afraid that soldiers would think that he wanted to deface it.

"Today you're going to colour in the trousers of Mr President and tomorrow his necktie in white. If you do it well, you can also do his teeth and the whites of his eyes."

"And his hands?" asked Sjahid.

"You're still a beginner. Sadly, though, we cannot let his white heart be seen in the painting." Naji laughed loudly. "Easy does it, no rush. There'll come a time when you can colour in the skin of Mr President. One day you shall be honoured with the colouring in of his arse and his balls." He laughed once again.

Sjahid kept quiet.

"Laugh, man, are you scared?" asked Naji.

But Sjahid never let on as to whether he found Naji's jokes about Saddam Hussein funny or not.

That night Naji gave him another half a dinar. "You've earned it. To me you're not just a worker, but also the valve in the pressure cooker."

Naji controlled what Sjahid did until he was sure of his skills. After that he made the sketches of Saddam Hussein out of his head, painted the face and the hands himself, and left the rest to Sjahid. Then he sat on his chair to smoke and drink whisky from a small bottle that he hid carefully, so that no one would think that he neglected Saddam Hussein and painted him while he was drunk.

Naji spent his days at home. At night he made murals of Saddam Hussein or painted over the faded images. He had long hair and a beard and a moustache, through all of which you could not see his mouth. Everyone respected him, but sometimes jokes were made about his clothes and his hair. When he had begun painting the murals of Saddam Hussein, the residents of Boran were scared of him, even Hadi the Rocket. "Through Naji's hands Mr President becomes bigger, even though he is already so big," said Hadi the Rocket.

A watermelon seller demonstrated to Naji how scared the people were. Naji had bought a heavy watermelon from him and wanted to carry it home, but the watermelon seller was afraid that if Naji carried the watermelon home by himself, he would hurt his hand and would have to say no to a request to paint a mural of Saddam Hussein, at which they would ask him why not and he would say he was not able to because he had bought a watermelon. Because the party members would be unable to take the watermelon away because Naji had already eaten it, they would instead take the seller. The watermelon seller already knew what the secret service would say. "You know that he is a sensitive artist and that his hand is important for the fatherland because he paints Mr President. You knew how heavy the watermelon was, because you weighed it." So the watermelon seller insisted on taking it to Naji's house.

When Ahmed Hassan al-Bakr was president and Saddam Hussein the second in charge, Naji's father referred to Saddam Hussein as the Party Butcher, because if Saddam's men picked up an enemy of the party, he would disappear from the face of the earth. When the people began calling Saddam Hussein 'Mr President', although he was still not in power, Naji's father knew that Saddam Hussein would remove Ahmed Hassan al-Bakr from power at any moment and he began teaching Naji not to be scared of him. Naji's father ensured that there were no photos of Saddam Hussein hanging in the house and never said "Mr President".

His father was a professor of biology and taught at the University of Baghdad. Because he never mentioned the president in the course of his lessons, he was sent as a teacher to the primary school in Boran, and because the professor did not teach the children to sing for the president, but for Iraq, he had to stop giving lessons. He was given an old bicycle and became a postman. The professor had little contact with others, not even his colleagues at the post office. When he came home, he read scientific books in his study, and when Naji came home from school, he asked him what he had learnt. Then he corrected the information his son had received and threw Saddam Hussein from Naji's brain.

"Listen, my son. In the beginning there was Iraq, and only after that did Saddam Hussein come. Saddam Hussein is not the son of Iraq, but the son of Sabha. And Sabha is a chicken thief from Al Odja."

Saddam Hussein was the chain that linked the mouth of the father to his son's ear.

"Don't talk about Mr President like that to your son. You'll murder him," said his wife.

"What Mr President? He's a dog, a pig and you call him Mr President in our house?" The professor exploded. "You poison the children with the virus that Saddam Hussein spreads."

His mother always called Saddam Hussein "Mr President". His father spoke about "the son of Sabha".[1]

One day the professor could not take any more, when the heavens, the earth, the sky, the windows, the walls and heads were all filled with one thing: Saddam Hussein. "The son of Sabha has stabbed me with a rusty knife," he said to his wife on his deathbed.

"If you say 'Mr President' and not 'the son of Sabha', you'll get up from this bed as healthy as a horse," said his wife, who believed that his hatred for Saddam Hussein had led him to death's door.

That evening when she slept, the professor thought about her words, while hearing the voice of Saddam Hussein in the distance from a radio or television. He wanted to ask his wife to close the window, but did not want to wake her. He got up from his bed and went to the window. Instead of immediately closing the window, he inhaled deeply, for the last time, the air of Iraq.

"Whoever is an enemy of the party or the revolution, will be pursued by spirits if he escapes from the hands of the party," screamed Saddam Hussein in the distance.

The professor felt a stabbing in his chest. He put his hand to the pain and tried to walk to his bed, but his knees betrayed him and he fell down. He supported himself against the wall and closed his eyes tightly. Early in the morning his wife found him dead beneath the window.

After the burial of his father, Naji's mother warned him day and night not to say "the son of Sabha", but "Mr President". As afraid as his father had been that Naji's head would rot if he said "Mr President, so afraid was his mother that her son's head would rot if he did not say "Mr President".

Years later Naji acquired a passport, thanks to his mother paying all the gold she had received on her wedding to an

official. He went to Catalonia to study at the art academy. At
the airport in Barcelona he looked around with amazement –
but he saw not a single photo of Saddam Hussein, not on the
walls, not in the windows, not on the pillars. Disoriented, he
wandered in circles until a fellow worker led him to the exit.

Four months later a female model stood before the students
at the art academy. Naji tried hard to concentrate on her face,
but could not see it. The face of Saddam Hussein sat on her
neck. He painted the beautiful body of the woman and in the
place where her face should have been, he painted the face of
Saddam Hussein. Everyone laughed at his painting that day,
as Naji saw Saddam Hussein everywhere. If he was walking
through Barcelona, all the statues had the head of Saddam
Hussein, just like the models on the posters. He saw women in
bikinis with the smiling face of Saddam Hussein with blonde
curls.

He consulted a doctor, who asked him what his trouble was.
"Saddam Hussein," he answered.

"I can prescribe medicine against fever for you, but I can't
prescribe an army to cure you of Saddam Hussein," said the
doctor.

So Naji bought a bottle of whisky for the first time and drank
until he no longer saw the face of Saddam Hussein.

When Naji heard that his mother was lying on her deathbed
and wanted to see him, he immediately travelled back home.
His mother was still alive when he arrived. He decided to stay
until she had died, so that he could bury her. After that,
because he was an only child, he could sell the house and go
back to Catalonia.

After four months his mother had still not passed away, but
because more soldiers were needed for the war, travel abroad
was forbidden and Naji was called up for national service. "I
came to bury my mother, but am burying myself," he always
said in the trenches.

His days on leave at home he spent sitting, drinking and
thinking about Catalonia. If his mother asked him what he was
drinking, he said it was medicine. If she asked him what sort

of medicine it was, he said it was a medicine for the head, because he did not want his religious mother to die afraid of God, if she knew that he was drinking alcohol, which he had learnt in Catalonia.

Two and a half years after his return from Catalonia his mother came down with a headache. She wanted to ask Naji to give her some aspirin, but he was going to sleep. She could not find the aspirin, but did find the little bottle out of which Naji always drank. She fetched a glass, put in two cubes of ice as Naji always did, opened the bottle and filled the glass. She found that the drink smelt like gasoline, but threw her head back and gulped it down. Her heavy head lightened, as if she had acquired two wings. She filled a second glass and a third, until she could drink no more.

She threw her headscarf off, shook her grey hair loose and switched the radio on. She could only find songs about Saddam Hussein, so she switched the radio off again and looked in her cupboard amongst all her old things. She found an LP of Lebanese songs that she had bought when she was young and had gone with her husband to Lebanon. She plugged the record player into the wall socket. The turntable began to spin. With drunken fingers she set the needle on the LP and the lively songs wafted through the room, songs that she had heard in the mountains of Lebanon in 1957, a year before the king of Iraq was murdered in El Rihab palace and Iraq became a republic. The name of El Rihab palace changed to "Termination Palace", because the Ba'ath party used it as a place in which to execute its opponents.

Naji's mother felt an ancient breeze coming in through the windows, saw a decaying sun shining and felt time turning back like a genie from a magic lantern. She switched the fan on, switched everything in the house on, even opened the fridge and turned the LP up so loud that Naji woke up. He saw his mother twirling around and her hands moving through the air like butterflies. He got up straight away and took his mother back to bed. He smelt the glass and knew she had drunk his whisky.

In her bed she gazed at the ceiling and smiled. "That

medicine is not just for headaches, but also for heartaches," she said.

She fell into a deep sleep and never woke up again.

Naji remained in the army until a bullet from a sniper perforated his knee. He did not go back to the trenches. He always said that he never respected anyone as much as the Iranian sniper who had done that to him. He cherished nothing so much as that bullet that had brought him home and, after the doctor had removed it from his knee, he hung it around his neck. "Without that bullet I would have rotted on the border," he said if someone he could trust asked about it.

Naji tried afresh to go to Catalonia, but travel remained difficult. Just as Simahen waited in the shadows of the party house for her husband and her sons, so Naji waited for a passport, but when, after a few months, he no longer had any money and had not sold any paintings, he began to paint murals of Saddam Hussein.

The sort of painting Naji made of Saddam Hussein depended on what his state of mind was. If he was lazy or lethargic – which occurred especially in the summer – he painted Saddam Hussein in black and white.

"This is Iraq. Black and white, and no place for any other colours," he said to Sjahid or to himself when he was drunk. If Naji felt bored, he painted Saddam Hussein without any weapons on a chair. If he was locked in a negative spiral, he painted Saddam Hussein shooting a rifle in the air. When he once thought with melancholy about the beaches of Catalonia, he painted Saddam Hussein lying down in his swimming trunks on the beach of El Habbaniya lake with a can of cola in his hand. When Hadi the Rocket complained about it, Naji let him see the photo on which he had based his painting. Hadi the Rocket kept quiet.

"I believe that Mr President is glorious in any position and any clothing. Don't you think so?" asked Naji.

"Absolutely, master Naji, absolutely," said Hadi the Rocket. "But as you know, our fatherland is at war. Therefore it is better to represent Mr President in uniform. Don't spare any

trouble when you do it again, the party will pay for it." Naji
climbed the ladder and painted a uniform over the hirsute hide
of the reclining Saddam Hussein. Instead of a cola in his hand,
he painted a grenade, in the other hand a rocket launcher. The
water of El Habbaniya lake was turned into fire, the flying
seagulls into enemy aircraft, the distant ships into tanks and
the small sailboats into cannons.

A few days later an old woman, walking from her village next
to the swamps to the town to visit Kamel the pharmacist, went
past the mural with her granddaughter when she suddenly
held her granddaughter back.

"I'm sure that we must have lost our way. This is not the
same street. The last time Mr President was naked and
drinking a cola and not fighting with an RPG-7," she said.

The granddaughter tried to persuade her that it actually was
the same street, but the grandmother remained convinced that
she had taken the wrong road. She believed that streets could
change, but did not believe that Saddam Hussein could put on
his uniform on a wall.

CHAPTER 7

Thanks to the rocket

On the day the first rocket came down in Boran, Rizen took a fragment of it to wear around his neck, just as Naji did with the bullet from his knee. Every time a rocket fell, Rizen had to think of Tenzile. If he was at home, on leave from the army, he hoped that a rocket would not fall behind the date palms, but that it would come down in Boran so that he could see Tenzile.

He tried to tell his mother that he wanted to marry Tenzile. He saw that she had become a woman, but was too embarrassed to mention it directly to Wasile. Wasile understood his hints, but pretended not to understand, because if Rizen married it would cost the home its cow. A cow lost from the house to bring a woman in was a troubling proposition for Wasile, who had spent her life in front of the clay oven to feed the family and to save for a car for Rizen, who had to free her from baking bread.

"I'll save up for it screw by screw," she said. In her dreams she once saw the four wheels with a steering wheel, a steering wheel and a seat, and if she was feeling good, she saw Rizen alongside a complete car standing at the station in Boran. When she was younger, she had hoped that Sjahid and Joesr would look after the household after completing their studies, but a few years on she realised that one must expect nothing from children who had finished at school.

When Rizen was not dropping careful hints to his mother at the clay oven, he sat with Simahen in the hope that she would raise the subject of marriage, and he had to listen to endless stories for hours on end. He once tried to get Mira to start on the topic of marriage, but she ran around the whole day after the chickens and did not listen to him. He even went inside to see Joesr once, but came out of his room half an hour later with a headache because Joesr explained to him that he had not only length, breadth and depth, but also a fourth dimension of time.

"There are many girls who want to marry Rizen," a woman called from behind the wall, when no one in the house wanted to hear what Rizen was trying to say. Rizen's hints, which Wasile did not hear on her side of the wall, she heard very well from the other side of the wall.

"Let that son of yours get married before he dies in the war without a son to bear his name," Simahen then said angrily. "You obviously don't want to understand that Rizen wants to get married." She turned her back, walked to Rizen's room and shouted: "Sell the cow and get married! Don't ask the women to help you get married, you're the man of the house."

"Anything but the cow!" Wasile cried to Rizen, as if he had suggested it himself. She would never dare say any such thing to Simahen. "Marry ten women and bring them here, but that cow is not leaving this house!"

Three months later Simahen counted her hidden gold in her head. Gold that she had been saving for dark days when she had been pregnant with her first child, but it was not enough to allow Rizen to get married. So after much hesitation she took a heavy gold necklace with pearls and shimmering jewels out from among her boxes. Her mother had given her the necklace when she had first menstruated.

"This necklace has been passed from mother to daughter for a hundred and thirty five years," her mother had said. "No man has ever seen it, except for the first one who gave it to his betrothed." She had carefully handed the necklace over, in a piece of cloth. "Hide it away! Never let any man see it," her mother had warned. Simahen had hidden the package away without looking at the necklace. She had then gone to the washroom and locked the door behind her. She had unwrapped the tatty piece of cloth, revealing a newer piece of cloth and then a piece of silk. She had also unwrapped this layer and there lay the glimmering necklace.

When she had seen the necklace, she felt joyous, as if the necklace had wings, letting her fly through the blue heavens among the seagulls. Eventually, she picked it up carefully between her thumb and forefinger and hung it around her neck. The gems rested on her small breasts. She looked at herself in the mirror and twirled round with happiness. It was as if it was not the necklace, but the hands of a prince out of one of her grandmother's stories that were embracing her. As the hormones rose to her head, she closed her eyes tightly, touched the necklace with her fingers, and then touched her nipples. Then she let her fingers slowly slide down and touched herself, as if making love with the necklace until her mother called from behind the door: "Do you just fall asleep sometimes?"

Then she woke from her dreams, carefully wrapped the necklace up again in the three layers of cloth, threw water over her body and left the washroom, as if she had just made love with a prince with a thick moustache, a strong chest and muscular arms. When she had come to live in the Bird family household, she had not let anyone see the necklace, until she decided to sell it. "Rizen has no father, no uncle and no grandfather. Who else will let him marry? It is time for the necklace to go. After all, Mira won't ever have a daughter to give it to," she said to herself.

She asked Rizen to take her to the jeweller in Najaf, whom she had known for many years. There she took the cloth bundle out from under her clothing, laid it on the table and began unwrapping it with her old, trembling hands as if opening the doors of a cage out of which her life would fly away. Tears ran down her cheeks as she remembered her time as a young girl when she had looked in the mirror in the washroom with the necklace around her neck.

"Leave it. Don't open it," said Rizen when he saw his grandmother's tears.

But she waved for him to go and sit down and embarrassedly wiped away the tears with a cloth. "Ah, young man, these tears fall not for the gold, but for the years that have disappeared."

When the three layers of cloth had been opened like petals on a flower, Rizen and the jeweller saw the necklace, the first men to have done so in many generations.

"These two youngsters must get married and have a son before he dies in Mr President's war," Simahen said to the jeweller.

"Hadja,[2] this is a unique piece. Are you sure that you want to sell it? You can borrow some money from me," said the jeweller, overtaken by the moment, but Simahen was firm in her decision.

The jeweller weighed the necklace and gave Simahen two rings in a small box and money in a plastic pouch. Carefully and without letting anyone notice, she stole one last glance at the necklace on the jeweller's table. It felt like a knife stabbing.

"Take my hand," she said to Rizen to help her stand up. "Tell the family of the girl that you have the money and give them half of it. If they say that it is not enough, leave and never go back. Then it becomes business and they don't want you to marry their daughter, they want you to buy her. If they say that they don't want any money, give it all to them and say that it is for the girl to buy what she will."

Rizen kissed Simahen on her hand and two and a half months later he married Tenzile. Wasile had first gone to Tenzile's mother to tell her that she would very much like Tenzile and her son to be betrothed. Tenzile's mother asked for some time, so that she could ask Tenzile what she wanted to do. When Tenzile gave no answer, it was clear that she had approved the proposal to marriage.

After that Rizen had gone with men from the area to Tenzile's family and asked the same of the father. The father asked Tenzile if she wanted to marry Rizen, and when she did not answer him, he left her room again and said that the girl had said yes. The following day Tenzile went with Wasile to town and bought clothes with the money from Simahen's necklace.

On the last Thursday of July, Rizen married Tenzile. He had not seen her again since the day when the first rocket had fallen on Boran. They sat on the edge of the bed in their bedroom. On her face a thick layer of make-up and creams were smeared. She wanted to wash her face, but was embarrassed because everyone was looking at her. Rizen could not believe that after all these years he was sitting with her under the same roof without having to expect the slipper of her mother on his head. He sat close to her and looked into her dark eyes, which he had dreamt about during his time in the army.

"Do you still remember when we were kids, in the summer on the banks of the Thirsty River?" he asked her. She smiled bashfully. Rizen told her of the yearning he had had for her all this time. With every passing hour Tenzile became less afraid, such that by midnight they were sitting and talking as they had done by the Thirsty River when they were children.

"Perhaps they're still waiting outside," said Tenzile.

"What for?" asked Rizen.

"For you to go out." She wanted to add 'with the bloody sheet', but dared not.

"Let them wait. I've waited longer than they have."

When he left the room much later to go to the toilet he saw that Wasile was still awake. She stood up immediately and came to him.

"Is she still a virgin?" she whispered.

"That I don't know," said Rizen. "But I certainly am."

Wasile kept trying to find out if Tenzile was a virgin and if Rizen had slept with her. She thought that something was not right, just like the buyers of the bread that she baked, because the bread was sometimes too dry if she had too many things going on in her head. The last night before Rizen had to go back to the army, she heard some creaking during the night. The next morning she saw a red mark on the white sheet and breathed a great sigh of relief.

Tenzile cried when Rizen went to the war and only stopped when he came back. That got Joesr thinking about the war. Who was it being fought against and why? Would there be an end to it and, if so, when? Who began it and why? He thought of Tenzile and what would happen to her if Rizen died in the war and never came back again. Would she keep on crying? At the book market on El Mutanabbi street in Baghdad, where the steps were piled with books, he swapped his box of books about Sufism for a box of books about the history of Iraq.

"Be careful," said the bookseller, who had known Joesr for years and knew that he could trust him. "It is a bloody history, there is not a single decade without famine or death."

Joesr shrugged his shoulders and left with the new box of books with stories and photos about the Sumerians through to the time of Saddam Hussein. He put the forbidden books at the bottom, the approved ones on top and carrots on top of them, so that no one would see that there were books in the box. That is how he travelled back to Boran.

Joesr devoured the books and after two winters he had read the whole history of Iraq. He discovered that there had been many Saddam Husseins. He got a fright with El Hadjadj, who had come to Iraq a hundred years ago and had said he was seeking ripe heads and that it was time to harvest. In one of the books he wrote a joke that he had heard on the street.

A man asked Kamel the pharmacist for a tablet to make him sleep for a hundred years so that he could be free of Saddam Hussein. When he woke up, he heard the same cheering. The man went back to the pharmacy and said that the tablet had not made him sleep for a hundred years, but for only a few days. The grandson, who looked just like Kamel the pharmacist, said that he had actually slept for a hundred years. The man was disconsolate and screamed: "Saddam Hussein still in power, I don't understand, so why are the people still cheering in the same way? Why haven't they come up with any new slogans?"

One day Mira came to tell Joesr that Tenzile had had a son. Joesr looked disinterestedly at Mira.

"Why do you look at me like that? It's good news after all."

"In my head I'm busy taking life away from someone. I don't have time to think about someone who has just come into this world," Joesr said to Mira, who did not understand what he was saying.

Joesr was the smallest person in the family. He was thin and had deep-set eyes, which sparkled with intelligence. He wore tattered clothes, Rizen's old clothes, which Mira adjusted, or clothes that Sjahid no longer wore. He disliked the dogs' barking, but did not want Djazil to drown them in sacks in the Thirsty River.

He had unkempt hair. When his hair was too long, he sat on the ground with a mirror in one hand and Mira cut the locks at his instruction, because he wanted to save money on barbers and have more left over to buy books.

Although everyone at school mocked him, he had just one friend, Samer, the only one who could deal with his idiosyncrasies. Samer was an only child. When Joesr went to visit him, his parents treated him as their own son. He could regularly travel with Hassan, Samer's father, who was a driver between Baghdad and Boran. In Baghdad he went to El Mutanabbi street, where he would exchange the books he had read for new books. Each time he received fewer books in return and when only one book remained, he read it over and over, until he had enough money to buy new books. He never earned any money for the house, because he never thought about that.

Wasile despaired sometimes. "He sits like a prisoner in his room and schoolbooks alone are not enough for him." Wasile did not understand Joesr.

One day as she was throwing wood into the clay oven, he came up to her. "Do you know how much oil there is under your feet? Like an ass, you make bread all day, while there's an ocean of oil under your feet?"

Because he had called her an ass, she laughed. "If I'm an ass, then you're the son of an ass. As I see it, they don't teach you good manners at that school," she said.

After much thought, Joesr realised that every Iraqi should

dig under his house and sell his own share of oil for himself. He told this to his history teacher, who took him aside from the class.

"Listen carefully," the teacher whispered with urgency. "Ask yourself where people go after they're dead. Ask yourself where the heathens go on the day of judgement, where the soldiers go, where the water of the Euphrates ends up. But never ever ask where the oil goes, because that will cost you the head on your shoulders."

When Joesr read the books about the history of Iraq, he discovered that the most powerful men in Iraq died a natural death, in their own beds, among their own wives. Almost none of them were murdered. That got Joesr thinking about the murder of Hadi the Rocket. Every time that Joesr thought about the children of Hadi the Rocket, he felt remorse and the idea weakened, but when he thought of the children of the victims of Hadi the Rocket, the idea became stronger.

While Joesr thought about murdering Hadi the Rocket, Djazil eventually arrived in the neighbourhood where Fatin lived. She was the daughter of Hadi the Rocket, a pretty girl almost fifteen years old, with firm, pert breasts, which gave Djazil a headache if he thought about them. Fatin wore T-shirts on which a photo of a smiling Saddam Hussein, a pensive Saddam Hussein, or a sleeping Saddam Hussein was sewn, so that whenever Djazil saw Saddam Hussein he always had to think about Fatin's breasts and got an erection.

"When any Iraqi sees a photo of Saddam Hussein their tongue moves, but with me, my dick moves," he told the woman in the market to whom he sold his stolen chickens and with whom he sometimes slept if her husband was at the front.

"Don't let anyone hear you, otherwise it'll be chopped off," said the market woman.

Djazil had children take treats to Fatin. Once he had a piece of warm bread taken to her. He had taken it from Wasile, who did not know that one of her sons was thinking of murdering Hadi the Rocket and another of trying to sleep with his daughter. Fatin laughed with her full lips, broke the bread before throwing it to a goat, and saw a ring. She turned to Djazil, who stood at a distance watching her reaction and thought that he had walked into her trap.

One day on the banks of the Thirsty River Joesr told his friend Samer that he was looking for a pistol to murder Hadi the Rocket.

"Hadi the Rocket? Why not Saddam Hussein himself?" asked Samer.

"To kill Saddam Hussein I'd need an F-16. For Hadi the Rocket a pistol."

"But then you'll be killing your family."

"Don't try and talk me out of it. Imagine that if every Iraqi now murdered the equivalent of Hadi the Rocket," he said enthusiastically. "Then after a few days we would be able to spit in Saddam Hussein's face."

"You're crazy. Books have made you crazy. Don't you know what happened in Didjil, when they tried to murder Saddam Hussein? Even the date palms were chopped down."

Joesr sold everything he had to be able to buy a pistol, and when that was not enough, he sold everything that Mira had, because she believed that Joesr would never ask for any money for himself, but when he and Mira had nothing left, he still did not have enough money to buy even a plastic pistol. He thought about stealing the money that Wasile had been saving and went to ask Sheikh Abdullah Al Najafi if you could commit one small sin to do a greater good.

"For example, could you steal a knife to kill the devil?"

"You cannot do that," said Sheikh Abdullah Al Najafi. "Because what is a sin, remains a sin. Whatever is built on sin, is a sin."

Joesr debated with himself for days. Should he steal from Wasile or not? He went to his history teacher, for whom he had a great deal of respect, and posed the same question to him.

"That is permitted," said the history teacher. "Man destroys over here to build over there, he steals over here to give over there, kills here to give life over there. Knowledge gained during the Second World War when the Germans conducted gruesome tests on the Jews is still being used for medicines which now cure thousands."

Joesr was not sure what to do and kept on pondering as to what the best decision would be, until Djazil's left ear convinced him that he would never succeed.

Djazil came home with a pale, bloodied face. He turned a tap on and washed the blood from the side of his face.

Wasile was cleaning the rice and asked him to slaughter a chicken, but he did not answer her.

"Do you have trouble hearing me sometimes?" she called.

"The ear with which I need to hear you is in my trouser pocket and not on my head, leave me alone," said Djazil. He took the severed ear out of his pocket, washed it, looked in the mirror and held it to his head. He called Mira to bring a needle and thread and when she came he put his ear in her hand. Mira took it, but was not sure was meant by it and looked at him questioningly.

"Sew it on," said Djazil and pointed to his head.

Mira looked at the place where there was no longer an ear, let her head drop slowly to her opened hand and collapsed in a heap. Djazil called Wasile, who threw cold water in her face, while he went with the needle, thread, his ear and a mirror to Joesr's room.

"Sew my ear on again quickly, before it dies," he said to his surprised brother.

Djazil held his ear to his head, afraid that Joesr would also faint.

Joesr did his best to thread the cotton through the eye of the needle with his trembling fingers and held the severed ear, without question. It was still warm.

"Push the needle in deep," said Djazil and clenched his teeth in preparation for the pain.

Joesr also clenched his teeth, pushed the needle through Djazil's ear into his skin and sewed his ear back on to his head. When he was done, he fell down sweating on his bed.

Djazil looked in the mirror, turning from left to right, like someone who had just shaved himself. "I hope that my ear doesn't die off. I ran fast to get here in time."

"What happened?" asked Joesr.

"I thought I had Fatin and jumped over the last wall, but three men began punching me. I couldn't get away. Hadi the Rocket ordered the men to stop hitting me. He looked at me and said that they should cut off my ear. 'But he's only got the one,' said one of the men. 'Cut it off, so that he never comes back again,' screamed Hadi the Rocket. I begged and promised that I would never come back again, even if he said I could, but they cut my ear right off. I knelt in front of Hadi the Rocket and begged him to give me the severed ear. He and the men laughed loudly and threw my ear to the cat. Before it could get it, I grabbed it and ran away," Djazil related the tale, as if it had happened in the distant past and not just half an hour ago. "One day I'll pay you back, Doctor Joesr. You've done a good job." He left the room with the mirror in his hand and looked at his ear satisfied, as if he had just bought it. He went to Wasile's room, where Mira was lying on the bed. She had just come round.

"Look at it, a beautiful ear," said Djazil. "It's a bit sore, but it looks really good."

For the next seven days Djazil watched carefully how his severed ear was growing back on. He only slept on his right side and prayed five times a day. Wasile thought that he had finally found the true path, just as when his right ear had been cut off, but on the eighth day he looked in the mirror and felt that his ear, which he touched every day to see if it still had sensation in it, would not fall off any longer. Without giving any thanks to God he stopped praying. For a while he avoided fights and stealing, so that his ear would not be troubled before it was completely attached in its place.

The market woman asked him why he no longer had any chickens for her to sell and asked if he sometimes felt remorse.

"No," said Djazil. "I'm just waiting for my ear to grow back on to my head."

A rocket fell in the distance behind the rice paddies.

"But your ear is sitting on your head."

Another rocket fell closer by and made the market woman's chickens stop their clucking.

"My ear is lodging and needs some time to feel at home."

"How long?" asked the woman.

"I don't know," said Djazil, laughing. "Only the ear knows that."

And a third rocket landed so close by that the water the woman had put next to the chickens trembled.

CHAPTER 8

Paint, blood and forgiveness

Simahen prayed day and night to God to bring her men back and sacrificed her most precious roosters for him. She promised him a camel if he would chase Saddam Hussein away. When she thought that the roof would delay her prayers from reaching heaven, she climbed the stairs to the flat roof and called for Mira to bring her prayer mat and to show her in which direction Mecca lay.

"*Hadja*, why are you going to the roof? After all, God is everywhere," said Mira.

"Up here there is nothing between me and God."

"But you can also pray from down here and look up to heaven."

"I'm closer to heaven up here."

After God she prayed to the prophets. She began with the most well-known prophets, which were mostly buried in Iraq, and then went down to the lesser-known ones. One day she asked Rizen to take her to the grave of the prophet Yunis. Rizen looked for it for hours, until he found it. Simahen entered the tomb made of clay.

"I've tried with those who could walk on water, those that could lie on hot coals, those who brought the dead to life, those who could see the invisible and those who could fly," she said to the prophet Yunis. "Now I'm trying with you." She spoke to the prophet Yunis in his grave as if speaking with an old acquaintance. "Please, save us from Saddam Hussein."

After the prophets, she prayed to the imams. She began with Shi'ite imams followed by those of the Sunni, but Saddam Hussein did not go away. Day and night he kept on appearing on the television and every year went swimming in the Tigris.

Once when Rizen brought her back from a visit to the graves of her family members, she saw a church. She went into the church through the small door in the archway and she saw someone hanging on a cross. Beneath him stood a woman with a radiant face and tears in her eyes, looking up at him. She asked a monk who the man was. He told her that he was Jesus, and the woman was his mother Mary. Tears flowed from her eyes, this time not for Iraq, but for Jesus. It was the first time in her life that she had been in a church and she only knew the story of Jesus from the Koran.

"Rizen, let's go now. This man," she said, and pointed at Jesus, "can't save Iraq from Saddam Hussein. If he could do that, he would have saved himself from the cross. That woman there also can't save Iraq because if she could, she would have saved her son from the cross."

Simahen was impressed by Jesus on the cross and asked Rizen to take her back to the grave of her brother Abbas. She sprinkled his grave with tears. Then she forgave him.

"When he was alive you didn't forgive him. Now you forgive him when he's dead?" asked Rizen.

Simahen clapped her hands together. "I did not forgive him when he was flesh and blood, because he made me marry your grandfather the weaver, but now I can forgive him because he is dust," she said sorrowfully. "I am almost with them there. Imagine that I see my mother and father in his company, without having forgiven him." She was quiet for a while. "He took my life and my land and gave me a cow and a calf," she said, as if she had forgotten that she had just, after years of grappling with her conscience, forgiven him.

On the way back, a long distance from the grave, she

suddenly turned angrily to Rizen. "But where will God send him? God never forgives him. My father always said to him that he was responsible for his sister, because he knew that Abbas was a rascal."

"Don't say that, you've just come from his grave," said Rizen.

Simahen wiped away the tears of anger, which covered the tears of forgiveness. "The dead deserve forgiveness," she sighed.

Simahen always made her spot near the party house clean for her mat. She swept the area with a small broom that she took with her, threw the stones and gravel away and in the summer threw water around it, so that the wind would be cooler. She took food and a thermos flask with water and sat for hours on end at "the party", as she referred to the party house, waiting for her husband and sons. Because the armed guards insulted her, she set her mat down a long way from the entrance, at the end of the wall, so far away that she could not distinguish who the people going into and coming out of the party house were. In the beginning she drove the guards to despair by calling out that she wanted to know, each time, who were the women visiting the party house to ask after their husbands and sons, but after a while they grew used to her presence and they asked, if she was not there for a while, whether she had passed away.

Initially Wasile's children took her to the party house in the early mornings and, Rizen usually fetched her at the end of the day. Later they took her and fetched her only when Wasile remembered and sent them to fetch her, because they preferred to run through the orchard, catch birds or throw stones in the Thirsty River. Eventually Simahen went there and back all by herself.

Sometimes she fell asleep in the shadow of the wall where she sat and woke up when everyone had left, except for the armed guard. At such times she asked herself why she was sitting there, and tried quickly to remind herself. If she could not work out why, she stood up slowly and asked the guard at the party house. The guards there were accustomed to her. If they saw her coming, they called out to her from their chair: "Go and sit down again. They're not coming back today."

Often she did not stop and came up to them and asked the question: "Who's not coming back?"

"The ones who you're waiting for," was the answer.

So every day she laid her mat a centimetre closer to the door of the party house, until, years later, she sat right next to the door and could clearly see who was coming and going. Eventually she could even make use of the toilet in the party house. Sometimes she brought food for the guards and gave them medicines from her bag for their sick children. Sometimes she told them if she was away for a while that someone had disappeared behind their wall and she should be on the lookout.

One hot afternoon she became faint from the heat, rested her back against the wall and fell asleep. She dreamt that she was young and that she was floating in a golden boat over the crystal-clear canals of her home town with banks of date palms. When she woke up from the rumbling of a distant bombardment, she saw a mural of Saddam Hussein, one that Naji and Sjahid had painted in white clothes a few days earlier.

"My son, is he the party? I want to ask him about them. They have taken them away and we have not heard anything about them," she said and pointed at the mural.

"That is not the party. That is Mr President," said the grinning guard. He looked around him and when he saw nobody was around, he began to laugh loudly.

"If he is Mr President, why is he standing there in the heat? Why doesn't he come into the shade?" asked Simahen.

Tears streamed down the cheeks of the guard and his belly shook.

After she had drunk a glass of cold water that the guard handed to her, she realised that it actually was the president, standing in a mural in the distance. "I think I have gone mad," she mumbled to herself. "I thought it was the party, or an angel of God."

Shaking her head, she gathered her things together, struggled to her feet and went home.

"The seed comes out of the earth in the place where it fell. They went into the party house and one day they will come out," she always repeated. One day there was a knock at the door of the house. Mira opened it and saw a young stranger standing there, who eagerly wanted to see Simahen. Simahen told Joesr to talk to the man. He was the only man at home and she did not want to talk to the stranger before one of the men of the house had done so. At the door Joesr saw a man with an ass. It looked like he had been on a long journey. The man said nothing to Joesr, only that he wanted to see Simahen. Joesr showed him to the visitors' room, had Mira bring tea for him and went to fetch Simahen. She remained standing in the doorway, because she did not want to sit close to a man. Hesitatingly, the man began exchanging pleasantries. Simahen looked at him closely and tried to recall whether he was a member of the family, but eventually the man told Simahen that he had come to ask after his son, who had been taken into the party house. He asked her if they had brought him out of the party house.

"Did your son have a weapon when they took him in?" Simahen asked.

"No."

"Many go into the party house, but apart from those with guns, no one comes out again."

The man began crying. He told her that he had nine daughters and had now lost his only son. He said he had not yet let him marry and so had no grandson to continue the family name. "It was nothing, he just didn't pin the photo of Mr President on his chest. That day he was carrying cow dung to the orchard and he was afraid he would be taken away if drops of dung accidentally got on to the photo. He ran away when I told him that someone had written a report about him for the party. When they came, I said that he had drowned. They asked where his grave was, to which I said that I had not found him. They gave me three days to find him, otherwise they would take his sisters and make them pregnant. Before the time was up, my son had given himself up and since that day I have not seen him."

After the man had told his story, Mira called Joesr to tell him his meal was ready.

Joesr went out to fetch it. This man had asked after the

elderly woman who had been waiting in the shadow of the
party's house for years, and then came to us to find out what
had happened to his son, he thought. If Sabha had borne,
cooked, eaten and shit out Saddam Hussein, would that not
have been better for the air, for the dates, for this man, for the
ass waiting for him at the door?

Despite Joesr's insistence the man would not stay for a while.
But after he had left with his ass, Joesr felt that he had to talk
with someone. Because his friend Samer was not at home, the
lights were not on at Mohamed Mansour's and, according to his
mother, Yasin Al Terref was at his uncle's, Joesr walked to the
Thirsty River. There he saw Djazil walking in a hurry. He had
not expected to see Joesr there and walked on anxiously. Joesr
hurried after him.

When they came to the street lights Joesr saw brown marks
on Djazil's wet clothes.

"What's that on your clothes? Blood?" asked Joesr.

"Paint," said Djazil quickly and disappeared into the
darkness.

Joesr remained behind. He did not want to be alone and
called out to Djazil to walk with him, but he was no longer
anywhere to be found. He stared at the street light, at the
dancing bugs and insects around it, and thought about the man
who had asked Simahen about his son. What had happened to
the man's son? he asked himself. Perhaps they had hanged him
from the ceiling by his balls, which were filled with millions of
sperm bearing the family name.

Joesr walked aimlessly on until he saw a spotlight at a
building. There he saw Sjahid standing on a ladder. He was
busy colouring in the shoes of Saddam Hussein. Naji sat below
on a small chair, smoking.

When Naji needed to piss and walked off with the can of
water to find a quiet place, Joesr appeared out of the darkness.

"What are you doing here?" said Sjahid from the ladder. "It's
dangerous to be out on the streets at night."

Joesr did not answer, but looked at the red marks on Sjahid's
clothes. He did not expect any red patches, because the shoes
that Sjahid was painting were black.

"What's that on your trousers? Paint?" asked Joesr.

"Blood," answered Sjahid. "Blood of my soul."

Suddenly the air-raid siren began blaring. All the lights around them flickered and went out, except for the spotlight.

"Shouldn't you switch that light off?" asked Joesr, while Sjahid continued painting in deep concentration.

"The siren turns everything off, even the light in the heart, but not the light that shines on the shoes of Mr President."

A jet fighter flitted across the sky. A while later the sirens screamed for a second time and windows began to light up here and there, and Joesr walked home.

That night Joesr dreamt about the day long ago when he had gone with Rizen, Sjahid, Djazil and Mira to the Thirsty River, which was dried up at the end of the summer, to collect the fish remaining in the puddles, each with a bag in their hand. It was a nice day. The heavens were blue. It was the first time that Mira had gone with them since the day she had begun wearing a headscarf. Simahen and Wasile asked them to look after their sister carefully. If she got tired, she stopped and sat on the ground where she was. This led to her becoming upset because she received nothing from her brothers but screaming. When she was rested, she walked further through the mud of the Thirsty River. When she saw a crack that still had some water in it, she mixed it with clay. Then the fish stuck their heads out of the mud and she could grab them and put them in her bag. At the next puddle she did the same, but she threw the smaller fish, that she had caught earlier, out of the bag. Joesr was walking behind her. Every fish that was still alive, he picked up and threw back in a puddle. Rizen, Sjahid and Djazil then called him to follow them, but Joesr stayed where he was until every fish was saved.

After that expedition Joesr became a vegetarian. "I'm not eating anything that has two eyes and a mouth or a beak, nothing that can look at me and can breathe," he said.

Wasile thought he was sick, that his belly would have no flesh on it.

"Mr President has two eyes and a mouth, he walks and eats

and breathes and talks. Give him to me and I'll eat him raw," said Simahen.

One day, when there were festivities in the streets of Boran after a life-sized statue of Saddam Hussein had been unveiled in the middle of the town, Djazil saw a girl walking to the river. The girl had a pitcher in her hand and walked uncertainly behind her mother, as if she were out of the house for the first time. Djazil felt he had to see this girl one more time and followed her without her mother noticing. Every time there was no electricity and no water, Djazil waited at the Thirsty River to see the girl with her mother. The girl was aware that he waited there for her and was afraid that her mother would guess that she knew that he wanted to see her. After a while she became so excited at the thought of seeing him there that she secretly looked for him if she did not see him. Not because she wanted to see him, because she did not dare think of that, but because he had to be there.

One day Djazil saw her alone. He followed her and asked her if she wanted him to fill the pitcher for her, not at the riverbank, but deeper in the river, where the water was cleaner and cooler. Without waiting for an answer he grabbed the pitcher and filled it with water. The girl dared not look at him. The time after that Djazil filled the pitcher, but did not give it back to her and walked with it in the direction of the trees. The girl did not know what to do, to go home without the pitcher or tell him to bring it to her. Djazil came up to her without the pitcher and, tightly, took hold of her hand. She pulled her hand away, but he grabbed her by her black dress and she followed him. Under the trees no one could see them. There Djazil began kissing the girl on her neck and on her face.

"Don't bite me on the neck. My mother will see it," she whispered. She stood still, as if she could do nothing, except what Djazil wanted her to do. Like dough in the warm hands of a baker.

He laid his hand on her shoulder and pressed her gently to the ground. He pulled her dress up slowly as far as her navel and began kissing her legs and panties. He kissed her belly and her small breasts. The girl lay unmoving on the ground, staring at the sky above her, filled her hands with soil and clenched her fists. She did not know what had come over her and did not know if she should let him continue or should say that she wanted to go home.

Carefully, Djazil turned her over and came between her buttocks. The girl pulled her panties up and her dress down and turned her back to him, because she dared not look at him.

"What's your name?" she asked.

"Djazil," he answered without thinking twice. "But you must go now. Otherwise your mother will come looking for you."

The girl just remained sitting there, as if she were evaporating. Then she walked to the Thirsty River, walked in until the water covered her breasts, took the pitcher and left. She did not look back.

He saw her again days later at the Thirsty River. He indicated to her that he would wait under the trees for her, but she never came. He watched her and was fixed to the spot until she disappeared in the distance.

One afternoon he saw her on the riverbank, he took her pitcher and walked under the trees. She followed him hesitantly. He began caressing her body, while she stood still.

She closed her eyes. "I want to go before my mother comes," she said with trembling lips, but he kissed her neck, forced her to the ground, pulled her dress above her navel, pulled her panties down and glued his body into hers. She felt a fire inside her, while his body trembled on top of her. Then he saw her blood on his clothes and on the ground.

Frightened he stood up. The girl remained lying down quietly. She stared into the distance and felt that she was lying next to him as a problem, and not as a beautiful girl. He ran away. She stayed lying on her back. Her blood on his clothes, his sperm in her womb. She liked him, because he was the only one who knew she was no longer a virgin.

For a few minutes she lay without thinking of anything. Then she was also frightened. She dunked herself in the Thirsty River and, with some clay, scrubbed the blood from her black dress that she had worn since the day her father had disappeared in the war. She filled her pitcher with water, but could not carry it because of the distress in her head and the pain between her legs. She spilt half of the water from the pitcher, walked a few metres in the direction of her house, but thought her mother would be angry if she came home with so little water. Her dread of her mother gave her the strength to carry the full pitcher home, while looking anxiously over her shoulder to see if she was leaving a trail of blood drops.

At the little house of clay her brothers and sisters began calling her. "Baan! Baan!" They ran happily to meet her.

CHAPTER 9

Waiting for the water

Djazil was used to stealing chickens and lambs, but not a girl's virginity. That is why he hurried away from the banks of the Thirsty River. Now and again he looked over his shoulder, afraid that Baan was following him. The dog of a passing shepherd barked at him.

"He's barking because he smells blood on your clothes," said the shepherd. "Who wounded you?"

Djazil threw sand on the stains. "My penis," he said.

The shepherd laughed and walked on.

Djazil thought of going back to the Thirsty River to wash the blood from his clothes, but he did not want to see the girl. He did not know if she was still sitting in the place where she had hidden away and cried because she was no longer a virgin, or if she had gone home to tell her mother. He was angry with himself because he had told her his real name.

"Stupid, stupid!" he cried and kicked at the dust. He walked a little further towards home, but turned around, because he was afraid of seeing the girl and her mother there. He hid away in an abandoned house behind the orchard. He took his trousers and shirt off, washed them with clay and water, hung them on a branch to dry and fell asleep naked in the shadows.

When he awoke, the sun was going down. He put his clothes on and went home, because he was hungry.

Arriving in Boran he was still angry with himself. He came across Joesr, next to a lamp post. Joesr asked him about the stains in his clothes. Before taking the lids off the pots in the kitchen to eat the day's leftovers, he left his clothes to soak in water with washing powder. He scrubbed them with a brush once he had stilled his hunger. The stains became faded.

The next day the market woman who bought stolen chickens from him asked about the blood on his clothes.

"From the chickens," said Djazil.

"Chicken blood doesn't stay in your clothes," said the woman.

She was surprised when Djazil, instead of laughing as he always did, repeated that the blood was from a hen that he had slaughtered for a woman because there had been no man in the house. Then he walked away suddenly, while she had wanted to ask him if he had any chickens left over.

Behind the house, Djazil burnt his trousers and shirt stained with Baan's blood, buried the ash in the ground and wore Rizen's clothes. He asked Mira if anyone had been asking after him.

Mira found it a strange question and told Wasile.

"He must have stolen a camel. In a few days' time there'll be Bedouins standing at the door again, mark my words," said Wasile. Now and again she asked Mira to look through the keyhole to see if a tent had been put up outside the front of the house.

Five days later Baan saw that Djazil was watching her house. She thought that he wanted to marry her because she was no longer a virgin, and so could not marry anyone else. He whispered at the door that he would wait for her at the same place, but she never came. He thought that perhaps she was afraid of her mother and did not want to go until there was no running water and she would have to go to the Thirsty River to fetch some. She and her body were never out of his thoughts. That night he went to the water pump that filled the town's water tank and furtively threw a piece of iron over the electric contact wires. There was a shower of sparks and the pump fell silent and the night could be heard, just like the time between air-raid sirens.

The following day he waited at the banks of the Thirsty River and saw Baan coming with her water pitcher. She did not go to the bank, but went straight to the place where he was waiting. She put the pitcher on the ground and went to sit next to him on her knees. She looked at him as if he was a harbour, without which the ship of her life would never be anchored. He was the only one who could be with her, he was the eye of the needle through which she had to pass. It felt as if she was paralysed and he was the wheelchair on which she would have to sit. And he knew that. That's why he came right up to her. With his hand her pushed her to the ground. She heard how his breathing became heavier. He held his penis in front of her mouth. She turned her head away, but he hit her so hard that the trees around her trembled. She looked anxiously at his pale, sweaty face and opened her mouth.

"Suck," he said and he hit her. "Not with your teeth."

When she began to gag, he kissed her neck and her breasts, and screwed her. Then he quickly put his clothes on again and ran away without looking behind him. He heard her vomiting and thought that he never wanted to see her again, but the next day he waited at the same place for her and she came. Without looking at her or talking to her, he had sex with her. Each time he became calmer, until after two weeks he began talking to her and after the sex even talked with her before leaving. She talked about her father, who had disappeared in the war. About her uncle, who would kill her if he knew that she was no longer a virgin. About her mother, who complained about headaches the whole day, and about the pain in her back the whole night.

He was hoping to erase his name from her memory, as if he had written it with a pencil on a piece of white paper.

"Your name is not Walid, it's Djazil," she said, not to suggest that he had been lying, but to prove to herself that she knew who he was. From this young man, who had broken her hymen without anyone else knowing about it, all she had was his name and she did not want to lose that.

One day, when the streets in the south had been swept clean and water sprayed over them because Saddam Hussein was going to visit one of the cities, he waited for her, because he had once again broken the water pump. After their sexual encounter she gave him a ring she had bought with her savings and told him that she was pregnant.

Her words fell on his head like the piece of iron on the wires of the water pump. He thought of his name in her head, which no one could know about, while she thought of the child in her belly, which no one could know about.

"How do you know?" he asked after a moment of silence, without the message completely sinking in.

"Know what?" she asked.

"That you're pregnant."

"I dreamt that I was getting fatter, until I couldn't walk any more. I called my mother to pull me out of the mud. My mother said that the mud was not on my feet, but was growing in my belly and she said, with tears in her eyes, that I must look after my belly and that my uncle would kill me. I wanted to get out of the mud, but couldn't," Baan said with a lump in her throat.

"You're crazy," he said, irritated. "Plain crazy. You're not pregnant, just crazy, like Simahen, who dreams and talks like a madman. All woman dream and talk like madmen."

"Who's Simahen?"

"Simahen? Forget that name!" said Djazil and bit his tongue, because he had given Baan another name.

"Why?"

"Just forget about it if you ever want to see me here again."

The sound of singing reached them from the opposite bank of the Thirsty River. Baan's face suddenly brightened. "Perhaps they're singing for Mr President. Perhaps he's coming on a visit." She stood up and looked between the branches to the other bank. A man was standing in the water up to his neck. He was singing to the cows on the bank.

"Djazil, come and look," she called softly, but he did not come. She turned round. He had disappeared. She thought he had gone to piss. After a while she went to look for him among the trees, because she thought that perhaps a scorpion had

stung him or a snake had bitten him, but she could not find
him.

The next day she came back to the same place. She put the
pitcher on the ground and sat down next to it, but he did not
come. The day after that she put the pitcher on the ground and
remained standing, but he did not come. On the third day she
stood waiting with the pitcher on her shoulder, but he did not
come. On the fourth day she called his name with a soft voice,
as if he was sleeping and she wanted to wake him. On the fifth
day she heard sparrows fighting in their hiding place and she
knew that he was not there. On the sixth day she cautiously
came right up to the sparrows so as not to frighten them. On
the seventh day she prayed to God so that He would send Djazil
to her. Every day, not only when there was no running water,
she went there when her mother had her afternoon nap.
Sometimes she sat for short while and felt safe. She waited for
Djazil, while grinding up dry bread for the ants.

When she had given up hope, she waited for her period, just
as she waited for Djazil, but this too did not come. When she
slept, she dreamt that someone was eating her up from the
inside, first her intestines, then her bones, and then she felt a
terrible emptiness. She managed to hide her growing breasts
from her mother Henadi, until she was washing clothes by
hand one day and a splash wet her swelling bosom. Henadi
immediately pulled her by her hand into a room. She looked
Baan in the eye and knew without asking her that she was
pregnant. Henadi slapped herself on the face with both hands,
while Baan stood facing her like a date palm facing a river
washing away the ground from beneath it, leaving its roots
naked. Then Henadi slapped herself on the face with one hand
and began slapping Baan on the face with the other. From that
day on, she felt the pain in her back and her head
simultaneously, day and night.

When the sun came up the following day, Henadi went in
search of a house where two people with the names of Djazil
and Simahen lived. After two hours she came back and waited
until it became dark. With Baan she slipped to the house of the
Bird family. Henadi trembled. Instead of other women pleading

with her to allow their son to marry Baan, she now had to plead with another woman to allow her son to marry her daughter to save her daughter from death, and the family from shame. She prayed to God that she would succeed.

"We're going to see them," she whispered in Baan's ear. "Either they open your grave and let you continue living, or they close it firmly over you and the scorpion in your belly."

As the sun was setting Joesr lay on his bed, where he had been all day, reading the saga of Gilgamesh. He listened to a cassette of Danza Andaluza, which he had got from Sjahid, who had got it from Naji. He threw stones at the barking dogs and saw a dog licking its four new-born puppies. He went to the kitchen and came back with wet bread and soup, and threw it to the bitch. Mira, sitting in the yard peeling aubergines, laughed.

"Why are you throwing the peel away? There's vitamins in there," Joesr said to her.

"There's what?"

"Vitamins."

"What's that?" She almost cut herself with the knife as a rocket fell nearby.

"Healthy stuff."

"But we're going to eat the aubergine, so it won't need it any more."

"I mean that the vitamins are good for people, not for the aubergines."

"Sjahid doesn't eat it if I don't peel it," said Mira. "He'll think that I forgot to peel it." She hit at a chicken that was trying to steal rice from the pot.

Joesr sat next to her on his haunches, while in the falling darkness Mira continued preparing the meal.

"You know," he said to Mira, "if Saddam Hussein had been shown love and respect when he was a child, he might well have become an artist or a writer or a postman."

"Or butcher," said Mira.

"Yes, perhaps he would have been a butcher, not of people but of animals," said Joesr. He thought that if Mira had studied, she would have been a fantastic playwright, philosopher or journalist. He wanted to tell her that and was looking for a simple way to explain it, but she was already busy frying the aubergines in oil.

Later on Mira brought him the evening meal. As she walked away, she heard someone knocking softly at the door.

"Who is it?" she asked, afraid that it was perhaps someone from the secret service, the army or the party.

"Me," said a woman's voice.

Mira opened the door. An unknown woman stood there with a girl behind her of about fourteen years or so. They were dressed in black. Mira let them in, called Wasile and when Wasile appeared, the woman began pleading. Wasile thought the woman was one of those whose husband had been killed by Saddam Hussein's men and went around begging at night because they did not dare do it during the day.

"Look at her, please. She is a child and he ..." said Henadi imploringly.

"Who?" asked Wasile.

"Djazil," said Henadi.

Suddenly Wasile grasped what the woman had come to do. Henadi, Baan, Wasile and Mira stood at the front door, while the voice of Saddam Hussein reverberated out of a television or a radio in the neighbourhood.

"Our people are civilised. Seven thousand years old. We are here to serve this glorious people, not to govern," said Saddam Hussein. "Our wonderful people do not need anyone to govern them. Everyone is their own leader. Here, on this ground, the first laws were written. Here, zero was discovered." Applause followed.

"Pimp!" screamed Joesr. "The Arabs discovered zero so that they could sink far below it. Arsehole. Son of Sabha. Mira! Switch that arsehole off!"

Henadi looked in surprise at Wasile. How could anyone refer to Saddam Hussein as a pimp and an arsehole?

"Shut that window!" Wasile called to Joesr.

"It is closed! Switch the TV off or I'll break it!"

"It's coming from the neighbours!" Mira answered.

"Switch those neighbours off!" screamed Joesr angrily.

"Go and tell him we've got visitors," Wasile hissed between her teeth to Mira and addressed herself to Henadi and Baan.

"No one with the name Djazil lives here," she said to the woman and the girl.

"He does live here," said Henadi beseechingly. "And there is also a woman who goes by the name of Simahen."

"Take your little whore and go," said Wasile.

She dragged Henadi by her black dress to the door, but Henadi stood firm.

Joesr came to the commotion at the front door and saw Wasile trying to drag another woman in the direction of the door. Baan stood behind her. Joesr held his mother back and asked what was happening.

"Go to your room and lock the door!" screamed Wasile.

Joesr felt insulted. He gave his mother a shove and screamed in her face that she should watch her mouth.

Wasile did not listen and spat in Henadi's face.

"Let's go home," said Baan, subdued.

Henadi turned to Baan and slapped her. She turned back to Wasile, who was stamping her feet and going wild. At this, Joesr took off his slipper and threatened to hit Wasile.

When Henadi saw what Joesr did, she knelt in front of him and wanted to kiss his feet, but he pulled his foot away. Wasile kept crying that Henadi's daughter was a whore and she was as well, while Joesr led them to the sitting room. There he heard that Henadi had come with her daughter because her daughter was pregnant from Djazil. Not because she came from a bad family, but because she was too young to know how these sorts of things happened and because there was no man in their house to protect her. She told Joesr that the father of her daughter had disappeared in the war and that her uncle would kill her if he found out. Djazil could marry the girl without paying a single cent in bride price. It was not necessary to build a room for her, she could live in the stable with the sheep. They could kick her out when the child was born and had his name, then he would never have to see her again.

"I'll persuade Djazil to marry her. And if that doesn't succeed, I'll marry her myself," said Joesr unconcerned. He asked Mira to make some tea for Henadi and Baan, but Henadi said she needed to go and see to her other children, who were alone at home.

Joesr went looking for Djazil in the dark streets of the town. Soldiers stopped him and asked him for his identity card and the reason why he was walking the streets at night. They let him go on his way when he told them that he was looking for his brother, who had to get married.

"In the dark you go looking for a woman to marry yourself, not for your brother," one of the soldiers said, laughing.

At the next checkpoint one of the soldiers took his identity card and told him he could have it back if he went to fetch a kebab for him. After he had brought the kebab to the soldier, he went back home tired. He went to lie on his bed, but could not sleep. Every time he closed his eyes, he saw Baan before him. He switched the light on, opened the saga of Gilgamesh and tried to read, but could not. He called Mira.

"Where do you think I can find Djazil?"

"I don't know," she said with sleep in her eyes. She dared not tell him that he had already come home and that she had told him that Joesr was looking for him. She did not tell him that Wasile had told Djazil not to come home for a while, at least not for as long as Joesr was looking for him.

In the evening when the speech by Saddam Hussein was over, in which he said he would poison like insects the Iranians invading Iraq, Wasile stayed awake waiting for Djazil. When she saw the light shining in the kitchen, she went there and saw Djazil eating bread and radish.

"She was looking for you," Wasile said to him.

"Who?" he asked, chewing.

"The mother with the pregnant daughter."

"I don't know any mother or any pregnant daughter," said Djazil.

That was just what Wasile wanted to hear. She wanted him to know that she had wanted to hear that from him.

"You're lying," she said to avoid being complicit in what was likely to happen with regard to Baan. "Her father will kill you when he gets back from the army."

"But her father's never coming ba ..." said Djazil without thinking. He stopped chewing, swallowed and looked to see if Wasile had heard.

"Her father what?" said Wasile, and looked at him through slit eyes. "Do you know her father?"

"Her father and I will never see each other, because I don't know him or his daughter," said Djazil.

"If you stay away for two months, the daughter's belly will be so big that it will no longer be necessary to find a man to prevent others knowing that she did it without getting married."

"I heard that mad Joesr wants to find me to make me marry the girl," said Djazil. He took a bite of the bread. "He must first find himself."

"If you tell him that you never slept with that girl, he'll marry her himself. Then he'll bring her here to let her give birth to that swine inside her. If he doesn't find you, he'll wait for you, like the mother and her daughter, and then he won't go to the girl, because he'll also consider that the child in her is your son," said Wasile.

Djazil was amazed at his mother's thought process. She persuaded him not to show his face in the house for a while.

Henadi waited for Joesr to bring Djazil or for Djazil, if he decided to come himself. She sat on a mat beside the door, just as Simahen had done in the shadow of the party's house. She regularly went to the house of the Birds, but before she could open her mouth she was chased away by Wasile with the words that there were no men living in this house who wanted to marry a whore.

Baan's belly and her breasts grew steadily. One day Henadi told her daughter to follow her. Baan walked behind her mother without question to a desolate place behind the date palm orchard. She had Baan lie down on the ground and jumped on her belly, so that the child would miscarry, but it was as if the child was bound to the womb with a steel cable and not with an umbilical cord. Sweat and tears flowed over Baan's face, but she did not cry out, scream or talk. Her mother shoved her into a pit and called her out much later. "Has it fallen?" Baan shook her head. Her mother shook her back and forth and threw her to the ground. She placed heavy rocks on her belly and sat down next to her to wait, but the child did not come out.

"Your father only had to spit in my face to make my first child fall out," she said crying, while taking the rocks off Baan's belly. "The snake inside you wouldn't even come out if a mountain fell on your belly." Henadi hit a stone against her forehead. "God save us from the shame. Compassionate God, save us from the gossip."

At night Henadi cried softly, so that the neighbours would not hear her. "If that child in your belly doesn't fall, you will."

"But he'll come to marry me," said Baan to appease her mother. "And if he doesn't come, his brother will bring him."

"But when? When that child in your belly is already with us?"

Henadi asked Baan once again to follow her, when Saddam Hussein sent the first Iraqi rocket into space, with the name El Abid, and he threatened to set fire to half of Israel, and so there was joyous celebration on the streets. Baan refused. She said that he would come but Henadi did not know whether she meant Djazil, Joesr or the child.

Day after day Henadi begged Baan, but Baan would not go with her. One afternoon, when the Thirsty River had begun drying up and bombardments filled the skies, Henadi saw Baan surreptitiously sewing clothes for the child. Her face radiated contentment. Henadi snatched the tiny jersey from her hands and began tearing it apart with her teeth, as if she wanted to devour the child that would be wearing those clothes when it was born, then she went to lie down on her bed and wept softly.

"If you want, we can go behind the date palms," said Baan anxiously, but her mother lay motionless on her bed.

Baan threw her black shawl over her shoulders and went to the house of the Birds. After a moment of hesitation she knocked, but so softly that she could almost not hear it herself.

She wanted to knock again, more loudly, when the door opened and Wasile looked at her.

"What do you want?"

"He said that he would come," Baan said quietly.

Wasile took her hand tightly and Baan followed silently inside, just as she had followed Djazil to the trees on the banks of the Thirsty River. Wasile broke a switch off a pomegranate tree and took it to her room.

"If I hear a sound from you, I'll throttle you," she hissed between her teeth and began hitting Baan with the switch, just as Kosjer had done to her after she had run away after the birth of Rizen. When the switch broke, she hit Baan in the face with her slipper. She did not hit the belly, afraid that if she did the child would come out in her house. Wasile, who had endured beatings and insults for her entire life, hit Baan as if she was everyone who had ever done anything to her; her mother, her father, her brothers. She hit Baan and imagined the stinking Kosjer when he had had sex with her. She hit Baan and thought of Saddam Hussein, whose voice could be heard from doors and windows and let his iron fall from the heavens.

Baan's face turned black and blue. Her nose bled and her cheeks were covered with scratches. When Baan could no longer stand, Wasile dragged her outside. She took care not to let Joesr see her and let Baan out of the door.

With her hands Baan gingerly touched her wounded face. A tear stung a scratch.

When the sirens wailed, Simahen called Mira. "Sacrifice a chicken to God. I dreamt that he was angry. When I opened the door for him, he refused to come inside," she said.

Mira looked for Tenzile to help her catch the rooster, but could not find her.

Tenzile had seen Baan sitting outside the door and had brought her a glass of water, warily, so that Wasile would not notice. Baan nodded thankfully and the glass fell from her trembling hands. Tenzile wanted to tell Joesr that Baan was sitting at the door, but when she got to his room, she saw a shadow from behind her. She turned around and saw Wasile watching her.

"Joesr has a sister who can look after him," said Wasile quietly, so that Joesr would not hear. "Or is one man in this house not enough for you?"

That was the first confrontation between her and Tenzile. Wasile was afraid that Tenzile would explode with anger, that Joesr would come out of his room and that she would lose her position in the house and that Tenzile would become the woman of the household after Simahen. But she also knew that if she oppressed Tenzile, she would be afraid of her mother-in-law for her entire life and then she would become the woman of the household after the death of Simahen.

Tenzile got a fright at Wasile's words. "I want to ask him to kill the rooster," she said with a shaky voice, because that was the only excuse she could think of, hearing the rooster cackling in the basket in which Mira had caught it.

Wasile sensed victory and told Tenzile to go and deal with the chicken. She did not mention the glass of water that Tenzile had given to Baan and was glad that she had let Tenzile see who would be the head of that house after Simahen. The bread in the oven was burnt and the dough had been eaten by the chickens.

Wasile tied a dog up at the front door. If anyone knocked, it would bark and so she knew she would be the first to see anyone coming to the front door. "If anyone asks why the dog is tied there, tell them that soldiers are looking for deserters," she said to Mira.

Once Tenzile had cleaned the chicken, she went to her room, scared by the idea that Wasile thought she wanted to do something with Joesr. She reproached herself for having thought of telling Joesr that Baan was sitting at the door and that she had told Wasile that she had wanted to call him to kill the chicken. "She couldn't have believed that, because I didn't believe it myself." She wrung her sweaty hands.

After Mira had sharpened the knife and was sure that Baan had gone, she called Joesr to kill the chicken, as Wasile had told her to do.

"I can't kill the chicken," said Joesr.

"So must I go down the street looking for a man to kill this chicken? What kind of man are you, then?" asked Mira.

"If manhood is defined by the ability to kill a chicken, then I am not a man." He took the rooster from Mira. "Look at it," he said. "It's still young. He wakes up when the sun rises to celebrate his life. He does not think about the destruction of the world. He doesn't poison any chickens in Halabja[3] and does not let the water in the south dry up. He has never written a bloody report for Hadi the Rocket about anyone. He will never complain, but he wakes you up and relieves you from the nightmares in your head," said Joesr. He stroked the rooster's head. "Don't be scared, white comrade. This knife will not cut your head off. At least not today."

"Do you need an aspirin?" asked Mira.

"What has this chicken ever done that you want to kill it? This rooster does not leave any hen pregnant and then disappear. Chickens do not judge unmarried pregnant chickens and do not look down on them." A chicken cackled and the rooster in Joesr's hands responded. Joesr threw it to the ground. "Go, brother, life is calling you!"

With the knife in her hand Mira went to Wasile. "Joesr must have gone crazy," she said to her mother.

"How so?" said Wasile, while taking bread out of the oven at the moment when a rocket fell in the distance.

"He says that chickens don't lay eggs, but become pregnant!"

When the muezzin called for the midday prayer, Joesr came out of his room to piss. Because the toilet was occupied, he opened the door and looked outside. He saw Baan's blood on the ground and called Mira.

"Whose blood is that? Did you kill that chicken after all?"

"Yes," she said.

"Why? I told him he wouldn't be killed today."

"Simahen said it had to be killed, because God will not want to come into this house."

"What do we want with God in this house? We don't need him. We need the rooster," said Joesr. "We don't need someone who forgives us, but someone who wakes us up!"

In the kitchen he stared at the plucked and gutted rooster.

"When can you tell from her belly that a pregnant girl is pregnant?" he asked Mira.

"After five months, perhaps."

"I have to find him before that," he said to himself. "Tell Djazil that I'm looking for him if you see him," he said to Mira as he left the kitchen.

Baan remained sitting at the door until her dizziness disappeared and walked home like a blind person. There she went to lie on her bed with her swollen face. Henadi turned the fan towards her and looked at her daughter, who stared vacantly at the ceiling. She tore her dress from collar to hem and screamed. She beat her slipper on the ceiling, as if she wanted to hit heaven. She kept on hitting her slipper against the ceiling, until she tired, and fell to the ground.

Baan fell exhausted into a deep sleep. Since the day from which she had no longer been a virgin, she had not slept so deeply, because every night in her dreams she saw her father. Sometimes he looked sadly at her and had shaved off his thick black moustache. When she asked him why, he said he was no longer a man and did not deserve his moustache, because she had lost her virginity on the banks of the Thirsty River. Sometimes he chopped down the trees on the banks of the Thirsty River and threw them into the water. He said he did that because then she could no longer hide herself under them and sleep with men. Henadi laid a wet cloth on Baan's forehead. Baan opened her swollen eyes and Henadi thought she was awake, but she was opening her eyes in her dream.

She was standing with a backpack on the banks of the Thirsty River. It was winter, the river was dry. Near her was a boat lying on the ground. A man dressed in white comes towards her. His face is radiant, making it difficult for Baan to see him.

"What are you waiting for?" he asks.

"I'm waiting for the water in the river, so that this boat can take me away from here," says Baan.

"But it is winter, the water only comes in the summer," said the man dressed in white.

"Are you God?" asks Baan.

"No," says the man, and he laughs with shaking shoulders.

"I am Saddam Hussein." He gathers some wood and makes a fire for her. "This fire will only go out when the river is filled with water and the boat is ready to take you on board," he said.

When Baan woke up, she no longer waited for anyone. Not for Djazil, not for Joesr, not for her uncle and not for the child. She only waited for the water in the Thirsty River.

"When the Thirsty River is filled with water, then I'll drown," she said to Henadi.

"Your uncle will have murdered you before that," said Henadi despairingly. "Ah, why can't people drown in the dry riverbed?"

Chapter 10

Bread, dinars, dollars and rockets

Ever since the day that Kosjer's ram had butted the antenna and Kosjer and the men of the family had disappeared, Wasile had worked to provide for the family's sustenance. She had thought that Sjahid and Joesr would take over from her when they had completed school, but she realised that as they got older they could not even look after themselves. They even stopped their hunting of starlings in the winter, which Mira had cooked with rice. Wasile no longer expected that someone who had studied at school would be able to help their family. She believed that if you went to school, you forgot what you had learnt in life.

When Wasile had given up hope that Sjahid and Joesr would help her in providing for the family, she decided after much consideration to save money to buy a car for Rizen, so that he could use it to earn a living when he came back from the army. She asked how much a car would cost. Two thousand dinars. An enormous amount. She saved up coins in bags and never used that money, not even when someone was sick and had to go to the doctor.

One day she walked past a garage. A car was standing on a platform. Two men were busy repairing it. Wasile saw that the car was made from diverse pieces of steel and screws.

Down in the mouth she told Mira what she had seen on her outing. "A car is not just chairs to sit on. A car is steel stuck to steel stuck to steel." She sighed. "A sheep is cut open in the blink of an eye with a knife, but a car needs two men and after a whole year they're still not finished ..." Wasile even began to doubt who was cleverer, God or people. "Anyone who can make a car, can surely also make a chicken," she said.

Simahen heard what Wasile was saying to Mira. "People made cars," said Simahen angrily. "No person can make a chicken, because a chicken lays an egg and out of the egg comes a new chicken. Out of a car comes absolutely nothing, just smoke and noise. Watch the bread!" Simahen smelt that the bread in the oven was burning.

"You're absolutely right. A chicken from God is better than a car from a man," cried Wasile, as she hurriedly took the bread out of the oven. "But a chicken from God is quite a bit cheaper ..." she mumbled because she did not want Simahen to hear.

Wasile's biggest problem in saving for the car was the Iraqi dinar.

"The dinar is rubbish," she always complained. "It goes up and down and doesn't know how to keep on a level path without rising or falling." When Saddam Hussein dropped a rocket on Israel, the dinar sank in value and the price of a car became eight million dinar and Wasile would have to bake bread for three hundred and seventy years to save that much. When Saddam Hussein dropped a rocket on Iran, the dinar rose in value and she could buy a car with six or seven years of saving. When Saddam Hussein dropped a rocket on Kuwait, she would have to bake bread for four hundred and twenty years for a car, and when Saddam Hussein began to drop rockets on the marines in the Gulf, you could no longer calculate the price of a car, because the dinar did not sink, but almost disappeared. A can of cola, which had previously cost fifty fils, now cost ten thousand dinar.

That day Wasile closed her bedroom door behind her and spread out in front of her all the bags of coins and piles of paper bearing images of Saddam Hussein. She began crying, because she had only saved enough for the car's steering wheel, as the mechanic had said to her recently. Mira came into the room and saw her sitting among the money.

"Look," she sobbed to Mira. "Years of sacrifice are turned into six falafel breads."

Mira tried to console her, but Wasile continued crying for two days. When she became feverish, they tried to get her to the doctor.

"I don't need to see a doctor, I know what my problem is," she said. "If Mr President drops a rocket on Iran and the dinar rises, my temperature will fall." She prayed to God that Saddam Hussein would send his rockets to Iran and did not think of the people on whom the rockets would fall, but only of the rise of the dinar.

She remained lying impassively on her bed, until she learnt an important lesson from Sjahid. She would never again save money that had the head of Saddam Hussein on it. She exchanged all of her savings for American dollars. Exchanging money into American dollars was forbidden. Saddam Street, where the money changers gestured to passers-by by rubbing their thumb over their index fingers, was secretively called Street of Dollars. Members of the secret police picked the money changers up if they saw them making that gesture and if they found Iraqi dinars and American dollars in their pockets.

As had happened to Remzi Dollar. He was sentenced to have his right hand chopped off and was given one hour to bid farewell to his hand. Some of those thus sentenced beat their hand against a wall to feel it for one last time. Others kissed their hand, as if it was their wife on the dockside at the start of a long journey, or put their hand deep into their pocket.

Remzi asked for pen and paper and he wrote. "These are the last words that I wrote with my hand." He folded the paper up and put it in his shirt pocket. A few weeks later he had a tattoo artist engrave the words exactly as they appeared on to his arm and proudly showed the text to everyone. "Look, my hand was so beautiful and that was its handwriting."

Remzi Dollar returned to the Street of Dollars with his one

hand, was picked up again and also lost his other hand. If they were to catch him once more, they told him, it would not be his hand that would be lost – as he no longer had any – but his head. "Gold decreases in value. Blood as well, but not the dollar," said Remzi Dollar and went without hands back to stand in the Street of Dollars. Because he no longer had hands and therefore no fingers, he was no longer caught in the act.

The secret police agents sometimes smiled at him and made jokes. "Look after that neck of yours, okay." But they discovered nothing more than seeing one of his three children disappearing into an alleyway: either the biggest with a case full of Iraqi dinars; or the quickest with a case full of dollars; or the youngest, who had to say whether the biggest or the quickest was needed.

Wasile trusted Remzi Dollar. She brought him hot bread when she wanted to change money and he always exchanged it at a good rate.

"Who have you come with and who do you want to go back with?" he asked her laughingly.

"I've come with Saddam and I want to go back with Bush," Wasile replied.

She hid the dollars in a bag in her room and was not concerned that they would constantly decline in value. She gained some experience in the exchanging of money. If Saddam Hussein dropped a rocket on Iran, she sold dinars and bought dollars. If Saddam Hussein dropped a rocket on Israel, Kuwait or the Marines in the Gulf, she sold dollars and bought dinars. If Saddam Hussein dropped rockets on the Kurds in the north or the Shi'ites in the south, she changed no money.

"The blood of the Kurds and the Shi'ites is free," she complained. "Ah, if only Kurdish and Shi'ite blood was as precious as the dollar ... Then not a drop of it would fall." In order to know where Saddam Hussein was sending his rockets, she asked where Iran, Kuwait, Israel and the Marines were situated and looked at the heavens to see in which direction the rockets were going. Because she was no radar and could not see everything, she bought a small radio and kept it close to her the whole day long at the oven. If the newsreader let fall the word 'rocket', she stopped her baking and listened carefully. Then she would throw on her shawl and go to Remzi Dollar to change money. If the newsreader was not clear, she took dinars and dollars with her and asked Remzi Dollar what she should do. He always gave her good advice.

When she heard on the radio that Saddam Hussein had developed the El Abid rocket and had sent it into space, she did not understand. 'Space' was not in any obvious direction.

"They said on the radio that Mr President has sent a rocket into space. Do you know who lives there?" she asked Sjahid.

"God, if he exists," said Sjahid. That day she went to Remzi Dollar and asked his advice as to what she should do if God were to be bombarded by Saddam Hussein. One day she took a flour sack full of Iraqi dinars and came back happily with a five dollar bill. Mira opened her eyes and mouth wide with surprise and thought that her mother had been swindled, but Wasile calmed her down, while holding the five dollar bill – earned from six months of baking bread – up in the air.

"The American who shaved off his moustache with no shame is better than Mr President with his moustache. These Americans never sink from gold to falafel, like Mr President." She kissed the image of Lincoln. "He never goes down, this American. If I had known that earlier, then I would not only have been able to buy a car, but a whole garage."

After many years and many rockets she had saved twelve hundred dollars. She bought a lamb to sacrifice in thanks to God for when the car would arrive and then asked Rizen to build a garage to protect it against bird shit and the heat of the sun.

"At least buy the car first," said Rizen. "You're putting the cart before the horse."

"First get the food and then the horse will never go hungry," said Wasile.

Rizen started work on the garage. He put windows in, as if the car could breathe. This made Tenzile angry. The garage for the prospective car was bigger than the room she had to share with Rizen and her children. Sometimes she had to wait for weeks to be able to have sex with Rizen without the children being able to hear. When they did have sex the bed creaked and the children woke up frightened. They thought the bombardments had started again and that their father had flown through the air and landed on top of their mother. The children asked Tenzile why the bombardments made their father fly through the air and land on her, and not them. Tenzile was not quite sure what to tell them, but thought of an answer, which she was proud of.

"Because your father is a soldier and the war only allows soldiers to fly."

As each child grew up and began to understand what was happening in the dark room between Tenzile and Rizen, they stuck their fingers in their ears. When Edjnaad decided to go and sleep in Wasile's room, his grandmother asked him why he no longer wanted to sleep in his parents' bedroom.

"I can hear the bombardments there," he said.

The older the children got, the less Tenzile and Rizen had sex. That is why Tenzile was angry that Rizen was building a garage for the car and not a room for them to be alone in. Rizen did not tell her that he actually did want to build a room, but that Wasile was against it, because she did not want Tenzile to have her own room. Whoever had two rooms, Wasile thought, and built a wall around them, had a home. Whoever had a home, had to have a kitchen and whoever had a kitchen would have to buy things to fill it. Whoever bought things for their own kitchen, would forget the kitchen of their family. Because nobody cooked in two kitchens. Wasile did not want Rizen to leave the house, because he was the only one of her children who could take upon himself the responsibility of the house.

Wasile, who was in charge of the kitchen, wanted to become woman of the house after Simahen's death, ahead of Tenzile. That is the reason Wasile bought a Victoria sewing machine for her, which had to be powered by a foot pedal, and she made sure from that day forward that whenever she came into the house Tenzile was tied to the sewing machine, so that she did not have much space to keep herself busy on other matters and Wasile could keep control over the kitchen. She ensured that

Tenzile had clients and also negotiated the price for which the work would be delivered.

When the garage became bigger than her bedroom, Tenzile became depressed. She could not talk to anybody about it, not with Rizen, because he was too busy building, and also not with Mira, because she would surely tell Wasile. In desperation she eventually went to Adam. She bent down next to him as flies encircled his head.

"This is a house for animals," she whispered. "They would rather make rooms for dead metal than for living people." She fetched the fan from her room and set it to blow in the direction of Adam's head to chase the flies away. Late that night as she was coming from the toilet, she met Simahen going to the toilet.

"Let me help you," said Tenzile and gave her an arm to lean on.

"Who are you?" asked Simahen, who could not see very well at night without her glasses.

"I'm Tenzile," she said.

"I dreamt about you. Before Selman went to Mashhad to visit Imam Reza and he never came back ..."

"Who's Selman?" asked Tenzile.

"I don't know any more. I dreamt that you came home and made a father of one of my grandsons and castrated the others." She laughed. "It seems I'm going crazy with these dreams. Who is Selman after all?" She turned to Tenzile. "Have you ever heard me talk about Selman?"

"No."

"Tomorrow I'll ask the man of the house about it," said Simahen.

"But Rizen has gone to the army."

"I mean Wasile," said Simahen. "She's a witch."

Tenzile was afraid that Wasile would hear them and would make her pay the price for those words. "I dreamt that Saddam Hussein himself went into her room and came out again without a head. Ah, the dreams ... Have I been to the toilet yet?"

"I don't know," said Tenzile.

"My days are numbered," said Simahen sadly. "If someone

doesn't know whether they are coming or going to the toilet, then it means that they're long dead."

Tenzile knew that Wasile was afraid of Simahen. And she knew that without Simahen, Wasile would treat her like a slave or a servant. So Tenzile looked after Simahen, afraid that she would die at any moment. She hurried to her when she called, which made Wasile angry, as she waited on Simahen's death so that she could become the lady of the house. Tenzile prayed to God to give Simahen time until her children were grown up, because then no one would dare insult her. Wasile used every opportunity to make Tenzile pay for everything she had endured in the house of the Birds.

"I thank Mr President for taking the men of this house away. They did not leave one branch in this house that was not broken on my head," Wasile once said.

"If anyone dared do that to me, Rizen would chop their hand off," said Tenzile.

Wasile laughed. "If Mr President had not taken the men, Rizen would have learnt from them how to break the branches on your head."

Tenzile believed that Rizen's love for her still filled his heart. She did not know that war, with its dead, wounded and hot metal, had buried her in him, so that his heart had long stopped beating for her. She had realised that only when Jakob, her only brother, died in the war.

During the time of the war with Iran, when Saddam Hussein was supported by the West, every family that lost a son in the fighting received a car from the government. So families began falsifying the reasons for the deaths of their sons. Tenzile's mother had only one son, Jakob. He was thirty, but he had the mind of a child. His mother decided to trade in her handicapped son for a car, one just like her neighbour had received. She wanted to pay money to get Jakob into the army and when she did not succeed, she began pestering Hadi the Rocket. She told him that she wanted one of her children to also defend Iraq. Eventually Hadi the Rocket took Jakob into the people's army, because he was afraid that his mother would go to Baghdad to complain to Saddam Hussein himself. When Jakob got to the frontline, he began to cry with distress. The soldiers thought that he was a coward and beat him to make a man of him. After a few days he ran in the direction of Iran. A mine exploded under his feet. His mother showed off her new car.

Tenzile tried talking to Rizen about her grief over Jakob.

"Why do you talk about the handicapped one, that your mother sold for a car? Why don't you rather talk about the car?" he snapped. His words struck deep in her heart, while Rizen continued. "I wish I was two people. One that died in the war and one that was given a car like your mother."

When Saddam Hussein invaded Kuwait in 1991, the market was suddenly flooded with plundered Kuwaiti goods. Rizen eventually bought a colour television, so that he could see Saddam Hussein in colour, and threw out the last black and white television in the south. He spent his time on leave with the remote control. Tenzile tried to talk to him, but he was busy zapping between channels. He was amazed at how the channels changed without him even touching the television.

"Perhaps there's an invisible Japanese sitting in the television. Those Japanese can do anything," he said.

"Don't believe in the Japanese more than in God," said Tenzile.

The army was Rizen's world, just like the room with books was Joesr's, Saddam Hussein was Naji's, the wall at the party's house was Simahen's and the clay oven was Wasile's world. Rizen never complained or nagged and was never tired, as if he was made of steel. As a child Rizen did not look like Kosjer, his father, but when Saddam Hussein began poisoning the Iranians with chemical weapons and Rizen began to come home even less, he began to look more like Kosjer. He smoked and he could not sit still; he got sick when he was not busy. When Rizen was at home, Tenzile tried to be alone with him, but almost never succeeded. Tenzile argued with him, because she wanted him to save money and build a house somewhere, so that they could live far away from Wasile.

"I'm going crazy," she whispered, afraid that Wasile would hear her. "Your mother sticks her nose in everywhere. Yesterday she said that I shouldn't stand so long under the shower, because the water costs money. I told her that I had fetched the water myself from the Thirsty River, at which she said that the river water costs money."

Rizen laughed loudly. "Let her stick her nose in everywhere. It's just a nose after all, not a tank?"

"I wish there was a tank that would drive over me," said Tenzile and she began crying. "You can take a break from the war of Mr President and there is a chance you will die, but here in this house, in the war of Wasile, there is no break and no chance of dying." She stared into his empty face. "I'm taking the children and going to back to my family."

"And who'll feed you and your children there? Your mother?" he asked her.

The following day Wasile glared angrily at Tenzile, as if she had heard everything. "The door is big enough for a camel if you want to go to your family," said Wasile.

During this time the party propaganda said that microphones smaller than a fingernail overheard what the party's enemies said. Tenzile searched her room for such a microphone, through which Wasile could hear everything she said, but when she could not find it, she knew she could no longer talk to Rizen about subjects that Wasile did not approve of. It felt as if she was slowly being throttled, because her throat was filled with words and she could not talk. She wandered through the house when she was finished on the sewing machine, while the silence covered her. One day, as the sun was setting, she sat in the yard to repair some of Edjnaad's trousers, when Adam, in search of somewhere quiet, softly came to stand beside her. Mira dragged him away and tied him up, but every time she untied him, he returned to Tenzile and remained standing next to her. No one realised that he was looking for the heavy silence that enveloped Tenzile, not for Tenzile herself.

"Perhaps we should castrate him," Wasile said to Mira. "He smells the scent of a woman and follows it."

Wasile thought for days of a way to castrate Adam, but did not know how to get it done. She went to a woman who castrated calves to fatten them up for slaughter, and asked her if she also castrated people or knew someone who could do it.

"I can't do it myself and I believe there is only one person in Iraq who does that: Mr President," said the woman. After much insistence from Wasile the woman took on the task of castrating Adam and went with her to the house. When she saw Adam, she opened her eyes wide.

"He's sleeping, why must we castrate him?"

"His dick doesn't sleep," said Wasile. The woman asked if it would not be better to wake him up before he was castrated, but Wasile told her that even a bombardment had not woken him.

"If he doesn't wake up when I castrate him, you'll have to bury him, because then he'll be dead," said the woman.

She asked Wasile and Mira to drive four stakes into the ground to which she tied Adam's hands and feet. Wasile filled his mouth with cotton wad and after half an hour the woman had castrated Adam.

Adam was in pain for weeks, but when the pain abated, he began walking like a blind person through the house again.

"Do you know what he's looking for?" Joesr asked Mira.

"I don't know."

"He's pale, perhaps he's sick."

"He was always like that," said Wasile. "And you, go and wash those plates," she said to Mira. She did not want Joesr to know that Adam had been castrated.

Tenzile pretended not to know. It made her even more afraid of Wasile, because if she could castrate one of her own sons, she would surely poison her daughter-in-law if she felt the need to.

On a peaceful night, without falling rockets or jet fighters flying over, Simahen dreamt about Adam. He was wearing a shirt with pale autumn leaves and was sitting in a yellow train passing through fields of sunflowers stretching to the horizon.

When she woke up, she called Rizen. "Build a room for your sleeping brother," she said. "Make sure that your children don't see him lying among the animals." Simahen was still under the sway of Adam in her dreams.

Wasile protested about the room, but after Tenzile had made it clear to Simahen with careful hints that Rizen had stopped building because his mother had intervened, Simahen screamed at Rizen, so that Wasile could hear, ordering him to build the room.

During every period of leave Rizen worked on the room with its four large windows. He put four doors in. "When he sleeps in this room, he'll wake up happy. Look, in every wall there's a window and a door, so he won't have to look for one." Rizen was glad that he could work on Adam's room, because then he did not have sit in his own room with its crowd of children and the noise of Tenzile's sewing machine or listen to Sjahid's long discussions in the sitting room with Mohamed Mansour and Yasin Al Terref about the war.

Sjahid, Mohamed Mansour and Yasin Al Terref listened to the news about the war on the radio, on stations from Monte Carlo, London or Washington, which broadcast in Arabic. Washington was the fastest with the news. London was the most detailed and Monte Carlo the most tense. They listened to news about the war on the radio and never thought to ask Rizen, who came from the war. They did make sure Rizen heard what the radio had to say about the war.

Rizen bought a small radio, although it was forbidden to listen to one in the army. He hid it, and between the booming of cannons and rockets held it tightly to his ear to hear how the war was progressing. Rizen was amazed that the three friends were now thinking about the war, while previously they had discussed literature and art. During the annual commemoration of the death of Sabha, who since Saddam Hussein had come to power was referred to as the holy mother of the fatherland and mother of the fighters and for whom everything was covered in the black of mourning – so that the television suddenly seemed to be in black and white again – Rizen asked Sjahid, Mohamed Mansour and Yasin Al Terref why they still discussed the war.

"Because shortly we'll have to go there." As their graduation drew ever closer, the friends became more afraid and listened more avidly to the radio. Thus Rizen discovered that you became more afraid thinking about the war than when you were fighting on the frontline.

When Adam's room was finished, Rizen began to sleep in it himself. So as not to be disturbed by Tenzile and her nagging, he washed Adam and took him to the room. Adam only stayed briefly, before feeling his way back to the stable. Tenzile went quietly into the room and stayed with Rizen. Each time she took something to the room, not too much at once, because she did not want Wasile to think that she had two bedrooms. She also spoke obviously about 'Adam's room'. Tenzile began filling her belly, in Adam's room, from Rizen and emptied it in her own room. After her last son Tali she could have borne more children, but one day she made the mistake of referring to Adam's room as 'my bedroom'. Wasile threw all of Tenzile's things out of the room, pulled all Adam's clothes off and tied him naked in the room, so that Tenzile would not dare go in there. Wasile kept the doors locked, until Tenzile no longer thought about 'her bedroom'.

When the Iraqi army was sitting in Kuwait and the American blockade of Iraq began, Rizen and Tenzile already had three children. Later they had even more. Of the five children who survived, the first child was a boy. Rizen named him Edjnaad, after the soldier who had saved his life when he lay unconscious from a bombardment in their trench. He had carried him fifteen kilometres and when he laid him safely on the ground, he was hit by a bullet, fell on top of Rizen and protected his body from flying bullets that night.

The second son was given the name Rasjad, because it rhymed with Edjnaad. Their third child was a son who was named Saddam by Rizen. Tenzile asked him how he could call one of his children after the man who had taken away his father, grandfather and uncles, to which Rizen replied that no one with the name of Saddam would be tortured, threatened or refused work. After that they had two stillborn children as a result of there being so little to eat during the blockade, and they were followed by a girl, who was named Shibe, and the last born was Tali.

When Edjnaad turned six years old, he began taking Simahen to the party's house. During Simahen's years of waiting, the wall next to the party's house had been transformed into a market. In the beginning an old woman came to sit with Simahen, asking after her son who had been taken away by comrades of Hadi the Rocket. Then another woman, who was looking for her husband, joined them. Then a boy began selling cold water to the three women in their black clothes. In due course a woman and her mother came, who asked Simahen and the other two women about their son and husband. A little later another boy came selling bread, and the women who had gathered there began quietly talking to each other about their disappeared men. If they were chased away by the guards at the party's house, they came back one by one and cautiously went to sit down again. The sellers began to bribe the guards at the party's house with a cola or some bread so as to be able to continue doing business with the women.

After a good few years a market had developed at the party's house, which was known as the Simahen market. Simahen bought treats for Edjnaad so that he would take her there, because she could no longer go by herself. When everything became hazy in her head and she had begun asking strange questions about her past, Edjnaad sat her down behind their house in the shade and told her that she was sitting next to the party's house. If she smelt Wasile's bread, she asked Edjnaad about it. He then said that the party was baking bread, because he was hungry.

One day Simahen fell asleep and when she woke up she realised she was sitting behind her house and that a thin young man with flies on his parched face was lying next to her. Because of the heat she did not know that she was lying next to Adam. Mira saw her looking around desperately and took her to her room. "I dreamt that I was sitting at the wall of the party's house and that the party gave me some bread and said that I was visiting him," she said.

Simahen continued to wake up ever earlier, shuffled outside laboriously and took up her place in the shade against the wall behind their house. "Earlier I walked long distances to the party's house, but now only a few steps. The world has really got smaller," she said.

One August day when it was so hot that the tar on the roads was melting, Simahen called Tenzile and asked her why she had been sitting at the party's house for all those years. Tenzile did not know.

Simahen walked laboriously to the kitchen where Mira was chopping vegetables. "For years on end I waited at the party's house. My waiting became a market. I want to know why."

"Because that's what they called it."

"Who?"

"The men in the house."

"Which house?"

"That house."

"Ah, my mind is disappearing from me." She smiled gently with her toothless mouth. "Now I can go to sleep," she said, relieved. "I thought that I went there because I was a member of the Ba'ath party."

CHAPTER 11

The journey of Baan's belly

Each time another child of Tenzile and Rizen was born, Sjahid felt less at home. The noise and the crying, which amused Simahen, irritated him. When he was in Baghdad he bought treats for the children, but at home he gave the treats to Mira or Tenzile to give to them. He did not give them to Wasile because he had often heard her say that she would not give them the treats from Uncle Sjahid if they did not listen to her. When the rumour spread that Saddam Hussein would visit Boran, the houses and streets were cleaned meticulously and the comrades accosted people on the streets all day long. Anyone who was not dressed neatly was ordered to go home and to wash and dress smartly, because otherwise Saddam Hussein would stay away.

If Saddam Hussein went on a visit somewhere, all the towns were told that he was going to come and would have to be ready to receive him, but no one knew in which town he would actually arrive.

So every time it was said that Mr President was going to visit Boran, Sjahid stayed at home because he did not want to see Saddam Hussein. Saddam, Rizen's son, could only just walk. Tenzile called to him from behind her sewing machine.

"Saddam! Saddam!"

Sjahid threw his slipper at the child, who fell over in a bundle on the floor and began to cry. "Couldn't Rizen think of any other name? Every time I hear that name, it's as if someone has spat in my face," he shouted irritatedly.

"Quiet down, don't let the neighbours hear you," said Wasile.

There are millions of names and Rizen calls his kid Saddam," mumbled Sjahid angrily. "Saddam's everywhere. In heaven, on earth. And even here in this house?"

"You yourself paint Mr President on walls and now you're irritated that one of Rizen's children is called Saddam?" said Wasile without realising that her words felt just as harsh as the rocket coming down in the distance.

Sjahid shuffled off in his slippers and went out without dressing in his smart clothes or putting gel in his hair. On the street he thought of Wasile's words. Just past the party's house he came to a stop and looked up at the mural of Saddam Hussein, which he had painted over many times with Naji and thought of the long hours he had spent doing that. He thought of the night that Naji had woken him up. "Someone has thrown a bucket of shit over Mr President. Come on, we have to paint over him before the sun comes up," Naji had said with sleep in his eyes. They had pinched their noses closed, carefully, so that no one would see and assume that they thought Saddam Hussein stank and send a report to Hadi the Rocket, and they wiped the soft shit off the mural.

"You know," said Naji, "that Hadi the Rocket himself woke me up? He trembled and stuttered. 'Mr Naji, my dear friend Naji, Mr President needs you.' And then I trembled as well. What did Mr President want with me? I was dead scared that I would have to look right at him and paint him. My hands would tremble like the wings of a hummingbird. Instead of the face of Mr President I might paint a goat." Naji coughed and cleared his nose like a diver just coming out of the water. "Hadi the Rocket whispered that I must get dressed and follow him. He brought me here. I smelt the stench, looked at the mural and saw Mr President smeared with shit. Hadi the Rocket gave the soldiers an order to arrest everyone out on the street and

posed the philosophical question to me ..." Naji cleared his nose
again and breathed deeply "...whether the night was long
enough. He did not specify what for, he did not want to put the
words 'Mr President' and 'shit' in the same sentence. I said yes.
What would Hadi the Rocket have done if I had said that the
night was not long enough to wipe the shit off Mr President?
Postponed sunrise?" Naji said jokingly and laughed cheerfully.
"I would gladly kiss the hands of the perpetrator. They are
more beautiful than the hands of presidents, kings, sheikhs
and generals."

Hadi the Rocket came regularly with kebabs or tea to check
on their progress. Naji painted and chatted with Sjahid when
there was no one else in the quiet night, because all the soldiers
were out on the streets arresting people. "Now I am proud of
this painting. It is painted on heroic shit."

Before the sun came up, Naji and Sjahid were finished. Naji
lit a cigarette. "The person who went out to find a bucket and
fresh shit and risked his life to deface this idiot, that person is
greater than the terror. He deserves to get a statue one day.
With the legend 'A hero in a time of terror, his weapon was the
shit of the people.' Sadly enough his sort are always unknown,"
said Naji, while walking with Sjahid to his house. Arriving at
the house, Sjahid wanted to leave the things, as he always did,
in the passage, but Naji told him to leave them outside, because
they stank. Naji fell asleep and Sjahid went to the kitchen to
fry an egg. His whole body was in pain.

Apart from Sjahid, Naji never had any visitors. At night a
woman came to clean the house and cook for the following day,
and before the sun came up, she quietly left the house again
and disappeared, cautiously, so that no one would see her.

"She comes here to remind me that I have a penis," Naji said
to Sjahid.

When Sjahid asked why he did not marry her, Naji said that
he did not want to be tied to any woman in Iraq, because a
woman in Iraq was like an anchor that fixes you in one place.
When Sjahid asked him if he wanted a child who could look
after him when he was old, Naji said what he needed was not
a child, but a tunnel under his house that came out on the

145

other side of the world. One day Naji came across Sjahid, Mohamed Mansour and Yasin Al Terref on the street and invited them for a cup of tea. The three friends politely walked home with him. Naji also treated Sjahid like a visitor and not as an employee, so as not to embarrass him in front of his friends. He brewed the tea himself and while he filled his own glass with whisky, he asked the three friends what sort of sex they liked.

The friends were in silent amazement.

"You," said Naji and pointed to Mohamed Mansour. "Who do you want to have sex with? A man or a woman, or with a goat perhaps?"

The question broke the silence. The three friends laughed, but Naji kept looking seriously at Mohamed Mansour.

"With a woman of course," answered Mohamed Mansour.

"Of course? Why of course? Why not with a man?" Naji asked Yasin Al Terref if he would like to sleep with a man or a woman or a goat.

Yasin Al Terref shook his head.

"And you, Sjahid?"

Sjahid also said nothing.

"And you, Naji?" asked Mohamed Mansour, who was starting to come to life as he discovered that Naji was a spontaneous youngster and not a difficult man.

"I actually tried it in Catalonia with a man," said Naji.

The three friends fell silent again and listened in amazement.

"Yes, with a man. But he was not like the men here. He had no hair on his body and his voice was softer than my mother's. But after a few minutes my penis let me down. It expected a soft hole and saw something else. That's when I knew for sure that I was only attracted to women."

Naji's openness was remarkable to the friends, who had never dared talk about masturbation or sex. Only Mohamed Mansour dared speak out and asked Naji how many women he had slept with. "Here I've only slept with a goat, but in my first year in Catalonia with twenty women. I still remember their names, their faces. After the first year I stopped counting."

"Did you ever actually sleep with two women at the same time?" asked Mohamed Mansour.

Naji laughed loudly. "Good question." He took an enthusiastic swig of his whisky. "Sadly not. During my studies in Barcelona I had a part-time job in a restaurant. There was a girl who worked there who fancied guys and girls. She had a relationship with a girl, but went off with me now and again and always said that she would bring the other girl in on it some time. I thought that she wanted to test me to see if I was faithful to her and always refused. A lost opportunity. For time to slip past is not difficult, guys, but for chances to slip by without grabbing them is."

"Is it so easy to get women there?"

"No, not exactly. If you live there, you discover that everything is the same as here, but that the women there are not treated like cattle."

"Women here are treated like women," said Yasin Al Terref, who always felt he was being attacked during discussions when anyone spoke positively about the West. "Women here are free to do what they want within tradition."

"Ah, are we going to be speaking like Mr President?" Naji filled his whisky glass with ice blocks. "If men themselves are not free and are treated like animals, how free can the women be? In Iraq only one person is free. One person does as he pleases. He is Mr President. He is more free than Margaret Thatcher or François Mitterrand."

"He's not free," said Sjahid.

"Look, your loyal friend has dared to say something about Mr President," said Naji. He was not yet drunk and saw that the expression of the friends subsided from excited and amazed to sombre and stern. So he stood up and showed the friends photos of the girls he had slept with, and the art academy he had studied at.

When they were leaving, he gave each of the friends a cassette tape with Spanish music and he gave Sjahid a calendar of naked Catalonian women. "Twelve women for twelve months," he said laughingly.

For weeks the friends were afraid that Hadi the Rocket

would come to hear what they had been talking about with Naji. If someone had seen them coming out of Naji's house, they would surely have thought they were holding a meeting. They never again went back together in the evening or went over the subject that they had discussed, and never again did Mohamed Mansour and Yasin Al Terref visit Naji.

When Sjahid was not accepted for the art academy after secondary school, he could choose between the army or one of the institutes for which no party papers were necessary. So he became a student at the Fashion and Textile Institute. To escape the boring lessons he began drawing murals of Saddam Hussein at the institute, and later on spent the whole day with Naji. By the end of the year he had passed all the exams without going to a single lesson and was accepted for the second year.

"I didn't spin a single gram of wool and was passed," he said to Naji. Naji continued to warn him that he had to get out of Iraq before he had completed his studies, because otherwise he would have to go to the army, but Sjahid then repeated that he would not go to the army.

"If ants spoke Arabic, Saddam Hussein would put them in uniform and get them fighting. Who are you not to have to go to the army? The son of Mao Zedong?" said Naji.

But Sjahid was adamant. He was convinced that the army would never be part of his life. The studies at the institute would take three years and each student could do only one year over again. Every young man ensured that they failed one year, so as to postpone military service. The problem with Sjahid was that lecturers would not dare fail him, because he made murals of Saddam Hussein, not even at Sjahid's request. So he took leave on medical grounds for a year and was able to spread his studies over four years.

A year before Sjahid would have to join the army, Wasile began digging a hole in the ground in which to hide him if necessary. At night she would surreptitiously empty the pots of earth into the Thirsty River. Sjahid said he would not go under the ground, but she contradicted him.

"Anyone who does not fight for Mr President, must go under the ground, dead or alive," she said and kept digging until there was a large hole. She made an air pipe that came up out of sight among the trees in the garden, a roof of wood, plastic, clay and straw. On top of that she tied up some goats and sheep.

Sjahid laughed when he saw her busy at it. How could she think he would go and sit in a hole under the grazing goats and sheep and into which the worms could fall. But the nearer he came to the end of his studies and the moment when he would have to present himself to the army, the thinner and more distant he became. Djazil offered to smuggle him over the border, but he dared not do that and chose to wait for a passport and permission to travel.

Every day he waited at the office where passports were issued, from eight in the morning until four in the afternoon. His waiting was more gruelling than Simahen's waiting at the party's house. Simahen often forgot why she was waiting and sometimes she even forgot that she was waiting. She went to the party's house because that is what she was used to doing. Sjahid felt every moment of the waiting for the passport, that small, green book with the photo of him that would be his salvation. He sat on the veranda and chewed over his thoughts, because he dared not read a book.

When he had run out of ideas, he counted the birds receding in the sky, the car's passing noisily by and rockets flying through the air from the border to Baghdad or from Baghdad to the border. He went to sit in the shadow of the wall and when he was thirsty asked one of the others waiting if they would listen out to see if his name was called. Then he ran quickly to get something to drink and went back to sit and wait until four o'clock when the window was shut. Sjahid felt that there were only a few months between him and the army. He began to feel how powerful Saddam Hussein was. His efforts to get a passport ended when the official behind the window called him.

"You see that donkey over there?" said the official.

Sjahid looked and nodded.

"Only when that donkey becomes a turkey will you get a passport."

"You've got thin," said Wasile when she saw him come in, walk slowly to the tap without greeting anyone and hold his head under the stream of water. "Perhaps you've got worms."

"I've got lots of worms," said Sjahid.

Wasile then hurried to her room and fetched her bag of medicines. She rummaged in the bag, took a small box out and read out from it. "Vermox, yes, that's what I was looking for. Here, against worms."

Sjahid suddenly burst out laughing. He had not expected his mother, who had never been to school and could read no Arabic, would be able to decipher the medicines' English names.

"Why do you laugh with your stomach full of worms?"

"I don't mean the worms that are eating me up from the inside, but from the outside," said Sjahid.

"I don't see any worms," said Wasile.

Saddam Hussein shouted on the neighbour's television. A rocket fell in the distance.

"Do you hear that? Those are the worms that are eating me up," said Sjahid. He wanted to say that he meant the rocket and Saddam Hussein, but Wasile closed her medicine bag and went back to the clay oven.

"Ah, I've let the bread burn because I thought you had worms and you're making jokes?" Mira took a glass of tea to Joesr's room. She hurried because she wanted to get to his room before another rocket fell and made her spill it. Sjahid followed her to Joesr's room and saw him on his bed reading an old book.

"What is th ...?" said Sjahid. A rocket fell.

"It is the book ..." said Joesr. A rocket made the town tremble. Sjahid fell against the wall. The siren wailed. "American rocket," said Joesr. "When the siren is too late, then the rockets are American."

When a rocket fell so close that the room not only trembled, but everything fell to the ground, Joesr and Sjahid jumped up and ran outside. Sirens and ambulances screeched in chorus.

"The silence after these rockets will probably last for a week," said Joesr, clutching his head, realising he had fallen against a wall and a bump had formed on the back of his head. He went, groaning, to lie on his bed without knowing that he would jump up the following evening from the noise of the bullet that would kill Baan.

After three months it looked as if Baan has just put on a bit of weight, and in the fourth month of her pregnancy her belly began travelling from wall to wall. First the woman next door looked over the wall. "Look at Baan's belly. She looks pregnant," she said innocently to Henadi. After that Baan's belly jumped from one wall to the next. Each time Baan's belly jumped, it was made bigger by the women's tongues than it was by the baby itself. With time Baan's belly was not only jumping from wall to wall, but passing from door to door and flying from window to window. Baan's belly began talking, sitting in rooms and drinking tea and telling how it was filled one summer afternoon on the banks of the Thirsty River. Baan's belly kept on travelling until it was five and a half months old and arrived at a wall behind which a woman with a colourless face sat minding children.

"Have you heard?" his wife said to him, when Baan's uncle came home on leave from the army, even before he had taken his uniform off.

"What is it that I must have heard?" he said.

"About Baan." So the uncle came to know everything, as if Baan's name referred to her belly and not to herself. He took his old pistol that had belonged to his father, left his house still in his uniform and perforated her skull with a bullet.

The sun had already gone down. That afternoon Baan had swept the house clean and brought the mats in from the washing line. From the courtyard she heard a knocking on the door. She opened it a crack and saw her uncle in uniform standing there. She was taken aback because he always came to visit on his second day after having returned, and then in the morning in his normal clothes with bags full of shopping.

He did not see Baan, but knew that it was her who had

opened the door, because she always opened the door ajar. "They say ..." said the uncle and he choked. "Your belly is big," he said, without seeing her clearly in the darkness.

She did not answer.

"Where's your mother?" he asked, pushing the door open and seeing her standing there looking pale in the light from the lamp outside. She waved her hand and pointed to the kitchen.

Before she could say "there" and her mother could ask "who", the shot rang out and the bullet penetrated her head. A second later she collapsed in a bundle on the floor in the courtyard, her hand pointing in the direction of the kitchen, as if she was pointing somewhere more distant than the clay wall and the insects dancing in the light of the lamp.

"He's killed her!" a woman's voice screamed. Her mother came outside screaming.

The uncle swung the pistol back and forth. "Ssssssshhhhhhh ..." he hissed and went inside the room. There he saw six small eyes trembling in a corner. "Don't be scared, don't be scared," he whispered and walked towards the children. He became aware of the pistol in his hand, threw his hand behind his back and stroked the children's heads with his other hand. "Don't be scared."

He took a blanket and threw it over Baan's body in the courtyard. Then he went to the kitchen, picked up a knife, hacked off her right hand and hung it, tied by the thumb with yellow string, to the front door of the house as proof that the family's honour had been restored. Then he gave himself up to the police and spent six months in prison.

Joesr had stopped searching for Djazil a month and a half after the meeting with Henadi and Baan. It put his mind at ease in the first days. Every time he came home, Wasile told him that Henadi had come to tell them that some other man had slept with Baan, had made her pregnant and was going to marry her. She swore that was the case, but Joesr did not believe her and did not speak to her. He knew that she was lying, and she knew that he knew that she was lying, but each time he heard that story, his head became a little less burdened and he thought a little less about knocking on Henadi's door, where Baan was waiting for him. It then seemed to him as if she lived not a few streets further up, but somewhere in a story that he had read. Wasile counted the days and thought that if Joesr did not go to Baan for four months, everyone would know about her pregnancy and even her marriage to him would not save her from any scandal.

One day Djazil appeared in the house.

"Go before Joesr sees you," Wasile whispered to him.

Djazil laughed. "Don't worry about it," he said.

Joesr heard him, but remained lying on his bed, as if Djazil had to come to him because he had been looking for him. Just as Baan was waiting for Joesr or Djazil, and Joesr for Djazil, Wasile was waiting for the sound of the bullet. Not because she wanted Baan to be killed, but because she wanted the trouble that had come with the arrival in her house of her swollen belly to be killed.

In the middle of winter, when there was no water in the Thirsty River and the riverbed had become a road, Joesr decided to become a veterinarian. He had discussed it with Samer, who had said the people in Boran had no money to go to a doctor, never mind a vet. The sick animals would not go to the vet themselves, but Joesr said that he would go to the sick animals and would not ask for any money.

Samer laughed. "You should go and visit my father. He's a sick ass," he said.

At four o'clock each afternoon Joesr sat behind the house with Simahen, who thought she was sitting at the party's house. He took a book out, ate grilled meat at six o'clock, burnt incense in his room and listened to one of Sjahid's cassettes. He listened to 'No soy de aquí' while lying on his back, with his hands on his chest until he fell asleep with his mouth wide open.

Mira quietly swept the room with the broom made of date palm fronds.

"Tell Djazil that he shouldn't throw puppies into the Thirsty River," he said to Mira in his sleep. She smiled, because the Thirsty River had dried up and no dog could drown in it.

She left the door ajar to allow the dust to blow out of the room, fed Adam and when she returned to close the door, she saw Joesr lying on his bed in the foetal position because of the cold. She put a blanket over him and quietly closed the door.

At a quarter past nine Joesr woke with a start at the sound of the shot, as if he recognised the bullet out of all the bullets ever fired. He ran to Wasile's room. "Her uncle has killed her," he said trembling. He saw Djazil sitting there. "They have killed her," he said shakily to Djazil. "Didn't you hear the shot?"

Djazil did not answer.

Mira came in. She had heard from a neighbour over the wall that Baan had been killed by a shot through the left side of her temple and that her right hand was hanging by a piece of yellow string on the door.

"I didn't know that he would come today," stammered Joesr. "I wanted to go and see her tomorrow. Or the day after tomorrow. I swear." Joesr hit himself on the forehead. "Oh God, oh God," he stuttered. He put his slippers on and went to Baan's house. Nearing the house he saw women dressed in black going into the house through the old wooden door. He saw the hand hanging from the door and threw up.

Children began to laugh.

"He's scared of the chopped-off hand!" one of them cried.

"If he sees her lying in the courtyard, he will die from shock," cried another child.

"I saw her lying there, dead. The child in her belly is still moving," said yet another.

"You're lying. You're just saying that because you want to be cool. The baby in her belly is also dead," said the next.

Joesr saw men listening to the children, who, because they were so young, could go into the house then tell the men what they saw. One child said that Baan had tried to run away, but that her uncle had caught her up at the door. Another child said that her mother had tied her hands up, had blindfolded her and had brought her into the courtyard. Yet another said that the uncle had also tried to kill Henadi, because she had let Baan sleep with men for money, but that then he did not know who would look after the rest of the children.

Joesr turned his back and walked away. When no one could
see him any longer, he began running, just as Dime had done
on her final day in Boran, and just as Rizen had done when he
was in love with Tenzile. At the dry Thirsty River he ran over
the riverbed and screamed. A peacock from Hadi the Rocket's
farm answered. Exhausted he fell to his knees.

"Oh God, I've killed her," he panted with a terrified voice.
"And the child in her as well."

He cried until the day began, stood up and went home.

Wasile had just stoked up the oven. The chickens scratched
around behind Mira in the hope of catching some breakfast.

"What is it with you?" asked Wasile, but Joesr did not
answer.

He began walking breathlessly back and forth to his room,
collected his books and cassettes and threw them into the oven.
Wasile wanted to hold him back, but she restrained herself
because of the wild gaze in his red eyes. After the books and
the tapes, he threw the recorder, his bed, the blankets, his
clothes, the carpet, the bookcase, his slippers and shoes into
the fire. Everything disappeared into the oven. Wasile and
Mira looked on. They dared not get too close. When he went
into his room and stayed away, Mira looked cautiously around
the corner. She saw him sobbing, sitting in the middle of the
empty room.

"There's nothing left to burn," she heard him say.

"Would you like some tea?" asked Mira.

He stood up abruptly, walked to the oven, took his clothes
off and threw them in. When he also took his underpants off,
Mira ran away, because she did not want to see him naked, but
Wasile called her back. Joesr screamed so loudly and so
frightfully that the doves and the stork flew away.

"Mira, help!" screamed Wasile as she grabbed him by his
feet, so that he could not throw himself into the oven.

CHAPTER 12

She even crucifies sleep

Mira would never forget how she and Wasile dragged Joesr away from the clay oven. They threw a blanket over his naked body and kept holding him until he calmed down. Then he stood up with the blanket like a cloak over his shoulders and walked calmly to his room, as if he had not just attempted to throw himself into the oven.

After an hour or so Mira quietly opened the door to his room and saw him standing in the middle of it. His hands were crossed over each other above his head, as if he was hanging from the ceiling. His head was bowed. Mira went into the room to see the rope with which his arms were tied to the ceiling, but she saw nothing. She moved closer and looked at his swollen face. She left the room but on hearing a thud went straight back. By the light of a lantern she saw Joesr lying on the ground. She held the lantern to his face, saw that he was crying and went away so as not to embarrass him. The quieter the night became, the clearer Joesr's sobbing could be heard.

When Wasile woke up early the next morning to make a fire in the clay oven, she saw Joesr, dressed in Adam's clothes that had been hanging on the washing line, going to his room with an axe. He swung the axe in the air and with great lunges began breaking down his room. Wasile did not dare hold him back, afraid that he would turn his axe on her.

"What's that noise?" asked Simahen from her bed.

"Bombardments," Wasile called back, at which Simahen recited what she knew of the Koran from her head, so that no rocket would hit their house.

When the room was completely destroyed, Joesr sat on the ruins of what had been his room. He sighed deeply, put his slippers on, went out and only came back as the sun was going down. He went up the stairs to the flat roof, stared at the birds in their cages, separated the cock pigeons from the hen pigeons and listened to their cooing.

When Mira brought him food, he was sitting in the moonlight drawing on a plank with a pencil. Mira put the plate of food in front of him and went without saying anything.

The next morning he came down from the roof with the plank under his arm. He had red eyes, as if he had not slept, and asked Mira for the key to the cellar. From the nail on the wall in Simahen's room she fetched the old rusted key that had not been used since the time of the Ottomans. Joesr looked at the stork's nest on Nadim's tower and tried to recall the last time that he had seen the stork or had looked at it. It was on the day during his childhood when he had tried in vain to persuade the storks to come down by throwing frogs on the grounds. He thought about what Simahen had once told him, that the tower had been built by the devil to be higher than the minaret and that God had broken it down and commanded the stork to land on it and peck the devil so that he would not build it higher again when God was not watching.

When the stork spread its wings and disappeared into the sky flapping noisily, Joesr felt an enormous weight on his shoulders again and walked slowly to the cellar. He removed the boards from the trapdoor and opened it. He felt Mira standing behind him, watching him.

"If someone asks after me, tell them I'm not here any more," he said without turning round. After he had nailed the plank to the trapdoor, he descended into the darkness and closed it behind him.

Mira called one of the neighbour's children to read to her what was written on the plank.

"Here rests Joesr," the youngster read politely. "Did you bury someone here?" he asked.

"We haven't buried him," said Mira. "He buried himself."

Every day Mira put food and drink at the trapdoor to the cellar, next to oil for the lantern. She took it on herself to also add a wick every three weeks. "I can look after one who's sleeping, but oh God, how can I look after someone who has buried himself," she complained.

So as not to forget Joesr, Mira tied the dog, which Wasile had tied up at the front door to watch for Baan and Henadi, at the trapdoor to the cellar. If it barked because it was hungry or thirsty, Mira thought of Joesr. Because the dog did not use a lantern and could not remind her about it, Mira eventually forgot about the oil and wicks and after three weeks Joesr lived in darkness.

Mira knocked on the trapdoor when she brought his food.

"Leave it at the trapdoor," Joesr always said. He said nothing more than that.

One day she called him, because Samer was asking after him. "Samer is here. He wants to see you."

"Leave it at the trapdoor," he said.

So Mira discovered that he could not hear what was being said.

When Rizen came home on leave, he did not notice that Joesr's room had been razed. This upset Tenzile. If he did not see that the room was now a pile of rubble, he would not see her either. When she pointed out the broken down room, he laughed.

"It's like the projectile from a 200mm rocket fell on it," said Rizen and he began talking about how far a T-55 tank could shoot and what it was used against.

"Enough!" screamed Tenzile suddenly and pressed her hands against her ears. "Don't you know any words other than 'rockets', 'cannons' and 'tanks'?"

"So what do you want?" Wasile called from the clay oven. "Poetry recitals?"

Rizen laughed out loud and that hurt Tenzile, especially because she thought that Rizen was laughing so loudly to let Wasile, at the clay oven, hear that he was laughing. Tenzile ran to her room and sat angry and upset behind her sewing machine. Instead of going to console her, Rizen went in search of something to do. He began by digging the earth from around an orange tree in order to replant it elsewhere. The onions could not grow well in its shade.

He replanted the orange tree and that made Simahen more angry than when the birds picked at the seeds, fruit and vegetables.

"Rather replant the onions, not the tree!" she cried.

As the effects of the blockade became more serious and Iraq could no longer sell its oil, the residents of Boran began growing vegetables in their gardens and even on their balconies if they did not have a garden. Simahen removed the stones from the garden and took the rubbish away. With Rizen's children she fetched more fertile soil from the banks of the Thirsty River, mixed it with the bird droppings and laid her vegetable garden out. When Simahen was not sitting at the wall of the party's house, she worked in the garden.

A scarecrow in the centre of the garden was supposed to scare the birds away, but the birds quickly realised that the scarecrow was a pole with rags and ate the newly planted seeds. Sometimes Simahen gave Rizen's children money to chase the birds away, but they were quick to run off to buy ice lollies or sweets. One night she went to the toilet and saw Adam standing at the closed front door. She came up with a plan to use him as a scarecrow.

The next morning she led Adam to the middle of the garden, where she had just planted some seeds, and said in his ear that he must stand still. A moment later he was back in the stable. Simahen asked Mira to fetch him and she drove a branch into the ground, to which she tied a second one like a cross. She put Adam against it and with Mira's help tied his hands and feet to the branches.

When the birds had also become used to the sleeping Adam

and landed on his arms, which looked like dead branches, Simahen had a fresh idea. She saw that if Adam moved and made a noise, the birds were frightened. So she began to burn Adam with a cigarette, because if he kept on groaning she could be sure that no bird would land in her garden. At night she smeared burn salve on his wounds so that he could lie down and the following day could stand groaning in the garden again.

Mira told Simahen that God would not approve.

"While God is a merciful God," answered Simahen, "he created this boy fast asleep. And so can I not, as a mere person, just use him for a few days to chase the birds away from the seeds to fill children's stomachs?"

So Mira also began burning Adam with cigarettes when Simahen was tired. And when Adam fell over with the branches, Simahen made a cross of more sturdy branches. If she could not hear his voice, but could hear the chirping of the birds, she called Mira. "Take a cigarette and chase those birds away with it." Mira understood what she meant.

One day Mira saw that Adam was trembling on the cross. When she put a cigarette out on his arm, he stopped trembling and began groaning. She told Wasile that perhaps Adam had a fever, because she had discovered that he began to tremble when he heard the birds. Wasile said that perhaps bird flu was going around and Adam had caught it, and she gave Mira a vial with drops from her medicine bag. When Rizen's children saw what Mira and Simahen were doing to Adam, they began collecting cigarette stubs and put them out on Adam's skin.

Tenzile got a shock when she realised what they were doing and when her children told her that they were imitating Mira and Simahen, she began hitting the children. The children scattered in all directions, but when Tenzile caught one of them, she stubbed a cigarette out on their hand to make sure that they would not do it ever again. Tenzile wanted to bring her children up as she thought right and hoped that they would later protect her from Wasile and build her a separate room, kitchen and shower, separated from the rest of the house by a wall, without Wasile ruling over the kitchen.

But Wasile never gave her any such opportunity. Wasile had

the money, with which she bribed the children by buying them sweets and ice lollies, and at meal times it was Wasile who dished up the food, and divided the meat if there was any. If a child favoured Tenzile, they got a little less food than the rest and if a child pestered Tenzile, they received an extra piece of meat. Tenzile only felt at ease if Rizen or Sjahid were at home, because the children were afraid of them, especially as the time for Sjahid to go to the army approached.

A week before the time was up he invited Mohamed Mansour and Yasin Al Terref out to eat at the Saddam kebab restaurant in Saddam street near Saddam square.

"In the Bible there's the story of the last supper. This ..." said Sjahid to his friends, "...is the last kebab." Then he told them that he would not go to the army. Mohamed Mansour asked him if he would escape across the border, but he said he would not venture that far.

"What are you going to do then?"

Sjahid answered with a smile, so as not to contaminate the kebab. "I'll go back to mother earth."

As the sun went down, Sjahid bade farewell to his friends. He stayed in his room for the last week before he had to present himself to the army. If the children made too much noise, he came outside threateningly with a slipper, chased the children down the street and disappeared into his room again.

On the seventh day he walked wanly through the house and looked at everything with a melancholic gaze. Then he picked up a shovel and removed the earth from in front of Dime's room, which they dared not come near when they were children, not even Djazil, out of fear of scorpions. He pushed the wooden door open. The smell of the past and the silence hit him in the face. Everything in the room was covered in a layer of dust and spiderwebs.

Sjahid picked up the mirror that Dime had used to harm her face. The passing of the years had made the blood drops look like rust. Sjahid looked in the mirror at himself and saw he was sitting under a spiderweb. A kohl pencil was lying on the ground, a wooden comb with long black hairs in its teeth and stripes of caked dust. In one corner a blue dress was lying on the ground. He turned round, held the dress up and saw that a tall, thin woman must have worn it and not a fat witch, as Simahen had always said when she was young.

Sjahid heard someone calling his name. He left the room, shut and door and pushed the earth back in front of it, as if he did not want the silence of Dime's room to escape to another time.

"Weren't you scared of the snakes in there?" Mira asked him.

"I think the only person who's ever lived in that room was a tall woman with long, black hair," said Sjahid absent-mindedly. A rocket made all the pigeons fly off.

"You're covered in spiderwebs, go and have a shower," said Mira.

"These aren't spiderwebs," said Sjahid. His throat felt as if it was pressed closed and breathing was difficult. When he realised he was speaking to Mira and that she would perhaps not understand him, a tender smile crossed his face.

In the garden Sjahid suddenly saw Adam standing tied to the wooden cross. His head hung on his chest and he was groaning. His skin was covered in burn marks. Flies buzzed around the bird droppings in his hair. Sjahid was alarmed, ran up to him and began untying the ropes.

"God touches the sleeping ants with a finger of moonlight," whispered Adam.

Sjahid broke the branches of the cross into pieces over his knee, but Adam's hands remained hanging, as if he was nailed to a cross of air.

"Mira!" screamed Sjahid.

When a rocket fell near the banks of the Thirsty River, he and Adam fell to the ground.

Sjahid screamed: "Mira! Who crucified Adam?"

"Simahen," said Mira hastily as she came running up thinking that the rocket had fallen in the garden and that was why Sjahid was making such a racket.

"She even crucifies sleep!" cried Sjahid and he took the axe that Joesr had used to break his room down. Mira pushed Adam quickly into the stable and went to fetch Wasile, while Sjahid swung the axe around. He began hacking at the trees and churned the ground where the ungerminated seeds were.

Wasile thought that Baan's soul had taken possession of her children's bodies, first Joesr and now Sjahid. Her soul made them break down everything around them. Wasile was afraid that if Baan's soul took possession of Adam, he would also take up the axe and would kill her. So she burnt the haft of the axe and threw the iron blade into the Thirsty River.

While Wasile lay nervously in her bed that night, Djazil crept up to the roof and kept watch on her room, where she hid the case with dollars at night, deep in the holes, until he fell asleep. That was the last night on which Joesr, Sjahid and Djazil all slept in the house; Joesr in the cellar out of a feeling of guilt for Baan, Sjahid on top of the cellar in his room, shocked by what had happened to Adam, and Djazil above them on the roof, snoring loudly.

Sjahid could not sleep well that night. He did not get much air. He did not understand why he had not noticed what was happening in his own house and thought of Joesr, who always had something for others. He regretted that while Joesr was busy trying to find a solution, he was merely busy with discussions to let it be seen that he was good at having discussions.

"The spiderwebs," said Mira the next morning, "are still there from yesterday or did a spider spin a web on your head while you were sleeping."

Sjahid did not answer, but his breathing was rasping.

"Do you need a pill?" asked Mira. "You sound blocked up."

Sjahid shook his head and asked Mira where Joesr was. Mira pointed to the cellar. Sjahid went to the trapdoor, below which Joesr had buried himself, and stared for a while at the plank on the trapdoor. He seemed to hesitate, but turned round a moment later with a bowed head and walked slowly to the hole that Wasile had made. Mira walked behind him, ready to catch him if he fell.

"Where's the door?" he asked Mira, coming to the place where he had seen Wasile working. Sweat of shame ran over his cheeks, because he was going to go into the hole that he had previously laughed about while Wasile was making it.

"What door?" asked Mira, hearing Sjahid's anxiety increasing.

"The door to go down." He avoided saying "the door into the hole".

Mira brushed dung and straw to one side until a small trapdoor became visible, just big enough for Sjahid. From his room he fetched the calendar with Catalan women that Naji had given him, and when he came back to the trapdoor he saw Wasile standing next to Mira with her hands covered in dough. Sjahid did not look at them. Wasile wanted to tell him that she had made a wooden ladder, so he could get down easily, but when she saw how ashamed her son was, she turned away with a lump in her throat, nudged Mira and walked away with her.

Sjahid lowered himself through the trapdoor and found a small, but fully furnished room. A carpet on the floor, a mattress, a mirror on the wall, a lantern. He sat down and looked up through the hole, which allowed the light to shine in. A sheep looked down and began bleating. Someone pulled the sheep away and closed the trapdoor. Sjahid sat in the space as if he had gone blind. A rocket fell nearby and Sjahid felt the earth around him, on him and under him tremble. He heard the mirror fall down and break. Mira threw a box of matches down, closed the trapdoor and spread the straw and cow dung over it.

Sjahid became anxious in that stuffy space under the ground and did not think he would be able to stand it for very long, but through the air pipe that Wasile had cleverly hidden, he suddenly heard a strange woman's voice calling: "That's his mother!" He heard men's voices, at which the woman called again: "Her son insulted Mr President!" Sjahid's heart began beating faster and he crawled back against the wall, as far away from the air pipe as possible, as if the hands of the men could pull him out through it.

"That is his mother!" cried Henadi again and she pointed at Wasile. "Her son sat in his room and swore at Mr President." She then pointed at Joesr's room, which was no longer standing. "That's the room, but God broke it down, because Mr President was sworn at from inside it."

One of the men from the secret police, who had been brought to the Bird household by Henadi out of vengeance for the death of her daughter, asked Wasile who had lived in the room before it was broken down.

"No one," said Wasile.

The man walked threateningly towards her and put his pistol to her head.

"No one?"

"Joesr," said Wasile with trembling lips. Sweat from the clay oven mixed with the anxious sweat that flowed from every pore in her body. Behind her stood Mira, Tenzile and the children all next to each other on the trapdoor.

"Where is he?"

"He's dead."

"Where?"

"In his grave. He sees no one and no one sees him."

"She's lying!" cried Henadi.

The men from the secret police looked at the two women, who would have started hitting each other if the police had not been there. They began searching the house. When they came into Simahen's room, she thought that Nadus and her sons had finally returned and she fell to her knees and began thanking God. At the trapdoor they saw ants crawling around the food that Mira had set down there and the plank that Joesr had nailed to it. They opened the trapdoor and saw Joesr sitting hunched in the darkness. They brought him to Henadi.

She got a shock when she saw him. His beard was greyish and long, the wrinkles on his thin face were black from the dust in the cellar and his clothes were rumpled. Henadi believed that Saddam Hussein had driven him mad, because he had sworn at him. She believed that Saddam Hussein had transformed the boy, who had said he would marry Baan if his brother did not come forward, into a monster.

"Is that him?" asked one of the men.

"More or less," said Henadi.

"Take him away," said the man.

Two men roughly pulled his hands behind his back and pushed him in front of them.

"Where are you taking him?" cried Wasile, who also got a shock at the state Joesr was in, but one of the men ordered her to shut her mouth.

"He is dead! He is buried!" screamed Wasile, but the men took Joesr away. Henadi walked behind them.

That day Mira took the dog away from the cellar and tied it up at the trapdoor where Sjahid was hidden, so that she would not forget to bring him food and drink.

In jail Joesr was held in a hall full of people. They did not question him, because they thought that he was crazy, but wanted even less to release him, because they were afraid Henadi would lay a complaint against them and a report would be written about them. Joesr sat in a corner next to Diary, a young Kurd from Arbil. When the secret police called Diary to the front at night to torture him, Joesr stood up and went in his place.

Three months later all the prisoners were sent to the army, because the war was becoming more serious. They signed a petition to Saddam Hussein in which they stated that they wanted to punish the enemies of the fatherland, before the fatherland punished them. After eight months in the army Joesr received five days' leave. Wasile saw him coming through the door in his uniform which was too big for him. In Sjahid's room, he put Adam's clothes on and told Mira to burn the uniform.

"Has the war finished then?" asked Mira.

"No, but I'm finished with the war."

Joesr slept for two days in Sjahid's room. On the third day he called Diary's phone number, which he had had tattooed on his arm. A Kurdish woman who could barely speak Arabic said that Diary had gone up the mountain. That evening he phoned again and asked for Diary. "On the mountain," said the woman again.

Every time he called, the same woman answered, until he got Diary on the line. He told Joesr that the only word his mother knew in Arabic was 'mountain'. Joesr told Diary in coded language that he needed someone to smuggle him over the border.

"I'm a smuggler," Diary said laughing, loudly and not afraid that the telephone was being tapped.

"You?" asked Joesr.

"Yes, me," said Diary and he laughed again. "Every Kurd is born as a smuggler or a refugee."

The next day Diary was at his door in a car. Joesr hugged him and left the house with an old coat in a suitcase, because he had heard that the mountains in the north would be cold.

"Where are you going?" asked Wasile.

Joesr did not answer her and would not accept the dollars that she wanted to give him. Before he got into the car, he went back to Simahen, who was lying on her bed.

"I dreamt that you come back running behind an American tank," Simahen said to Joesr. "But if you're here, how can you come back with the Americans?" Simahen fell silent when a rocket fell. "Make sure that you sit inside the American tank, because in my dream I see the Americans laughing at you. Don't run in front of an American tank. If you trip, it'll run over you."

"Don't you worry," said Joesr. "I'll come back running next to the American tank."

"That's better," said Simahen and she began coughing.

Joesr kissed her hand.

"Say good-bye to your mother," she said. "Otherwise the journey will be difficult."

"I'll do that ..." he said. He wanted to say he would try to do that, but the words stuck in his throat.

When Samer came a few days later asking after Joesr, as he had been doing for his entire life, Mira gave him the letter Joesr had written for him.

For my best friend Samer,

I am going to a distant corner of this world to rebuild my brain. I am not going to look for a new life, but with my new intelligence I will try to understand the life I have left behind. I have learnt a great deal and shall learn a lot more.

Your friend Joesr

CHAPTER 13

The Catalan calendar and
the new Saddam

After the men from the secret police had taken Joesr away and Sjahid had heard their voices over his head, he no longer thought about emerging from the hole. Every night Mira opened the trapdoor. Sjahid sat like a sick chicken in a corner, still afraid of the secret police. He looked smaller and stared at her with an unsettled gaze.

"I've switched off the light up here," said Mira. "Do you want to go to the toilet?"

"Not today," he said.

When Mira opened the trapdoor the following night, he immediately asked if the light was on.

"There's no electricity," she said.

"So what's that light then?"

"It's a full moon."

Sjahid climbed out and went to the toilet. After that he breathed deeply in the breeze coming from the Thirsty River and looked at the moon. When he noticed that Mira was standing waiting for him to go back into the hole, so that she could go to bed, he went to the trapdoor and climbed down.

Each night the number of words he and Mira exchanged

became fewer and fewer and after a while they said nothing to each other. Sometimes as she opened the trapdoor she heard him whispering: "Not today." After a few weeks she no longer heard his voice and she waited. If, after quarter of an hour, he had not come out, she shut the trapdoor and went to sleep. If he did not come out for a few days and did not touch the food that she put out for him, she put her head down the hole and smelt to see if he was dead. If he left the lantern at the trapdoor, she knew he needed oil and a new wick.

The calendar he had received from Naji, with Catalan women in bikinis next to the blue sea, hung on the wall in the hole. By the lantern's light he looked at the women's naked feet on the sand of the Mediterranean and began to dream. Very slowly he allowed his gaze to rise. He concentrated on each and every part of their body, until he reached the hair. Then he assembled the pieces in his imagination and fantasized a voice. The seagulls and the waves behind the woman began to move and the clouds drifted across the sky.

Silently the woman walked towards him. The flying seagulls and the clouds left the calendar to swirl around in the air of the hole. Sjahid smelt the sea and fantasized about walking down the beach with the woman next to him. He felt the sand between his toes. At the moment when he touched the woman, he leapt out of the hole into the skies above Boran, filled with smoke from the war, and dust. Then he pushed through the clouds and went higher and higher. When Mira opened the trapdoor, he woke from his dream.

He began to avoid any contact with Mira. Sometimes he came outside on his own after he had heard her footsteps receding. Emerging he would look to see if any of his clothes were still on the washing line. Then he would take them and throw them into the Thirsty River so that the neighbours would not know that he was still at home. If it was too dark to be able to see the clothes, he would throw all the clothes that were hanging there into the water. So then Mira made sure that there was nothing left on the washing line before she opened the trapdoor. Sjahid would walk along the washing line whispering. "Surely there must be some clothes."

Like a nocturnal creature he rushed carefully past Mira if she stayed and waited for him. Most of the time the outside world was dark and Mira could not see him very well, but on one ocassion during a full moon she was shocked at how thin he had become and at the length of his beard.

"Should I bring you a razor?" she asked, while he stared at the moon.

"The dead in their graves don't need any razors, just prayers."

From that night on Mira prayed for Sjahid. Wasile heard her and said that it was not necessary because he was not dead yet, but Mira told her that Sjahid had requested it. That surprised Wasile because she had not expected that Sjahid, who did not believe in God, would ask anyone to pray for his soul. Wasile gave thanks to God. She believed that it was the hole that had brought God into Sjahid's heart. When Rizen came home during his leave, Mira asked him to kill a rooster for Sjahid's soul.

When Rizen was on leave in the winter, he took his children to the market and bought baklava for them. In the summer he took soap and a sponge to the Thirsty River and washed his sons there one by one. He also let them kill chickens, so that they would become men in the future. If there were puppies, he put them in a sack, which he took along and let his sons throw into the Thirsty River. After a while he stopped doing that, because the children fought amongst themselves as to who would throw the puppies into the Thirsty River, and once he saw the children trying to put the head of a big dog into a sack. He told Tenzile that if Mr President set the children of Iraq loose in Israel, they would throw the Jews into the sea. To which Tenzile said that perhaps the Palestinians would also be thrown in the sea by them.

If the children heard a rocket coming down, they ran to that place and collected the shards of metal. They hoped that they would see dead bodies, so that they would be able to tell exciting tales when they got home. If an execution was taking place nearby, they hurried to it. One day Edjnaad stood in the throng, near a soldier standing tied at a wall ready to be executed because he had been absent for three days from the army. His hands were tied behind his back.

The soldier looked at Edjnaad and whispered: "Hey, boy, come closer."

Edjnaad shuffled up to him.

"Take the money out of my trouser pocket and buy a cigarette for me."

Edjnaad felt in the soldier's dusty pocket.

"There's no money."

"In the other pocket," said the soldier. He urged Edjnaad to hurry up.

Edjnaad shuffled even closer up and smelt the clay air hovering around the soldier. Carefully he put his hand into the other pocket. One of the soldiers saw him and thought that he was stealing from the condemned soldier. He gave Edjnaad a kick on his arse, at which Edjnaad ran away through the throng. The soldier came after him to give him a beating. The children saw what was happening to Edjnaad and stood further away from the condemned soldier standing tied at the wall.

"Hey, you there," hissed the soldier and winked at Saddam. "Take the money out of my pocket."

Saddam was lucky enough to be able to take the money from the trouser pocket without being seen. From a boy hawking bubble gum, cigarettes and water among the spectators to the execution he bought a packet of cigarettes and showed it with the change to the soldier.

"Keep the money and the rest of the cigarettes," he said. "One is enough."

Saddam opened the packet and took a cigarette from it.

"Light it," whispered the soldier.

Saddam lit the cigarette with a lighter from the hawker, shuffled back through the mass of people and tried to put the cigarette in the soldier's mouth, but the soldier was too tall. Saddam stood on his toes and the soldier tried to bend over, but the ropes prevented him from doing so.

Suddenly Saddam felt two hands grabbing his ears. They lifted him into the air until the cigarette reached the soldier's mouth.

Behind him stood one of the soldiers who would be an executioner. "Put it in his mouth," said the soldier.

Saddam put the cigarette between the condemned soldier's lips. The executioner put him down and took the packet of cigarettes and the rest of the money for himself.

For months Saddam related how the cigarette remained burning in the mouth of the soldier and did not fall to the ground when his head fell forward after he had been shot dead.

The children tried not to make Rizen angry, because then he would scream and hit them hard. He would put their hands in the fire and throw stones at them. Sometimes he would put one of them in a sack and lower it into the Thirsty River, only to lift it out just in time. If Rizen was not angry at them, he let them wear smart clothes, saw to their wounds and combed their hair, sang songs and changed from a wild animal into a gentle lamb. Sometimes the children could ride on him as if he were a donkey, hit him with a slipper on his head or his arse and grab his moustache like reins.

That is why the children liked Rizen while at the same time were afraid of him, except for Saddam, who did not like Rizen and was not afraid of him. When Rizen was at home, he avoided him. If Mira asked him if he did not want to see his father, he pursed his lips. Saddam never said much. Sometimes he spoke with Edjnaad, when he helped him with his homework. Edjnaad discovered that if Saddam had an idea in his head, he ignored every counter argument so that his idea could flourish. Saddam thought long about the television and the remote control and eventually told Edjnaad that there should be two remote controls for every television. One that changed the channels and one to turn the television around, so that you would not have to move if you wanted to watch. Edjnaad laughed and said that a television was not a tank.

Saddam got on well with his oldest brother Edjnaad, but he had a dislike for Rasjad, never calling him by his name, but always 'hey' or 'you'. After Edjnaad once said to Saddam that he should choose another name, because he would be without a name if Saddam Hussein disappeared, he then only sat with Edjnaad if he was helping him with his homework.

Before Saddam, Tenzile had two miscarriages because of the bombardments. Saddam survived. He grew up thinking that Saddam Hussein was his father. Always and everywhere he saw him and heard him, on walls, on the television, over the radio, through windows, in the air. He heard and saw more of Saddam Hussein than of Rizen, who was in the army most of the time. If he heard Saddam Hussein on the television, Saddam would go up to it. "Papa Saddam, Papa Saddam!" he called.

"I want Papa Saddam," he sometimes said to Tenzile and started crying.

"Where must I find Papa Saddam for you?" said Tenzile. "Not even God and the Americans know where he is so they can free us from him."

From his earliest years Saddam had frizzy hair that was full of lice, because no one looked after him, just as was the case with his younger brother Tali. Saddam was never scared. When he was three years old and there was not enough to eat during the time of the blockade, he crawled after the goats, pushed the kids aside, grabbed the goat's udder and sucked the milk straight from it. Mira caught him like this once and pulled him away from under the goat. Saddam looked angrily at her, as the milk dribbled from his lips. Mira told Wasile what she had witnessed. Wasile asked Tenzile and Mira to prevent Saddam drinking goat milk like that, because otherwise he might grow horns and become a goat.

"That child is only good for the army. Mr President can then teach him to become a man," said Wasile when Saddam was six years old and did not appear to be the brightest student at the school.

Mira saw Saddam putting puppies into a sack and staggering to the Thirsty River. "Not just by name," she screamed, "but you are also just like Mr President. One day you'll put us in a sack and throw us in the river."

Then Saddam laughed happily at the compliment that he was strong and brave.

When Mira told Tenzile about Saddam, Tenzile complained: "It's not his fault. It's his father's fault. He gave him the name of Mr President." He had done so because a rocket had once landed among a group of soldiers. Only one had survived, the one who went by the name Saddam.

Sometimes Simahen found it pleasant if one of the children sat with her in the shade. "Bring me the son of Sabha!" she would call out to Tenzile. She complained to the child, as if he understood her. "Ah, Saddam, you know no mercy. You have a heart of iron."

When Saddam turned seven years old, he began to kill the chickens. Mira watched amazed at how he slaughtered a rooster and, with its head in his hands and a glitter in his eyes, watched the headless rooster jumping around. Sometimes he disembowelled a sparrow with a razor and watched the final beat of its tiny heart.

"Your son is wild. Not even Djazil was so bad when he was a child," Wasile once said to Tenzile.

Tenzile straightened her back with pride. "Naturally. He's named after Saddam, isn't he?"

When Saddam Hussein appeared on the television, the young Saddam stared at the screen, as if drawn by a magnet to the president. When Rizen was home on leave, Saddam avoided him, as if he did not want to know that Rizen was his father and not Saddam Hussein.

One day Rizen asked his children to go and fetch water from the Thirsty River, because there was no running water and there were fifteen soldiers visiting as they travelled through Boran on their way to Basra. Each child took a pot or a bucket from the kitchen and hurried to the river. Saddam, not paying attention to what he was doing, hurriedly grabbed a sieve.

"What's that in your hand?" asked Rizen.

"This," said Saddam and held up the sieve. Then he noticed that it was a sieve and not a pot.

"Fool, do you want to go and collect water with a sieve? Wash your mother's arse with a sieve?" shouted Rizen and hit Saddam over the head with it.

Saddam, unperturbed, looked at Rizen. "Why don't you wash your mother's arse," he said.

Rizen laughed loudly. "Take the sieve, wash your mother's arse and the arse of my mother and then wash my arse," he said.

Saddam went and stood in a corner in the kitchen and grumbled, while a rocket fell in the distance.

"Why have you come back without any water?" asked Mira.

"He ...he didn't think that I knew that a sieve couldn't hold any water," said Saddam.

"Why do you call him 'he' and not 'father'?" asked Mira.

Saddam did not answer and went to Simahen's room. He softly opened her door and went in. Because she was sleeping, he turned the fan on himself. It was not spinning because there was no electricity, but when it did return the cool air would blow in his direction. He lay down and fell asleep.

The first one to notice Saddam's link with Saddam Hussein was Joesr. One day Saddam asked Joesr why the sky did not fall to earth although it was not resting on poles.

Joesr told him it was like that so that the birds could fly underneath it.

"That's not true," said Saddam.

"Well, what then?"

"The sky is blown up," said Saddam. "Like a balloon, look. He took a balloon out of his pocket and blew it up to prove his point."

Joesr gave him some money to go and buy some sweets.

A few days later Saddam again came to Joesr's room. "Wasile said that God can create everything," he said. "Can he create someone who is cleverer than he is?"

Joesr laughed loudly and threw some money down for him. "Probably could," he said between laughs.

"Like Papa Saddam?"

When Joesr heard that, he began screaming. "Papa Saddam? You son of a bitch!" Joesr stormed over to the television in the sitting room, picked it up, went outside and threw it to the ground. Then he began breaking it into pieces with a hammer, as if he was raining blows on Saddam Hussein. "Look," screamed Joesr, "now you no longer have any Papa Saddam!"

Saddam never forgot what Joesr had done to "Papa Saddam". That's why sometimes, when Joesr had gone into the cellar and Mira left a plate of food at the door when the dog barked, he pissed on Joesr's food. Saddam was used to seeing Saddam Hussein on television, circled by dancing children, in white clothes and with a white smile. So when the television was no longer there, he then went to the neighbours and sat in front of their television.

"No," he said when the neighbour asked him if he was sitting and waiting for Tom and Jerry. "I want Papa Saddam."

Because no one knew how Saddam thought, everyone considered him stupid. He picked up one of the sentences from the blackboard and worked through to its furthest point, deeper and deeper, wider and wider. Other information was unimportant. Every year he was kept back. After six years at school he was still in the third grade. Because he was so much older, he was the biggest in the class and he sat at the back, so that the other children would be able to see the blackboard.

Once he scratched noisily at his hair, which was full of lice. The teacher sent him home. "Wash your hair, get rid of the lice and come back tomorrow," he said loudly, so that the other children could hear. The following day Saddam still sat scratching. This time the teacher sent him away with a letter. Saddam threw the letter away, just as he did the next one, and began showering carefully, so that not a single drop of water would disturb the lice on his head. He hated the teacher, who had ensured that the other children sat far away from him, because they did not want any lice.

When the teacher saw that Saddam kept on scratching, he called him to the front and pointed at the door. "Go away and come back with your father!"

"I don't have a father," said Saddam.

The pupils fell silent in shock.

"You don't have a father," cried the teacher. "So where do you come from then?" He directed the stick in his hand at Saddam's head and scratched around with it in his hair.

The children laughed and Saddam stood still, as if nothing was happening. "Answer me; where do you come from then?"

"Out of my mother's cunt," said Saddam.

The children laughed even louder, until the teacher swiped at his desk with a bang and it became dead quiet in the class.

"Choose a punishment," cried the teacher. With red chalk he wrote the three options on the blackboard: forty canings on the feet, sixty canings on the palm of the hand, five canings on the back of the hand. One of the pupils had to read the punishments out, so that it was clear to everyone.

Saddam was given fifteen minutes to decide. The pupils stared at the red words on the board and at Saddam, deep in thought. Sixty canings on the palm of his hand would tire the teacher's hand and that was good, but his hand would swell up and would take days to get better. With forty canings on the soles of his feet he would have to lie down and there would also be swelling, and together that was not good. So he chose five canings on the back of his hand, which was more painful than sixty canings on the palm, but he would be able to use his hands immediately.

The teacher prompted Saddam to read out clearly the punishment he had chosen.

"Five canings," said Saddam, and he held out his hands. "Three on the right and two on the left."

The teacher asked him why.

"Because my right hand is stronger and can stand the pain better than the left."

"Then I'm changing the punishment," said the teacher. He wiped the sentences from the board and wrote the chosen punishment down: five canings on the back of the right hand or five canings on the back of the left hand. With each caning the children closed their eyes in unison, but Saddam stood still and looked right in the teacher's eyes without making a sound. The sweat streamed from his face and the lice fled from his head, which had become too hot. The teacher, who always had the pretty boys stand at the board and name the parts of the body as he touched them, sent Saddam to the bathroom to wash his face.

On the way to the wash rooms Saddam began to think over how he could take his revenge on the teacher. His brain was working hard and intensely and kept doing so for some two months. Tenzile thought he was sick, because he could not sit still, with his eyes like a chameleon's taking everything in, until he had thought of the appropriate revenge for the teacher.

Nesrien was the teacher's four-year-old daughter. Saddam had kept a close watch on the teacher's house and had discovered that sometimes in the afternoon, when everyone else slept during the hottest part of the day, the girl played in the sand outside the door of the house. She built houses and dug rivers. With an empty rice sack, Saddam lay in wait one afternoon, ready to pounce, while Nesrien made a house for her doll. He walked up cautiously and sat next to her on his haunches, opened the sack and told her with a smile that he would take her to the swings at the Sugar Festival if she would sit in the sack. When he saw that the girl became scared, he quickly stood up and left. The following day he went past her and smiled until she waved back with her doll. With this he went up to her again, knelt next to her and let her see a young, white dove that had just grown feathers and which he had put in the sack. Next to it were some sweets. The girl looked at the dove.

"If you go and sit next to the dove, I'll take you to the swings at the Sugar Festival," said Saddam with a gentle voice.

The girl went to sit next to the dove. She put her doll down beside her and held her hands around the dove like a nest. When Saddam saw that no one was watching, he tied the sack and picked it up. He walked with big strides to the Thirsty River, afraid if he ran the girl would scream and people would notice what he had in the sack. The girl kept asking if they were at the swings at the Sugar Festival yet. On the bank of the Thirsty River he chose a place between the trees where no one could see them, opened the sack and saw the girl sitting with the dove in her hands.

"Where are the swings?" she asked.

"Just wait," he said to set her at ease. He carefully placed stones around the girl, as if he was building a wall around her.

"What are you doing?" the girl asked.

"I'm building a nest for the dove," said Saddam. When he thought there were enough stones, he winked at the girl. "There, now we're going to the swings at the Sugar Festival."

He closed the sack, took a piece of string out of his pocket and tied it up. He threw it into the Thirsty River and watched how it sank. Air bubbles appeared on the surface.

That evening Edjnaad called Saddam to help him with his homework, as he always did.

"It's not necessary," said Saddam. "The teacher's not coming tomorrow."

"Why not?" asked Edjnaad.

"He caned ten times and not five."

Chapter 14

Shi'ite, Sunni and English medicine

When Edjnaad was fifteen years old, he no longer liked sleeping in the same room as Tenzile, Rasjad, Saddam, Shibe and Tali, and especially not when Rizen was at home on leave. So he began building a room in the place where Joesr had demolished his room.

"Build no room in this house," screamed Simahen, when she saw Edjnaad tidying up the place. "The house will be blown up." She hit him with her stick, but laughing, he jumped out of the way of the mother of his grandfather. Simahen chased away the friends Edjnaad had rounded up to come and help him, but they waited behind the house until she fell asleep and then began building. When she awoke, shaking her head, she let the boys continue with what they were doing, but she never went into that room. When she needed Edjnaad to translate the English leaflets that came with her medicines, with a medical dictionary that he had bought with her money, she called him.

From the day on which a fridge had arrived in the Bird household, she never believed that the medicines should be kept in it. She sniffed at the medicines as she did with meat or vegetables to see if they were still okay and did not check the expiry date. For her the only expiry on medicines was when they were finished.

Edjnaad could not sway her even when he told her that medicines past their expiry date were not medicines at all, but poison. "This tonic expired two years ago already, you mustn't drink it," he said to her.

"Medicines that have expired are better. Then they understand me and can help me, because I too should have expired a long time ago."

Just as she did not believe in expiry dates, she did not trust Arabic medicines. "Don't buy them and don't let them into your body," she said to Edjnaad.

"Why not?"

"English medicines don't differentiate between Sunnis and Shi'ites. Just look at the English when they came to Iraq. Arabic medicines are different. If they are made by Shi'ites they are no good for Sunnis and if they are made by Sunnis, they are no good for Shi'ites. If they are made by someone who does not believe and is Arabic, they're not even good enough for the Kurds."

"I don't think medicines differentiate between Shi'ites and Sunnis," said Ednjaad.

"They do so," said Simahen. "One day I gave some drops to a Sunni woman. Her eye was healed, but I got such an itch from it that my eye became like a tomato. So Sunni medicines are for Sunnis and Shi'ite medicines are for Shi'ites and English medicines are for everyone."

Simahen believed that all medicines that came with leaflets not written in Arabic came from England. Because Edjnaad had to translate them, he thought seriously about studying pharmacology, especially during the blockade when he saw people breaking down the roofs of their houses and selling the steel in them to buy medicines for their sick relatives.

Tenzile was not happy that Edjnaad was building another room to the house. After she had given up hope that Rizen would build a house for her and free her from the family home, she turned to the hope that Edjnaad would go to work after his studies, earn money and marry a woman who also worked. A

wife who would not accept that her mother-in-law still lived in
the Bird family household and would take Tenzile to live in
their own home. There she would cook for them and clean and
she could look after the children. But Edjnaad built a room and
simultaneously broke down Tenzile's hope of him disappearing
from the house.

Because of the blockade that Wasile imposed between
Tenzile and her food, Tenzile became weak. Simahen called
her.

"You must eat. Make sure you get a bit fatter than you are,
you have a husband. Your flesh is not just for yourself, but also
for him," she said. Tenzile did not tell Simahen that Wasile
blockaded food from her, just like the Americans had blockaded
the Iraqis, but as her intellect became ever weaker, her power
became less and Wasile's blockade of Tenzile grew more
intense.

The only way in which Tenzile would ever be free of Wasile
would be through Wasile's death. Because Tenzile believed that
women only died from old age and men from the war, she
believed that she would she would first have to wait for the
death of another, Simahen's death. Tenzile was not inclined to
hope too much for something, like for someone' death, but she
did not think of Wasile's death as death, but as a solution.
Tenzile had a kind heart that was filled with tenderness and
thirsted for warmer times. If she had been born in another
country, where women were able to make their own decisions,
she would have studied psychiatry or become a hairdresser.
She would have lived in a small flat with a dog or a canary with
two balconies, on which the sun would shine when it came up
and when it went down. Her balconies would be filled with red
flowers and she would always have been in love.

If Tenzile thought back to the times when she meant
everything to Rizen, she became depressed and cried, but she
told that to no one, because then they would think that she
needed another man. When she was alone in her room, sitting
behind her sewing machine, she let the wheel spin and cried
over her lifelong imprisonment. She tried to strike up a
friendship with Mira, to be able to talk with her about her

problems, but Mira ran through the house the whole day long between the kitchen, the garden, the chickens and the stable where Adam lay, and had no time for any friendship. So Tenzile unrolled her prayer mat in the direction of the Kaaba and directed her complaint in a quiet voice to God. She could not pray for too long, because then Wasile would think that she was sleeping. So she complained briefly to God and quickly went back to sit behind the sewing machine.

One August 29 a pleasant feeling came over Tenzile. It was a quiet evening. She could not hear the voice of Saddam Hussein on any television or radio and there were no ambulance sirens wailing. She lay on her bed and immediately fell asleep. She dreamt she was walking through a field of sunflowers. Her hair was flowing behind her because she was not wearing a headscarf. Because she was afraid that someone would see her hair, she picked blossoming sunflowers and put them in her hair while laughing out loud and then stopped, because no one must hear her and think she had gone crazy. When she heard the sound of running water, she felt thirsty and went to the Thirsty River, in which clear water was flowing. On the bank Saddam Hussein was standing in his white clothes, just as in the dreams of Wasile, Baan and Simahen. He smiled. Behind him stood someone who looked like Djazil, dressed in dusty, old clothes. He had wings on his shoulders and was wearing sunglasses. Tenzile laughed and went towards Saddam Hussein until she could smell his cologne. His face radiated light.

"Who's that man behind you, Mr President?" she asked softly.

"He is my angel," said Saddam Hussein.

"Why is he wearing black glasses?" She did not know the word 'sunglasses'.

"So that his eyes stay healthy in my radiance. If you look for too long, you'll go blind, Tenzile."

"Why aren't you wearing any?"

Saddam Hussein laughed out loud. "What comes from me, does not make me blind."

Tenzile began rubbing her eyes.

"Look, it's starting already. I'll soften my radiance a little," he said. The light around him dimmed.

"That is Djazil behind you, Mr President, but with wings," Tenzile said, amazed.

"That's right. That's Djazil and because he is standing behind me, he has the wings. He is my angel and he will free you from Wasile."

When Saddam Hussein said the word 'Wasile', Tenzile felt the apprehension piling up in her heart. She began pulling the sunflowers from her hair and the laughter disappeared from her face. She knelt before Saddam Hussein so that she could touch his shoes and began crying.

"Look, Mr President, my hair has turned grey because of my suffering under Wasile." She repeated the sentence over and over with an ever-softer voice.

Saddam Hussein touched Tenzile's head with his finger in the dream and she suddenly awoke to see that she was kneeling beside Wasile's bed. She had been sleepwalking and was suddenly aware that Wasile was staring angrily at her.

"Go to your room. You're talking in your sleep."

As Tenzile went back to her bed, Wasile decided that she should receive even less food, but when she felt a stabbing pain in her back, she had second thoughts. Perhaps the pain in her back was a warning from God not to do that, because then Tenzile would surely die of hunger.

That night Wasile tossed and turned in her bed from the pain in her back, but she could not sleep. Groaning she went to the sitting room, where Edjnaad and Rasjad were watching television with the volume turned down. The screen was filled with a talking Saddam Hussein in military uniform.

"If you're not watching the television, why do you turn it on?" said Wasile.

"After Mr President, there's a horror movie," said Edjnaad.

"You're just trying to make Mr President angry with us." She turned the volume up.

Saddam Hussein began talking. Wasile forgot her back pain when she heard the voice of Saddam Hussein filling the sitting room. Because he was looking at her, she politely sat upright, as if he was there with them.

Edjnaad and Rasjad began giggling next to their grandmother and winked at each other.

"Mr President is looking at you, gran," said Edjnaad seriously. "He wants to talk to you. Listen carefully and call us for the horror movie when he's finished."

He left the room with Rasjad. They took the remote control with them and left Wasile alone with Saddam Hussein. Wasile felt her skin prickle when she saw Saddam Hussein smiling at her. She forgot about her back pain and suddenly began crying, which she also did not understand. Edjnaad and Rasjad looked once through the curtains at their grandmother and did not understand why she had to cry. Wasile thought of the day she had dreamt about Saddam Hussein and he had ordered her not to become pregnant again.

"Why are you crying?" Wasile heard Saddam Hussein saying in her head at the moment when Edjnaad turned up the volume on the television to fill the sitting room with Saddam Hussein's voice, which sounded like the screeching of a raven. Wasile saw his eyes, staring at her from the television screen.

"I'm crying, Mr President," she said.

Edjnaad turned the volume down with the remote control. Wasile thought Saddam Hussein had gone quieter so as to hear her answer. That was the moment at which she could actually talk about herself after all those years in the home of the Birds.

"I'm crying because of the pain in my back, Mr President."

"She's speaking to Mr President," Rasjad whispered in Edjnaad's ear.

"Ssshhhhh," hissed Edjnaad. "Not so loud, she'll hear us."

"Can you hear what she's saying?" Rasjad asked.

"She's speaking so softly, she's afraid of Mr President."

"Make her talk louder," said Rasjad.

"What? You've also lost your mind. I've only got a remote control for the TV and Mr President, I can't make her go louder!"

"She's starting to talk again," said Rasjad.

They strained to listen to their grandmother.

"Not just my back, Mr President, but my whole body is in pain. My shoulders, my legs, my feet and this ..." said Wasile and hit herself on the chest.

When Edjnaad saw that her lips had stopped moving, he made the television even louder.

"What do you want to relieve the pain?" Wasile thought she heard Saddam Hussein saying.

"I want you to bomb Iran with a few rockets. I've saved up Iraqi dinars and have been waiting such a long time for your rockets, so that the dinar will rise in value and I can change them into dollars to buy a car for Rizen. You've been too late with your rockets this time, Mr President ... Too late ..."

Edjnaad pressed the volume control to make Saddam Hussein laugh.

"Tomorrow or the day after tomorrow," said Saddam Hussein.

Edjnaad made the TV quieter again.

"Don't worry about it, tomorrow or the day after tomorrow I will bomb Teheran with rockets, although I ended the war with the Persians a long time ago," Wasile heard Saddam Hussein say in her head.

What happened after that, Edjnaad and Rasjad never understood. The remote control fell from Edjnaad's hand while he was watching his grandmother. Wasile said to Saddam Hussein that she had a terrible pain in her back now and again from standing and baking bread and wanted him to free her from the pain. He asked if she could come right up to the television so that he could touch her back. She shuffled up to the TV, turned her arse against the screen and pulled her dress up. Edjnaad and Rasjad saw that her underpants were made from the curtain that had disappeared from her room, because during the blockade there were no longer any underpants in the shops, and so they discovered why there were no longer any curtains in her room. Edjnaad and Rasjad jumped back from the window, because they thought that she was touching the screen because she wanted to make love with Saddam Hussein.

An hour later Wasile called them because Saddam Hussein had finished his speech. Rasjad no longer dared go up to the television, but Edjnaad noticed that Wasile's face was more peaceful and happier and that the pain had left her face.

"Tomorrow or the day after tomorrow the price of the dinar will soar. Then I'll buy a fountain pen for you," Wasile said before making the tea and going to watch the film with Edjnaad, happy that the pain in her back had disappeared. When the American horror film began, she asked Edjnaad to read the subtitles.

Wasile had never seen any films apart from the black-and-white Egyptian ones, in which boys with no money always fell in love with girls, after which they emigrated to Saudi Arabia, Qatar, Dubai or Kuwait to earn money and forgot their beloved in an ocean of wealth. In the middle of the film they suddenly thought about the girl, who had been waiting for years without hearing from them, and then they decide to return to Egypt in a luxury limousine. After a long search they find their girl. She has become a belly dancer and he feels guilty. The film always ends with the buying of a villa and in the final scene the man and the woman sail along the Nile in a hired boat at sunset.

The American horror film that Wasile watched that evening was different. In the darkness, a man with red eyes looked through the window at a sleeping girl. The full moon shone down on her half-naked body. Suddenly the man's fangs became longer. He leapt inside and bit the sleeping girl on her neck. The white sheet turns red with blood. The following day the police come and she is buried, but the next night she appears out of her grave with long fangs and red eyes to go and bite a sleeping girl.

Wasile sat watching, numb with terror. "Oh God, help us. This film has turned the TV into a butchery."

Wasile went to her room terrified. She was sorry she had seen those few minutes of the film, because now she could not sleep. Eventually she fell asleep with difficulty, but she dreamt that Baan came out of her grave and knocked on the window. She woke with a start and heard something in the kitchen. She went there to investigate and heard the crackling of hot oil in a pan. Through the kitchen window she saw Djazil standing and frying an egg. His hand was white like a woman's. She looked at his feet, which were the feet of a woman, with blue slippers. He turned round and stared at Wasile, who saw that he had the face of Baan. There was a bloody hole in Baan's forehead. She held her severed right hand in her left hand, as if she wanted to fry it in the oil.

Trembling, Wasile dragged Mira to the kitchen, but there was no one to be seen. There was no hot pan and no smell of eggs being fried. From that time on, Wasile had nightmares every night. Sometimes she saw a red light in the window, to which she was drawn, and then she saw Baan standing in the darkness with a red light that was like the eyes in that horror film and which shone out of the hole in her forehead. Then she wanted to scream, but could not get it out. When she fetched Rizen, he saw no one. Sometimes she saw Baan in her room, holding the severed hand in her other hand and trying to untie the yellow string. Sometimes she woke up drenched in sweat with a burning spot on her forehead, as if the severed hand had touched her with a finger, as cold as ice.

When she could no longer sleep, she went to the mosque and told Sheik Abdullah Al Najafi that the devil had come to her during the night. Sheik Abdullah Al Najafi advised her to read a passage from the Koran that would chase the devil from her room. Because she was illiterate, she had to buy a cassette recorder and listen to recorded passages. With the lilting voice reciting the Koran, Wasile could sleep for a while again, but after a few weeks she awoke and saw Baan's severed hand with two wings doing its best to turn over the cassette recorder.

After she had spent the night outside, she went to the mosque and complained to Sheik Abdullah Al Najafi. This time he advised her to go to Mecca. With passport photos in her hand she waited at the window in the passport office. The official, who spent the whole day doing crosswords after travel had been forbidden, asked her what she was doing there.

"They say that you should wait here if you want to go to Mecca."

The official waved for her to come up to the window. She handed over the photos to him, because she thought she was going to get a passport.

"Go home. Find a people smuggler to take you to Mecca," he said. "Getting a passport is more difficult than getting wings on your back. Why did God not create a Mecca in every country, so that Muslims could go there without having to make use of smugglers?"

Because Sheik Abdullah Al Najafi could not help her, she went with two cockerels to a fortune-teller and told him the story of Baan. The fortune-teller told her that Baan appeared to her because she had not been buried according to Muslim tradition. Wasile decided to search for Baan's grave. She pulled a burka over her face, so that no one would recognise her, and asked around for the place where Baan had been buried.

Because Baan had been killed in a matter of family honour, she had not been buried in the usual cemetery. Eventually one of the women told her that a taxi driver had willingly taken her with Henadi to be buried among the date palms. Wasile went in search of the driver and asked him to take her to Baan's grave.

"Henadi cried the whole way and said that it was not her uncle who had killed her, but a woman who goes by the name of Wasile," the driver said to put her at ease, because he did not know that he was talking to Wasile.

When Wasile knew where Baan was buried, she took Djazil to one side in her room. She shut the door and pulled out the bag filled with dollars from under her bed. She took fifty American dollars out of the bag and gave it to him.

"What's this money for?" asked Djazil.

"To make a grave for your child."

"What child?"

"The one in the belly of the girl."

Djazil looked at the fifty dollars and said nothing. Wasile opened the bag again and took another fifty dollars from it. Djazil saw that there was a lot more still in the bag.

"You'll get this when you're done with the grave. I'll only give it to you once I've seen the grave." She pushed the bag with the dollars between her breasts, afraid that Djazil would steal the money now that he knew where she had hidden it and she told him where Baan was buried.

Djazil disappeared and came back two days later. He swore

that he had made a grave at the place where the taxi driver had stuck a palm frond in the ground. Because Wasile did not take him at his word, he took her to the place, where she saw that he had built a grave with stone and cement. There was also a gravestone at its head, but because she could not read, she did not know that it had been stolen from a man named Abid Ali Abd-al Hassan. The stones were also stolen. She opened her bag of money and gave him the promised fifty dollars. She recited the Al Fatiha sura from the Koran, which she knew by heart, and felt herself released.

That same day she bought a lamb and sacrificed it for Baan's soul. Everyone could eat as much as they wanted, even Tenzile. That night she slept like a rose. With renewed energy she lit the oven the following morning and thought of her bag filled with dollars, which she had put under her bed as she usually did when she went to sleep. Suddenly she ran to her room, because she had forgotten to hang the bag around her neck. She felt under the mattress for the bag, which would have had exactly the right amount of dollars to buy a car if she had not had to pay the hundred dollars for Baan's grave. It was not there. She turned the mattress over, put her hand between her breasts and felt around her neck. She took off all her clothes, searched them thoroughly and turned in circles in front of the mirror to see where the bag of dollars had gone.

Without putting her clothes back on she ran to Mira's room. "Djazil! Djazil! Have you seen Djazil?" she screamed.

Mira got a fright seeing her mother naked. "I saw him leaving just half an hour ago," she said.

Wasile ran behind the house in the direction in which Mira had pointed, naked, just like Dime, and screamed: "My son is a thief. Grab him!"

Everyone in the house ran after Wasile. Edjnaad threw a blanket over her, after which she put on her clothes and scoured the streets and the date palm orchards in search of Djazil, who remained out of sight. The next day she took a stick and walked for hours through the town to find her son. On the third day she asked Edjnaad to go with her, while she went through the streets calling his name.

The morning after that she could not get up. She remained groaning on her bed. "Everything's gone. Years of my life have been wiped away. Between the clay oven and Djazil, they've stolen it away," she groaned. "Djazil has killed me. Just as he killed that pathetic girl with the child in her belly, just as he buried his brother alive in the cellar, so will he bury my life."

She got up from her bed once more and took a taxi with Edjnaad to the party's house. There she told one of the party members that they had to find Djazil, because he had insulted Mr President. Because she thought that she would find her dollars if she found Djazil."

"Who is Djazil?" asked the party member.

"My son," she said.

The party member looked angrily at her and began screaming in her face. "When you run away from each other, you want Mr President to find you, but when you run away from Mr President, you won't find each other." He asked for Djazil's full name.

"Djazil Kosjer Nadus Bird," she said.

The man stood up and went from behind his desk over to a wall lined with shelves, on which lay a file for every family in Boran. Using a stepladder, he took down a file from the top shelf. He began reading. "The Bird family have been fighting against Mr President from the very moment he became leader of Iraq in 1979." He leafed through the papers. "And now Joesr has fled, Sjahid has fled and so has Djazil as well," he said.

Wasile's face became pale.

The party member stood up, put the file back, took hold tightly of Wasile's hand and led her to the door of the party's house.

"Never come back here again," he said. "The party does not find what you want, but what it wants for itself."

Wasile kissed the party member's hand and thanked God that she had encountered a good comrade that had not incarcerated her in the party's house. Then she went to lie down in her bed and she became one of the people whom Mira looked after. From that moment on Tenzile could walk through the house without feeling she was being followed by Wasile's eyes or making her angry. If Tenzile had had any money, she would have sacrificed a ram with big horns to thank God for releasing her.

CHAPTER 15

How Saddam Hussein's shoes closed the market

As Rasjad grew older, he became ever more gentle. He had inherited his mother Tenzile's tender heart. From the day when he had first gone to school, he had stopped throwing puppies into the Thirsty River. When he thought back to how he had burnt Adam with cigarette butts, he begged God for forgiveness. Tenzile was concerned about him because he no longer fought with the children on the street or came home with a black eye and torn clothes. She complained to God that Shibe, who was scared of no one, had been given the heart of a boy and Rasjad the heart of a girl.

So she set Rizen the task of schooling Rasjad, so that he would become a man and that his heart would become stronger. Rizen taught him to butcher chickens, took him to the date palm grove at night, where foxes and wolves howled, and forced him to walk back alone with a dagger in his hand. When it became clear that Rasjad's heart was becoming stronger, and Rizen began leaving him to his own devices, his gentle nature returned. In about his tenth year he began looking interestedly at girls and to think about them under the trees in the garden.

One day Edjnaad cornered him. "Why are you crying like a girl?" he asked, seeing the tears running down his cheeks.

"I've got toothache," Rasjad said, and held his hand against his cheek.

"So why are you sitting here all alone?"

"I don't want to go to the dentist." Edjnaad saw the hearts pierced with arrows that Rasjad had carved into the tree trunks and could not understand how his brother could think about hearts when he had holes in his teeth.

When Rasjad began to grow a moustache, he began to search for English songs. A friend had given him a tape by Abba. He played it all day long in the kitchen, where the tape recorder was. Mira quickly became fed up with it, pulled the plug from the wall and gave the recorder to Rasjad. He went to sit in Sjahid's room and listened to the tape until he knew all the songs by heart. He listened to English radio broadcasts, which did not have as much interference as Arabic broadcasts.

"Mr President will send you to jail if he finds out you're listening to foreign broadcasts," said Mira.

"Why?"

"He'll think that you're an American."

"Then I'll be the happiest person on earth."

"What do you mean?"

"Like I said: I'll be so happy if some miracle would now turn me into an American. They'll quickly send an aeroplane, throw a rope down and take me to America."

"But the Americans are our enemy," said Mira.

"Maybe that's why I want to be an American so badly."

"Do you also talk like this at school?" Mira asked anxiously.

"I only talk like this with you and to myself."

"You must stop thinking like that. Americans are filthy. They eat pigs, like Jews and hate Muslims. They're barbarians. If I catch an American, I'll put a rock in his pocket and throw him into the Thirsty River myself."

A rocket saw to it that silence settled in the area and the birds suddenly stopped their chirping.

"You sit here the whole day. You know nothing," said Rasjad. "Americans are filthy because they eat pigs. We are filthy, because we are pigs. The Jews kill their enemies, but they don't kill each other, like happens here."

"If you keep on thinking like that, you'll disappear just like your Uncle Joesr or hide yourself under the stable, like Uncle Sjahid. It's dangerous to think like that."

"I never think, I just wait."

"What for?"

"To go to America. Every time I see an American film, I want to go there. To freedom."

"Freedom? Aren't you free here?" Rasjad laughed out loud.

"Yes, Mira, I'm completely free here. I'm free to be a thief like Djazil, to run away like Joesr, to hide myself away like a rat like Sjahid, to sleep my whole life away like Adam, or to fight like Rizen. Or to cry that the years of my life are disappearing like Wasile, or to wait for something that will never come, like Simahen."

"I'm not giving you any more money to go to the movies. Those American movies are making you crazy."

"You've actually just opened my eyes. Now I know that I'm living like a bird in a cage."

"You've only just grown a moustache and you're already talking like that. What will you be saying when you have a real moustache?"

"I'll shave it off and throw it down the toilet for the cockroaches."

Mira laughed and pressed what money she had in his hand, as Tali and Shibe came running up and jumped into her arms.

"What are Americans?" asked Tali.

Mira put him on the ground and hurried to the kitchen because she could hear the chickens there.

Every time a new American film came to the Sinbad cinema, Rasjad nagged Mira for money to go to the movies. The Sinbad cinema had air-conditioning. In the heat of summer when it was fifty degrees outside, the cinema was filled with soldiers escaping from the heat. They slept in the cinema, snoring through the film, and woke up at the end to go to the station and travel on towards the war. The cinema had a generator.

Even when there was no power, there was air-conditioning and the film kept going. After the first show of the day, almost no one went, unless they heard that there were 'snacks'.

Snacks, in the language of the patrons of the Sinbad cinema, meant that there were sex scenes in the film. Normally these were cut from the film, but Paulus, the owner of the cinema, now and again let the entire film be seen without warning and then it became dead quiet in the cinema until the snacks were finished. The more snacks, the more patrons. As soon as the snacks were over, the visitors left the hall, except for those patrons who had come to sleep or to see the film, but these could be counted on one hand. News that snacks were to be had spread like wildfire. Then the hall would be jam-packed for the matinee performance, but if Paulus decided that there would be no snacks in that showing, the patrons went angrily back to the ticket booth to demand their money back.

Paulus was a small, bald man with a round belly. His shirt was always open to display his chest hair, in which a gold cross glistered. He would stand against the throng and address them.

"Guys, it spites me to say, but no snacks today. I run a cinema and not a restaurant. You must learn to come and watch, not eat," he would say to the protesting public.

"But with the previous showing there were snacks, why not now?" the filmgoers screamed angrily.

"They're all finished!" screamed Paulus. "All eaten up."

Nevertheless, Paulus still regularly provided real snacks. 'Real snacks' meant real sex, not just kisses and caressing of bras. It was always the same five-minute clip. In a farmyard a girl with blonde curls slowly took her clothes off in the straw, while a boy in overalls watched her every movement. When her dress became a circle around her feet, he walked up to her. Then they kissed and fell in to the straw. The boy kissed her mouth and her panties. When he pulled the panties down and her pubic hair became visible, the five minutes of real snacks ended and the lights of the cinema flickered on. Then everyone went quietly outside, satisfied and a little uncomfortable.

The government would rather have had the youngsters

watching war films instead of westerns with sex in. The films that showed in the cinema were mostly war and action films, and for that reason the posters that appeared on the street mostly showed kung fu, taekwondo and karate, archery, sword-fighting or fencing.

One day after long debate, Paulus did not show the five minutes of real snacks. He was afraid of the police.

"Guys," he shouted, "no farmyard and no flesh on the straw. If it's sex you want, I'll fetch my mother and a volunteer can fuck her."

Everyone laughed loudly and then went on their way. It was obvious that Paulus really could not show any snacks.

Rasjad regularly played truant and went eagerly to watch the ten o'clock performance at the Sinbad cinema. The hall was almost empty at that time. When the showing was over at twelve o'clock he went home, crept into Sjahid's room and looked at the paintings in his drawing book, where flowers grew on the edge of small lakes and women with exposed breasts lay on large beds embroidered with gold and above them naked angels hovered on their wings, as if they had only been created to flap about in rooms and not in heaven.

Through those pages, Rasjad's masculinity was stirred for the first time. He spent his afternoons among the trees in the paintings, on the edges of the lakes, under the cloudy skies, where the burning sun did not exist. He walked along shaded paths, climbed in the branches, made love to women, after having chased away the angels and closed the windows and the curtains to be alone with them and their sleeping faces, which were filled with peace and not anxiety.

In the beginning Mira asked him not to go into Sjahid's room, but when she saw that he sat there to draw, she let him be. Months later Rasjad sometimes thought that Sjahid's room was his own, but he never changed anything or left anything behind when he left. He played Catalan music or the Abba tape and disappeared in a world of painting, far from the war, from Saddam Hussein and Hadi the Rocket, from soldiers and women dressed in black, holding their emaciated children in their arms, malnourished thanks to the blockade.

While Sjahid sat in the hole, Rasjad always locked the door when in his room. This was because Sjahid, one day before his disappearance, suddenly came in while Rasjad had a book open on a page of naked women and was busy pleasuring himself. Sjahid pretended not to notice anything. In consternation, Rasjad wanted to leave the room, but Sjahid told him to stay.

"Can I come and watch you and Naji when you next make a mural so I can learn to paint?" Rasjad asked.

"You won't learn anything about painting from Naji and me, except for Saddam Hussein," said Sjahid, and he gave him an art book. "Take this. It is Da Vinci. From him you can learn the Mona Lisa." He gave him another book. "And this is Goya. From him you can learn De fusillade."

"Can I keep these books?"

"Yes, and use my paint, brushes and pencils." With that Rasjad began painting Adam, because he did not move, unlike Mira when he tried to use her as a model. It was as if Rasjad was only really seeing Adam for the first time, and he stared intensely at him for a few minutes. Then he put his pencils down and wanted to ask Mira about Adam's story, but a rocket landed on a house a few streets away, which made all the windows shatter. Rasjad ran to the kitchen and forgot Adam and his painting.

One evening Rasjad was in the sitting room when he heard Adam groaning. He took him to the Thirsty River, because he thought he was feeling the heat. There was a full moon. There were no trails of smoke blocking the moon and it bathed the water and the trees with its soft light. Rasjad went into the water and carefully pulled Adam with him. Adam walked into the water as if he were entering another world. He was not afraid, but became calm and stood in the water mumbling in his own words that no one could understand. "The wind sweeps the steps," whispered Adam when the water reached his knees, but he went no further.

Rasjad splashed him. "Perhaps he'll wake up tonight, because the moon is really beautiful," he whispered to himself.

When he saw a rocket explode in the distance, he became scared that another would come down closer to them and Adam would fall in the river and be swept away by the water.

From that night on he took Adam with him whenever he went swimming in the Thirsty River. He let him stand up to his knees in the water and splashed him. He spoke into Adam's ear to teach him to speak, but he received only repetitions of old words as an answer, words like those that Mira said when she chased the chickens, or words from Simahen before she went to sit in the shade.

"He is not a man, he is an old tape recorder," Rasjad said to Mira, when he took Adam home.

Days later he listened in amazement as Adam, in the water of the Thirsty River, repeated those words.

"I am not a man, I am an old tape recorder."

So Rasjad discovered that Adam did not only have his own incomprehensible language, but could also repeat words that he had heard. Rasjad began listening carefully to him and came to hear Simahen's words, Wasile's words when she asked God to free her from that house, the monologue Joesr had with Mira when he was in puberty, when he read books and wanted to save the world, Sjahid's words about his dream of going to the art academy and the song 'No soy de aquí', which stuck in Spanish in his head. Rasjad began whispering words in Adam's ear. He discovered that he received the words back in sentences.

"Joesr, school, cellar," he whispered, and dribbled water on Adam's lips.

"Joesr left school and left home and went into the cellar, because Wasile chased away Henadi and Baan who was pregnant with Djazil's baby," said Adam, in Simahen's words to Mira.

Rasjad never revealed how he knew what had happened among the family. He was afraid that Wasile would cut Adam's tongue out if it said anything more about her, that Simahen would tie his hands and throw him into the Thirsty River, or that Hadi the Rocket would shoot him dead if he repeated a speech by Saddam Hussein, which were always and everywhere resounding from radios, televisions and windows, through which the president changed from a communist comrade into a Muslim leader.

Wasile was shocked by some of the questions Rasjad asked about past events in the family. She thought that Simahen had become senile and had started telling everything. When Adam was standing in front of Rasjad one afternoon, with his head hanging like a rag doll, he uttered the first sentence that he had ever said to anyone.

"My heart is calling you."

Rasjad asked him for the reason behind his long sleep, but Adam repeated the same sentence.

Rasjad did not believe that he had actually said it to him and thought that it must be one of the sentences that Adam had once heard. That was the first and the last sentence that Adam said to Rasjad, because Tenzile called Rasjad to tell him that she had chosen him to leave school and go to work to earn money for the family, and not Edjnaad, because he was cleverer.

When Djazil had stolen the dollars from Wasile, she began lying in bed all day long and baked no more bread. The money that Tenzile earned with her sewing was not enough to buy food for the whole family. From the wages Rizen received, he could not even come home sometimes. So Rasjad went to seek work in restaurants and shops, fruitlessly. Eventually he went to Naji's house and asked him if he could work for him.

"There's no longer any space for new murals," said Naji, as he took a gulp of his whisky. "I'm waiting myself for the paint to fade or for someone to throw shit over one so that I can work."

"But there's lots of work," said Rasjad. "The clothes that Mr President is wearing are no longer in fashion. Maybe it would be best to change them on the murals."

Suddenly Naji's face lit up. He clapped his hand to his forehead. "Why didn't I think of that?" He quickly stood up. "Come tomorrow. There'll be lots of work." He got dressed and hurried to see Hadi the Rocket.

A while later Naji stood in the office of Hadi the Rocket. A comrade gave him a glass of cold water and tea while from behind his desk Hadi the Rocket lauded the presidential election, in which 99.99 per cent of the votes had been cast for Saddam Hussein. The air-conditioning blasted cold air into the room. On the wall hung photos of Saddam Hussein.

"Historic election. Never before has a people chosen so overwhelmingly," said Hadi the Rocket.

"I cannot imagine Iraq without Mr President," Naji offered in response.

"Iraq?" said Hadi the Rocket. "I cannot imagine the world without Mr President. In Israel even a child in the womb is given a gas mask, because they're scared of him. Spectacular, inspiring. Netanyahu himself sleeps with a gas mask, if he is able to sleep at all, of course."

"Mr President is the leader of all Arabs," said a comrade standing at the door.

"The leader of Arabs and others," said Hadi the Rocket.

"I do not want to take up your precious time, but I have something very important to discuss," said Naji politely. "Mr President must change his clothes."

"What?"

"I mean on the murals," said Naji. "His clothes and his shoes are out of date. As you know, his head, his hands and his hair have not changed, but his clothes have. He is old fashioned and must be renewed. This is a great responsibility."

Hadi the Rocket immediately decided that the clothes on the murals of Saddam Hussein had to change. It had to be done quickly, before the visit of Saddam Hussein to Boran, which had been expected for years. Hadi the Rocket was afraid that Saddam Hussein would see himself in clothes from the time of Brezhnev. That same day he established a commission to collect funds from the people in order to renew the clothes of Saddam Hussein on the murals.

Some time later, in a little village, a woman and her family were shot dead by the soldiers from the commission. The woman had lost her husband and sons in the war and had nothing to eat, but the commission saw the ring on her finger and wanted to take it. She lost her patience, which she had maintained for years. With a kick she threatened the commission. "Arseholes, we have no coins and no food, and you want to change the clothes of Mr President on the murals? You and your Mr President can bugger off."

The day after the visit to Hadi the Rocket, Naji and Rasjad began changing the clothes on the murals. In the beginning Rasjad passed the paint to Naji, fetched tea for him and painted Saddam Hussein's shoes. With time he moved up and after a year Rasjad was allowed to paint the shirt collar. The day that Naji tapped him on the shoulder and told him that he was ready to paint Saddam Hussein's face was a special day in Rasjad's career. Although he had longed for that moment, he was afraid.

"Master Naji, do you really think I'm good enough for the face of Mr President?"

Naji spat angrily on the ground. "Look, master Rasjad, when we are not alone, then say 'Mr President'. But if no one is around, then don't say that word. Otherwise I won't pay you one red fils."

"What should I say then?"

"Whatever you want. God, motherfucker, son of Sabha. But never ever say 'Mr President', not even when you hear me say it."

Rasjad had long waited for the moment that he could paint the face of Saddam Hussein, but because Naji saw that he was afraid, he painted the face himself and did not ask again. Until one day he said that Rasjad should sleep well that night, because the following day he would actually be painting the face of Saddam Hussein.

Rasjad entered the house quietly with his clothes smeared with paint and told Tenzile and Mira that tomorrow he would be painting the face of Saddam Hussein. They began praying and asked God to help Rasjad. Mira made rice with saffron, raisins and lentils, so that he could eat well and sleep, but Rasjad could not sleep because he was so stressed. When the cockerel crowed, he had a glass of tea and walked to the mural in clean clothes, but with his nervousness showing on his face.

He was too early. He waited far from the mural until he saw Naji coming and then walked with him to the painting.

Naji smoked and Rasjad prepared the paints.

"Don't forget that it's the face of Mr President that you're painting," said Naji. "Don't let the paint drip, otherwise it'll be your own blood that'll be dripping. Is that clear?"

"It's clear," said Rasjad from above.

At the moment when Rasjad went to take the first brush stroke, he saw a girl walking by with a big suitcase. She walked behind a man, also with a big suitcase, and behind them a woman with a child in her arms. The girl looked at the mural of Saddam Hussein and Rasjad looked at her. She turned her eyes from the face of Saddam Hussein to the face of Rasjad and looked at him with her shining eyes as she walked on. Then she walked slower. Rasjad felt it.

'Ferdous, hurry up," said the woman.

The girl took a few more valiant steps. Her body leant to the side on which she carried the suitcase and her eyes were fixed on Rasjad's. She turned as she walked so that she could keep on looking at Rasjad.

The paint fell from his hands to the ground.

Naji thought that the paint had fallen out of nervousness at the prospect of painting the face of Saddam Hussein. "Come down. You're not ready for it yet," he called.

Rasjad hurried down the ladder, while images of the girl flashed through his head.

"It took you months to get from Saddam Hussein's shoes up to his face and you're still scared? Take this." Naji threw some money at him so he could go and fetch breakfast.

Rasjad picked the money up and ran in the direction in which the girl had gone. She was carrying a suitcase, so she had to be going to the railway station, where it was always busy with hawkers, buses and taxis. He saw the suitcases tied to the top of a car. The girl was sitting beside the woman in the back seat. When she saw him, she looked surreptitiously at him. Rasjad went closer and asked the woman through the open window where the car was going.

"To Amman," said the woman.

"When is it coming back?" he asked, as he looked at the girl and felt his heart in his throat.

"I don't know, you'll have to ask the driver."

Rasjad wanted to hear the girl's voice and to know where he could see her again. "Are you coming back from Amman?" he asked hurriedly.

"We're coming back," said the woman. "But Ferdous isn't," she said and patted the girl on her shoulder. "She is going to marry her cousin and go to Germany."

Rasjad wanted to ask more questions, but saw the man looking angrily at him, because he was talking to his wife and looking at his daughter. As he walked through the throng, he thought about Ferdous. He felt waves surging from his belly, through his heart to his head, and ran back to the car. It was just beginning to move through the throng. He ran next to it and saw the eyes of the girl searching for him and looking at him as she spotted him. He wanted to touch the car window, but was afraid of the driver and her father. Emerging from the throng, Rasjad stood in the middle of the street. The car disappeared in the distance, with Ferdous looking out of the back window, not daring to turn round.

Rasjad heard a hooter and realised that he was standing in the middle of the street.

"Ass," a driver shouted at Rasjad, who ran to the pavement. He bought breakfast for Naji and took it back. Just as he had been unable to sleep the night before because he had been thinking about the face of Saddam Hussein, Rasjad could not sleep that night because he was thinking of the face of Ferdous. In the dark, he went to the station, as if she would be waiting there for him. He sat down and stared into the emptiness.

When some soldiers arrived to catch the day's first bus on their way to the war, he walked around until the sun came up then went to the market to ask for the price of a people smuggler to Amman. It cost one hundred and fifty dollars. Because he earned a quarter of a dollar from Naji and had to give at least half of that to Mira for groceries, he would probably have to change the clothes on every one of Saddam Hussein's murals seven times before he could travel to Amman.

Every time he thought of Ferdous's eyes, or of the few minutes he had seen her, he almost went crazy. He did not have as much time as his grandmother Wasile had when she had been saving for a car, because Ferdous would be married to her cousin within a few months and go to Germany. Instead of Amman, he would then have to be smuggled into Germany. He spent half the day working, and the other half thinking about Ferdous.

In September he and Naji worked at night, because the heat during the day was too fierce. At the mural, Naji clipped on the builder's lamp and began painting a uniform over Saddam Hussein's normal clothing. He changed the cigar between his fingers into a gun. Rasjad had not slept well for days. While thinking about Ferdous, he painted one of Saddam Hussein's shoes green, and the other one blue. Naji was drunk and did not notice it. Before the sun came up, they went home.

"Come round tomorrow at the same time," said Naji as Rasjad set off home. "We'll do the mural at the police station."

Just as Naji was falling asleep, he heard his door being broken down. He switched his bedside lamp on and saw his room filled with soldiers.

"Are you Naji?" they asked him. They gave him no opportunity to answer, but dragged him outside.

"Let him bring some black paint," said a soldier in the car that was in front of the house.

Two soldiers allowed Naji to fetch a brush and a pot of black paint and took him to the mural. Soldiers were standing everywhere. The market was empty, because everyone had been turned away, apart from three men who had been chained up, and a donkey laden with vegetables. One of the men held in his bound hands the rope to which the donkey was tied.

"Sir. We didn't see Mr President, but the shoes ..." said the man, who was the father of the other two.

"Shut your mouth," said one of the soldiers. He hit the man in his face with the butt of his Kalashnikov. "And you, get up there," the soldier ordered Naji and pointed at the mural.

Naji looked but through his nervousness and tiredness was

unaware of what he had to do. "What's the problem here?" he asked.

"You were here the whole night long and look what you've done!" The soldier pointed at Saddam Hussein's shoes. It was as if Naji had been pricked with a needle when he saw that one of the shoes was green and the other blue. With the black paint, he climbed the ladder like a monkey, up to Saddam Hussein's shoes. "I hope I manage to stay alive after these shoes," he whispered with trembling lips.

When the colour of Saddam Hussein's shoes had been changed to black, Naji climbed down. Before he could say anything about Rasjad, the soldier ordered him to shut his mouth. Two soldiers took him to a green jeep. The brush in his hand dripped the last of the black paint on to the dusty ground.

"What must we do with them?" one of the soldiers asked and pointed at the three men and the donkey who had inadvertently seen the shoes of Saddam Hussein on their way to the market to sell their vegetables.

"Take them along!" said the officer, but when he saw that the donkey followed behind them to the jeep, he laughed. "Let them go," he said. "Did you see anything?"

"We saw nothing, Sir," said the father. Flies sat on the blood on his face.

"Go then," said the officer.

When the three men saw that the jeep carrying Naji and the soldiers was heading away, they threw the vegetables from the donkey and ran in the direction of their village. The donkey ran after them. When they saw that, they stopped, the father sat on the donkey, and they ran on.

Naji sat in the jeep. Each time he wanted to say something, the soldiers hit him. That morning soldiers with a megaphone in front of his house told everyone that they could take whatever they wanted. Not even two hours later, everything had gone, even the doors, the electrical wiring and the trees from the garden.

At sunset Rasjad walked with a pot of food in his hands, to Naji's. With his mind on Ferdous he stopped at the place where there had always been a door. He wanted to knock in the darkness, but there was no door. Inside only bare walls remained. Rasjad got a fright. He thought that there was a wild animal in the house and that it would devour him, just as it had eaten the doors and everything else. He called out to Naji, but received no answer. He ran outside and hurried home through the empty streets.

"Halt! Halt!" he heard.

Rasjad stopped.

"Hands above your head."

Rasjad put his hands in the air, still holding the pot of food for Naji.

From behind him, a soldier with a Kalashnikov came into view. "Why are you running?" asked the soldier. A rocket came down and made the ground beneath them tremble. "Answer me. Why were you running?"

"I've got diarrhoea," said Rasjad, breathlessly.

"Don't move and don't shit in your pants," said the soldier sternly. He frisked him and found nothing, but when he smelt the food, he told him to lower his hands. The soldier took the pot of food, removed the lid and saw by the flame of a lighter that it was rice and chicken. "Leave the pot here and run home before you shit yourself," he said.

Rasjad ran home, this time because he really did have diarrhoea, from nervousness.

Mira saw him hurrying to the toilet. "Why are you back so soon?" she asked him when he emerged.

"Everything's gone," he said fearfully. "Doors, windows, things and Naji."

"Go and look for Naji and stop talking like Adam," said Mira.

"Tonight I don't have to look for Naji, but for a people smuggler."

"You're not thinking straight," said Mira. Another rocket fell nearby.

"Ah, Mira, I have to go to Amman before a rocket falls on my head or before I go crazy."

"Perhaps it's better to run away. If I wasn't a woman and didn't have to look after Sjahid, Adam and Wasile, I would have run away from this house long ago," said Mira and she fetched the gold ring from her room, which she had been given by Simahen when she had been unwell for the first time. "Sell this when you need money." She gave the ring to Rasjad.

"That is not enough," said Rasjad. "I need a hundred and fifty dollars to get to Amman."

Mira took Rasjad by his hand and dragged him to the back of the house, where no one could hear them. She whispered in his ear that he should go to the market and ask for Abid-the-harelip. On his left ball he had a birthmark. Rasjad asked her how she could know that, at which she told him that when Abid was still a child she had looked after him for a week. Abid would take him to Djazil. She took off her watch and gave it to Rasjad.

"Give this watch to Djazil. Tell him that you've got nothing else and he will smuggle you to Amman, because he won't want you to know where he is and tell it to Wasile, who's looking for him to get her dollars back," she said.

Rasjad did not want to take the watch that she had long ago been given by Joesr, but she insisted. "It is just a weight on my wrist. I don't need it. Joesr and Sjahid once used to ask me for the time, but no one asks me any more. I haven't even asked myself."

Rasjad was amazed at the information provided by Mira, whom he never saw outside of the house. In the market he asked after Abid and after half an hour he was standing in front of a man with a harelip, just as Mira had said.

"You get vegetables from my aunt," said Rasjad. "She once looked after you and washed you in the Thirsty River. She said she paid careful attention to the birthmark on your left ball."

Abid laughed out loud. He turned his back, unbuttoned his trousers, looked at his left ball and saw the birthmark, which he had never noticed before.

He embraced Rasjad. "Your aunt knows my ball better than I do," he said, proud that someone had remembered the birthmark on his ball from so long ago.

Rasjad felt that the birthmark on the left ball of Abid-the-harelip would help him to get to Ferdous and he was thankful for that. Abid took him to a pick-up truck and two and a half hours later Rasjad was sitting in front of his uncle Djazil.

"Does your grandmother know you're here?" he asked.

"She doesn't know." Rasjad gave him the watch. "Mira knows, but she won't tell."

Djazil looked at the watch, which he had always wanted. He tried it on his wrist, but because it was too small, he put it in his pocket.

Rasjad stayed for a week in a small room built of clay. Every night Abid brought a new person. Abid's blind mother looked after everyone. In the small house she only had one small gas stove, a mattress, a few pots and one large plate. She cooked for herself and for Abid and Djazil's clients. Each night she counted the number of people in the room, by touching them on the head, to cook for them. Then she knew how much rice and beans she had to prepare. If they were hungry, Abid and Djazil's clients would let themselves be counted twice in the line.

When she was done with counting she would grumble. "People have lost their sense of direction. Once upon a time all you needed to cross the border was a camel, now you need a smuggler. It's a hard land. It doesn't care much for its smugglers either. My son Abid has smuggled half of Iraq over the border and still has nothing, except this clay house and half a pick-up truck."

Rasjad would often later think of Abid's mother and what she had said when he helped her wash the dishes. "I wish God had created a smuggler who could smuggle Iraq away from the Iraqis." Rasjad scribed that sentence into the clay wall with a nail.

When there were sixteen young men to be counted, they were loaded into a truck filled with sheep. That night the truck headed in the direction of Samawah. Each time the truck stopped, the refugees trembled among the sheep and choked with fear until it began moving again. At the checkpoints someone always asked what was in the truck.

"Sheep," came the answer. Sometimes a soldier shone a torch on to the sheep, or walked around the truck without looking into it and told the driver to drive on. At one of the checkpoints, a soldier saw the refugees. He negotiated with Abid and Djazil, and would not let the truck proceed until he had been given three sheep.

As a joke, Djazil grabbed hold of one of the refugees, who began stuttering.

"I ... I'm not a sheep."

Djazil, Abid and the soldier laughed.

At a farm in the darkness, the refugees climbed out of the truck and Rasjad went with a quiet, thin man in a car. After another half hour, they stopped.

"Guys, this is Jordan," said the man, who told the men to get out.

"Is that Jordan?" asked Rasjad, as if he had been expecting something different.

"Of course. And that is the highway to Amman."

It was still dark. Rasjad stood still and tried to decipher the number plates on the passing cars. The other refugees went their separate ways and a little later it was just Rasjad and the man left standing there.

"Which way is Amman?" asked Rasjad.

"That way." The man pointed to the highway, turned the car round and left.

Rasjad had never felt so alone. He had nothing apart from seven dollars, the ring and the eighteen years of his lifetime. He waved down a truck loaded with watermelons and got a lift to Amman. In the back of the truck, on top of the watermelons, his heart was beating faster because he was nearing the city where Ferdous was. The towns through which they drove became bigger and busier, but nowhere did he see any murals of Saddam Hussein or soldiers, checkpoints or comrades in uniform. Even the air was different.

CHAPTER 16

Rasjad, don't climb that mountain!

Adam stood for days on end in front of Sjahid's room, where Rasjad had resided in the final days before he had disappeared from the house. Mira was amazed that Adam had begun to use his hands. When she opened the door for him, he went and stood in the middle of the room. His head was bowed in the direction of where Rasjad had always sat in the winter to draw while talking to himself, so that Adam could hear him.

Rasjad had opened his heart to Adam but was unaware that Adam heard his voice in his sleep like drops of water. Adam had missed the sound since Rasjad had left. He turned on the tap and listened to the drops, which sounded like the voice of Rasjad. If there was no water, Mira saw him putting his ear to the tap. When Tenzile cried and repeated Rasjad's name, Adam would walk slowly to the tap and watch it, as if Rasjad would appear out of it. Every day as evening fell he would walk to the Thirsty River, stand knee deep in the water and listen to the babble of the waves, as if he was listening to Rasjad.

One day Shibe heard him saying 'the late'. She went to Mira. "Perhaps he's going to die," she said.

"Who?"

"Adam."

"He's long dead," said Mira.

Shibe swallowed hard. Someone in the house was dead and walking. Now and again she got a fright at night when there was no power and she saw Adam feeling his way through the house, but Shibe, who was just as fearless as Simahen, was not afraid of the tales and did not disturb Adam.

Shibe was said to resemble Simahen when she had been a child. One day Simahen was sitting behind the house on her mat. She saw Shibe coming from the Thirsty River with a bucket of water and thought she was dreaming and seeing herself as a child. She waved for Shibe to come to her. Shibe put her bucket down and came closer. She looked at the mother of her grandfather, who began complaining about her long wait that would not end with death, but would live on beyond it. Tenzile called Shibe to bring the water.

The following day Simahen stared at Shibe and thought she was still asleep. Because she was thirsty, she called for someone to wake her up. She became confused and when Mira realised what was happening, she told Shibe to hide herself, so that Simahen would not see her and think that she was dreaming.

Shibe did not realise that she was a dream to Simahen, but while still young, she learnt that it was a good thing not to attract attention. She passed invisibly and silently through the house, just like Adam. When Mira or Tenzile told her to, she hid herself from Simahen's gaze, so that the old woman could eat and drink.

Apart from Mira, no one in the house knew that Rasjad had run away. Tenzile abandoned her sewing machine, sat the whole day behind the door, cried and looked through the keyhole to see if he had returned. Rasjad had left a letter on top of the television for Adam. He had written on it: "For Adam when he wakes up." Tenzile had Shibe read the letter to her.

"On a beautiful evening I take you with me to the Thirsty River. You stand in the water up to your knees and you gaze at the full moon. Rasjad."

Tenzile did not understand the letter very well, but she understood one thing: that she would not see Rasjad for a long time, because he had written "For Adam when he wakes up" on the letter. Perhaps it was his way of saying he was never coming back.

When Simahen heard Tenzile's crying, she recalled a dream about Rasjad. She called Mira. "Tell me, in which country are there mountains? I saw Rasjad in my dream climbing a mountain and he never came down again."

"They say that the land of the Kurds has mountains," said Mira.

"Where is the land of the Kurds?"

"In the north," said Mira.

Simahen did not know how she could prevent Rasjad from climbing the mountain, which was at one time red in her dream, and black or blue at another.

"Why did God create mountains? There's no need for them?" she said to Mira. She thought that Mira was still in the room.

Arriving in Amman, Rasjad went with a pounding heart through the streets in the hope of finding Ferdous. It was a city of brick houses, encircled by arid, desolate mountains. When he was hungry, he bought some bread at a bakery and searched further. After his first day in Amman he sat behind some houses in a poor suburb thinking about the home he had left behind, about the sparrows chirping in the trees in the last hour of the day and about the chickens on the wall, and he was lonely. He wanted to cry, but when he thought of Ferdous, his heart leapt and he wanted the sun to quickly rise again so that he could continue his search. In the distance someone played a flute.

Rasjad felt his body against the ground and fell asleep, until the sun woke him. He stood up and continued his search for Ferdous. He felt he would go crazy if he could not find her or if he stopped looking. When he was tired, he sat for a while in the shade or in a mosque and fell asleep without attracting any attention. Thousands of Iraqis, out of fear of Saddam Hussein or because of hunger due to the blockade, had fled and the streets were filled with people.

By the third Friday Rasjad had seen thousands of faces, but not that of Ferdous. He was getting desperate. People gave him alms or chased him away, but his heart kept pounding for that one girl. After he had sold the ring to buy bread and water and he had nothing left, he thought he would never see Ferdous again.

That night he crept tired and hungry into a cemetery. A gentle breeze blew. He dreamt that he was sitting in Sjahid's room and had opened an art book on a page with a woman with naked breasts. He wanted to wake up to close the book so that no one would see it, but he was not able to, so soundly was he sleeping. He heard running water and smelt the wind of the Thirsty River. Mist filled the room from under the door. Rasjad opened the door and walked to the Thirsty River. On the bank, through the dense mist, he saw Saddam Hussein dressed in white and smiling at him.

Rasjad went closer and saw that the cigar in his mouth was also white. "Does white tobacco exist, Mr President?" he asked.

"Only in dreams." Saddam Hussein laughed while his shoulders danced up and down.

Tenzile called in the distance. "Saddam! Saddam!"

"I must go, I'm going to your mother. She's calling me from another dream," said Saddam Hussein and he patted Rasjad on the shoulder. He moved off in a white boat with white sails and white ropes. "And you, Rasjad, go to Al Hashemia square. There you will find what you seek."

In the Roman amphitheatre at Al Hashemia square Rasjad sat staring in front of him, when he heard someone speaking with an Iraqi accent. He turned round and saw Ferdous sitting listening to a man. She was different. She was wearing new clothes, had kohl pencil under her eyes and held a handbag under her arm. She got a fright when she saw him. He wanted to go up to her, but dared not because of the man next to her. He followed the pair to a shop, into which the man went to buy a drink. Rasjad seized his chance.

"What are you doing here?" whispered Ferdous.

He heard her voice for the first time. The voice about which he had dreamt for nights on end.

"I came looking for you," he said.

"You're crazy," she said and looked cautiously towards the shop. "I'm married and tomorrow I'm flying to Germany."

A bolt shot through his heart.

Ferdous took a step backwards when the man came out of the shop. "He's an Iraqi beggar," she said.

The man dropped some coins into Rasjad's hands.

The next day Rasjad waited at the airport. He had washed his hair and clothes to be able to gain entry. At a quarter to four he saw her through the windows, pulling a large suitcase behind the man with whom he had seen her the day before. An official looked at their passports. Then they disappeared. Rasjad stood there not knowing if his search for her was beginning or ending. He remained standing outside the airport building until he heard that passengers to Berlin should proceed to Gate Three and saw her going up some steps into the aeroplane.

A short time later he watched the plane disappear from view. His chest burst open and his heart flew out. He left the airport and hitchhiked back to the Roman amphitheatre. He climbed the stairs and looked up at the sky, through which Ferdous was flying. Her voice still resounded in his ear. By the time it was dark, Rasjad had decided to go to Germany to find her. He slept on the stairs of the Roman amphitheatre and when the sun rose, he went to Al Hashemia square.

After a few hours among the Iraqis there, he learnt that he needed between three and four thousand dollars to get to Germany. In Jordan that would mean four to seven years of working, said the Iraqis. That is if he was lucky enough not to be caught and thrown back over the border.

He quickly discovered that there was a way other than hard work in which to earn money: selling a part of your body to a hospital. Rasjad had vaguely heard about the market for body organs in Jordan, but until he found himself in the market that day, he did not know that there was more than one broker in organs. The Iraqis met each other there and spoke quietly and carefully, afraid of the Jordanian secret police. If a police agent approached, they dispersed in all directions, only to come together again not too quickly and not too slowly.

Brokers sought new clients there and clients sought trustworthy brokers. When someone wanted to sell an organ, the brokers would take him to a hospital for the transaction. The seller then signed a contract donating his organs to the hospital. The sick person, or the family of the sick person would give the money to the broker and he would give it to the seller – less an amount for himself, which was sometimes more than the seller received.

Rasjad heard someone on Al Hashemia square saying that the price for white beans was high today, because there were buyers, but there were no offers. The previous month the offers had been greater than the demand. Rasjad understood nothing of this. A man smiled in a friendly way at him and struck up a conversation. When he found out that Rasjad was an Iraqi alone in Jordan, who had no passport or money and wanted to get to Germany, the man told him that Germany would cost him one white bean, but advised him not to sell his white bean before he had been tested to make sure he could go without it.

"What does white bean mean?"

"Your kidney," the man whispered in his ear.

"And grape juice?"

"Blood," said the man. "The apple is your heart and bread the skin. Everything that you can sell has another name here."

"Are there people who sell their hearts?"

"Not that I know of, but there is a rumour going round that a man sold his handicapped son for ten thousand dollars. And another man sold his lantern for twenty thousand dollars."

Rasjad looked at him questioningly.

"His eye, for the cornea," the man explained. "But listen, if you want to sell something the most important thing, I believe, is the test. If you sell a white bean when you can't do without it, you won't be able to use the money to run away, you'll have to use it all just for medicines. The tests take one week. You get good food and sleep in a hotel. The operation and recovery period cost you nothing. During the operation there's someone from your side there, to make sure they take just one white bean and nothing else."

Suddenly the man walked briskly away. The other men also disappeared in all directions. Only Rasjad was left standing on the square along with a man in smart clothes who remained sitting. When a police agent walked past, the smartly dressed man turned away.

"Look what's happening to us," said the man to Rasjad. "We're selling ourselves." The man stood up and approached Rasjad. "Be careful of the police." He held out his hand to Rasjad and introduced himself as Abdulmehdi. After a short chat he invited Rasjad to his small apartment.

"What do you do here in Amman?" Rasjad asked the man.

"I'm waiting to go to Sweden. And you?"

"To Berlin."

"Why Berlin?"

"I have someone there."

When Abdulmehdi heard that Rasjad had left Iraq to search for Ferdous, he laughed.

"All the Iraqis I know are here out of fear or poverty, except you. You came here because of love."

"How are you going to get to Sweden?"

"I sold a white bean for four and a half thousand dollars. I sent a thousand to my family and used five hundred for my upkeep here. The rest is for the smugglers."

"Was the operation serious?"

Abdulmehdi picked up a book, opened it and let Rasjad read. "It says there that there is no danger in losing one kidney. Perhaps God gave Iraqis two kidneys so that they could sell one to smugglers."

Rasjad spent that night in Abdulmehdi's apartment. At nine o'clock Abdulmehdi left him there alone and went out, saying that he would be back.

"He is between seventeen and twenty. And healthy. He knows absolutely no one here," said Abdulmehdi to the Jordanian he had known for more than five years.

"How much will he cost?" asked the Jordanian.

"Thirty five thousand dollars."

"That's too much."

"Just the heart will earn you twenty five thousand. And it is a good heart."

After some stormy negotiations Abdulmehdi said that he would not do it for less than thirty thousand, stood up and made as if to leave.

"Next week Thursday, four o'clock," said the Jordanian. "The money after the anaesthetic, just like the previous time."

"Thirty thousand?"

"Thirty thousand."

That week Abdulmehdi bought cassettes with love songs, books about lovers who gave up their lives for their beloved, and fruit. He listened for hours to Rasjad, who talked about Ferdous. At the same time as Simahen cried that Rasjad must not climb that mountain in her dream, Abdulmehdi told Rasjad about his love for a woman whom he could not marry, because she had to marry her cousin. Abdulmehdi wept while talking about her. Rasjad asked Abdulmehdi if he could look for work to pay him for the food and the place to stay, but Abdulmehdi said that he could pay once he had received a good price for his kidney.

Rasjad was glad that he had met Abdulmehdi, a compatriot whom he could trust. He decided to sell his kidney to be able to go to Germany.

"Do any of your family have health problems?" Abdulmehdi asked during dinner.

"What sort of problems do you mean?"

"Heart problems, for example."

Rasjad stopped eating and looked suspiciously at Abdulmehdi.

"But I'm selling my kidney, aren't I?"

Abdulmehdi was visibly shaken. "I meant, if you had a heart problem, you mustn't sell your kidney."

After dinner, when Abdulmehdi knew that Rasjad enjoyed American films, he rented a video and a television. The film was Florida Straits in which a man travels the oceans in search of a lost love. After the film Rasjad was even more enthusiastic about his trip to Germany.

On the Thursday, Abdulmehdi woke him at half past six.

Rasjad had a shower and some breakfast. Then Abdulmehdi went with him in a taxi through the streets of Amman. Rasjad thought of the Thirsty River, of the doves on the roof, of the taste of Wasile's bread. Dogs barked and Mira quickly took the washing from the line because it was going to rain in that distant winter. He saw himself during that summer holiday after the first year at school with Edjnaad and Saddam, swimming to the far bank of the Thirsty River for the first time. There they each stole a watermelon from a plot, threw them in the water and swam back to take them home. The sky was distant and summer's clouds were racing to the north.

That morning Simahen walked from room to room, knocking on the doors with her stick.

"He mustn't climb that mountain," she cried, while Rasjad looked through the car's window at a girl turning to him as she crossed the road holding her mother's hand. Not knowing that all his organs had been promised to sick people in hospitals in many countries, and thinking he was going to sell a kidney, Rasjad rode that taxi up the Al Hussein mountain.

CHAPTER 17

The job interview

"Tonight we're going to be turned into ash or chopped into pieces," Rizen said to Hamid, who came from Amara and had been a good friend since their first day in the army. There were heavy bombardments going on through the night at that moment in the war with Iran and they huddled up together in their trench. "We will never be able to make love to our wives again. I hope Mr President does it for us."

That night Rizen and Hamid had made a solemn promise to each other. If they were to survive the war, return safely home, sleep with their wives and each have a child, the one a girl, the other a boy, then the boy and girl would marry each other. Hamid had Enhar and Rizen Edjnaad. Rizen forgot about the promise as the two friends lost contact with each other after the war, until the day Hamid came knocking on the door and offered his daughter to Rizen's son.

Rizen asked Edjnaad to be ready the following Thursday.

"What for?"

"For your betrothal. You're going to get married."

"But I've got tests."

"Marriage is also a test, but you don't only use your pen, but your penis," he whispered in his son's ear. "And you don't have to study for it." Rizen laughed.

Edjnaad blushed, as a rocket slammed into the neighbourhood.

"If you like another girl or if your penis doesn't work, you can refuse."

Neither of those were the case, so Edjnaad did not think of refusing. Suddenly he began fantasising about what the girl looked like. Then he said her name out loud and tried hard to see her in front of him. Tenzile had gone to meet her family with Rizen and tried to describe his future spouse's appearance to Edjnaad.

"She has long hair, like a horse," she said from behind her sewing machine. "Her eyes are like those of a gazelle, her teeth are like pearls, her lips like mulberries, her cheeks silver and her voice golden."

Edjnaad became ever more confused. In his head he had the idea of a mixture between a safari, a greengrocer and a jeweller. Sometimes Edjnaad had nightmares that he was marrying a horse and had vegetable children, until he went with his parents to the house of the betrothed girl. The journey took six hours through many checkpoints. When they arrived in the village among the reeds of Al Ahwar[5] in Amara, they took their place in the reed sitting room. Enhar brought them pomegranate juice, which she served without daring to look at Edjnaad. Edjnaad began to stammer out of embarrassment because Enhar was more beautiful than he could have wished for. Her father followed her out of the sitting room and asked her if she had seen the boy and if she wanted to marry him. When she said nothing, he knew that she was in agreement. That was the happiest day in Edjnaad's life. In a few minutes he fell in love and became engaged to her.

Rizen did not discuss with Edjnaad what he should do on the first night with his wife. Tenzile insisted that he should do so, but Rizen said that Edjnaad would learn it when the moment came.

"If he doesn't learn it from you, then from who?" Tenzile nagged him.

"She is no tank that he can learn to drive. She is a woman and he a man."

Tenzile kept insisting and when Rizen no longer had any patience, he called Edjnaad.

"Do you know what a man does with his wife?" he said to his son, before Tenzile had left the room.

Tenzile ran away at the moment Edjnaad opened his mouth.

"I think I know," said Edjnaad timidly, because he was discussing such a matter with his father for the first time.

"Your mother is concerned that you don't know," said Rizen. "When you're with your wife, don't use your mouth, but something else."

Edjnaad thought that he knew how to make love, but because his mother was becoming ever more pale, he began to think that there were obviously many things he did not know. But he dared not ask this of people who had at any time slept with a woman, so he just sat uncomfortably. What made him most nervous was that everyone would be waiting outside and he would be inside having to prove to Enhar how much of a man he was.

What if he failed, he asked himself. When he was alone and thought about the woman on the television, the blood began flowing faster between his legs, but when he thought of Enhar, his heart pounded, not his penis. He so wanted to be alone with Enhar, somewhere where no one knew them and he could walk with her under the trees along the riverbank, her hand in his, while he looked out for wild fruit to give her. When he thought of that, he was the happiest person on earth, but before he could be alone with her, he first had to prove to everyone that he was a man.

On their wedding night, he was led to the new room, built so that he could study in his own room, where Enhar waited for him in her white dress. She sat near the bed on a bench. He went and sat next to her, looked at her hands, which were painted with henna, and lifted her burka away from her face. She smiled timidly at him. At that moment he forgot his concerns of the past four weeks.

"Are you tired?" he asked her.

She closed her eyes and smiled again without answering.

Edjnaad took off his waistcoat and went to sit on the bed. She smelt of orange blossom. He took her hand, felt she would fall from the bench, stood up and carried her to the bed. He wanted to kiss her on her mouth, but she turned her head away in surprise.

Enhar had never seen television and thought that a man kissed his wife on her cheeks and grabbed her neck and breasts. She knew nothing more.

"Wait," she said. She gargled in a corner of the room with some water, cleaned her teeth with her finger, bit on a piece of cardamom and came back with the taste of cardamom in her mouth.

While Edjnaad experienced the best time of his life, Tenzile cried quietly for Rasjad behind the house. She did not know where he was and Mira dared not tell her what she knew, so as not to be accused of helping him. If Rasjad was in a safe place, she thought, he would have sent her a letter. But no letter came.

Tenzile sat behind the door and watched through the keyhole for his arrival. Because her eyes were weak, she bought some glasses. She asked all her clients if they knew of fortune-tellers and asked Edjnaad to go to every address she was given, to ask after Rasjad. One day she heard of a man in Fallujah who accepted no money from his clients and knew everything. Accompanied by Edjnaad, she went to visit him. The whole way there she complained to other travellers about the disappearance of Rasjad and showed them a photo of him. When new passengers boarded the bus, the old travellers told the story they had heard from Tenzile. Tenzile listened in amazement at how some travellers told her story and even had to shed a tear.

In Fallujah they went to a hut under the date palms, up to a thin man sitting on a mat of palm fronds. There was nothing in the hut apart from a kettle and a rusted mirror. Tenzile began crying and told him her story. She asked the man for Rasjad's address because she wanted to send him a letter. The man wrote down Tenzile's name, that of her missing son and that of his father on a piece of paper, threw it in the water, dribbled the water on to the mirror and stared into it, while reciting verses from the Koran and burning incense. Edjnaad looked on inquisitively.

"How is he?" asked Tenzile, but the man kept on looking vacantly into the mirror.

"He's alive," said the man after a while.

"Where?"

"I don't understand what I'm seeing," said the man. "Your son is living all over the place at the same time. In the north his heart is beating, in the south his skin is coloured by the sun. His left eye runs over the snow and his right eye climbs mountains. His blood flows here and there through arteries." The man scratched his head. "Your son is alive, but not in one place."

He looked at Tenzile in the hope of elaboration from her, but she was even more confused than he was. She could not understand how Rasjad could be alive in different places. If he was alive, why he had forgotten her and not written a letter to set her mind at ease.

"Is he scared?" she asked.

"No, he is not scared. He is without himself," said the man.

Tenzile looked incomprehendingly at Edjnaad, who was trying hard not to burst out laughing. "Is his heart thinking about us?"

"His heart is beating in the chest of a woman next to a river that does not flow and into which the rain falls," said the man.

"Ah," said Tenzile and began crying. "He has forgotten about us. He has found a woman and has forgotten about us." She pushed a note under the man's mat when he refused to accept any money, and left.

The man stared at Edjnaad. "Do not follow the dogs," he said to him, before Tenzile called for him to take her back home.

"I thought that his heart would beat for his mother, who gave him her milk," said Tenzile without knowing that Rasjad's heart had been transplanted into Johanna's chest, who was on the banks of the Mosel river in Europe. His heart had managed to arrive in Germany, but did not beat for Ferdous or Tenzile. From the moment it left Rasjad's chest, it was no longer afraid of bombardments, soldiers or rockets. Apparatus tested his heartbeat and music attempted to calm his heart. Far from the anxiety, restaurants and bars ensured that Rasjad's heart felt more at home in Johanna's chest than in Rasjad's at the Thirsty River. Windows that opened on to green and rain allowed his heart to beat more quietly than with the view of fire and smoke trails.

The same evening that Tenzile came back from her journey to Fallujah, she realised that Saddam was not yet at home, and soldiers were everywhere. Mira said she had been waiting for him all day so that he could go and drown some puppies, but he had not yet made an appearance. The day before, he had been walking through the orchard when he was stopped by a soldier.

"Halt!" The soldier walked around Saddam. "What are you doing here?"

"I'm walking."

"Why are you walking?"

Saddam did not answer.

"Talk! Why are you walking?"

"I don't know why I'm walking."

"If you don't know why you're walking, then why are you walking?"

Again, Saddam gave no reply.

"Talk!" screamed the soldier. "You're an informer for Israel, Iran or America."

Another soldier came up.

"He is a spy," said the soldier who had stopped Saddam. He turned back to Saddam, after a moment of silence to hear if a rocket that had come down nearby had done any serious damage. "Have you got any cigarettes?"

"I don't smoke."

"You don't smoke and you don't know why you're walking?"

"Let him go," said the other soldier. "He's just a pitiful guy."

The soldier pushed the tip of his bayonet against Saddam's chin. "He's an informer. And now: stand like a stork."

With the threat of the sharp point, Saddam stood on one leg. He was only allowed to change legs if a red car went by. The two soldiers sat in the shadows nearby and talked to each other.

After an hour an officer in a jeep came driving up. He screamed at the soldier.

"Idiot, why is that man standing there like that?"

The soldiers saluted.

"Let him go." Then the officer drove off.

"Now you can go," the soldier said to Saddam. "But next time, if you don't smoke and don't know why you're walking, I'll shoot you dead against the nearest wall."

The following day as Saddam was walking through the date palm groves, he was stopped by another soldier. This time he had to show his identity card, which the soldier examined meticulously. He declared that the card must be false. He took Saddam to the secret police. They went in through a door in a high wall with barbed wire, an electric fence and cameras. Saddam was placed in a large hall with all the people who had been apprehended that day.

At nine o'clock that night a soldier came in. Everyone had to take off their clothes. As the women began to get undressed, the men tried to stand in front of them, but the soldiers sent the women to one corner and the men to another. The children had to stand in the middle between their parents. They were forced to bark and to bite their parents until the blood flowed. If they did not do it, they received a shock, administered by one of the soldiers with an electric wire, on their naked bodies. The soldiers laughed and ordered everyone to put their hands in the air.

When one of the soldiers saw the tattoo of Saddam Hussein on Saddam's chest, and the name Saddam Hussein on his arm, he became afraid. He asked Saddam to put his clothes back on and go home.

When Saddam arrived home at about midnight, Tenzile was sitting pale-faced waiting for him.

"I thought they had taken you away, there are soldiers everywhere," she said, still terrified.

"I was."

"Who set you free?"

"Mr President."

Saddam went to his room, Sjahid's old room, which he had inherited when Rasjad had disappeared. He went to lie on the bed and thought that the most suitable place for him was the one from which he had been saved by the tattoo of Saddam Hussein. That place with walls holding in fear, screams and blood.

The next day Mira asked him to throw the sack with puppies and stones into the Thirsty River, but he was in a hurry and left without drowning them.

"No time for dogs," he said.

At eight o'clock in the morning he stood at the door of the secret police, at which people dared not even look. The guards asked him the reason for his visit.

"I want to serve Mr President," he said.

One of the guards frisked him and he was sent to a hall where men were standing in a line. When it was his turn, Saddam went into a small room, where two soldiers were sitting, and between them someone in civilian clothes.

"What's your name?" asked the man in civilian clothes.

"Saddam Rizen Kosjer," said Saddam.

The man looked to his left and to his right at the soldiers. "I think he's okay." The soldiers smiled. "Imagine it, you're standing on a beach. Mr President, Iraq and your mother are lying in the sea. A hyena goes towards them. Who do you save?"

"No one," said Saddam.

"Why not?"

"No one needs to be saved. The hyena would not dare go into the water anywhere near someone like Mr President," said Saddam.

"Congratulations," said the man. "You're hired." He gave him a folder and instructed him to come back with four passport photos and the form filled in from the dossier, so that he could join up to the fidaï Saddam.[6]

The next day Saddam shaved. He borrowed some money from Mira to buy shoe polish and go to the barber.

"Are you getting engaged?" she asked.

"I'm going to Baghdad."

"They'll soon catch you on the way."

"They'll never catch me again, Mira. I'm becoming a member of the fidaï Saddam."

Mira prepared some food for him to eat on the journey and asked him at the door when he would be coming home again.

"I don't want to come back here. I'll live there," was his answer.

"And the dogs? Don't you want to throw them in the river?"

Saddam smiled. "Just do it yourself for once. You must get used to it," he said and left.

Mira took the sack with the puppies to the Thirsty River. The dogs' mother walked with her, sniffed at the sack and licked at it. Halfway there, Mira put the sack on the ground and opened it. One by one the dog took her puppies back to the house.

"There'll be more dogs living in this house than people," Mira whispered when she saw the dogs lying in the shade waiting for night to fall.

CHAPTER 18

Trussed up cocoons

During Simahen's final summer Edjnaad asked her about her life.

She counted carefully. "I am eight wars old," she said.

He asked her if she knew how old she was in years, but she could give no answer to that.

While Edjnaad continued with his studies and she was busy working out how old she was, the dogs disturbed her. She called Mira to throw the puppies into a sack.

Mira replied that no one wanted to throw them into the Thirsty River and that she did not want to do it.

Simahen screamed angrily: "Then shove the barking into a sack and throw that away."

Mira left, confused. She told Edjnaad, who was sitting in the shade, what Simahen had said. He started laughing.

"Instead of laughing, throw the dogs into the river, please," Mira said to Edjnaad.

Edjnaad put his pen between the pages where he had been reading and closed the book. "Did you know that killing a dog is half killing a person?"

"Then what is the solution for all these dogs that are being born?"

"Castration," said Edjnaad. "I read that in Sweden they don't kill dogs, but castrate them."

"Shhhtt ..." Mira put her finger to her lips. "Be careful that Mr President doesn't hear you and stops killing Iraqis and castrates them instead."

Edjnaad laughed. He did not think about doing anything about the problem with the dogs because when the dogs started barking in the early evening, he took the opportunity to make love with Enhar, when no one could hear them. After a while he waited for the barking before making love to Enhar and the barking itself became exciting. After making love he threw stones at the dogs to shut them up.

"Beware of the dogs," Edjnaad said one evening in January to Enhar. "Don't go behind the house at night. They might not be used to you yet and they'll bite you."

Enhar told him that there was no need for concern, because the dogs always disappeared at night.

The night was cold. Enhar had washed herself after everyone in the house had gone to bed. She had shaved her legs for the first time with the razor that Tenzile had bought her on a trip to Fallujah and had given to her in a plastic bag, so that no one would see it.

"Take it," said Tenzile. "It is a medicine for legs."

Enhar took the bag, opened it in her room and saw five razors. She was upset, because she thought Tenzile must have thought she had too much hair on her legs, but was confused because Tenzile had never seen her legs. That night she had dripped olive oil on to the blade, so that it would not rust, then perhaps the blades would last for five years. She was glad, because now she would not feel self-conscious when Edjnaad kissed her legs. She hurried back to the room, afraid that someone would discover her late shower for Edjnaad. With some tweezers she tried to thin her eyebrows, put some make-up on her cheeks and lipstick on her lips. She was satisfied when she looked at herself in the mirror.

Edjnaad sat in the study. He was preparing for the half-year exams. He had put his science book down next to him and was thinking about alternating current when Enhar came into the study.

"Are you tired?" she asked.

"A little," he said. "I think that oil heater has used up all the oxygen in the room."

"Would you like some tea?" Enhar asked.

He looked closely at her. "Yes, love some. You're looking nice."

She giggled and ran to the kitchen.

He stretched and went outside to get some fresh air.

Back in the room with the tea, Enhar did not see where he had gone. She thought he had gone to the toilet. She put the tea on the floor close to the mattress on which he sat to study and she smelt the wick of the heater beginning to burn. She turned the heater down, fetched some oil, filled the heater, smelt the oil in the room and thought it would be better to take the heater outside to fill it up. She opened the window and the door, and lit some incense in the room. She went to sit next to the science book, which was open on a page about alternating current, and she decided that the next day, when the sun was up, she would air the mattress outside so that it did not become mouldy. She drank her tea before it got cold and thought she would make fresh tea when Edjnaad came back.

Edjnaad felt he needed a bit of cold air to get the sleep out of his eyes. He pulled his woollen winter coat tightly around him. He yawned. From behind the house he heard a strange sound that was repeated regularly. It seemed like the screech of a cat, of a newborn baby, of one animal calling another in the distance, or of a seagull. He saw the moon appearing from behind the clouds and the dry bed of the Thirsty River being lit up. He no longer felt sleepy and was energised by the cold wind, which blew into his face as he came out from behind the wall.

The oil heater consumed all the oxygen in the room, that's why I felt so lazy, he thought. Suddenly he saw the dogs walking past him in a line, like prisoners of war in an endless desert. They walked quietly, like ants, like a nocturnal train to the bed of the Thirsty River. Edjnaad followed a little behind the dogs, with the intention of going back and drinking the tea that Enhar had made, but when he wanted to turn round he still kept following the dogs, because he felt there must be something where the dogs were headed. A chill went down his spine when he thought about it and he knew it would be dreadful, but he still had to know where the dogs were going.

The further the dogs went, the colder it became, until he stopped, wanting to go no further. He looked back and saw that the lights of the town lay far behind him, but when he saw that the dogs had almost disappeared in the dark, he ran after them over the bed of the Thirsty River. The dogs all gathered around him, wagging their tails. He shouted, the dogs took a few paces back and walked on in a line.

Edjnaad followed them. The darkness became pitch black as clouds hid the moon. The wind grew stronger and colder. Edjnaad thought of the oil heater, which he would have to fill before the wick burnt out, and wanted to go back, but his curiosity won over his anxiety, even as that increased. At a spot that the dogs seemed to know well, they left the bed of the Thirsty River. Edjnaad followed behind them. On the river bank he became scared. He wanted to stop but this time felt that he should stay with the dogs. An enormous force drove him forward, behind the dogs, which were walking ever faster.

Then they came to a desolate place, out of which the earth rose as if it had just been ploughed. Edjnaad's heart began beating faster and his lips trembled when he saw that the dogs were beginning to dig and fight with each other. The moon reappeared, by the light of which he could see a dog had grabbed hold of a foot that was still wearing a shoe. The other dogs pulled at the leg, growling.

Edjnaad stood nailed to the ground. He dared not run away, afraid that the dogs would attack him and rip him to pieces. One of the dogs found another corpse, at which the pack divided into two. Edjnaad threw a stone at the dogs, as if hurling it at his own fear, but they kept on biting at the clothes and body of a man. Edjnaad picked up all the stones he could find, threw them at the dogs and screamed. The dogs shrank away from the two bodies and glared at him with their bloodied snouts. They yapped with a hungry sound. He threw another stone and screamed until the dogs were afraid of him and stood a little further away.

Edjnaad walked up to the foot wearing the shoe, fell to his knees and hesitantly touched it, just as the moon began disappearing behind the clouds. He bent over the furrowed earth and felt body parts everywhere. Elbows, hands, heads sticking out of the ground. Edjnaad stood up, started running, tripped over the bodies and fell on the rutted ground, which seemed endless. He heard the dogs fighting, ran towards them and in the gathering moonlight could see them devouring a corpse. He shouted loudly and threw stones, as the dogs bit into the flesh. He screamed as if he was feeling the pain of the flesh that was being eaten.

Suddenly the dogs fell quiet and tilted their heads up. In the distance Edjnaad saw a light approaching. He ran in the direction of the dry riverbed of the Thirsty River, but in the darkness could not easily see where he was going and fell into a deep hole. His heart was in his throat and his whole body trembled. He wanted to climb out of the hole and run away, but over the edge of the hole he saw cars approaching and he ducked down. The headlights were like enormous eyes spreading terror to the horizon. They stopped at the edge of the rutted field. The dogs trotted up to the soldiers getting out of the cars, and began wagging their tails, as if they knew them. An excavator and two trucks followed behind the cars.

The excavator began digging at a place one of the soldiers pointed out. When a big hole had been dug, one of the trucks reversed up to it and tipped its load into the hole. From the vehicles' lights Edjnaad saw people with their hands and feet tied up, falling out of the truck. Screams filled the space between heaven and earth. The people writhed like creatures trying to escape from their cocoons. One soldier stood near the hole and guided the excavator to dump the excavated earth on to the people and the screaming. The more earth was dumped, the more muffled the screams became, until they stopped completely.

The excavator began digging a second hole.

"I don't think those dogs are going to be hungry today," shouted one of the soldiers.

"Or perhaps they don't like the taste of them any more."

"Over there!" one of the soldiers shouted suddenly. "The dog over there." He pointed at a dog standing and wagging its tail at the edge of the hole where Edjnaad was hiding. The soldier came over to the dog, with a Kalashnikov over his shoulder and a torch in his hand.

Edjnaad threw himself to the bottom of the hole and rolled in the dirt like a hedgehog. He became a ball of fear. Like a blind person he scratched around the bottom of the hole, in search of an escape through which to slip his body, but he could find nothing. He wanted to dig his way out with his fingers when he saw the light swinging to and fro over the hole. He could hear the footsteps of the soldier in his army boots. The light became ever brighter, until it shone directly into the hole. Edjnaad looked up and saw the soldier standing there next to the dog.

"Aha. I was asking myself why the dog was wagging its tail. Out!" yelled the soldier. Then he shouted to the others: "We've got a snooper here."

A soldier shouted from a distance, but through the rumbling of the excavator they could not understand him.

"Another one," called the soldier, ordering Edjnaad to climb quickly out of the hole, as his nervousness made him slip down to the bottom again. "Stand up and turn round!" The soldier shone the torch in his face, held out his hand to him and pulled him up. Then he ordered him to walk in front of him to the cars.

Edjnaad kept stumbling and fell over, and the soldier eventually grabbed him by his shoulders to help him walk. The dog trotted with them up to the excavator, which had finished digging the second hole. The other dogs ran up to Edjnaad wagging their tails.

"What's that?" an officer asked the soldier.

"I found him over there in a hole."

"Alone?"

"Yes, alone."

"Abdul Hussein!" called the officer. "Go over there and check that there are no more of them."

Another soldier saluted and ran with his torch to the hole.

"Tie up his hands and feet," said the officer to the soldier who had caught Edjnaad.

When Edjnaad heard that, his knees could no longer support him and he fell over. He looked pleadingly at the officer. "Please, let me go home. I swear to God that I haven't seen anything," he sobbed.

The officer lit a cigarette and said to Edjnaad that he need not worry himself.

With his teeth the soldier tore a T-shirt, from one of the prisoners in the truck, into strips with which to tie Edjnaad's hands and feet.

"Stand over there," he said, but Edjnaad could not move. The soldier dragged him over.

"Please, please," begged Edjnaad, as the soldier threw him over the edge of the second hole. Edjnaad stood up.

The officer gave a signal, at which the truck reversed.

A soldier guided the driver to line up the back of the truck with the hole. "Okay, okay," he called. "Just a little further. Stop!"

Edjnaad saw the bed of the truck rising up. The tailgate opened with a screeching noise. The trussed up people in the truck piled on top of the screaming Edjnaad.

When Edjnaad did not come home, Enhar went to the toilet and whispered his name, but there was no answer. She wanted to look behind the house, but she was afraid of bumping into Adam, who scared her with his deep eyes that bored their way into hidden worlds.

"Edjnaad," she whispered again, but she received no reply. She wanted to wake Mira up, but was embarrassed with her lipstick and perfume, which she only put on when everyone else had gone to bed. She went back to the study, switched off the oil heater and the light and waited in her room, because he might well come back soon. She switched the colour television on and on the first channel saw Saddam Hussein, who was visiting some village. The people were applauding him. "Saddam, your name makes America tremble!" they shouted. She switched to the second channel and saw Saddam Hussein walking in another village, while the people shouted: "With our souls, with our blood we offer ourselves up for you, Saddam!" She switched back to the first channel, turned the volume down and every few minutes peeked through a crack in the curtains of the study window to see if Edjnaad had appeared.

When the newsreader smiled and the national anthem played, she knew that the day's broadcast was over and it was midnight. She washed her face and knocked on Mira's door. Sleepily Mira opened the door. Enhar told her that Edjnaad had gone out and not come back. Mira went to the study and began to look for him under the blankets lying there, among the books and behind the heater.

"What are you doing?" Enhar asked.

"I'm looking for him," Mira answered.

"I don't think you're completely awake. I've already told you he went out. Why are you looking for him between the books?"

"Where do you want me to look? He'll definitely be back soon," said Mira, yawning as she went back to her room. Enhar stayed up until three in the morning, going back and forth between her bedroom and the study and began looking between the books herself, under the blankets and behind the heater and the radio, which was still droning softly on with the voice of Saddam Hussein. Then she began knocking loudly on all the doors in the house, waking up everyone, except Adam.

Four days after Edjnaad had disappeared, Rizen came home on leave. He immediately began searching, until the sun went down, but could not find him anywhere.

Simahen came to him on her walking stick. "Follow the dogs," she said, and went back to her room.

The next day, when the sun had gone down, Rizen took a torch, a knife and a sack and followed the dogs along the bed of the Thirsty River. He turned the torch on to the place where the dogs began digging and saw shoes, torn clothes and blood. He chased the dogs away and began searching, but could not find Edjnaad. When he decided to head home, he called the dogs to follow him, because he was afraid they would eat Edjnaad.

The next day he took a shovel, a torch, sacks and poisoned meat. In the dry river bed he fed the meat to the dogs, lit a cigarette and waited until the last dog had stopped moving. Arriving at the mass grave he began looking for the place where the bodies were about five days old. He covered his mouth with a shawl against the stench. He hoped that the dogs had not devoured Edjnaad because they knew his smell. From his experience in the war, after seeing thousands of bodies, he knew how long a corpse remained as a corpse, and after two days of digging from dusk until dawn, he found Edjnaad. He recognised the woollen winter jacket that had been Sjahid's. He pulled his son's body out and untied the strips of T-shirt that bound his hands and feet, afraid that if he was stopped on the way back, the soldier would know that Edjnaad had been executed. Then he would also be found guilty, because he was the father of someone who had been killed by soldiers. He quickly put him in a sack and that sack inside another. Before he left, he covered the other bodies as best he could, in case other dogs or scavenger birds came by. He put the sack over his shoulder and started walking home as the dawn was breaking.

In the stable where Adam lay, he put the sack down and rolled a cigarette.

When Mira came in, he sat crying and smoking. He could not get a word out.

Mira began crying silently, because the neighbours could not be allowed to hear her, and went to Wasile.

She asked in a whisper from her bed if he had been found.

"He's lying in the barn."

"Take me there," said Wasile. She leant on Mira's shoulder, who led her to the barn. She saw Rizen sitting there. His face was like stone and was wet from the tears.

"Do not scream," said Rizen, when he saw his mother coming in. "There are hundreds more lying out there. If the party knows that we know, they'll kill us all."

Wasile looked at the sack. She fell down beside it and sobbed quietly. She put her hand on the place where she thought his head would be, began feeling, until she felt his nose. She kissed him on his face through the sack. Her tears mixed with the dried earth encrusted on the sack.

Enhar came crying into the stable, but Tenzile pulled her away and locked her up in her room.

Rizen went to Simahen before the sun had set on the night that he was to take Edjnaad to Najaf[7] to bury him in the family grave that Simahen had bought, so that her children could all be buried together and she would not have to search for them on judgement day.

He kissed her hand and her forehead. "I followed the dogs," he said.

She smiled. "Didn't you have anything better to do, you're not a child any longer?" she said.

"Do you want to bid farewell to Edjnaad before I take him to Najaf?"

"Where are you taking him?"

"To Najaf."

"Why's the boy going to Najaf? It's dark outside. Let him sleep and take him tomorrow morning. He is not married. Don't disturb him," she said, and smiled. Simahen thought for a while as to whether she had any acquaintances or family in Najaf, but could not recall.

Rizen gave Simahen his hand and helped her up. He took her to the stable, where Mira had lit a lantern along with Enhar's incense. Enhar had given Mira some of the incense that she sometimes burnt in Edjnaad's study to chase away the smell of the oil heater. Before Simahen entered the stable, Rizen told her that he was dead, but Simahen did not know who he was talking about. When she smelt the incense in the barn and, with her troubled eyesight, saw the tearful faces, she walked up to Adam, who was lying in his corner, and thought that it was Kosjer's body.

"Finally, before I die, I can shed tears over your body," she said. "I have waited for so long. My waiting has become a market." She began kissing Adam.

"Here, Edjnaad is in this sack," said Rizen.

"Edjnaad?" said Simahen surprised. "What's he doing in a sack?"

238

"He's dead." Simahen crawled on her knees from Adam to the sack and felt over it.

"Ah, now I know. Ah, now I know," she whispered, touching the sack, as if a lightning bolt had restored her memory. She lay her head on the sack as if praying and did not move. After a while Rizen held her by the shoulders because he thought she was dead and he saw that she had fallen asleep. He carried her to her bed. She weighed almost nothing.

Then he went to fetch a friend who had a car and they put the sack containing Edjnaad in the boot. He covered it with a bag of straw. Rizen drove with his friend to Najaf. Every few kilometres they were stopped at a control point by the secret police or the police and were afraid they would be caught. A soldier or policeman would ask for their papers and want to know what they were transporting in the car.

"Straw," said the driver.

Each time Rizen prayed to God that they would not open the boot. He had brought Edjnaad's student papers along to show that he was not a soldier, and fifty dollars in case they came across a corrupt soldier.

He sighed with relief when they arrived at the cemetery with millions of graves. He did not carve Edjnaad's name into the gravestone.

Hiding Edjnaad's death was more difficult than hiding him away when he was alive. Tenzile washed his clothes, as if he were still alive and hung them on the washing line, so that the neighbours would see them and not ask where he had gone. Sometimes she called him. "Edjnaad! Your food is ready."

Weeks later the neighbours began asking after Edjnaad. No one saw him coming or going any longer or heard his voice.

One day Tenzile called him. "Edjnaad, come on, why are you taking so long in the bathroom?"

One of the neighbours laughed. "Are you crazy? He's not in the shower, the water's not running!"

So it came about that Edjnaad's name was no longer mentioned in the house, except in Tenzile's silent weeping.

Forty-four days after the burial, after Simahen had returned from her visit to his grave, Simahen asked Rizen to take her to a cardiologist.

"What's wrong?" asked the cardiologist, smiling.

"Ah, doctor, test to see if my heart is still working." The doctor placed his stethoscope on her chest, measured her blood pressure and did an ECG. After careful consideration he told her that her heart was in perfect order and that there were no problems.

"Take me home," said Simahen to Rizen, disappointed.

"Big problem," she said when Mira asked her how it went. "The heart doctor says my heart is still working, working well even."

Six months after Edjnaad had been buried, Rizen and Tenzile took Enhar back to her family. The whole way back she thought not of her bleak future as the wife of someone who had been killed, found and buried in secret, but of the short, beautiful time that she had had with Edjnaad.

CHAPTER 19

The third sheep

When Wasile lay in bed for days on end after Djazil had stolen her dollars, and no longer earned any money by baking bread, and no money was coming in any longer from Rasjad, all that remained was the little that Tenzile earned from her sewing. Every mealtime Simahen walked, mumbling, on her walking stick, to the kitchen, because the meals she was receiving were becoming smaller and smaller. She carefully felt the pots.

"Not yet," she whispered if they were warm and she went back to her room.

Simahen trusted Mira's soul, but not her heart, which she thought was weak, because with just a few words or tears anyone could get from her what they wished. If Simahen heard that Mira had given someone money, for which she usually had to sell a chicken or a lamb, she became angry and spoke sternly to her.

"You mustn't do that. You don't have a son who can look after you when you're old. Save your money and buy gold. Save it for a rainy day, so that it can look after you when you're old."

"I don't think I'll be growing old in this house," Mira replied. "If Adam wakes up or dies, then I'll die." It sounded as if her caring for Adam was her reason for being alive.

When rockets began falling to earth and others were

launched, Simahen became afraid that she would be struck by one of them and the secret of the gold she had bought and hidden in the floor and between the bricks of her room would die with her. So she told Mira in a roundabout way.

"When I die and come to you in a dream and say that you must dig somewhere, believe in the dream and go and dig."

Mira did not understand this, but because Simahen had locked the door before she would tell her, she knew that it was important and she held on to it.

A few weeks later she dreamt that Simahen asked her to dig in the party's house to uncover the bones of her father Kosjer, her grandfather Nadus and her uncles. Excited, Mira told Simahen about her dream, but she said the search and the digging must take place among the bricks and walls of her room and demarcated the place for her. She did not use the word 'gold'. Mira grasped from Simahen's hints that it had to do with something yellow that did not rust and which she had hidden years ago in her room for the rainy days, when there would be no fire under the pots in the kitchen. She knew it was a big secret that she must not reveal.

When Wasile no longer earned any money from selling bread, Mira began selling things from the house that had any value, and this was followed by the sheep and the chickens. Each time she could only sell a little less. When Simahen was being given only tea and bread, she still did not believe that the rainy days, for which she had been saving the gold, had arrived. She dipped the bread in her tea and did not complain.

Wasile, however, did complain. She lay on her bed and clasped her head in her hands. Ever since Djazil had stolen her dollars, she had been plagued by headaches. Wasile liked the sound of Tenzile's sewing machine. When there were fewer clients, Wasile sent old clothes for Tenzile to repair, not out of necessity, but to make sure that the sewing machine kept on making its comforting sound.

When there were no longer any old clothes, Wasile asked Mira to go outside and see if there were any naked people.

"Then ask them why they don't want any clothes sewn for them," she said when Mira said they were all wearing clothes.

That the sewing machine kept turning was more important for Wasile than the money from the customers, because it meant that Tenzile did not exist in that house, but the sewing machine did. For years on end Wasile slowly starved Tenzile until she was nothing more than skin and bone. Rizen had stopped considering her as a woman from the time she had been pregnant with Tali. Despite everything, Tenzile remained a thorn in Wasile's foot. If Tenzile had been able to live as a divorced woman with a roof over her head and her own income, she would probably have done so. She let her mother know that she wanted to get divorced, but she began screaming in her face.

"Divorced? And come back here, I suppose?! Who's going to look after you? And if I decide to do that, then who's going to do it after I'm dead?"

After a little thought, Tenzile realised that her mother made sense. A woman got divorced only if she could not have any children or if she did not want to become the second wife. That is why Tenzile prayed regularly. If she was not going to get her chance in life, she should at least not squander her chance in the afterlife. She did not think much about her life before, when Rizen had waited for her on the bank of the Thirsty River, when her heart leapt for the man who walked panting through the dusty heat of the streets to sell bread. The man whose eyes shone full of love for her. When he appeared in her life again when the first rocket fell in the centre of Boran, he was like a bolt of lightning; he came suddenly and then disappeared into the war. After that she waited to be freed from Wasile and even later she waited at the keyhole in Rasjad's door, not knowing that his organs had been divided into other lives. The despair almost became too much and one day she washed herself and prayed to God to free her, not from the Bird family household, the sewing machine, Wasile, the waiting for Rasjad or the despair of Edjnaad, but from her life. She prayed so earnestly that her tears fell on to her prayer mat.

That night she dreamt that she was waiting behind her door for her death. Suddenly the keyhole became bigger and bigger.

Tenzile became concerned, because everyone going past would be able to see her sitting there, but she saw no one. She stood up and walked through the keyhole, which had become a doorway. Outside there was no sound of army boots, which had been walking those streets for centuries, and there was no metal falling from the skies. Tenzile went to a large garage that was surrounded by a high wall. Green cars and buses were chained to tanks trying to pull them out of the mud. Tenzile understood nothing of what she saw. With a questioning gaze she looked around, when suddenly a wagon drawn by ten flying horses on golden reins, came down from the sky into the garage.

"That must be God," whispered Tenzile. On the ground around her all she could see was a lot of military clothing, full of bullet holes and dried blood, nothing with which she could cover her head. When the wagon touched the clay, the muddy field was instantly transformed into a green pasture. The buses and cars began driving by themselves. A man dressed in white from his shoes to his Adam's apple climbed out of the wagon. She tried to see his face, but the bright light radiating from him prevented her. She closed her eyes tightly and covered her face with her hand.

"Oh, most gracious God, blessed is thy name," she cried.

"I am Saddam Hussein," the man said, laughing.

Suddenly she began crying, knelt down and clutched at the white shoes of Saddam Hussein.

"Stop, Tenzile," said Saddam Hussein. "If you kneel in front of me like that, God will be angry with me." He laughed and his shoulders shook. "I'm not God, just a person," he said.

His words touched Tenzile deep in her heart. "Ah, Mr President," she said crying. "Wasile still lashes me with her hoarse voice, even when she's lying on her bed. Mr President, please, release me from her."

"So Djazil did not free you, as I had instructed him in a previous dream?" asked Saddam Hussein.

"Not yet, Mr President. Kill her, please," begged Tenzile.

"A little patience. I will kill her," said Saddam Hussein and he began laughing again.

Tenzile grabbed him with both hands by his jacket and began shaking him back and forth and shouted: "Kill Wasile! Please, kill her!"

Then Tenzile felt rain failing from the skies. She calmed down, opened her eyes and saw Wasile staring at her angrily from her bed.

Mira put down the bucket that she had emptied on Tenzile's head to wake her up.

When it filtered through to Tenzile that she was holding the handle of Wasile's door, she ran terrified to her room. That day she received no piece of bread and no tea. She thought Wasile was punishing her, but Mira simply no longer had any money with which to do any shopping.

When Simahen also did not receive her piece of bread and tea and found no warm pots in the kitchen, she went back to her room.

"The time has come," she said, and began digging in the ground. She brought out a gold ring and gave it to Mira to sell.

Mira let her see the twenty dollars she had received for the ring.

"I don't know what's happening with the world," said Simahen. "We swap Iraqi Muslim gold for American Christian paper to fill our pots with food."

"Where did you get the money?" Wasile asked her when she brought the food. "Have the Americans lifted the blockade?"

"Not the Americans, but Simahen," said Mira.

Each time the money ran out, Simahen dug in the ground of her room or removed a brick from the wall and took out a piece of gold or jewellery. She always waited until there was no longer any food brought to her. Despite the many years that had passed, she never forgot the places where she had hidden the gold. She knew exactly how deep she had buried it and how it was wrapped. With the last piece of jewellery she had hidden, a gold ring with a blue stone that she had bought from a Bedouin, she took her glasses off and wept. Her tears fell on to the ring.

"You are our final bread," she whispered, because she believed that the ring on her finger that she had been given on her wedding day would go with her to the grave. She kissed the blue stone and gave it to Mira. "Ask a good price for this. After this only God, Mr President and the Americans can end our hunger."

Simahen felt that her days were numbered and that she would not see the next summer, especially after she had seen Edjnaad in that sack. "I no longer think," she sighed, "that I have the will to live, no more time for waiting." She took a deep breath, at which a rasping voice came from her throat. "No more fire in my heart and no more gold for the kitchen."

That night she had a dream. She stood in an enormous palatial hall. She was young and strong again, as she had once been. Her hair had curls and was pitch black. God sat on his throne, clothed all in white. Light shone from his head, such that Simahen could not see the colour of his heart. He held a sword in his hand. Strong prophets holding spears stood on his right-hand side, thin, weak prophets holding lanterns on his left-hand side. Behind the throne Simahen saw a sea of angels. Tall angels stood on the ground, small angels flew around above the throne. In Simahen's dream Moses walked up to God's throne. He took God's sword and passed it to a man.

"Go to Baghdad and throw Saddam Hussein out," God said to the man.

Simahen was amazed, because the man who took the sword had no moustache and no beard. He stood before the throne, as if he had been riding a horse for the whole day to be able to be there. He did not kneel before God, but looked at him impolitely.

"Praise be to God," he said loudly. He turned round and staggered out of the hall with the sword in his hand, past Simahen, who looked at him with big eyes and looked into his face to remember it.

Simahen asked God why the man who was going to save Iraq from Saddam Hussein had no beard and no moustache, as all the other prophets, sheiks and imams did. God said to her that this man was an American.

At that moment, Simahen woke up. Everyone laughed at her

dream when she told them about it and thought that she was going senile.

Not much longer after that, when the streets had been cleaned and palm fronds and banners were hanging on the walls for the expected visit of Saddam Hussein to Boran, Simahen was sitting in her room. She passed her black prayer beads between her fingers and mumbled the names of God. Mira put her lunch down on the ground in front of her, placing the tray with rice and aubergines on the newspaper that served as a tablecloth. Simahen gently laid down her prayer beads next to her and picked up the bread from the newspaper. Suddenly she pushed the plates roughly aside, picked up the newspaper and stared at a photo.

"Who is that man without a moustache or a beard?" she asked Mira, but Mira did not know who it was.

Simahen stood up and walked, without a stick this time, to Rizen. She waved the photo in front of his face and asked him who the man in the photo was.

"That," said Rizen, looking at the photo in the newspaper, "is George W. Bush."

"That is the man from my dream! That is the man who took up the sword of Moses!" cried Simahen and threw her hands into the air with happiness.

Rizen laughed loudly, took Simahen to her room and fetched a glass of water for her from the kitchen.

That night Simahen could not sleep, but the next day she walked in a sprightly manner, holding her gold wedding ring in her hand, to Rizen and gave him the ring.

"Sell this ring and buy a big sheep. Kill it and give the meat to the poor. It is a solemn oath to Ayatollah Bush."

"Bush is not an ayatollah, he's a pig!" said Rizen, but Simahen, who clearly saw Bush in her dream, muttered to God for forgiveness for Rizen.

"Do not say anything bad about someone that God has chosen as the one to remove Saddam Hussein from power. He is a sacred imam," she said and swore on her mother's honour that she would not go back to her room until Rizen had bought the sheep for Ayatollah Bush. Rizen went to the sheep market, bought a large sheep, killed it and gave the meat to the poor, as Simahen had decreed. Thankfully no one asked why the sheep was being killed. The sheep for George W. Bush was, after Dime's sheep and that of Kosjer, the third significant sheep in the history of the Bird family.

In the days that followed, when everyone thought Simahen had forgotten about her dream, she came every day from her room, leaning on her stick, and asked if the war had begun yet. Every day the answer was no and she turned round, disappointed.

"But he will come here, that American whose name I've forgotten, the one who took Moses' sword," she would hiss.

Everyone thought Simahen had gone crazy, because for her the waiting for the end of a war had turned into the waiting for the beginning of a war. After a few weeks she began walking without her stick to the neighbours' houses. She knocked on their doors and told the whole neighbourhood that they no longer needed to be afraid. She held the newspaper up with the photo of George W. Bush. He had a drop of dried aubergine soup on his lip.

"He's coming with his sword to throw the son of Sabha out of Baghdad!"

The news that Simahen really was senile spread quickly. Everyone discussed how she knocked on their doors and talked about Ayatollah Bush. In the house everyone was afraid.

Simahen was not only a supporter of Bush, but she also prayed for his grandmother, because she was the mother of the president who had saved Kuwait and the grandmother of the president who would save Iraq from Saddam Hussein. If anyone said to Simahen that the Americans would only come to Iraq for its oil, she shook her head.

"Let them take the oil to burn in their heaters and cars. It's better than us burning up here with the oil," she would say.

When Simahen prayed to God and asked him to protect and bless Ayatollah Bush, Wasile called Mira. "Take your grandmother to her room before someone hears her. Soon they'll break the house down," she said in fear.

Mira would then turn the radio up loud, so that the neighbours would not hear Simahen.

One day Simahen lost the picture from the newspaper of George W. Bush. She had hung it above her bed, stuck with a date, but had forgotten what she had done. She wanted to tell the neighbours that he would save Iraq from Saddam Hussein, but she had forgotten his name and wanted to show the picture to them. In a newspaper she saw a photo of Saddam Hussein in cowboy clothes. Because she was not wearing her glasses, she thought it was a photo of George W. Bush. She tore it out of the newspaper and knocked on the neighbour's door. She pointed at the picture of Saddam Hussein in the newspaper.

"He is the only one who can save Iraq from the son of Sabha. Only him," she said, as the sweat dripped from her face.

One Thursday Rizen took her to Edjnaad's grave. Once there she did not cry over the grave of her great-grandson, nor did she touch it. She spent the whole day shuffling round the piece of land that she had bought as the family grave, in search of a place where the sun did not beat down too harshly and where there was also not too much shade. When she had found the right spot, she breathed a sigh of relief and looked at Rizen, who was rolling a cigarette.

"Don't fight against Ayatollah Bush. God is sending him here, not the Pentagon," said Simahen, and smiled. "Ah," she said and clapped her hand to her forehead. "The old people of today, instead of knowing the names of prophets and imams, know the names of Bush and Clinton and Carter and Reagan and the Pentagon. Oh God, help us if we get to heaven with all these American names." She told Rizen where she wanted to be buried.

"You haven't greeted Edjnaad," said Rizen on their way home.

"No need to. Soon I'll be with him."

The following day she went outside, with the last bit of energy in her body. She went to the Simahen market next to the party's house, where women dressed in black waited for their missing relatives. Simahen went to stand among them with a stick in one hand and a picture of Bush, which she had taken off her wall, in the other.

"This American is coming here," she cried out, and pointed with her stick at the newspaper and then at the mural of Saddam Hussein. "And he will run away. The days of the son of Sabha are numbered. Go home now."

The women and hawkers scattered in all directions, terrified at Simahen's words.

One of the guards who had seen Simahen sitting at the wall through the years, went up to her. "That was long ago," he said to her.

"Ah, my son, this will be the last time that you see me."

The guard gave Simahen his hand and walked home with her. When Mira saw the guard coming into the house with his Kalashnikov, with Simahen on his arm, she screamed in terror. The bucket of water she had just fetched from the Thirsty River toppled over.

"Don't worry. Don't be scared," said Simahen. "I've known him since before he had any grey hairs."

Mira took Simahen to bed.

In the courtyard the guard looked around for something to take with him, but could find nothing. "Don't let her outside, she is for the Americans," he said sternly, as he left.

Mira locked the door to Simahen's room.

Simahen slept for an hour and woke with a start. She had dreamt that the cars were flying round like birds, with chickens' wings, and exploding in the sky. She crawled on her hands and knees to the door. When she could not open it, she called Mira, who found Simahen breathing with difficulty behind the door.

"Why is the door locked?"

"The guard said that you were an American."

"If I really was an American, he would bow before me," said Simahen.

Leaning on Mira's arm she went to all the rooms and asked everyone for forgiveness.

"When the sleeping one awakens," she said to Mira when she

was lying in her bed again, "ask him for forgiveness on my behalf."

On her final Friday, Simahen woke up because her breath was sticking in her throat. She fell to her knees. When Mira came to bring her tea, she found her praying, but not in the direction of the Kaaba.

"Gran, the Kaaba's not in that direction," she said.

"I know that," sighed Simahen. "But I think God has relocated in this direction."

Tired, Simahen went to lie on her bed. Mira dribbled water into her mouth, but Simahen turned her head away. Mira held the bag of medicines out to her. With a trembling hand, she took a small bottle of tablets out. Mira ran with them to Wasile, who told her that they were sleeping tablets. Mira did not give them to her grandmother.

"Have they found him under the ground with his hideous beard?" she asked Mira.

"Who? Sjahid?"

"No, Saddam Hussein," said Simahen.

Mira left the room shaking her head and locked the door behind her.

That night Simahen woke up concerned. She searched for her bag of medicines, but could not find it anywhere. She crawled to the door, but it would not open. A rocket came down behind the date palms. Simahen's room rattled and when the silence resumed, Simahen had become a part of it forever.

Three months after Simahen's funeral, Saddam Hussein released all prisoners. He had the Ba'ath party members, the army and the police lay sandbags around their departments. Public address systems, radios and televisions began spreading the voice of Saddam Hussein louder than usual through the atmosphere. He threatened the betrayers of the fatherland, and the Americans.

Mira had given out the last of the money from the ring with the blue stone. As night fell she went on to the roof, packed the doves into a basket made of palm fronds and the next morning took them to the market to sell. People were busy stocking up on flour, rice, sugar and lentils before the looming war. In a corner she put down the basket with the doves and sat down next to it. She looked at the ground, because she was not used to being in a market.

"Go home," she heard a familiar voice saying, but she dared not look up.

She stood up and took the basket, while keeping her gaze fixed on the ground. She wanted to go home and thought that perhaps the sale of doves had been forbidden on that day.

"Mira," she heard the voice saying.

She looked up and saw Djazil. He was thinner and older. He had a short beard with grey hairs. The beard made his face look more peaceful.

"Take this money," he said.

"Maybe you'll need it yourself," said Mira. She thought that he was ashamed when he saw her sitting on the veranda.

"Don't worry," said Djazil. "Buy some food. Put enough away for the coming times. The Americans are coming here. Buy what you can store."

He said this cautiously, so that no one else would hear, and looked around to see if there were any policemen or party members in the vicinity. From his pocket he took the watch he had received from Rasjad and gave it back to Mira.

"Did he get safely over the border," she asked him.

He nodded. Then he bent over the basket, opened the flap and watched the doves as they flew back home. Three men stood waiting for him next to a pick-up truck.

Mira went to the market with the empty basket to buy groceries.

The spring of 2003 drew nearer, just like the Americans on the border. Djazil waited for news from the smugglers at the border and he listened to the small radio that he always carried in his trouser pocket. He waited with his men and when he saw the soldiers and party members packing sandbags around their buildings, Djazil gave Hadi the Rocket eight hours, until it became dark.

With his armed men, Djazil went to look for Hadi the Rocket

at his house. That night he arrived with his men at the farm, which he had not been back to since that day he had sneaked there with Rizen to steal peaches and see the party in his house. The night was quiet when the men climbed on to the high wall and sat on top of it. A dog barked from below. A newborn child cried.

The men on the wall saw Hadi the Rocket in his pyjamas coming out of the house with a torch in one hand and a pistol in the other. He walked cautiously through the garden and looked carefully around him. When he stood below the men, they jumped on him. He immediately threw the pistol down, as if it was a scorpion that was going to sting him, and he put his hands in the air even before he was thrown to the ground and Djazil's men went to sit on his back. The dog came closer and barked loudly. The soft voice of a girl called "Hadi! Hadi!" and she came walking from under the trees in the direction of where the dog was.

Djazil took the torch from the trembling hand of Hadi the Rocket and shone it on the girl. She was perhaps sixteen years old and carried a baby in her arms. Two men who had covered their faces with a headscarf, took the nervous girl inside and pulled the telephone wire from the socket. Djazil threw a stone at the dog, which kept on barking.

"Comrade Hadi, could you please tell comrade dog to shut up?" asked Djazil.

Hadi the Rocket tried shouting at the dog, but his nervousness prevented any sound coming out of his mouth.

"Bring him a glass of water," Djazil said to one of the men.

After a gulp of water, Hadi the Rocket shouted at the dog, which sauntered off. "What you're doing is treason," he then said to them. "The Americans are at the border and you're attacking an Iraqi citizen."

"We're also American," said Djazil and hit Hadi the Rocket hard across his face. "If you say anything without being asked, you'll cut short the minutes you have left to live. Motherfucker! The Americans are at the border and you're walking round in your pyjamas?"

He instructed his men to put Hadi the Rocket against a wall

where a light was hanging. Djazil then removed the scarf from around his face, lit a cigarette and smoked it calmly.

"The fatherland needs us," said Hadi the Rocket, terrified, as he looked into Djazil's impassive eyes.

"The fatherland needs you, comrade Hadi, and not us," said Djazil. "It's your fatherland, and not ours. It gave you a farm, cars, guns, pistols, women." He came right up to Hadi the Rocket's ear. "And it gave you boys ..." He desperately wanted to let Hadi the Rocket see his left ear, which the man had hacked off when he had followed Fatin, and which Joesr had sewed on again, but did not want his men to know about it.

"Do you want money?" asked Hadi the Rocket.

"Yes, comrade Hadi. We want money, but we don't need you to help us take it."

Hadi the Rocket began to beg in a whining voice. From the house the girl called him in a shrill scream, as one of the men raped her. The child was crying.

"God does not approve of what you are doing," said Hadi the Rocket, confused.

"God? Has God become a member of the Ba'ath party? Has he become a comrade?" Djazil slapped him across the face. "Why don't you answer me, comrade Hadi?"

But Hadi the Rocket kept quiet.

"Is there a shovel?" Djazil asked him, and when he did not answer, he hit him again in the face.

"Comrade Hadi doesn't know where a shovel is, because other people work for him on his farm," said one of the masked men and laughed.

"Ah," said Djazil. "I'm so sorry that I asked you for a shovel. It was not intended as an insult."

He ordered the men to look for a shovel and then had Hadi the Rocket dig a hole. Djazil went into the house, in which photos of Saddam Hussein were to be found on all the walls and on all the tables. He heard the girl and the child crying in one of the rooms. On the stairs he found a radio from which the voice of Saddam Hussein wafted softly, as he called on the Iraqi people to fight as one against the Americans. Applause and cheering sounded around him.

254

Djazil took the radio outside. The men were sitting around the hole smoking, waiting for Djazil. He turned the volume of the radio up. The voice of Saddam Hussein shattered the evening's silence and overwhelmed Hadi the Rocket's sniffling and the men's mumbling.

"Comrade Hadi, you can go," said Djazil.

Hadi the Rocket turned towards the house to go and find his latest wife. When she was fourteen, he had forced her father to give him her hand in exchange for her brother's freedom, whom Hadi had had thrown in jail.

"No, comrade Hadi. I didn't mean that way. Here!" Djazil shouted loudly and turned the torch on to the hole. "Go and stand there, filthy dog."

Two men shoved Hadi the Rocket into the hole. He knelt down and begged for mercy.

"Here, a present, comrade Hadi." Djazil threw the radio into the hole. "Perhaps you'll miss the voice of Mr President in heaven."

The threatening voice of Saddam Hussein and the whining voice of Hadi the Rocket emerged from the hole.

"Bury Mr President and his dog," said Djazil to the men. With the shovel, their hands and their feet, they threw earth into the hole, until the voices of Hadi the Rocket and Saddam Hussein had been silenced.

"The party and the president will disappear. If we are the first to dare to do it, we can be the first to take everything the party gave to its members," said Djazil, and he went into the house to drink tea with his men.

Rodaan Al Galidi

Chapter 20

The sky is the Americans', the earth Saddam Hussein's

The Americans set an ultimatum. George W. Bush gave Saddam Hussein and his sons Uday and Qusay forty-eight hours to leave Iraq. Mira heard it whispered around the market, but it was not clear to her who should be fleeing from whom. Would Iraq bomb America or America Iraq?

It was quiet in the market. The streets were empty. Many people had left their homes and gone to stay with acquaintances and family members in the countryside. Those who remained had boarded up their windows. Battery-operated radios were no longer to be found, as was the case with cigarettes and matches.

Arriving home, Mira made breakfast for Wasile and told her that Saddam Hussein had given America a time limit of forty-eight hours to deliver Bush and his father, otherwise he would bomb America. "They're saying in the market that Mr President will fight with the Americans after forty-eight hours or days, I'm not sure which."

Later that morning Wasile heard a child outside shouting: "It's raining dollars!"

256

Wasile called Mira to help her stand up. Together they went out into the courtyard. They saw pieces of paper falling from the sky. Mira picked one up and saw a photo of Saddam Hussein with Arabic writing next to it and a palace with a target over it.

"Who's throwing that from the skies?" asked Wasile, amazed.

"Mr President?" said Mira, while the paper quietly and slowly floated down like snow.

"Why is he throwing himself from the sky? Perhaps they come from the Americans. Oh God, have mercy on us," said Wasile, as if they were rockets and not paper. She grabbed Mira by the shoulders, so that she would not fall over.

When Mira took Wasile to her bed, she asked her to cover the windows with blankets. Then Mira took the broom and began sweeping up the sheets of paper and burnt them in the clay oven, afraid that a party member or someone from the secret police would see her, as if it was her fault that the papers had fallen from the sky and she lived right underneath them. Mira sweated and swept as if she were running after hundreds of chickens at the same time. She called Tenzile to help her, but the paper kept falling from the sky.

She hurried to Wasile's room. She stood panting in the room with the broom in her hand.

"Please, throw the papers away," said Wasile and pointed at the photos of Saddam Hussein still stuck in the bristles of the broom.

Mira went to the clay oven with big strides so that she would not step on a photo of Saddam Hussein, threw the broom in and ran back to Wasile. She dared not go back to her own room.

"God no longer wants Mr President," a pale Wasile said from her bed. "That's why he's throwing papers from the sky."

"They say that America's throwing the papers, and not God," said Mira.

"If the Americans can throw all that paper from the sky, they can also throw iron everywhere," sighed Wasile.

Through the blankets covering the window Mira saw a thin man walking in the courtyard. He was wearing old clothes, had a thick beard and unkempt hair. He caught a paper falling from the sky and read it, as papers fell on him and around him.

"Sjahid!" cried Mira, alarmed at seeing him in that state.

She ran up to him. His eyes were deep in their sockets. The black of his irises had changed to grey in the darkness of the hole. He picked up a piece of paper, read it and picked up the next one. Then he looked at the ground, which was covered with Saddam Hussein. Mira heard him crying softly.

"The Americans are throwing Mr President from the sky," he sniffed.

"What are you saying?" asked Mira, who saw him mumbling, but could not understand him.

"The Americans are throwing Mr President from Al Awja[8] in Baghdad and now they're throwing him from the sky down to earth. Mr President will govern the earth."

Mira could still not understand him.

"The Americans are coming here," he said, but Mira shook her head, not comprehending. "To free the Iraqis from Iraq," he added and went outside, into the empty streets, which were covered with white leaves that were still falling from the sky.

The papers that came from American planes spread a deep silence over everything. No one dared walk on them out of fear of standing on a picture of Saddam Hussein. Sjahid saw the sandbags around the buildings and all the curtains drawn in the windows. Soldiers sat on the veranda. Next to the Saddam Hussein bakery on Saddam Hussein square he saw an anti-aircraft gun with two soldiers alongside it. One of them called Sjahid over and gave him some money.

"Buy some bread for us," he said.

Sjahid went to the bakery and returned with bread.

"Run away, far from here," said the soldier. "The Americans will destroy all the towns."

"And you?" asked Sjahid.

"If they didn't shoot deserting soldiers on the spot, I would have run away long ago."

"Don't talk like that," said the other soldier. "Just shut your mouth."

"You shut your mouth," said the soldier, breaking the bread

and taking a bite of it. "Everyone has fled. No one brings us food any more. The Americans will make mincemeat of us. And then, just like after every war, Mr President will appear on the television and say that he fought and won. The Arabs will applaud him and hold his photo up high, just like in 1991."

"Shutting your mouth would be better," said the other.

"You must shut your mouth." The soldier turned to Sjahid. "And you, go, shave your face and wash yourself, before the Americans send you to heaven like you are now."

Sjahid wandered through the empty streets like a vagrant. He scratched his head, which was full of lice. A man tried to walk without standing on a photo of Saddam Hussein, but because that was not possible, he stood still.

"The Americans," Sjahid said to the man, but he did not respond.

Sjahid walked on and saw a girl sitting on her haunches. She seemed to be glued to the ground. With gentle movements she pushed the papers aside, as if brushing butterflies aside so that she could walk through them.

When she saw Sjahid looking at her, she smiled. "Mr President," she said. "Careful."

Sjahid walked on and saw a man and a woman with a child in her arms standing next to each other among the white papers. They did not know how to go any further. Behind them two older children jumped up and down, trying to catch the papers in the air before they touched the ground. They screamed with pleasure. "Papa Saddam! Papa Saddam!"

A man with three sheep was standing motionless. The sheep were eating the papers. "Go to your house, if you have one here," he said to Sjahid. "That is better than treading on Mr President."

Sjahid walked back and went to stand next to the anti-aircraft gun.

"Why are you standing there like a dog at the butchery? Go away!" shouted one of the soldiers.

Sjahid went home. From behind the blankets covering the windows Mira saw him standing in the courtyard among the falling papers.

"Mira!" he called.

She went up to him.

"Where are all the chickens and sheep?"

"They've all gone," said Mira.

"There's nothing left apart from Saddam Hussein," said Sjahid.

This time she understood him.

"The sky is the Americans', the earth Saddam Hussein's. Birds can no longer fly through the sky, no foot can walk on the earth any longer. It's over. It's over," Mira heard him repeating, as he walked out of the house for the last time.

On 20 March 2003 Mira waited up until five in the morning for the start of the war. When nothing happened, she said her morning prayers and went to bed. She woke up a little later. The house trembled from the bombardment, as if it was an earthquake. Her room filled with dust. Mira ran from her room and dragged Wasile outside, so that she would not be crushed by the roof if the house caved in. Then she called Tenzile, Shibe and Tali.

The bombardments ended as the sun began to rise and were followed by a sandstorm, which turned the world orange. After the Iraqi army had later set the oil wells alight, so that the American aircraft could no longer find their way in the smoke-filled skies, Mira lit an oil lamp to find her way through the house, but there was so much smoke hanging in the air that even with a lamp she could see nothing, and she went through the house like a blind person. There was no electricity, no running water, no telephone. Only the voice of Saddam Hussein still sounded from the radios the people had bought.

On 9 April when the Americans tied an American flag over the face of the statue of Saddam Hussein on Ferdous square in Baghdad, and a rope around its neck, Saddam Hussein ordered one of the soldiers who had remained with him to drive the car away from there. He fled from Baghdad.

At that moment a heavy feeling came over Mira. She thought that she would fall over with tiredness if she did not go and lie down immediately. From her bed she saw that there was a crack snaking across the ceiling. She immediately remembered that she had forgotten to give any food to Adam, stood up and walked over the trembling ground to the kitchen in search of powdered milk. She scooped two spoonfuls into a glass of water and went to the stable, with the glass trembling through the bombardments, which had begun again. A plane passed overhead with such a noise that the glass in Mira's hand broke and blood and milk dripped from her hand.

A boy from next door came running into the courtyard. He screamed: "Sjahid is sitting behind the anti-aircraft gun on Saddam Hussein square, just like in Rambo III[9], and fighting against the Americans!"

"Like who?" asked Mira.

"Rambo III!" The boy ran away as another aircraft flew over.

Mira put her shoes on and ran to Saddam Hussein square, from which the lone anti-aircraft gun was still being fired. All the soldiers, police and party members had fled after throwing their uniforms away. From Saddam Hussein Bakery, Mira saw Sjahid sitting behind the anti-aircraft gun. He was screaming and shooting into the air. Through the racket Mira called out his name. He turned round and saw her standing there. He put his hand in the air to greet her.

At that moment Mira saw Sjahid's hand come flying towards her through the air and fall down in front of her. A rocket had come down on the anti-aircraft gun. Mira bent over and looked at the hand. Then she walked like Adam to where the anti-aircraft gun had stood. Smoke drifted out of the crater. The anti-aircraft gun had been transformed into black chewing gum.

At the Saddam Hussein Bakery Mira asked for a plastic bag so that she could gather up what remained of Sjahid.

"He was crazy," said the baker. "We told him that the Americans were flying over us, but he screamed 'Long live Iraq' at us, and those sorts of slogans. We told him that even Mr President had fled, but he just carried on shooting. We wanted to take him away from there, but he threatened to shoot at us if we did not let him fight against the Americans."

Together with the boy who worked in the bakery and a friend of his, Mira put what remains of Sjahid she could find into the plastic bag. Then she went home and went to Wasile with the bag, which was covered with blood and ashes.

"What have you got there?" asked Wasile.

"Sjahid's remains," said Mira, but Wasile did not hear her through the bombardments. Mira put the bag down beside the door and went to Adam to give him a drink. He was lying in the stable in the place where Rizen had laid out the bag that had contained Edjnaad's body. He was lying on his back and staring at the ceiling. When a jet suddenly flew low overhead and the walls of the stable trembled, Mira fell over. She jumped up, as if waking up from her life in the Bird household, bent over Adam, grabbed him with both hands by the shoulders and shook him roughly.

"Wake up!" she cried.

Suddenly Mira saw Adam's head moving. He opened his eyes, but not as she had often seen him do when he was sleepwalking at night. He looked at her as if seeing her in a dream. Light and life slowly began to appear in his face.

"What?" he said sleepily and sat up.

Mira collapsed in a heap.

Adam, who had just woken up, was not aware of Mira's collapse. He saw her for the first time. The noise of the exploding bombs began rushing into Adam's head like two rivers emptying into his ears. He groaned as the American jets opened the skies with their metal. Disoriented he looked around. He saw Mira as if recognising someone from a dream and wondering where he had seen her before. He looked at her for a few minutes, but he did not recognise her. A long sleep had come between him and the world. He could not stand the noise of the world, he fell over and groaned, while in the distance the final cries for Saddam Hussein could be heard: "With our souls, our blood, we offer ourselves up for you, Saddam."

On 9 April when people were jumping on the statue of Saddam Hussein that had been pulled down on Ferdous square, and hitting its face with their shoes, Saddam Hussein reached the suburb of Al A'adamia in Baghdad in his car. The people there cheered, carried him on their shoulders, kissed his shoes and his clothes, and put him on the roof of the car. He stood there in his uniform with his pistol in his belt for a full one minute and thirty-four seconds. When he almost fell over, he climbed down and sat in the car. The car hooted, drove slowly through the throng and stopped again. Saddam Hussein climbed out of the car again and was put on the bonnet by the crowd. For two minutes and four seconds he waved at the cheering people, climbed off when he heard the Apache helicopters and ordered the soldier driving the car to leave.

The car began driving through the streets, which were just waking from the fear they had endured for thirty-five years. Through the window of the car Saddam Hussein saw a woman dressed in black clapping for him. He waved at her, and felt some pain, because he was leaving Baghdad for the last time. The pain ran like a waterfall from his head to his chest to his stomach, as if the marines he had left behind in Baghdad were not fighting there, but in his stomach. He rubbed his stomach with his hand but it did not help. He felt that he needed a toilet.

"Stop!" he ordered the driver, at an isolated rubbish dump. He climbed out, wanted to go behind a wall to squat there and picked up a stone on the way with which to wipe his arse.

A child saw him and began to cry out: "Papa Saddam!"

Suddenly a man emerged from behind the dump and cheered: "With our souls, our blood, we offer ourselves up for you Saddam!"

He was followed by men, women and children who all called in chorus: "With our souls, our blood, we offer ourselves up for you, Saddam!"

Saddam Hussein acknowledged them with the hand holding the stone. He wanted to smile, but could not manage it.

"Mr President, if there are no longer any weapons, we will fight them with stones, just like the Palestinians," shouted one man, because he thought Saddam Hussein was holding the stone in his hand as a symbol of the struggle against the Americans, and not something to wipe his arse with.

Saddam Hussein hurried back to the car, while the people followed behind him, cheering. He climbed in and ordered the driver to leave. He felt that he was going to explode if he could not sit somewhere and open his arse to let the pain out. He saw a date palm that was big enough to sit behind, ordered the driver to stop and walked to it. When he was standing behind it and began to undo his belt, an old woman saw him.

"Mr President," she cried. "Mr President!" She began to jump about and dance. "With our souls, our blood, we offer ourselves up for you, Saddam!"

People came from all directions, out of their houses and began applauding. Saddam Hussein went back to the car. The pain in his stomach and intestines made him double over. He saw someone throwing a bucket of faeces over a mural of him. Someone else was breaking a statue of him with a hammer. He heard children shouting: "America! America!"

The word stabbed him in the stomach. He screamed in agony. "Aiiiii."

"Mr President do you want to go to the hospital?" asked the driver.

"I want to go somewhere where there are no Iraqis and no Americans," said Saddam Hussein, and he held his stomach with both hands. "Aiiiii."

The two soldiers who were also in the car, thought that he had perhaps eaten something poisonous.

"Stop here!" cried Saddam Hussein.

"Mr President, perhaps it would be best if we get out of Baghdad quickly."

"Stop!" cried Saddam Hussein with pain in his voice.

The car stopped suddenly. Saddam Hussein climbed out, but people approached from all directions. Wherever he stopped, people appeared from everywhere, from behind walls, out of houses, from under bridges. They shouted out, so the crowd became even bigger. Nowhere could he find a place to do what he needed. The pain began to flow through his body in waves, threatening to send his intestines sailing out through his arse. He almost shit in his pants. The pain became an octopus with knives for legs. Saddam Hussein concentrated with all his might on his arse, afraid that he would shit in his pants and that people would think that it had happened because he was scared of the Americans, and not because of his despair over the loss of Baghdad.

"A toilet! A toilet!" he whispered. "Drive!"

"Where to, Mr President?"

"Straight ahead!"

"But Mr President, straight ahead is the south," said the driver.

"Straight ahead! Straight ahead! To a toilet!" cried Saddam Hussein, who, due to the pain in his stomach, had not heard what the driver had said.

The driver put his foot on the gas and kept it there until the car arrived in Boran. A few minutes from the large mural that Naji had paid for with his life, Saddam Hussein ordered the driver to stop. He climbed out of the car, which could go no further because of all the people blocking the street, and they began cheering for him.

Saddam Hussein went up to an old wooden door, behind which Tenzile sat, peering through the keyhole to see if Rasjad was coming back. The people followed him and applauded. "With our souls, with our blood, we offer ourselves up for you, Saddam!"

When Tenzile saw Saddam Hussein walking towards the house, she ran with Tali and Shibe to the cellar and closed the trapdoor behind her. She thought that the Americans would bomb everything. When the people's cheering reached Wasile's room, she felt an enormous energy rising up in her body, just as Kosjer had, when he had returned with the ram and had heard the applause from the tearoom. Without any trouble, she stood up and went into the courtyard, clapping. There she saw Saddam Hussein opening the door and coming into the courtyard. She knelt in front of him and wanted to kiss his shoes, but he pulled his feet away.

"Where's the toilet?" he asked.

"Here, Mr President." Wasile pointed to her room, because she did not want him to go to the old toilet filled with cockroaches. That would be too disgusting for Saddam Hussein.

He hurried to the room and closed the door behind him, squatted in a corner of the room and had a shit. Wasile walked around looking for Mira, Tenzile, Shibe and Tali so they could greet Saddam Hussein and saw Mira lying on the ground in the stable.

"Wake up," cried Wasile, confused. Then she went quickly to the toilet, filled the can with water from the fridge, because there was no water in the taps, and gave the can to the soldier at the door to her room.

"Drink some," the soldier said to Wasile to make sure the water was not poisoned, as if Saddam Hussein would drink from it and not clean his arse with it.

Wasile took a sip, after which the soldier took it and waited a while to see if anything happened to Wasile. He opened the door a crack and pushed the can in. When Saddam Hussein was done, he came out relieved. He face was peaceful, as if it was not only his insides that had been emptied of shit, but Baghdad of the Americans.

"Who lives here?" Saddam Hussein asked Wasile, who looked at him as if the angel of God had appeared to her.

"Mr President, I live here with my daughter, my son and daughter-in-law and their two children."

Saddam Hussein said something to the soldier and went to the front door. Suddenly the soldier pulled Wasile into the room in which Saddam Hussein had just had a shit, and after three minutes came out alone.

"The others as well, Mr President?" asked the soldier.

"No time," said Saddam Hussein. He went outside, greeted the people who were still applauding and cheering and he drove off in the car.

Half an hour later the Americans arrived in Boran. The people threw plastic flowers and sweets on to the American tanks and cheered. "With our souls, with our blood, we offer ourselves up for you, Bush!" Djazil searched for more men to occupy the offices and houses of the government, from which the Ba'ath party members had fled.

Before the sun had gone down, Rizen came home with his

uniform in a plastic bag. He wore old clothes that he had begged from somewhere. It was dark in the house. He called out.

Shibe answered him from his room and came up to him with a lantern.

"Where is Mira?" he asked.

"In the stable."

"Is she sleeping?"

"No, she's dead."

"Where is your grandmother Wasile?"

"In her room."

"Is she sleeping?"

"No, she's dead."

"And your mother?"

"On her bed."

"Dead?"

"No, she's sleeping."

Rizen took the oil lamp from Shibe and went to his mother's room.

Wasile lay on the ground with her feet bare. He smelt the stench and thought that it was from the corpse, but when he shone round with the lamp, he saw Saddam Hussein's pile of shit in the corner of the room and the can next to it. He threw a cloth over it, not realising that the shit was the reason why Saddam Hussein had given his last soldier his last order to strangle Wasile.

Rizen carried Wasile to Simahen's room and laid her down there. Next to her he laid Mira and the bag of remains, not realising that those were the remains of Sjahid.

When the sun began to rise on the first day without Saddam Hussein, the people set to plundering. They invaded government buildings, schools and hospitals, stole everything they could carry and burnt or destroyed what they could not carry.

In the intensive care unit of the Saddam hospital, someone was wearing an oxygen mask. The mask was taken off his mouth and nose and the oxygen tank was taken as well. When someone else pointed out to the plunderer that you could not use that type of gas in the kitchen, he put the tank down and left it behind. A woman grabbed another man's drip and ran away, with the patient running behind her, because the drip was still in his arm.

It seemed like one great relocation. Everyone carried chairs, benches, tables, chests, machines, apparatus, carpets. Even the museum of antiquities was emptied. Tenzile felt as if a new era was beginning, because she could talk with Rizen without a rocket falling in the midst of their conversation.

Before noon Saddam appeared from behind the house. He was wearing clothes he had taken from a shepherd in Kut, after he had thrown away his fidaï Saddam uniform. In the kitchen he took the lid off the last pot of rice Mira had cooked and began eating with his hands, before disappearing into Sjahid's hole, afraid of the Americans and of the people who knew that he had been a member of the fidaï Saddam.

"Won't you just go and get something for us," Tenzile said to Saddam as he went down into the hole.

"No, Mr President will return, just like in 1991," said Saddam. "And then he will chop off all the hands that have stolen anything."

Shibe called from the roof: "The Americans!"

Rizen, Tenzile and Tali went up to the roof. They saw lines of soldiers approaching. They were young and were red from the heat. Some of them wore glasses. Sometimes they rested a little, then continued on their way, as the people applauded them. They went into a school. Some went to stand on the roof with their weapons in their hands. Others began playing volleyball in the sports hall, as if it was not their first sight of that place. Apache helicopters flew low overhead. The soldiers in them waved at the people standing on their roofs.

At three o'clock in the afternoon Rizen went with a shovel to the place where he had found Edjnaad, so he could bury the dead.

"Please stay at home. It's safer," said Tenzile, when she realised that he wanted to go out to bury the dead and not to plunder.

"Nowhere is safe any longer, except the Ministry of Oil," said Rizen, and he left. He walked through the streets and saw bodies everywhere, burnt out cars, uniforms, boots and people fighting to get more plunder.

"Is that shovel all you managed to get?" asked an old toothless woman.

Rizen tried to smile, but could not manage it.

American soldiers stood in front of a building with their hands on their weapons, ready to shoot. Rizen stood in front of them and began rolling a cigarette, while looking at the bodies on the veranda and wondering whether he should bury the new bodies or dig up the old bodies with his shovel.

"The new bodies are rotting and have no history," he mumbled, as he smoked.

After smoking his cigarette he went to the market and bought plastic bags to put the skeletons in and a stapler so that he could staple any papers he found in their pockets to the bags.

He followed the banks of the Thirsty River until he arrived at the mass grave where he had found Edjnaad. He went to sit in the shade of a date palm, smoked another cigarette, picked up his shovel and began to dig.

CHAPTER 21

The cable of democracy

Even before the arrival of the Americans the government officials and Ba'ath party members had fled. Djazil and his men occupied their houses and farms and the party's house, took possession of the government vehicles, even fire-engines and ambulances for their own use. On the advice of an old party member who had joined up with him, Djazil hired three signwriters. They painted over the names on the buildings and the vehicles. With green paint they painted the words 'Army of God' on everything. He had his armed men stand in front of every building he had occupied, so that no one could plunder anything from them and ensured that he took occupation of the town hall with the printing press for identity cards. A former colleague from the town hall who had also joined up with him, designed an identity card for him. Everyone with such a card was a member of the Army of God.

Djazil was surprised at how easy it was for someone with guns and men to rule. He even thought of flying the American flag from the buildings and cars of the Army of God, but his men advised him not to do that, because the two did not go together, an army of God and an American flag.

"Why not?" asked Djazil. "When my grandmother Simahen

died, she believed that her soul would not be taken up to heaven on the wings of an angel, but on an F-16."

But when Djazil saw men everywhere with long beards and Korans in their hands coming over the Iraqi border to fight against the Americans, he changed his attitude. His theory was that there were two types of people one should never fight against: the Americans and the mujahideen. Not against the Americans because they were afraid of everything, except God, and not against the mujahideen, because they were not afraid of anything, except God.

Djazil had a notebook in which one of his men wrote down the names of all those who joined up with him. A few hours after the arrival of the Americans, Djazil's band of six men had become eighty-five and was steadily growing. Every man who became a member of the Army of God received from Djazil a Kalashnikov from the barracks, abandoned by the Iraqi army, that he had occupied, and an identity card.

By the end of the day on which the Americans came, there were four armed men standing in front of the former party house, which was now called the House of the Army of God. In the office of Hadi the Rocket, which was now Djazil's office, instead of a photo of Saddam Hussein there was a photo of Djazil. People began coming to the Army of God to complain if they received no help from the Americans. Every member of the Ba'ath party who paid Djazil received protection and an identity card for the Army of God. Former Ba'ath party members or office bearers who were betrayed by other people, were killed for a fee by the Army of God. Every street that paid the Army of God was protected at night by Djazil's men when the Americans returned to the protection of the green zone outside the city.

At nine o'clock in the evening Joesr arrived in the suburbs. He walked through the streets full of rubbish that had been piling up for days, and thought of the times he had been there with Samer, as they had discussed the most recent solutions to the world's problems that he had thought up in his room, when he had told Samer that being a vegetarian was not an illness, when he thought of becoming a vet.

"Halt!" he heard behind him.

Armed men wearing masks appeared out of the darkness. "What have you got there?" someone asked him and pointed to the case in his hand.

"A laptop," Joesr answered.

"That means nothing to me," said the masked man.

"It's a small computer."

"Are you a Shi'ite or a Sunni?"

"What do you mean?"

"Are you for Saudi Arabia or for Iran?"

"I'm for my laptop."

"For who?"

"For my laptop," Joesr repeated and he held up the rectangular case in his hand.

At this, the man ordered other masked men to take Joesr along, who then thought that it would have been better to have waited until the following morning to go to town. The men searched Joesr's bags, in which they found Iranian, Afghan, Russian and American money, which they confiscated. Half an hour later Joesr was standing in front of the House of the Army of God.

"No talking," said the man who left Joesr in a poorly lit corridor.

Joesr had to sit on the floor with the others who had been picked up that evening, to await a hearing. After two hours he was led to an office. A man with a beard sat behind a table with an oil lamp, behind him stood two large men with their hands behind their backs. The bearded man was smoking and writing in a file.

"No, no, no!" sounded from somewhere in the building. After three shots it went quiet.

The bearded man turned to the man on his right. "Please tell them that with all this noise we can't work. There has to be discipline in the system."

Joesr saw the photo of someone who looked like Djazil hanging above the desk. The man began talking to Joesr.

"Who is that man in the photo?" asked Joesr.

"You're here to provide answers, not questions," said the bearded man. "I have extraordinary powers to have you executed behind this building," he continued when Joesr kept staring at the photo.

"If that man in the photo is who I think he is, then I am here to ask questions and you to provide answers," said Joesr.

"What do you mean?"

"If that man in the photo is Djazil, then I want to go home," said Joesr and he looked at the man. "Tell him that the doctor who saw to his left ear must be paid back."

The bearded man took a mobile phone out of his pocket and spoke politely to Djazil. A short while later Joesr was given his money back and was taken home in a car of the Army of God, with his laptop.

He opened the wooden door, behind which a stone had been placed. It was quiet and abandoned. The smell of freshly baked bread, which had remained in Joesr's nose for years on end, had disappeared. Joesr went to the cellar. At the trapdoor he lit a match. He saw the plank hanging on the trapdoor, on which he had written with a pencil on the roof in the moonlight. Then he went to the place where his room had been and where Edjnaad had built his study, he opened the door and went in. He lit a match and saw the room just as Edjnaad had left it when he had followed the dogs. He bent over an open book, threw the match away when he burnt his fingers and lit a new one. In the book he saw that someone had been studying science and had been reading about alternating current. Joesr turned his head to the place where he had lain before he had broken his room down. The second match burnt his fingers. He lit another match at the place where he had stood on the night that Baan had been killed and walked out of the room. Outside a gentle breeze blew the match out. He walked around and when he heard Adam, he thought that Mira must still be alive. He went to her room, knocked softly and waited.

"She is in Najaf," he heard from behind him.

He turned around and saw Rizen with an oil lamp in his hand. They embraced.

"What is she doing in Najaf?"

"She's lying in her grave."

That night Joesr lay on a reed mat on the roof, looked at the stars and thought of Mira on the day she was catching fish in the cracks in which there was still water on the bottom of the dried-up Thirsty River. In the morning, he was woken by the cooing of the doves, after which he took a bucket to fetch water from the Thirsty River and wash himself. He saw Adam leaning with his back against a wall.

"Who are you?" Adam asked him.

"I'm the Thirsty River," said Joesr, thinking that Adam was still sleeping and was talking in his sleep.

Adam thought about Joesr's answer for the whole afternoon.

"But rivers don't talk in houses," he said to Shibe, who had taken to looking after him after Mira's death and brought him his lentil soup.

"What are you saying?" asked Shibe.

"Thirsty River was here."

Shibe put the lentil soup down in front of him and walked away. Adam waited until the soup was cold, dipped his fingers in it, then put them in his mouth and thought about Joesr's words. Tired of thinking, he went to lie down on the ground and looked anxiously at the sky, which was so vast, so far away and so deep.

After Joesr had washed himself, he went out, where people were still busy plundering what they could. Even land where nothing had been built was being divided up and marked out with chalk lines. When the new owners saw that there was no way of getting to their land, they began arguing with each other over where the streets should be. Joesr saw a wardrobe, to which a table and three chairs were tied. Under it walked a thin old woman, carrying it all on her back. A child of about ten had a wooden door with the face of Saddam Hussein carved into it in fine detail. People climbed the walls and broke in the windows of a bank to grab any money that might still be there.

At one of the open computer shops, Joesr asked if there was any internet yet.

"Strange," he said to the man in the computer shop, when he heard that it was not available yet. "The Americans are here, but still no internet."

When the sun came up the following morning and Rizen was going to the mass grave, he asked Joesr if he wanted to come along to bury the dead.

"I want to bury the living," said Joesr and went out to see if there was any internet connection.

Rizen picked up his shovel, the bags and the stapler and went to the mass grave, where he had been spending his days. He dug there carefully, like an archaeologist, put each skeleton in a bag, tied it up and stapled the papers from the shirt and trouser pockets to it. At midday he ate the little he had and then continued until the sun went down.

When Rasjad failed to come home days after the arrival of the Americans, Tenzile, Tali and Shibe went with Rizen to search for him among the dead. Rizen dug the earth away from the skeleton, Tali brushed it clean, Tenzile watched to see if she recognised the clothes and Shibe took the papers out of the pockets and stapled them to the bag. In one shirt pocket Shibe found a photo of a smiling girl. Her face was circled with a pen in a heart shape. There was a plastic packet with sunflower seeds in. The identity card was perforated with a bullet hole.

Shibe called everyone to let them see what she had found.

"This one really liked that girl. I think she liked eating sunflower seeds," said Rizen.

"Perhaps she just liked sunflowers," said Shibe.

"Perhaps the boy wanted to give her the seeds to plant, because he knew he was going to be shot," said Tali.

Shibe planted the sunflower seeds at the place where she had found the boy's bones. She watered them and kept the photo of the girl to hang it on the sunflowers if they sprouted.

"I don't think they're going to grow," said Tali. "Haven't they been in the ground all this time?"

"Yes, but they were in a plastic bag and now they're free to grow," said Shibe.

"They were set free by you and not by the Americans," Rizen called from where he was digging. "Long live Shibe." He uncovered a skull with the false teeth still in and the blindfold still tied on.

Shibe watered the sunflower seeds every day. Days later

they began to sprout. Everyone was surprised at how fast they grew.

"This is good ground for sunflowers," said Tenzile, who had never forgotten her dream of leaving the Bird family house. "Perhaps we must start a farm here and begin again."

"But all the souls of the dead are here," said Tali.

"The souls of the dead will leave when their bones are buried in Najaf," said Tenzile.

The streets began to be filled with banners from the new parties, the verandas with new newspapers and magazines and the roofs with satellite dishes. Computer shops and internet cafés were opening everywhere. Politicians began talking about freedom on their own television channels. Ba'ath party leaders who had fled to other countries, broadcast over their channels about the American occupation of Iraq. The mujahideen did the same about jihad in the mosques.

"The war between Mr President and the Americans was over before it began and now the war between the Americans and the mujahideen begins," Rizen said to Tenzile. "Even razors will be outlawed here."

"But Bush junior will surely bring those wooden boxes for elections?" asked Tenzile.

Rizen laughed when he heard that Tenzile had been thinking about something that happened not in their house, but in the streets.

"Elections are good," he said. "But will the rooster be happy if the hen receives more votes? Will the rooster jump down from the wall to sit on the eggs, because he lost the election?"

"Iraqis are not hens, they're all roosters," said Tenzile.

"That's the problem," said Rizen. "How can you persuade roosters not to attack each other?"

When Tali heard the word 'democracy' being repeated everywhere, he asked Rizen what it meant. He thought it was an unusual word for freedom, but had heard someone at the market shouting through a megaphone that the Americans had brought democracy to Iraq, but had taken freedom away.

"Where did you hear that word?" Rizen asked.

"At the market?" said Tali.

"Ask your uncle Joesr about it."

At seven minutes past eleven Tali saw Joesr, who was just arriving home with a cable for an internet connection. While Joesr tried to connect the cable to his laptop, Tali asked him what democracy meant.

"Democracy?" asked Joesr.

"They're talking about it in the market."

"Ask your father about it."

"Father sent me to you."

"Then ask an American on the street about it."

"But they don't speak any Arabic and no one can approach them when they're on the street, or you'll get shot dead right there."

"You're a child. They don't shoot children." He saw that Tali was still waiting for an answer and pointed to the internet cable. "Look, Tali. This is democracy."

Tali looked questioningly at his uncle.

"Watch," said Joesr. He typed in the word 'democracy', clicked on 'Enter' and the screen was filled with search results. He clicked on one of them and let an amazed Tali read the definition of the word 'democracy'. Then Joesr typed in 'America + occupation + Iraq'. Tali saw hundreds of entries appearing in front of him. Joesr went on and typed 'America + liberation + Iraq', at which Tali saw hundreds of different results. He took the laptop to the cellar and left a disappointed Tali behind. Joesr came back with a shovel and began burying the cable, as thin as a mouse's foot, under the ground.

"Why are you burying it?" asked Tali.

"This democracy is American," said Joesr. "So no one must know that you have it. More importantly you must protect it from the chickens and dogs."

When Joesr went back into the cellar, Tenzile called for Tali. She closed the door behind him and asked him what the cable was that Joesr had just buried.

"Internet," said Tali.

Then Tenzile asked him what he had seen on the laptop, which she referred to as 'the book with the screen'.

"The Americans," he answered.

Tenzile was shocked at how Joesr had changed. If she looked into his eyes, she knew that it was someone else standing in front of her and not the thoughtful boy she once knew. The compassion had disappeared from his eyes. He did not even go looking for his best friend Samer, who had kept coming to the house to ask after him, until he had been killed by the fidaï Saddam. He had stuck a photo of Saddam Hussein on his windscreen and the chickens in the cage that was tied to the roof of the car had shit on it. He was summarily taken away, together with the chickens and the old woman who had hired him to transport her and her chickens.

Twenty days after Joesr had returned, one of the men of the Army of God knocked on the door. Shibe came to the cellar and told Joesr that a man wanted to see him, but when Joesr realised that he had been sent by Djazil, he refused to see him.

"Tell that man that no one by the name of Joesr lives here," he said to Shibe.

Thus Djazil knew that Joesr did not want to see him. The following day he sent him an Army of God identity card so that no one would imprison him. Just as Mira had once always found him busy with books when she brought him tea or food, so Shibe found him behind the laptop. After a few times he asked Shibe to stop bringing him food.

"I'll come to the kitchen when I'm hungry," he said.

When he had eaten something in the kitchen, he left some money behind for Tenzile.

"What's up with him?" Tenzile complained. "He treats us as if this is a restaurant. We even get a tip."

When Joesr had finished eating he went back to the cellar, which he had furnished with a bed, a small table with two chairs, a lamp and an oil lantern, a box of shirts and heavy crates, the same as those used by the army for munitions, which he dragged into the cellar at night.

"Materials for my laboratory," said Joesr when Tali once asked him what sort of crates they were.

Tali asked for more detail, but Joesr became angry and said nothing more, from which Tali knew he should no longer ask about the activities in the cellar.

Tali waited for an opportunity to go into the cellar to see what was in the crates. He did not know that Tenzile was also waiting for such an opportunity, because then she could have found out about it from him. When Joesr was away, Tali ran to the cellar to see if it was locked, but Joesr always locked it when he left, until he one day found the cellar open. When Joesr returned from the toilet, he saw Tali in the cellar trying to open one of the crates. He sensed his uncle coming into the cellar again and looked up without turning round.

"You probably want to know what is in those crates?" Joesr looked at Tali, who nodded, almost imperceptibly. "There are things in them that a person can turn into a weapon."

"Books?" asked Tali, who had heard from Tenzile that Joesr had once locked himself away in his room and read books.

"No. Books turn people into victims," said Joesr. "But you gave a good answer." He gave Tali a five dollar bill. "Don't ever talk about the crates," he added.

Tali ran outside and was happy that Joesr had thought his answer was good.

Tenzile, who had anxiously been watching the trapdoor through her keyhole, suddenly pulled Tali into her room, while looking at the bill in his hand. She asked him what he had seen in the cellar.

"Nothing," said Tali.

"You're lying," she said quietly. "You saw something and you were given money to not say anything."

"In the crates," said Tali, who saw that his mother was paying careful attention to his words, out of curiosity as to what was in the crates, "are medicines that turn people into rockets."

"Ah, just a little longer and everyone will have become Hadi the Rocket," said Tenzile, who would never forget the shame Simahen felt in her last days for Joesr and the cellar. "And you, don't ever dare go in that cellar again. You'll get hurt." She lifted her hand threateningly in the air.

After two and a half months Saddam dared to venture out of the hole during the day. He went swimming in the Thirsty River when it was hot in the afternoons, when he knew that no one would dare pick him up because he was family of Djazil. At sunset he sat outside the front door, against the wall and watched the Americans. He thought of his days in the fidaï Saddam, where he had quickly achieved success in the secret barracks. On the first day of training there were five hundred young men lined up.

"Men," a man with a moustache and thick chest hair, which grew up his neck, said to them through a megaphone, "you are the fidaï Saddam. You are directly linked to the name of Mr President. This is no place for cowards or traitors, only for men of steel."

They put their black uniforms on, from which you could see only the eyes, mouth and nose, and went with a corporal out on to the training ground. The corporal took a rabbit out of a basket and told them that after nine months of training they would be men and would be able to tear up that rabbit with their teeth and fingernails. Saddam put his hand in the air and told the corporal that he could already do it. The corporal called him to the front. Bursting with pride, Saddam grabbed the struggling rabbit by its ears and began tearing it up with his nails and teeth. His face and hands were soon red. Some of the young men fainted or looked at the ground.

"Go to the dormitory and have a shower," the corporal said to him. "You don't need to take this course."

Saddam completed the training, that usually took nine months, in two months. The men trained on blocks of wood and dogs, and by the end they were all ready to chop off someone's head with one blow and they could break someone's arm or leg with one swipe of a steel cable. Saddam was proud when he was selected from the barracks to chop a head off for a secret service film. They showed these films to prisoners. Then torture was not always necessary, because the prisoner would immediately tell them what they wanted or what the secret service wanted to hear. After the arrival of the Americans the torture films were found in a secret service building and were broadcast on the internet.

Saddam laughed proudly, when Djazil watched the film on a computer screen and said that the executioner in the film had hands and an arse just like his.

"Idiot, are you really the masked man with the sword?" Djazil slapped him on the shoulder.

"I'm not saying anything," said Saddam.

Tenzile encouraged Saddam to join up with the Army of God.

"Djazil is your uncle. He's sure to help you."

"Yesterday with the fidaï Saddam and today with the Army of God? Not likely," said Saddam.

Tenzile decided to take the matter into her own hands, went to the House of the Army of God and asked to see Djazil. After waiting for four hours, one of his men led her into his office.

"What can I do for you?" he asked without looking up, like all Muslim leaders, in order not to look at women.

"Saddam," said Tenzile, and she thought that he would recognise her voice.

"What about Saddam?"

"He wants to work for the Army of God."

"How do you know Saddam?"

"He is my son." Djazil waved her away in dismissal.

"Go home, there is no place in the Army of God for anyone who goes by the name of Saddam."

"But isn't the Army of God his uncle's army?" said Tenzile angrily.

Djazil looked up and saw Tenzile. He immediately stood up, gave her a chair and ordered the two men behind him to leave the office and bring some tea.

"I don't want tea," she said. "I'm looking for work for my son in the Army of God."

"Don't worry any longer," said Djazil.

When Tenzile climbed out of the car of the Army of God that

had brought her back home, Saddam got in and never came back to that house, which had never felt like home to him.

After quarter of an hour he was sitting in front of Djazil.

"From now on you're called Abdullah the Pious and not Saddam," said Djazil.

"What must I do?" asked Saddam.

"Let your beard grow."

From that day on Saddam became Djazil's shadow. He followed him everywhere. Even in the photos of Djazil published in the Army of God's newspaper, Saddam stood behind him with a Kalashnikov in his hand.

One day Tenzile proudly brought a newspaper to Rizen.

"Look at our Saddam behind Djazil. He looks like Mr President when he stood behind Ahmed Hassan Al-Bakr."

"That's true," said Rizen, irritated. "Congratulations, we have a new Saddam Hussein."

After three months Saddam's comrades from the fidaï Saddam had become members of the Army of God and had begun training the new members of the Army of God in the barracks. These had been abandoned by the Iraqi army when it had been disbanded by the Americans.

"Maybe the Americans will get angry if they see that we are training soldiers in the barracks," Djazil said to Saddam.

"We have seven lawyers, ten journalists, a newspaper and a television station. Just what the Americans wanted ..." Saddam said. "An army with lawyers and journalists. But ..."

"But what?" asked Djazil.

"We need a party," said Saddam. "An army without a party is like a computer without a screen."

Djazil hired four former Ba'ath party members who established the Party of Heaven for him, with which Djazil became the leader of the Army of God and leader of the Party of Heaven. Before elections took place, Saddam would ensure that many people were members of the Party of Heaven. At night, when the Americans withdrew to the green zone, a list of names rolled out of the Party of Heaven's computer of those who were not members and had to be killed or kidnapped, and Saddam's masked men headed off in all directions into the dark.

People lined up to become members of the Party of Heaven. They could do this at a window in the old security services building, which Saddam had taken over. On the door he wrote 'Human rights building'. He gave the Red Cross and the Red Crescent an office in the building and even opened an office there where anyone could go to find those who had gone missing. Far from there he had an underground prison built below the training barracks, in which eyes were pulled out and necks hacked through. From there the bodies were thrown in the middle of the night in bags into the Thirsty River. In the Army of God Saddam found the freedom he needed to practise his violence.

When complaints reached Djazil, he summoned Saddam.

"Do anything, except one thing," he said to him. "Do not make the Americans angry. Do not bark in their face, do not bite, just wag your tail."

Hundreds of women dressed in black stood outside the human rights building to ask after their missing from the time of Saddam Hussein and from the time of Saddam Rizen Kosjer Bird. They held up the photos of their missing relatives in their hands. In front of the human rights building a market developed, larger than Simahen had ever accomplished. In the market computers were traded, alongside marijuana, DVD players, software, porno films, virus scanners, digital cameras and CDs about the jihad. Every woman in the queue was given a file, on which the photo of the missing person was attached next to their name, address and the date on which they had last been seen. Then they were sent to another queue to receive a number, with which they could wait at another counter to see someone from the Red Crescent or the Red Cross.

When Rizen found Kosjer's skull, which he recognised from the gold tooth that Wasile had told him about, he put it in a bag and went home, this time before nightfall. He wanted to buy a lamb and sacrifice it for his father's soul, now that he was sure that he was dead. He walked through the town, saw the queue of women stretching from the veranda through the sheep market and he followed the queue until it reached the human rights building. A man from the Army of God kicked a woman trying to get into the building. Rizen helped her up.

"What do you want here?" he asked her.

"My son was taken away a month ago by men from the Army of God and I've heard nothing more of him," she sniffed.

Another woman came up to him.

"The security services of Mr President took my son in 1987. Ever since then I have heard nothing about him."

Then more and more women came to stand around him, glad that someone was listening to them, and Rizen became surrounded by black shrouds and complaining voices.

"My father was taken away in 1979," cried Rizen.

The women quietened down.

"Today I found his skull." He took the skull with the gold tooth out of the bag and held it up, so that the women could see it.

As if he had been sent by God, all the women came up to him.

"There!" cried Rizen.

He walked to the mass grave and the women followed him, until he came to the bags.

"Do not mix the bones up!" Rizen shouted loudly.

The women walked carefully down the long row with pale faces and trembling lips alongside the bags and looked at the clothes that had been pulled out of the ground and at the papers that Rizen had found. Now and again a woman wailed, if she recognised a piece of clothing, the hair or a photo of her missing relative. When evening fell, peddlers arrived and began selling candles and oil lamps to the women. Taxi drivers stood ready to take the women home, with their missing ones. The night was lit to the horizon by the candles and oil lamps and by crying to the heavens.

When the sun began to shine, everything had been taken away, apart from a few bones here and there and the sunflowers. Rizen took the remaining bones home with him. From that day on he went every time a mass grave was discovered and any bones that were left over, he took home. After a few months Rizen had seen three hundred and sixty mass graves. From the remaining bones he had assembled his father Kosjer, his grandfather Nadus and his uncles, took it all to Najaf and buried them alongside the graves of Simahen and Edjnaad, exactly as Simahen had instructed.

Arriving home, he slept for two days and felt unwell, as he always did when he had nothing to do. While he lay in bed, Tenzile's idea of building a house near the sunflowers grew on him and on the third day he stood up and went to the sunflowers, which were growing quickly in the fertile ground. He sat there on a rock and smoked until the middle of the day, until he could envisage the house, just as he could the orchard in front of the sunflowers and the canal that would bring water from the Thirsty River. For about an hour Rizen dreamt about the time he would spend in the shade of the fruit trees, sitting and looking from the sunflowers stretching to the horizon, and how the water would flow through the canal, as birds flitted on the branches.

"Here, on this ground, far away from the guns, we can begin a new life if Mr President does not go back to Baghdad and I don't have to go back to the army," Rizen said to himself. He rolled a cigarette and wished that he had brought things with which to make tea for himself.

CHAPTER 22

Joesr's laboratory

There were rumours that Saddam Hussein was busy somewhere bringing the army and the party back together to begin a new war against the Americans. Some people were still afraid that Saddam Hussein would return to power, others hoped for it. The fear surged when Saddam Hussein sent a cassette tape to the media and the television began broadcasting his speech, in which he called on the Iraqi people to rise up in opposition against the Americans.

Tenzile was anxious that day. She walked from one corner of the house to another.

"I think Mr President is going to return to Baghdad," she said to Rizen when he came home. "Thankfully you didn't burn your uniform or throw it away."

Tenzile began frantically searching for a photo of Saddam Hussein to hang up if he came back to power, but could not find one anywhere, except on the Iraqi bank notes. She would not rest until Tali had the photo on a note enlarged by a former Ba'ath party member. When Tali brought the photo of Saddam Hussein back, covered in newspapers so that no one would see him, Tenzile hid it in the hole where Sjahid had stayed.

Every time Tenzile saw Joesr coming out of the cellar, she

wished the house next to the sunflowers would be built even faster. It surprised her that Joesr did nothing in the house's empty rooms and chose to sleep in the cellar.

When Joesr took his clients down into the cellar, she could take it no more and went to Rizen.

"Joesr is taking people down into the cellar," she said.

"Perhaps he's starting his own army, just like Djazil," said Rizen. "From the day the Americans came here, everyone's been setting up armies, parties and newspapers."

"When they go into the cellar with Joesr, they're still thin, but when they come out, they're fat," said Tenzile.

"Perhaps he's blowing them up."

"Don't you even want to see what he's doing down there?"

"Why would I? Perhaps Joesr's doing something he doesn't want anyone to know about."

"But this is your house as well."

"Since the arrival of the Americans, no one has their own house any longer," said Rizen. "Yesterday a man killed his daughter because she was watching a sex film on the internet. Someone else threw his son into the river because he wanted to be a woman. A son killed his father, because he had smoked hash and raped his daughter."

Tenzile was deterred by Rizen's stories and waited in even greater distress for the moment when the house by the sunflowers would be ready. Then she would be able to get away from those streets full of Americans, the mosques full of mujahideen and the skies full of Apache helicopters. But what made her most afraid was that from 9 April, when Saddam Hussein had fled from Baghdad, her dreams had become darker. Saddam Hussein no longer brightened her dreams with his white shining clothes and his glowing skin.

From 9 April 2003 she dreamt in the darkness, in which she felt her way and called out searching for a path. "Mr President! Mr President!"

Rizen tied her to the bed, so that she would not wander outside in her sleep while calling "Mr President". Once when he forgot about her, Tenzile called Tali, who untied her hands and feet. Tali became disconcerted when he saw his mother like that, but was put at ease after he went to the internet café and typed in 'woman + bed + tied" and saw Sharon Stone appear before him in the film Basic Instinct. He wanted to watch to see what would happen to the blonde American woman, but the man from the internet café came to stand behind him and said that he must not watch those sorts of films, otherwise the internet café would be blown up by the fundamentalists.

When tying Tenzile to the bed proved ineffective, Rizen eventually decided to hang the picture of Saddam Hussein, which he had hidden in Sjahid's hole, above the bed. He put a candle near the photo, to light it up, and put a recorder with songs about Saddam Hussein within earshot, so that he could find his way through the dangerous Americans to Tenzile's dream. When Saddam Hussein reappeared in her dreams, she slept deeply and the noise of the chickens, the screaming of the Americans, the car bombs and Joesr's clients could not wake her up.

At twenty to six in the morning the first client came to the cellar, which Joesr called a laboratory. It was a boy of seventeen years old. He was calm, not as if he was going to explode in two and a quarter hours. He sat on the chair in front of Joesr, who sent an e-mail from the laptop saying the boy had arrived. Then he asked him to take his shirt off. Joesr saw that the boy had the name Fatima tattooed on his left arm.

"Is she your sweetheart?"

"Who?"

"Fatima."

"She's my mother," said the boy.

Joesr was amazed that anyone would tattoo the name of their mother on their arm, because the names of mothers and sisters should remain secret, but he did not want to ask the boy about it.

"Does your mother know that you're going to blow up?"

"Not yet, but she soon will."

"Have you said goodbye to her?"

"I'll see her in heaven."

From his composed and quick responses Joesr understood

why the boy had been chosen to be the first in Iraq to commit a suicide attack.

Joesr opened a crate, picked out the explosive and began sticking it with tape on to the boy, who remained breathing calmly.

"What are you getting to do this?" Joesr asked and tried to smile.

"Heaven," said the boy. "I was lost, my life had no purpose. I only thought of myself, until I met them and they showed me the truth and gave meaning to my life by letting me fight for what I believe in. And what are you getting?" the boy asked, full of self-confidence.

"A lot of concentration and two hundred dollars."

After Joesr had covered all parts of the boy's chest with explosives, he asked him to keep perfectly still.

"Now I am going attach the detonation device to it."

The boy saw that sweat began to drip down Joesr's face and that his hands were beginning to tremble.

"Are you ...?"

"Sshhh," said Joesr.

The boy had wanted to ask if he was nervous, but kept quiet and looked at Joesr, who was concentrating with anxious eyes and a sweaty face.

Joesr had never before tried the type of detonator he was using now. He had heard from the Afghans, who had heard it from the Palestinians, that a Chinese detonator was less reliable than a German one.

"Sit still," said Joesr. "Every movement will throw this cellar twenty metres into the air."

The boy smiled surreptitiously. "Just keep calm," he said.

Joesr knew that the boy had to do the same. He wiped the sweat off his face with a handkerchief and began with the detonation device, as if operating on an eye, as he had learnt in Afghanistan. Then he asked the boy to put on his shirt again. But it no longer fitted. So he took a larger shirt out of one of the crates.

Joesr looked into the eyes of the boy and wanted him out of the cellar in a hurry before something went wrong and the boy exploded. "In three-quarters of an hour the timer will go off.

You won't feel any pain because in less than a second you will become ..." He searched for the right word.

"Charred mincemeat," said the boy, smiling.

"Just so," said Joesr and he led the boy outside. Behind the house he watched the boy leave, walking like a pregnant woman. Joesr went back to the cellar to catch his breath. He had not worked with explosives for two and a half years and wanted the first operation to go well.

Suddenly he remembered that he had not asked the boy where he was going to blow himself up, but it would probably be somewhere near the Americans.

After forty-five minutes Joesr heard an explosion and he knew that it had been a success. Then ambulances and the fire brigade could be heard. He went in the direction of the blast and found that the boy had blown himself up in the bird market. The dead were still lying on the street, among bloody feathers and cages that had been thrown around by the force of the explosion. Some of the dead had been burnt, others bled out. Joesr saw people running with buckets of water to the shops where birds were still chirping, to save them from the fire. A girl of about six years old was cut in half. She was still holding a cage with a dead bulbul in it.

Joesr went back to the cellar and after half an hour fell asleep. When he woke up, he switched his laptop on. In his e-mail was a photo of his next client, with the place and time where he would meet him.

Because there was no running water, Joesr went to the Thirsty River to wash himself. There he saw Adam standing in the water up to his knees with all his clothes on. He walked into the water with the soap. Seagulls screamed from the opposite bank of the Thirsty River when a fisherman pulled his net out of the water. Adam groaned. He stared at the flowing water.

"Rasjad," Joesr heard him whisper.

"Rasjad what?" he asked, but Adam kept looking at the flowing water and repeating the name of Rasjad.

Adam kept on repeating the monologues and conversations of the family from the past, but when the wind died down and the suicide attacks stopped, especially as evening settled in, he stood up and went past all the doors of the household. He knocked on them and asked for Rasjad to continue with the first conversation he had ever had with anyone in his life. If anyone told him that he was not there, he closed his eyes and went to another door. His knocking on the door sounded like drops of water falling from an old roof.

"I'm Rasjad," Tali said to him one day, to see what he would do.

Adam slowly raised his hand and laid it on Tali's head.

"Still," he said and kept quiet.

"Still what?" asked Tali.

"Branches, afternoon birds, fire. Still and still," whispered Adam.

Tali removed the hand from his head and went away without Adam, who was looking down, realising it.

Adam remained standing at the door for the whole evening, believing he was standing in front of Rasjad and then went back there every night.

"I called Rasjad but his answers cannot reach me," he said when Shibe asked what he was doing at that door.

"Why are you calling Rasjad?"

"Steel everywhere ... Cold steel ... Hot steel ... Steel everywhere ... Ask Rasjad if he is a door," he said to Shibe.

When Shibe told Tenzile what Adam had said, Tenzile warned her to keep him off the streets.

"His soul left his body with Mira's soul," she said. "And now there are spirits living inside him, because he was not buried as a Shi'ite should be."

But Shibe did not believe her and looked after him. When Shibe went with Tenzile and Tali to help Rizen in building the new house by the sunflowers, Shibe never forgot to take Adam along. She tied a piece of string to his finger so that he had to follow them and did not stop every few steps. After a while he followed their voices without a string on his finger. At the sunflowers, he sat in the shade of a date palm. If he disappeared, they would find him back at home in the stable.

Tenzile kept on complaining, even after everything had been plundered or stolen. "Look, everyone's taking their piece of Iraq, except you. As if we don't live in this country and haven't endured all the wars, fear and pain."

But Rizen's fear of Saddam Hussein was too great. Rizen, who for his whole life had seen how men fought at the order of Saddam Hussein, did not believe that the man could disappear just like that.

"Then at least take a door or a window from somewhere," Tenzile said when she saw him stripping doors and windows from the house and taking them to the new house.

"And what if Mr President comes back? What then? Will we then have time to get the door or the window out of there and throw it back in the street?" Rizen asked her. "Just you wait. Mr President is coming back and then everyone will throw everything they've stolen out into the street." He told Tenzile what he had seen in 1991, when Iraq had lost the war in Kuwait and the south and the north had risen up against Saddam Hussein, as Bush senior had ordered, following which General Schwarzkopf with the Republican Guard, Saddam Hussein's private army, under the protection of American Stealth bombers, had crushed the uprising in the south. A hundred thousand people had lost their lives as a result.

On the roof of the Bird's house a satellite dish appeared, through which they could receive 485 Arabic channels, while television in the time of Saddam Hussein had two channels, one of Saddam Hussein, one of his son Uday. Thanks to this Tenzile became less afraid of Saddam Hussein, but Rizen's fear increased, especially when the films showing torture and killing, which were found in the secret services' building, were broadcast. Rizen did not want to work for the Army of God, not even at Tenzile's insistence.

"I spent my best years in the army of Mr President and I don't want another army to steal my remaining years," he said.

Tenzile warned him not to use the term 'Mr President' any longer, because people would think he was still in favour of Saddam Hussein.

"My tongue was shaped by Mr President, I can't help it," said Rizen.

Tenzile was worried that Rizen's fear of Saddam Hussein, which had previously saved him, would now get him killed. Every night she prayed to God to save Rizen from his fear. She burnt incense while reciting what she could remember from the Koran and the holy scriptures.

She once heard a voice calling her in her sleep. She opened her eyes.

"Who's there?" she said in the darkness of her dream.

"It's me, Saddam Hussein," said the voice.

A match flared for a second.

Tenzile got a fright. She saw a tramp in old clothes, a long beard and long, unkempt hair. "Are you really Mr President?"

"Yes."

This time Tenzile recognised his voice. "Should I light the oil lamp?" she asked politely in the dark.

"No," said Saddam Hussein. "There's a price on my head and the Americans are everywhere."

"Ah, Mr President, I'm sorry I didn't recognise you, but why do you have that beard? Don't you have a razor?" asked Tenzile.

"This beard is not here because I don't have a razor but because the Americans brought Islam to Iraq. Ah, Tenzile, you should feel how the lice plague me."

"Take a shower, Mr President. Do you perhaps want a bucket and some soap?"

"The time for a shower will come, but now is the time for the Americans and the lice," said Saddam Hussein. "But I heard you calling me. That's why I came here. What can I do for you?"

"Rizen, Mr President. He is still scared of you." Saddam Hussein laughed quietly.

"Don't worry yourself. Wait for six days, and on the seventh day sacrifice a white rooster, at which Rizen will be freed of his fear for me. Now I must go. The Americans are everywhere, except in your dreams."

Tenzile counted off the seven days, bought a white rooster and had it killed by Rizen. That was on 13 December 2003.

On that day Rizen left the house, not knowing why he had killed that rooster. There was no electricity. Suddenly he saw people running to a house, where they had a generator. Curious, he followed them, especially because the owner of that house was shooting into the air with his gun and shouting.

"Come and look at the rat!"

Rizen clapped, just like his father Kosjer had when he had come back with the ram and had heard the applause in the tearoom. He hurried into the man's overfull living room. It was stuffy. Rizen only just squeezed in. Breathless he waited with the others to see what would appear on the television.

An American filled the screen. "Ladies and gentlemen," he said in English. "We got him."

No one understood what was being said, but everyone remained dead quiet watching the screen. Suddenly it was as if Rizen had been slapped in the face. He saw Saddam Hussein standing with a long beard and wild hair. And Americans wearing gloves looked with a torch into his mouth and in his hair. Rizen felt light-headed. He could not get any air, as he watched the man who had taken him from his home at the age of sixteen to fight for him until he had become grey.

In a daze he walked back home. Tenzile had just plucked the rooster.

"Why are you so pale? Did a car bomb explode?" she asked.

"Not a car, Saddam Hussein," he said, confused.

"What are you saying?" she asked him, surprised because he simply said 'Saddam Hussein' and not 'Mr President', without thinking about it.

"The Americans were looking for lice in Saddam Hussein's hair and chemical weapons in his mouth," said Rizen. "They caught him."

He went to lie on his bed and recalled that what Simahen had told of her dreams had become reality. He was sorry he had not paid more attention to the rest of her dreams. Then he would know what was going to happen after Saddam Hussein had been found in the hole and when the Americans would leave Iraq.

When the electricity came on again, Tenzile ran to the

television and called Rizen. "Is that our Mr President?" she said when he came into the room.

"I think so, that's him."

"Perhaps it's a double."

"Saddam Hussein has no double."

"Why not?"

"God would not allow that another like Saddam Hussein ever be created. Now you can burn my uniform."

When Tenzile burnt the uniform, she also found the photo that she had had enlarged and stared at it. She could not imagine that the lice had dared infest his hair and his beard. She even thought of also burning the photo, but considered that it would be better to wait a little before doing anything so rash.

Chapter 23

On the way to Abu Ghraib

Simahen's prayers for George W. Bush during her final months and Rasjad's dream of going to America, ensured that Tali held the Americans close to his heart. He was curious about them, when they came to Boran. They walked in their khaki-coloured uniforms down the street, their hands on their weapons, ready to shoot. Little by little he got closer and closer to them.

One day he saw an American soldier wearing glasses. Tali examined him from top to toe. Then he walked around the soldier and kept watching him. The soldier smiled at him. Tali looked inquisitively at the things he was wearing and asked him if he had ever tasted berghi dates.[10] The American soldier spoke no Arabic so thought that Tali was perhaps asking him about his weapon and gave him his helmet. Tali took it and put it on his head, found it too heavy and gave it back. The soldier took a sweet out of his pocket and gave it to Tali. He took it and thanked him with a salute. He could not believe how civil the American soldier had been to him.

The following day he took a bag of berghi dates along for him. He searched for him throughout the town and when he found him, he handed the bag over to him. The soldier indicated that he should first open it. When he saw what was in it, he smiled and took it. Tali did not understand why he had to open the bag. He wanted to ask him, but could not do it in English. At home he looked through Edjnaad's books for one that would teach him to speak English, but he found only dictionaries. He began pleading with Tenzile until she gave him some money, with which he bought a book in the market about how to learn English in five days, looked for questions in it that he wanted to ask the American soldier and underlined the sentences with a pencil.

The next day he searched for the American soldier until he saw him with other soldiers standing in town. The soldier recognised him and smiled. Tali could not get any closer because they kept the people at least twenty metres away from them, but he did not give up. The next day he saw him standing at a barricade they had set up. Tali walked up to the barricade and greeted the soldier in English with the sentence he had once learnt in school and had found in his book.

"Hello, how are you? I am fine. Thank you very much, my friend. And you?"

The American soldier laughed and began speaking slowly in English to Tali. Tali turned round, sneakily read a sentence from the book in his back pocket, turned back and asked the soldier.

"What is your name, mister, now?"

The soldier walked up to Tali, put out his hand, like they did in the American films and shook his up and down. "My name is Bill, and you?"

"Bill Clinton," said Tali and he laughed. "My name is Tali, and you."

"Bill Clinton. And you?"

Tali was so happy that this time he forgot to turn his back to read from his book. Bill did not understand all the questions he asked. Tali bent over and concentrated on his book and saw a question. "Do you like to eat a hamburger with me?"

Bill read the question aloud and laughed.

Tali went red when he turned the page and read the translation of the question. He wanted to tell Bill that he did not mean that question, but the question that was above it: "What kind of food do you like?"

"McDonald's," he said when he saw that Tali was embarrassed and he read the intended question. He never ate there, but wanted to give his new little friend an answer.

Tali, who did not know what McDonald's was, quickly paged through the book, from the pages about food and restaurants to the pages about making introductions. Bill saw many of the sentences had been underlined in pencil. He began reading the sentences out slowly and answered them. A Humvee stopped and a soldier winked at Bill. He took a sweet out of his pocket, gave it to Tali, bade him farewell and went to the Humvee.

Tali was in seventh heaven. He could not believe that he was so good at English that he could communicate with an American soldier. He went home as happy as could be. Every day he walked through the streets until he encountered Bill. After there had been attacks on various schools, Tali no longer had to go to school and he was happy about that. Every day he took a bag of berghi dates with him, gave them to Bill and talked to him. At home he told Shibe about it. She wished that as a girl she could also be able to do that. When Shibe heard that Bill did not eat the dates, but only took them, she said to Tali that perhaps the American soldiers were afraid that the dates had been poisoned.

"Poisoned?" said Tali, surprised. "But we're friends? I wouldn't poison my friend."

"The television says that the Americans are our enemy. That's why they go around with their weapons on the streets."

"Do you also think they're our enemy?"

"Of course not, I hope that they stay until I turn eighteen."

"Why?"

"When I'm eighteen and the Americans are here, then I can join the army," said Shibe. "Then I can learn to use weapons and work for the United Nations, so that I can travel to other countries."

"How did you come to that?"

"From the satellite," said Shibe. "When I'm on my own, I watch the American TV broadcasts."

"But you don't speak any English."

"No, but I'm not blind."

The arrival of the Americans had created new dreams for

Shibe, while Tali thought about her remark that perhaps Bill thought that he wanted to poison him. The next day he walked for an hour to the furthest date plantation and an hour back again to find delicious berghi dates for Bill. He gave him the bag and received a sweet in exchange. Bill took the bag without opening it or looking what was inside, and also without even tasting one. Tali opened his book to make sure of the sentence that he had engraved on his mind over the past hour.

"Mister my very good very friend Bill. Dates very good for healthy if not poison," said Tali, and took the sweet he had been given by Bill. He put it in his mouth, looked Bill intensely in the eye through his glasses and waited expectantly for what he would do.

Bill took a date, looked at it and ate it up. When he had swallowed it, he suddenly clutched at his throat and began groaning. "Tali, no, Tali, no!" he cried out.

"Mister very friend ... mister very good!" said Tali, concerned.

Then Bill burst out laughing and looked at Tali's pale face. "American joke," he said and ate all the dates in the packet.

Tali felt that their friendship was now so strong that they were almost brothers. He wanted to tell that to Bill, but his English was not up to the task.

Bill took a piece of paper out of his pocket and gave it to Tali. 'Tali@hotmail.com, password: veryfriend' was written on it. Tali went home and waited for Joesr so that he could ask him what it was that he had been given.

Tali had the walls of his room, where Mira had once slept, covered with posters of American pop stars and basketball players. The walls of Shibe's room, where Edjnaad and Enhar had once slept, were covered with posters of female American soldiers landing in the swamps, fighting against an unseen enemy or surrounded by children with their fingers making the V-for-victory sign. The documentary about the arrival of the Americans at the zoo in Baghdad had a profound effect on Shibe. All the employees from the zoo had fled. Most of the animals were dehydrated or had already died of hunger and thirst. Shibe saw a pelican that still had a little water left in the pond in its cage. He saw two female American soldiers opening a tin of sardines and giving it to the pelican. Soldiers sprayed water from a fire engine to fill the pond, at which the pelican began flapping its wings. Tears flowed down Shibe's cheeks when he saw the pelican frolicking in the water.

"I think the Americans are going to heaven, even if they aren't Shi'ites," he announced to Tenzile after the documentary.

"What?" said Tenzile who was busy washing some rice before cooking it.

"The Americans are going to heaven. They saved the pelican."

"Where?"

"In the documentary."

"Not one single American is going to heaven," said Tenzile. "Not even if they take a thousand documentaries with them on the day of judgement. God is afraid that they'll also start a war in heaven. And be careful that the terrorists don't hear you. They'll make you wear red pyjamas and kill you with a knife." Tenzile was not happy with her children's fondness for the Americans and always became angry when she saw the posters on their walls.

One day Tali came back after a meeting with Bill and proudly let Shibe see the sweets he had been given. Tenzile saw them, grabbed them and threw them on to the ground.

"What are you doing?" asked Tali, taken aback.

"They're tainted. They come from the Americans. They don't believe in God."

"But you still use American medicines?"

"You have a long tongue. You mustn't support the Americans, because when you grow up, you'll hate them."

"Why then?"

"Because they're American. They like Jews and hate Muslims."

When Rizen came home from building the house next to the sunflowers, he found Tenzile upset, like a clucking hen with a red head looking for somewhere to lay its eggs.

"What is it?"

"Your children like the Americans."

Instead of Rizen getting angry and smacking them, he did nothing.

"I said that your children like the Americans and you do nothing?" cried Tenzile, whose voice sounded ever louder in the house after Wasile's death.

"What would you have me do?" said Rizen. "Burn them? Get into their hearts and burn the Americans? Our own men ran away and left Baghdad behind for the Americans. And Saddam Hussein, who always vowed that he would save the last bullet for himself, has been found in a hole!"

Tenzile looked at Rizen, who was rolling a cigarette.

"When the Americans came, we woke up in our trenches and there was no longer anyone to give us orders. Our officers had disappeared during the night. They left us behind for the American's fire and what did the American's do?" Rizen looked earnestly into Tenzile's eyes. "From their Apache helicopters they threw rubbish bags so that we could put our uniforms in them, because they knew that we did not want to leave our uniforms behind, like in 1991, out of fear for Saddam Hussein." He lit the cigarette and inhaled deeply on it. "Let the children like the Americans. Perhaps it's better than the hate that poisoned our lives."

"You also like the Americans," said Tenzile.

"Do you think that someone who has spent his whole life fighting, knows love?"

Tenzile walked away. She felt tears welling up when she thought back to the time when he wore a shard on his neck from the rocket that had ensured that they saw each other again.

Tenzile could not sleep that night. She was afraid that someone would realise that there were people in their house who liked the Americans and would blow the house up. She had prayed furiously for God to protect the house from car bombs that were exploding everywhere and the sharp knives of the fundamentalists.

When she eventually fell asleep, she heard the voice of

Saddam Hussein calling her. She was standing in an endless tunnel in which a crowd screamed and applauded loudly for Saddam Hussein.

Suddenly everyone went silent and the voice of a newsreader from the time of Saddam Hussein could be heard. "Hail the holy mother."

The ground under Tenzile became grass with flowers. Colourful butterflies flew around her knees. Children waved little flags in their hands. Behind her stood armed soldiers and behind them people stretching to the end of the tunnel, cheering and jumping like slaughtered roosters. "With our souls, our blood, we offer ourselves up for you, Saddam." Tenzile also wanted to jump and shout, but Saddam Hussein came up to her, in the clothes he was wearing in the dock during his trial, which she followed on television when there was electricity. He held the Koran in his hand and was followed by hundreds of lawyers from the East and the West as disciples.

"Holy mother. You don't have to clap," said Saddam Hussein.

"Ah, Mr President," said Tenzile. "My children, Mr President. They like the Americans."

Saddam Hussein laughed and spoke to his lawyers with a cheery voice, like the one he put on when he visited his birthday gifts museum, which was filled with golden guns, knives and shields.

"You don't have to do that because you are the new mother of Iraq." He turned to Tenzile. "Don't worry about it. Fast every Thursday until the second April of the Americans in Boran. Then the love for the Americans will disappear from the house. And now the recess is over, I must get back to the dock."

Saddam Hussein walked to the dock, the lawyers behind him, and behind them the soldiers and thousands of applauding people. "With our souls, our blood, we offer ourselves up for you, Saddam."

Tenzile looked at the green earth beneath her, where the colourful butterflies were dancing about her, and when she looked up again, she saw an enormous chair, on which her son Saddam was sitting. She looked at him.

"Where did you get that chair?" she asked.

"I got it from my father," cried Saddam.

"But Rizen doesn't have a chair like that."

"Not from my father who sleeps with you, but from my father who slept with Iraq." Saddam laughed and tried to make his shoulders dance, just like Saddam Hussein when he laughed.

On the third Thursday that Tenzile fasted, she heard a knocking on the door and the bleating of sheep behind it. Standing behind the door was an old man and a young woman.

"We're looking for Rizen, the father of Abdullah the Pious and the brother of the leader of the Army of God," he said, after he had greeted Tenzile.

She suddenly felt proud and powerful and wished that Rizen had heard it. "You are at the correct address. What can I do for you?"

"Abdullah the Pious's men have taken my three sons away. This woman is married to the middle one. We have heard nothing more of them. We are afraid that the men of Abdullah the Pious will take us away as well if we go and ask about them. The Americans said we must go to the Red Cross, the Red Cross sent us to the Red Crescent, who directed us to the mujahideen to hell and gone, who said we should go to the police, but as you may know, there have been no police since the arrival of the Americans."

Tenzile began crying when she heard her son mentioned in the same sentence as the Americans, the mujahideen and the Red Cross.

"Rizen is not home, what can I do for you? I am the mother of Abdullah the Pious."

The man and the woman immediately knelt at her feet. The sheep bleated louder and the woman began kissing Tenzile's hands.

"If Abdullah the Pious or Djazil do not release them, then we'll find their heads on the banks of the Thirsty River. Here are three sheep, one for each of them," the man pleaded.

"Bring the sheep in," said Tenzile and she took them to the stable, where no animals had been since Mira had sold the last sheep in order to buy groceries. Then she went with the man and the woman to Saddam. Half an hour after she had made it clear to the guards that she was his mother, the three men were back with their father. That day animals and chickens began returning to the house. People knocked on the door to ask Tenzile to bring their missing back. After four days Rizen noticed the animals and the fighting roosters.

"I didn't buy them," said Tenzile proudly when Rizen asked her where she had found the money. "Every lamb and every rooster is a person saved from death."

"You've brought death to this house." Rizen was surprised at the number of people Djazil and Saddam had taken captive in four days. "Idiots," he hissed between his teeth and looked at Tenzile. "We must get out of here before it is too late."

The Army of God became a large militia, especially when it became apparent that the American army did not concern itself with what was happening on the streets and only protected the oil wells and the Ministry of Oil. The name of Abdullah the Pious began to invoke fear. Just as the television was the instrument of fear in the time of Saddam Hussein, so was the computer in the time of Saddam Rizen Kosjer Bird. Militias and armed gangs filmed the torture of their victims and posted the recordings on the internet. On their foreheads they wore headbands bearing the names of the militia or group.

During a big party by the Army of God and the Party of Heaven on Djazil's birthday, which had been made a holiday, Djazil called Saddam to his office.

"Didn't I ever tell you not to come into conflict with the Americans," he said angrily.

Saddam kept quiet.

"Look at what your men have done!" he screamed. On the computer screen a film was showing in which a group of men wearing black clothes and headbands of 'The Army of God' were killing an American in red pyjamas with a knife. A voice said that that was the retribution by the Army of God and the Party of Heaven for the American occupation of Iraq.

From that moment on, Djazil slept in secret locations out of

fear of the Americans. After a few days a member of the Party
of God phoned Djazil and told him that he was one of the
leaders who had been invited by Paul Bremer, the American
administrator in Iraq, to Baghdad to discuss the current
situation. Djazil called in sick and sent a delegate.

After four days the delegate returned. He said that Paul
Bremer wanted to phone him, because he was concerned about
his health. At the appointed time, Paul Bremer phoned Djazil.
At that moment Apache helicopters appeared above the farm
where he was.

Paul Bremer asked what he was hearing.

"The Apache," said Djazil with his heavy Iraqi accent. "Mr
Boel[11] Blemer, you got me." He put the phone down, took his
pistol out of his belt and put it on the table.

"If you want, we can open fire on them," said one of his men,
as the Apaches landed.

But Djazil told them to lay their arms on the ground. "Only
attack the American when he believes he is safe and do not do
it like a snake in the air, but like a scorpion in the dark at a
moment when their guard is down."

The door was kicked open by screaming soldiers. Djazil's men
were tied up with their hands behind their backs and laid on
the ground, while Djazil was blindfolded and flown to Abu
Ghraib in an Apache helicopter.

The walls of Abu Ghraib prison had been painted by the
Americans to hide the blood from the time of Saddam Hussein.
The nails with which chopped-off ears and tongues had been
hung up, had been removed. Instead of the rusty old bars, new
ones had been put in, with locks that were not opened by keys
but by electronic cards. In the corridors and the cells moving
cameras had been installed.

On arriving Djazil had to take his clothes off and his body
was searched by the American guards. He had to remain on his
hands and knees and a female soldier ordered him to bark.

"Good dog," she said when Djazil barked loudly as she made
him crawl to his cell and threw him some red pyjamas.

Chapter 24

Pyramid of naked arses

Tenzile fasted every Thursday, as Saddam Hussein had told her to do, in her dream. In the second April of the Americans in Boran she began counting the days.

"Just you wait," she said to Rizen. "Shortly there'll be no love lost for the Americans in this house."

"How do you get to that?" said Rizen.

"I dreamt it."

"You're old-fashioned. After the coming of the Americans people were talking about what they see on the internet and you're still fixed on your dreams."

After the third Thursday in April she listened diligently to the news which came via the satellite dish when there was electricity, and otherwise through the keyhole.

"April is almost over and still nothing has happened," she complained to Rizen.

At the end of April Rizen went to the market to buy something Tenzile could burn under her pots, because the logs were finished and there was no longer any wood in the empty rooms. At the market, all eyes were focused on the newspapers hanging up in the shops and lying on the verandas. People stood in groups around them.

A deep silence reigned, which was not normal for that time of day, following the loud cry of the newspaper sellers. "Abu Ghraib! Abu Ghraib!" they cried, as if the newspapers were buses that could take people to Abu Ghraib.

"Can you help me?" asked an old woman with a trembling stick in one hand and a fluttering piece of newspaper in the other.

"What can I do for you?" asked Rizen.

"The newspaper," said the old woman. "I heard that the Americans put photos of the prisoners in the newspaper. They're naked, so that their families can recognise them. I'm looking for Mohamed and his son Arkaan and his nephew, whose name I've forgotten … The Americans took them away, because they had beards. They had beards because otherwise they would have been killed."

"But you have a newspaper in your hand. Did you not find them in it?" asked Rizen.

The woman sat wearily on her haunches. "I can't see very well. Someone told me that the newspaper I bought isn't the right one. He said that there were no naked people in my newspaper. He said it's yesterday's newspaper, and not today's. I don't know what the difference is between yesterday's newspaper and today's newspaper."

"I believe yesterday's newspaper is all about yesterday and today's newspaper about today."

"The Americans didn't take them away yesterday and not today, but four months, one week and three days ago," said the woman. "Please can you exchange this newspaper for me for the one from four months, one week and three days ago?"

Rizen took the newspaper from the woman.

"Tell him I want the newspaper with Mohamed and his son Arkaan and his nephew, whose name I no longer recall, in."

Rizen walked through the crowds of people to go and exchange the newspaper.

"The pigs! The savages!" screamed someone with a sword in one hand and a newspaper in the other, and running in the direction of the green zone. He was wearing a headband bearing the words 'God is Great'. Behind him men were running with the same headband and the same swords.

Before Rizen reached the newspaper seller, a bomb exploded. A bus and the cars around it flew into the air. Bodies, fire and steel were thrown in all directions. More cars exploded and shots rang out. In the chaos people ran in all directions, over the newspapers that they had been looking at before the explosions.

The newspaper seller screamed: "Not on the newspapers … Not on the newspapers!" He began gathering up his newspapers and throwing them into his cart.

"The old woman says she bought yesterday's newspaper," Rizen said to the man, as the ground under his feet trembled.

"What?" screamed the newspaper seller.

"This is yesterday's newspaper," shouted Rizen.

"It's a better one," cried the man, busy packing newspapers into his cart.

"But the old woman is looking for her son Mohamed and his son Arkaan and his nephew, whose name she no longer knows. These aren't in the newspaper."

"My idiotic mother is also not in yesterday's newspaper," cried the newspaper seller, getting irritated with Rizen.

A bomb fell on the old woman. The newspaper seller flew through the air and fell to the ground. "She no longer needs today's newspaper," he said to Rizen, who looked at him as if nothing had happened around him.

When a second bomb fell, the newspaper seller ran away and left everything behind, but Rizen was thrown on to the newspapers by the shockwave. As he stood up, on one of the front pages of the newspapers he saw photo of naked bodies stacked up. He got a fright when he saw a tattooed eagle on one of the arses. An Apache helicopter overhead blew all of the loose newspapers into the air.

"Djazil's arse," whispered Rizen, dazed as he looked at the third layer of the neatly packed arses, in which Djazil's arse was fifth from the left. He stared at the tattoo made when Djazil was a child, to chase the scorpions away. The bird looked more like a chicken as Djazil's arse became fatter, and like an eagle when he was thinner. As a result of the torture the bird had become more like a heron than an eagle.

"Out of the way!" screamed a man running past him with a

wounded child in his arms, but Rizen looked through the photos in the newspapers to see if he could find Djazil's face anywhere. As bombs were falling around him, Rizen walked up to the old woman, who was lying on her back on the ground, and he laid a newspaper over her. Then he wandered home with the newspapers in his hands.

"Look," he said to Tenzile and threw the newspapers on the ground.

"Did the bombs make you crazy? You don't bring such dirty newspapers home," said Tenzile angrily, because she thought they were erotic pamphlets.

"Look at that arse," said Rizen.

Tenzile wanted to send Tali and Shibe out of the room. They were looking inquisitively at the newspaper. Their father, who was illiterate, never picked up a newspaper.

"Let them look," said Rizen. "It is their uncle's arse."

Tenzile remained still and looked carefully at the newspaper. She was taken aback on seeing the photo. "Why in heaven's name did the Americans build a pyramid of arses?"

Tali and Shibe stared with wide eyes and open mouths.

"It's him." Rizen put his index finger on the arse with the eagle. "That is the arse of their uncle Djazil."

Tenzile picked the newspaper up and gave it to Shibe to read what was printed next to the photo.

He read the article and then cried out cheerily: "The arse of my uncle Djazil is now famous all over the world, just like Elvis Presley! We have a world famous member of our family!"

"Read out loud. We also want to hear," said Tenzile.

Shibe began reading the article aloud. Her face, at first delighted because of Djazil's now famous arse, became concerned. She slapped the newspaper to the ground.

When Tali heard what was in the newspaper about the torture of prisoners by the American guards at Abu Ghraib, he stormed to his room and tore down the American posters from his walls and threw them into the clay oven. Then he gathered up all the sweets from Bill into a bag, took a newspaper and ran with it to town in search of Bill. Tali tripped, grabbed a stone and threw it angrily at an Apache helicopter overhead.

Then he ran on through the smoke of destroyed houses, bodies and burning cars. He found Bill with a group of American soldiers. Their faces, hands and clothes were covered with ashes.

"Stop!" shouted one of the soldiers when he saw Tali approaching them with a bag in his hand. Tali stopped, panting, put his hands in the air and looked at Bill, who was standing next to a group of men who were squatting on the ground with their hands on their heads.

"Let him come!" Bill called to the other soldiers.

Tali walked up to Bill with his hands up.

"Okay, Tali, okay," cried Bill to put him at ease.

Tali threw the bag down, sending the sweets scattering in all directions. Then he threw the newspaper at Bill. "You not my friend. You American!" Tali cried angrily. He turned round and ran back home. There he saw that Shibe had also pulled down the posters from the wall in her room.

That evening Tenzile laid out her prayer mat in the direction of the Kaaba and prayed: "Merciful God, just as you have saved this home from the Americans, save us from this house, before it falls on our heads, as Simahen predicted."

The days following the publication of the photos from Abu Ghraib were busy days in the Bird household. Tenzile began packing her things in bags and boxes for the move, as soon as Rizen was finished with the roof of the new house and Joesr was receiving ever more clients. He gave discounts to clients who came of their own accord, without having joined up with anyone. On Wednesdays he even worked for free for clients who wanted to blow themselves up because they had nothing better to do.

In the first week of May Djazil was released from Abu Ghraib prison. The torture he had endured had weakened him. By the time he arrived in Boran, he was a famous national leader, because the Army of God and the Party of Heaven had let it be known that the tattooed eagle in the newspaper photo belonged to Djazil. During demonstrations by the Party of Heaven against the Americans, people held up photos of Djazil's arse.

Djazil went into his office in the House of the Army of God

and sat behind his desk. On the wall behind him hung a photo of his tattooed arse in Abu Ghraib, next to the photo of his face. On his orders, all the photos from Abu Ghraib in which he appeared were spread out on a table. He handed them out to journalists and political leaders who came to visit him.

He would then proudly point at his arse. "In this photo my arse is third from the left, second level," he would say. Or: "That's the bag on my head."

Half a month later Djazil was standing on a big podium in the middle of Boran, encircled by armed men. Thousands of people were clapping and chanting slogans against the Americans.

Djazil began speaking. "Brothers." Applause … "Sisters." Applause … "Americans." Applause … "America." Applause … "Iraq." Applause … "No." Applause … "Yes." Applause … Applause … Applause …

Djazil turned to Saddam, who was standing behind him. "Do you understand anything of what I'm saying?" he asked.

"No," said Saddam.

"Then why are the people clapping?"

"They're standing further away from the microphone, so they can hear you better."

"I think they're clapping for the microphone and not for me," said Djazil, but Saddam could not hear him as an eruption of applause rose up into the blue skies.

On that same sunny day, Rizen moved with Tenzile, Shibe, Tali and Adam to the new house alongside the sunflowers. When Rizen stopped at the front door in the truck and went inside to load the boxes and bags that Tenzile had packed, he found Tenzile sitting on the floor crying.

He silently picked up a box and wanted to go to the truck, but she asked him a question with a lump in her throat. "Aren't you going to ask me why I'm crying?"

"If you weren't crying, I would ask you why not?" said Rizen, and he wanted to walk away with the box on his shoulder.

"I'm crying because our lives are in boxes and bags," she said.

Rizen put the box down and waited for her to say what was

on her mind. When nothing came, he said: "But in an hour's time we'll be in the new house. Wash your face."

"And what about Joesr in the cellar and the stork in its nest? They'll be all alone."

"They don't need us," said Rizen. Joesr has the internet and the stork its two wings." He picked up the box and quickly went to the truck.

When everything had been loaded, he let Adam sit with it. He remained in the back of the truck until everything had been unloaded and taken into the new house. That night Shibe found him looking in the empty boxes and bags.

"What are you looking for," she asked him.

"Rasjad," said Adam and continued looking with the thin hands that still bore the scars from the cigarette butts put on him by Simahen, Mira and Rizen's other children.

"Don't look for him. He's not here," said Shibe. "Go to bed."

"But he must be in one of the boxes," said Adam.

Tenzile took his hand and pulled him to his new room.

An hour later Adam got up and walked back to the old house.

When Joesr came out of the cellar, he saw his brother standing in the courtyard. "Did they forget you here?" he asked him and went to the toilet.

When he returned, Adam was standing at the cellar's entrance.

"I found Rasjad in the drops but not in the boxes," he said to Joesr.

"What do you want with Rasjad?" said Joesr.

"For him to pull me out of the water," said Adam. "My knees in the water, my eyes on the moon." He looked at the infinite stars and performed in the same rhythm as that song that he had heard one distant June. "No soy de aquí, ni soy de allá ... no tengo edad, ni porvenir ... y ser felíz es mi color ... e identidad."

Joesr, who had still not quite grasped that Adam was awake, was surprised that he had remembered the Spanish song for all those years. He listened to the same intonation as had been on one of Naji's cassette tapes, which he had been given by Sjahid, one June evening long ago.

"What a memory," whispered Joesr.

"I'm not a man," said Adam. "I'm an old tape recorder."

After a short silence he repeated the speech by Saddam Hussein, in which he thanked France for the Super Etendard jet fighters and their pilots, with which he bombed the Iranian oil installations during the war.

Adam put his hand in the air, slowly lowered it on to Joesr's head and looked at the ground. "I did not find Rasjad in the rooms or in the boxes," he said with a weary voice.

"Go and lie down," said Joesr. He wanted to say that Adam should go and sleep, but thought that he was already asleep.

"I can't lie down with my knees in the water," answered Adam and he carried on with reciting what he had heard that day in June.

Joesr heard his own conversation with Mira from then, when he had followed her to tell her about her rights as a worker in the house, while she chased chickens. Joesr followed his words from when he was a dreamer who wanted to change the world, until the moment he left the house. He discovered that his friend Samer had often come to ask about him during his absence. In the middle of the night he heard what had happened in the years that he had not been there. When Adam repeated what Simahen had said about her grandson Joesr, he threw Adam's hand from his head and went down into the cellar, sweating.

The next day he could not find Adam anywhere. Shibe had taken him back to the house and locked him in his room, so that he would not walk away before he was used to the new place.

"Adam! Adam!" Joesr called out in the empty rooms.

On the floors lay ashes from the garden's trees, which Tenzile had burnt beneath her pots.

CHAPTER 25

Sunflowers

On an evening during the fourth December of the Americans in Boran, the Bird household was empty of women and a lone lamp still burnt in the cellar. Joesr ate cold tinned meals when he was hungry. His clients were more concerned about the stench of the empty tins than about the explosives being wrapped around their bodies, but they did not complain, because they thought it was part of the atmosphere of that place. At about the time at which the rope that would hang Saddam Hussein was being tied to the ceiling, Joesr threw an old blanket over his shoulders and went outside for some fresh air. He heard a newborn child crying. He went to the place where the sound was coming from and heard a song by Enwar Abdulwahab[12] coming out of the only lit window in the ocean of bullet riddled walls. The child had stopped crying.

"Emel," said a woman trying to talk softly. "Turn the radio down. If the terrorists hear that they'll tear this house down."

The radio was turned down and when the song ended, the tuner button was turned.

"Go to sleep instead of looking for songs," said the woman, who had begun to lose her patience in the night, throttled by terror.

314

"I can't sleep," said a girl's voice.

"That's your own fault," said the woman. "You stay awake the whole night and sleep during the day or are tired. Give the radio to me."

A little later the silence returned and Joesr heard nothing other than the wind whistling through broken windows.

Suddenly a gunshot broke the silence, followed by machine-gun fire from all directions. Joesr jumped behind a broken-down wall until the silence returned and then ran away. A few shots followed him, he disappeared behind a wall again and when it became quiet, he ran home. He walked, breathing heavily, down into the cellar and when he had caught his breath, he realised he had lost the old blanket. He went to lie on the bed and thought about the six clients he had to prepare the following day for attacks. One of them was named Murad. His face was familiar, but he did not know from where.

At ten past eight in the morning, Joesr woke up from the sound of gunshots. He saw on the clock that he had missed the seven-thirty appointment with his first client. Within half an hour he had to be at the place where the second client would meet him. Joesr switched on his laptop to see why there was shooting, but there was no internet connection. He got dressed and went outside. People on their roofs were shooting into the sky. Joesr saw a man on the street shooting with a pistol into the air. He was being followed by a girl pressing her fingers into her ears and a boy with a seagull on his shoulder, which raised its wings every time the man let off a shot.

Joesr asked the man why everyone was shooting.

"I don't know. I'm shooting because everyone else is doing it."

Each time he posed the questioned, he received the same answer. After half an hour he went back to the cellar and waited for the internet connection to come back so he could watch Saddam Hussein's final steps and see the thick rope that lay around his neck like an anaconda.

Joesr took the laptop out into the courtyard, because he felt that this scene had to be seen by more than one person, but there was no one in the house to watch it. Then he went to his client. In some streets there was celebration, in others mourning. Some screamed, in tears: "They've hanged Mr President, the prince of the mujahideen." Another called, laughingly: "Ah, if only I'd had a rope to put around the neck of that parasite."

Joesr saw his client standing uncertainly, waiting.

"I don't understand any of this," said the boy.

"Do you want to postpone our appointment?" asked Joesr.

"Maybe that would be better," said the boy. He told Joesr that he knew of a good restaurant, where they could have a meal together.

"During his lifetime Saddam Hussein transformed Iraqis into bloody wolves and timid sheep, but after his death they've become crying Sunnis and laughing Shi'ites," said Joesr.

After the breakfast the boy made a new appointment for the following day in the same restaurant and left.

After his next three clients, Joesr took a nap, ate a tin of beans and went to the last client of the day. It was Murad, who wanted to commit suicide out of despair over love. He was in love with a girl by the name of Mejade. He had been following her for two years, but she never paid any attention to him and averted her gaze when she saw him. Eventually he wanted to end his life by slitting his wrists with a razor, but was prevented from doing that because after the death of his father at the hands of the fidaï Saddam and his mother and grandfather in a car bomb, he was the only one remaining to look after his blind grandmother. When a militiaman assured him that they would look after his grandmother after his death, he decided, there and then, to commit suicide to be freed from the heartache over Mejade. When Joesr set the detonator on him, he asked him how much time he needed. He thought he would need a quarter of an hour to find Mejade, half an hour to try to get close to her and then half an hour to get to the centre of town to blow himself up.

Then Murad set off in search of Mejade. He walked round and round her house, but only found her after an hour. This time he did not wave to her with his hand, as he did in the afternoons if no one else was around, or with his eyes if there were people on the street, but had the courage, for the first time, to walk up to her. His heart was going crazy. He looked at his watch, afraid that he would blow up right next to her if the quarter of an hour he had left was over.

"You've got fatter," said Mejade. "Yesterday you were thin and now you're fat. I think you've put on lots of clothes to make me think that you've got lots of muscles." She laughed.

When she saw that he did not find it funny, she continued talking to put him at ease. "Actually I think you're nicer without muscles."

Murad was amazed. He was sorry that after all these afternoons he had not walked up to her before. "What did you say?" he asked. When he saw how late it was, he wished that detonator would not take ten minutes, but an eternity.

"I said that you're not saying much. You're looking at your watch while I'm talking to you for the first time. Are you a professor that time is so important for you?"

"I don't have much time today," he said.

"Why not? Do you have to give a lesson at the university or are you going to the United Nations instead of Kofi Annan?"

"I'm going and you'll never see me again," said Murad.

"What?"

"I'm going and you'll never see me again."

"Don't do that," she said. "I'll really miss you."

Murad could not believe his ears. He looked at his watch and saw that he still had six minutes. He ran to the Bird house, to Joesr, the only one who could free him from the explosives. He ran, while looking at his watch. When he only had a minute left and knew that he would not get to Joesr in time, he stopped in the middle of the road. He tore open his shirt to pull the wires loose. "A terrorist!" someone screamed. Everyone ran away, as soldiers aimed their rifles at him and shot him before he could explode.

When night fell, Joesr switched his laptop on and read the news about Murad. In the article was his full name: Murad Samer Hassan. He ran in shock to the house where he had always gone to visit his best friend Samer or gone with his father Hassan to El Mutanabbi Street in Baghdad to buy books, and he knocked on the door.

"Who's it? Murad?" It was the voice of an old woman.

Joesr went in, lit the oil lamp with a match and saw the old blind woman lying in the darkness.

"Where have you been?" she asked. "I was getting worried."

Joesr looked at the wall and saw a photo of Samer with his father and his son Murad.

"Close the door," said the old woman. "It's cold."

Without saying a word Joesr went out of the room and walked into the darkness, with trembling lips, up to the wooden door behind which Baan had once waited for him.

He knocked on it and called out: "Baan! Baan!"

He pushed it open and went in, but found no one there. In the same place where Baan had stood in her last moments, he saw that he still had the oil lamp in his hand and he let it fall. The lamp broke. He fell to his knees and looked around him in the darkness.

"I should have been here to save a life," he whispered. With his last energy he stood up, walked back home and went into the cellar.

Half an hour later there was an enormous explosion. The house of the Birds was blown into the air and fell in ruins back to earth.

The following day it was said that the Americans had bombed the house, because a terrorist meeting had been taking place. It was said that the Army of God had bombed it, so that no one would know about the beginnings of Djazil's life as a chicken thief and of Saddam as a member of the fidai Saddam.

Tenzile believed that the internet cable had made the house implode and decided that no such cable would come to their new house. "If the internet comes to this house, the Americans will follow," she said.

Even a long discussion with Tali could not persuade her otherwise, but she kept giving Tali money so he could go to an internet café. "Here, buy a kilo of internet with this, just stop nagging me all the time," she would say, except when there were attacks, because then she would not give him money for even a single gram of internet.

Tali could not make her understand that internet was not bought by the kilo, but by the hour, so took the money and followed the same path back along the Thirsty River as Edjnaad had followed, behind the dogs, until he arrived in town.

When the Thirsty River had filled with water and the banks were green, Tali sat behind the computer and opened his e-mail, which Bill had set up for him. In his inbox he found an e-mail from him:

Hello my friend Tali,

When you were so angry with me, I began to think about the point of this war. I realised that I had to get away. Not because the war is good or bad, because it is not good or bad, but because the war is a human illness. I have deserted and flown to Mexico via Turkey. I am now living at the address you will find below. I would be really glad if you could send me a bag of those delicious dates, it would be a great present for my birthday on 11 August. Our friendship saved me from the war and I hope that it will save you from any hatred. Without war and without hate the steel between New York and Baghdad will be a train, and not a tank.

Your good friend Bill.

Costera Miguel Aleman 216, Plaza Condesa, Acapulco, Mexico

Tali's English was not up to the task of properly understanding Bill's letter. He wished that he had money to print it out and then translate it using Edjnaad's dictionary, but he wrote the e-mail out and was busy at home for days translating it. He did not help out in the sunflower fields until he had thoroughly understood the mail and had written an answer to it.

He asked Tenzile for money to use the internet. She asked if he wanted to help in the fields before she gave him money, but he said that he had to send an important e-mail. Tenzile did not know what an e-mail was but it was clearly something important and had something to do with the paper with which he had been busy for days. She gave him money after he promised to help when he returned. Tali sat behind the computer and typed the e-mail in with his index finger:

For my American friend Bill,

I am so happy with your e-mail. Is Mexico nice? We have a big farm with sunflowers. At the end of the season mother and father often argue. My mother wants to sell sunflower seeds and my father wants to make oil. We have our own canal and if the Thirsty River is dry in the winter we have a well with a pump and a generator. Lots of cars are being blown up and lots of people dying. I once saw some broken glasses on a veranda and thought that you had been killed. I hung the glasses on the wall and drew two eyes behind it. It looked a little bit like you. Hahaha. You will have to wait for the dates for the high season, but then I will send you some. As you can see, I have the internet here, but not my own computer. It would be good for the internet if there could be a computer. Is it difficult to send a laptop here?

Your very best friend, who will never forget you, Tali Rizen Kosjer Bird

P.S. Laptop with Explorer

Tali looked at the e-mail and wanted to delete 'I have the internet here' because it was not true, but dared not ask for a laptop for himself and thought that it was easier to ask for a laptop for the internet. Before the money for his kilo of internet was used up, he clicked on the button and sent the e-mail.

He began to work hard in the sunflower fields to earn the money to send dates to Mexico. He thought about the laptop and the internet, which would arrive in the house one day. He thought about how many friends he would have around the world and how many distant places he would visit through the screen, as he walked from sunflower to sunflower to give them water and the Iraqis began going from street to street to round the terrorists up. With the sunflowers, peace grew.

"Tell Shibe that she must look after Adam well," Tenzile called and she went to fetch eggs from the chickens to make breakfast, without forgetting about the lentil soup that Adam liked and ate with his fingers.

The sunflower fields suited Adam well. He followed Shibe all day long and did what she told him to do. If Shibe was not there, he walked behind Tali or Rizen. With a watering can he gave the sunflowers water. He remembered the words that he heard and made unintelligible sentences, but in the evenings he kept on knocking on doors and asking after Rasjad. He did not go to bed before someone said that Rasjad would be on his way soon. When the sunflowers reached their highest point and reached for the sun, Adam suddenly stopped walking behind Shibe, in his shirt with pale autumn leaves, as she continued on to the house for lunch.

"Come on, why have you stopped, aren't you hungry?" called Shibe.

"A big problem," said Adam.

"What is it? Were you stung by an insect?"

"No," said Adam. "I slept my life away."

"Ah," said Shibe angrily, because she wanted to get home in a hurry to eat. "It's better that way. You missed four wars."

"No," said Adam. "I missed four peaces."

"Why are you standing there in the midday sun?" cried Tenzile. "Food is ready!"

Shibe walked to the house with Adam behind her.

"I'm going to go behind the mountains on a train. I'm going to look for Rasjad. I'll go with him to a distant village to get to know someone who was born on the same day as me, at the same time. I'll ask to see photos and his diary to find out exactly what I missed."

"What are you saying?" asked Shibe, who was walking faster. "Speak up, so that I can hear you."

"Somewhere, behind the mountains is a photo album of the days that have been saved for me and which I never lived." He tried to recall a train that he had once mentioned somewhere more distant than his memory.

"Hurry up! Don't stand and dawdle!" Shibe left him behind and went to eat.

The sky was an azure blue, filled with birds returning to

their nests, after the steel of the war had departed, the shadow of the trees and the smoke of the violence had dissipated in the sky. On that beautiful summer's day Rizen sat eating his lunch and he thought about the future, about the sunflower oil factory that he wanted to build. He was happy with the most perfect and fertile sunflower fields in the south. He discovered that Iraqis were not only good fertilizer for guns, but were even better fertilizer for sunflowers. Tali, who had inherited a love of birds, stopped his constant clapping with two pieces of wood when the stork eventually landed in the field.

"Perhaps we must chase the stork away," said Tenzile, concerned. She felt that it was bringing back the history of the family and would perhaps make everything happen all over again. "One stork brings the devils home."

"Don't be so silly," said Tali. "Internet brings the Americans, the stork brings the devils ... perhaps you must go to school. It's just a bird."

Tenzile remained unsettled for a few hours, but then thought no more of the stork because of the chores in her new house, which was filled with life. After Shibe had finished lunch, she went in search of Adam, to show the stork to him. She saw him with the watering can at the sunflower on which she had hung the photo of the girl with a heart around her face, as she did every year, in the exact place where she had found the body of the man who had had the photo in his pocket.

In his hand Adam was holding the letter from Rasjad, with 'For Adam when he wakes up' on the envelope. "Look, these flowers are beautiful," he whispered. "Each sunflower is a dead Iraqi." He sighed.

"Each sunflower is an Iraqi looking up at the sun," said Shibe, as a gentle breeze made the sunflowers, stretching to the horizon, dance.

ENDNOTES

1. In Iraq it is a great offense if someone is referred to by his mother in this fashion.
2. Honorific title for women who have made the pilgrimage to Mecca. Older women in Iraq are also referred to by this title out of respect.
3. Halabja was attacked with chemical weapons in 1988 by Ali Hassan Al Majid, one of Saddam Hussein's lieutenants, who became known as Chemical Ali after this event.
4. Chapter from the Koran which is recited by mourners at a graveside, or celebrants at a wedding.
5. Marsh region in the south-east of Iraq.
6. Saddam Hussein's commandos.
7. The world's largest cemetry is to be found in Najaf. It is the Makbaret Wadi Al Salam, the Cemetry of Peace, where Shi'ites from the world over bury their dead.
8. Town near Tikrit where Saddam Hussein was born.
9. Rambo III was one of the most popular films during the time of Saddam Hussein, especially during wartime.
10. There are more than four hundred varieties of dates in Iraq; berghi dates are the tastiest and most expensive.
11. 'Paul' pronounced in Arabic sounds like 'Boel', which means urine. It was a joke when Paul Bremer was US administrator in Iraq.
12. Iraqi singer.